Bill Manhire has edited a number of major anthologies, including the prize-winning *100 New Zealand Poems*; a pioneering anthology of Antarctic fiction and poetry, *The Wide White Page*; and (with Marion McLeod) the classic collection of New Zealand short stories, *Some Other Country.*

The VUP Classics collection
celebrates more than half a century of stellar publishing
at Victoria University of Wellington

The End of the Golden Weather by Bruce Mason *1962*
Ngā Uruora by Geoff Park *1995*
Breakwater by Kate Duignan *2001*
Lifted by Bill Manhire *2005*
Girls High by Barbara Anderson *1990*
Portrait of the Artist's Wife by Barbara Anderson *1992*
Wednesday to Come Trilogy by Renée *1985, 1986, 1991*
In Fifteen Minutes You Can Say a Lot by Greville Texidor *1987*
Eileen Duggan: Selected Poems edited by Peter Whiteford *1994*
Denis Glover: Selected Poems edited by Bill Manhire *1995*
The Vintner's Luck by Elizabeth Knox *1998*
Man Alone by John Mulgan edited by Peter Whiteford *1935*
Six by Six: Short Stories by New Zealand's Best Writers edited by Bill Manhire *1989*
A.R.D. Fairburn: Selected Poems edited by Mac Jackson *1995*
R.A.K. Mason: Collected Poems edited by Allen Curnow *1962*
Ursula Bethell: Collected Poems edited by Vincent O'Sullivan *1985*

Six by Six

Edited by
Bill Manhire

Victoria University of Wellington Press

VICTORIA UNIVERSITY OF WELLINGTON
TE HERENGA WAKA

Victoria University of Wellington Press
PO Box 600, Wellington
vup.wgtn.ac.nz

First published 1989; reprinted 1991 and 1997; this edition 2021

A catalogue record for this book is available from the National Library of New Zealand

ISBN 9780864730879

ACKNOWLEDGEMENTS
Stories are reproduced from the following sources, and grateful acknowledgement is made to publishers and copyright holders. Katherine Mansfield, *The Stories of Katherine Mansfield* (OUP, 1988). Frank Sargeson, *The Stories of Frank Sargeson* (Penguin, 1982); reproduced by permission of the Sargeson Trust. Janet Frame, *You Are Now Entering the Human Heart* (VUP, 1983); reproduced by permission of the Janet Frame Literary Trust, c/o The Wylie Agency (UK) Ltd. Maurice Duggan, *Collected Stories* (AUP/OUP, 1981). Patricia Grace, *Waiariki* (Longman Paul, 1975), *The Dream Sleepers* (Longman Paul, 1982), *Electric City* (Penguin, 1987). Owen Marshall, *The Master of Big Jingles* (McIndoe, 1982), *The Day Hemingway Died* (McIndoe, 1984), *The Lynx Hunter* (McIndoe, 1987), NZ Listener (December 10, 1988).

Printed by Bluestar, Petone

Contents

Introduction

Six by Six is a big book of stories. The title, which sounds a little like something from the timber yard, indicates the principle of construction. There are 36 stories here, six stories each by six writers: Katherine Mansfield, Frank Sargeson, Maurice Duggan, Janet Frame, Patricia Grace and Owen Marshall. The authors are ordered according to date of birth. Only a matter of 50 years separates the first and last: Mansfield was born in 1888, Marshall in 1941.

This anthology is not meant to be a comprehensive survey of New Zealand short fiction. But it does try to show both range and depth – the variety and richness of achievement to be discovered when some of our best short story writers are put between the same covers. In choosing from each author's work, I have attempted to show individual range and development. Stories appear in chronological order, so that it is possible, for example, to see Frank Sargeson's work developing from an early sketch like 'Conversation with my Uncle' towards the garrulous, articulate manner of 'Just Trespassing, Thanks', or to watch Maurice Duggan move from the accurately named 'A Small Story' to the exuberant reach of 'O'Leary's Orchard'.

Six by Six is a big book for a further reason: it includes long stories, even a couple – 'O'Leary's Orchard' and 'Prelude' – which move towards the dimensions of the novella. This tendency in New Zealand fiction could as easily have been represented by works like Frank Sargeson's 'That Summer' or Janet Frame's 'Snowman, Snowman'. But Sargeson and

Frame are novelists, as well; and it seemed more useful to represent the longer story with choices from the work of Mansfield and Duggan – writers who specialised entirely in the short story form.

It is a truism to say that the short story has flourished in New Zealand. Writers here have given it their full attention. Owen Marshall, like Mansfield and Duggan, has published only short stories. Frank Sargeson wrote several novels as well as three volumes of autobiography, yet his reputation continues to rest on his work as a short story writer. Both Janet Frame and Patricia Grace published story collections before their novels (and further volumes of stories) began to appear.

Perhaps most writers of fiction try their hand at the short story when they first start out. All the same, the popularity of the form here does not indicate a nation of apprentice writers. It would be truer to say that most New Zealanders have been obliged to be part-time writers – snatching the time to write from their leisure hours, from evenings and weekends. Thinness of population and market have made life difficult for the aspiring full-time writer. Where magazine editors have always been able to find room for short stories, publishers have found it harder, at least until very recently, to envisage a market for hardback novels. The unusual vitality of the short story in New Zealand, however, must also stem from the fact that this is the form in which our very best writers have done much of their best work. The examples of overseas fame (Mansfield) and local doggedness (Sargeson) have been a powerful combination in shaping the imaginative ventures of many later writers.

A collection like this builds its variety on a base of consistent elements. All of these writers are participants in

what one of them calls 'the dangerous experiment of taking words seriously': they are interested in the medium they work with, in the power and slipperiness of words. They all touch, in different ways, on dislocation and loss; they notice covert and overt violence, and various kinds of social and emotional repression. The peculiarly New Zealand mixture of the raw and the genteel is a constant presence – from Mansfield's 'The Woman at the Store' to Marshall's 'Off by Heart'.

Mansfield and Marshall, at either end of *Six by Six*, share another preoccupation which is general: an anxiety about memory. Such an anxiety is hardly surprising in a land which often thinks itself lacking in 'history' – 'a little land with no history' was Mansfield's phrase in 1909. But worry about memory is also appropriate to the short story form itself, which finds its roots in rootlessness, in the instabilities of experience, which works best with the moment and cannot, like the novel, easily accommodate the process of time passing.

When short stories do deal with time, it is usually a simple matter of setting *then* against *now* – with the *then* (as in Maurice Duggan's 'Along Rideout Road that Summer') far more immediately and richly represented than the vague, perfunctory present of the tale's telling. Such stories and others focus repeatedly on moments of threshold and epiphany; and they often see growth and wisdom as inseparable from loss and betrayal.

The senses of dislocation and sadness in many of these stories also flow from the fact that the moments they record have passed away. Perhaps this is why the short story is more often surprised by melancholy than by joy. Like photographs, stories set out to fix the present moment forever, but find that

as soon as they do so, they enter the past, where their very preoccupation with the moment makes them vulnerable – less complete, less secure than, say, a historical novel. And time continues to pass, so that Mansfield's stories seem sadder now, more touched by transience, than perhaps they did in the 20s and 30s.

But there also surfaces in these stories a mischievous quality, a subversive comedy – sometimes subdued, sometimes exuberant – which offsets the passages of darkness. It is there in Sargeson's 'The Hole That Jack Dug', in Patricia Grace's 'The Wall', in Owen Marshall's 'A Poet's Dream of Amazons' – all stories which might easily be grim or unhappy but refuse to succumb to the circumstances they describe. Many of the stories in *Six by Six* are of this sort: they give the reader a conspiratorial wink – like the one at the end of Katherine Mansfield's 'The Voyage'.

The last story in *Six by Six*, Owen Marshall's 'Off by Heart', emphasises the way in which stories, like memories, take their characters and moments from the greater richness of the human community. The writer's job is to select and shape – as Sargeson's 'inarticulate' narrators like to remind us. In this book Patricia Grace is probably the writer who celebrates a sense of community most vigorously. And it is probably true that the Pākehā writers here tend to pinpoint the absence of community, or locate it only in the vanished worlds of childhood. But they chart its absence because they believe in it; stories which sketch failures of community, like Janet Frame's 'Insulation' or Maurice Duggan's 'Blues for Miss Laverty', reveal a deep desire *for* community. Patricia Grace's 'Waimarie', apparently about age and dispossession and death, ends with the voice of the title character calling to and sustaining her community: it touches past and present,

and it lifts out, 'weaving amongst the sheddings of light, encompassing the kinsman and his family, bearing them forward.' It is something like this that all these writers do – just when we need it, just when we least expect it.

Bill Manhire
1989

A Note from the 21st Century

This edition of *Six by Six* is a reissue, not a revision or a re-visioning. It continues to celebrate the remarkable life of the short story in twentieth-century New Zealand. The six writers here are perhaps even more secure in their reputations than they were back in 1989 – several of them through new ventures as well as new short fiction. Janet Frame died in 2004, but a range of posthumous publications has included poetry and longer fiction, along with a volume of new and uncollected stories. A fresh selection of Frank Sargeson's short fiction, *All to Blazes*, has just appeared in the UK. Owen Marshall, who has by no means abandoned the short story, has also gone on to publish half a dozen novels and several volumes of poetry. Likewise, Patricia Grace has added several novels, as well as children's stories and a significant memoir, *From the Centre*, to an already rich list of titles.

I was tempted to find space for contemporary short story specialists like Breton Dukes, Tracey Slaughter and Alice Tawhai, but *Six by Six* doesn't willingly translate to *Nine by Nine*. Still, it is well worth saying that the short story continues to thrive, both on the page and, these days, online. There are important practitioners, and a range of well-supported competitions. Where there used to be the Mansfield award, now there's the Sargeson. One day aspiring writers might aim to win the Slaughters.

The one visible change on the horizon has been the recent growth of 'creative nonfiction', particularly the personal essay, which freely uses all the techniques of traditional story-telling.

I find myself wondering if an anthology of contemporary short stories might soon abolish the sometimes misty distinction between fiction and non-fiction and include, say, Ashleigh Young and Madison Hamill alongside writers like Vincent O'Sullivan and Airini Beautrais. Maybe there's an editor out there who will let us know.

Bill Manhire
May 2021

KATHERINE MANSFIELD

The Woman at the Store

All that day the heat was terrible. The wind blew close to the ground – it rooted among the tussock grass – slithered along the road, so that the white pumice dust swirled in our faces – settled and sifted over us and was like a dry-skin itching for growth on our bodies. The horses stumbled along, coughing and chuffing. The pack horse was sick – with a big, open sore rubbed under the belly. Now and again she stopped short, threw back her head, looked at us as though she were going to cry, and whinnied. Hundreds of larks shrilled – the sky was slate colour, and the sound of the larks reminded me of slate pencils scraping over its surface. There was nothing to be seen but wave after wave of tussock grass – patched with purple orchids and manuka bushes covered with thick spider webs.

Jo rode ahead. He wore a blue galatea shirt, corduroy trousers and riding boots. A white handkerchief, spotted with red – it looked as though his nose had been bleeding on it – knotted round his throat. Wisps of white hair straggled from under his wideawake – his moustache and eyebrows were called white – he slouched in the saddle – grunting. Not once that day had he sung 'I don't care, for don't you see, my wife's mother was in front of me!' . . . It was the first day we had been without it for a month, and now there seemed something uncanny in his silence. Hin rode beside me – white as a clown, his black eyes glittered, and he kept shooting out his tongue and moistening his lips. He was dressed in a Jaeger vest a pair of blue duck trousers, fastened round the waist with a plaited leather belt. We had

hardly spoken since dawn. At noon we had lunched off fly biscuits and apricots by the side of a swampy creek.

'My stomach feels like the crop of a hen,' said Jo. 'Now then, Hin, you're the bright boy of the party – where's this 'ere store you kep' on talking about. "Oh, yes," you says, "I know a fine store, with a paddock for the horses an' a creek runnin' through, owned by a friend of mine who'll give yer a bottle of whisky before 'e shakes hands with yer." I'd like ter see that place – merely as a matter of curiosity – not that I'd ever doubt yer word – as yer know very well – *but*. . . .'

Hin laughed. 'Don't forget there's a woman too, Jo, with blue eyes and yellow hair, who'll promise you something else before she shakes hands with you. Put that in your pipe and smoke it.'

'The heat's making you balmy,' said Jo. But he dug his knees into his horse. We shambled on. I half fell asleep, and had a sort of uneasy dream that the horses were not moving forward at all – then that I was on a rocking-horse, and my old mother was scolding me for raising such a fearful dust from the drawing-room carpet. 'You've entirely worn off the pattern of the carpet,' I heard her saying, and she gave the reins a tug. I snivelled and woke to find Hin leaning over me, maliciously smiling.

'That was a case of all but,' said he, 'I just caught you. What's up, been bye-bye?'

'No!' I raised my head. 'Thank the Lord we're arriving somewhere.'

We were on the brow of the hill, and below us there was a whare roofed in with corrugated iron. It stood in a garden, rather far back from the road – a big paddock opposite, and a creek and a clump of young willow trees. A thin line of blue smoke stood up straight from the chimney of the whare, and

as I looked, a woman came out, followed by a child and a sheep dog – the woman carrying what appeared to me a black stick. She made frantic gestures at us. The horses put on a final spurt, Jo took off his wideawake, shouted, threw out his chest, and began singing, 'I don't care, for don't you see . . . .' The sun pushed through the pale clouds and shed a vivid light over the scene. It gleamed on the woman's yellow hair, over her flapping pinafore and the rifle she was carrying. The child hid behind her, and the yellow dog, a mangy beast, scuttled back into the whare, his tail between his legs. We drew rein and dismounted.

'Hallo,' screamed the woman. 'I thought you was three 'awks. My kid comes runnin' in ter me. "Mumma," says she, "there's three brown things comin' over the 'ill," says she. An' I comes out smart, I can tell yer. They'll be 'awks, I says to her. Oh, the 'awks about 'ere, yer wouldn't believe.'

The 'kid' gave us the benefit of one eye from behind the woman's pinafore – then retired again.

'Where's your old man,' asked Hin.

The woman blinked rapidly, screwing up her face.

'Away shearin'. Bin away a month. I suppose yer not goin' to stop, are yer? There's a storm comin' up.'

'You bet we are,' said Jo. 'So you're on your lonely, missis?'

She stood, pleating the frills of her pinafore, and glancing from one to the other of us, like a hungry bird. I smiled at the thought of how Hin had pulled Jo's leg about her. Certainly her eyes were blue, and what hair she had was yellow, but ugly. She was a figure of fun. Looking at her, you felt there was nothing but sticks and wires under that pinafore – her front teeth were knocked out, she had red pulpy hands, and wore on her feet a pair of dirty 'Bluchers'.

'I'll go and turn out the horses,' said Hin. 'Got any

embrocation? Poi's rubbed herself to hell!'

'Arf a mo!' The woman stood silent a moment, her nostrils expanding as she breathed. Then she shouted violently, 'I'd rather you didn't stop – you *can't* and there's the end of it. I don't let out that paddock any more. You'll have to go on; I ain't got nothing!'

'Well, I'm blest!' said Jo, heavily. He pulled me aside. 'Gone a bit off 'er dot,' he whispered, 'too much alone, *you know*,' very significantly. 'Turn the sympathetic tap on 'er, she'll come round all right.'

But there was no need – she had come round by herself.

'Stop if yer like!' she muttered, shrugging her shoulders. To me – 'I'll give yer the embrocation if yer come along.'

'Right-o, I'll take it down to them.' We walked together up the garden path. It was planted on both sides with cabbages. They smelled like stale dishwater. Of flowers there were double poppies and sweet-williams. One little patch was divided off by pawa shells – presumably it belonged to the child – for she ran from her mother and began to grub in it with a broken clothes peg. The yellow dog lay across the door step, biting fleas; the woman kicked him away.

'Gar-r, get away, you beast . . . the place ain't tidy. I 'aven't 'ad time ter fix things to-day – been ironing. Come right in.'

It was a large room, the walls plastered with old pages of English periodicals. Queen Victoria's Jubilee appeared to be the most recent number – a table with an ironing board and wash tub on it – some wooden forms – a black horsehair sofa, and some broken cane chairs pushed against the walls. The mantelpiece above the stove was draped in pink paper, further ornamented with dried grasses and ferns and a coloured print of Richard Seddon. There were four doors – one, judging from the smell, let into the 'store', one on to

the 'back yard', through the third I saw the bedroom. Flies buzzed in circles round the ceiling, and treacle papers and bundles of dried clover were pinned to the window curtains. I was alone in the room – she had gone into the store for the embrocation. I heard her stamping about and muttering to herself: 'I got some, now where did I put that bottle? . . . It's behind the pickles . . . no, it ain't.' I cleared a place on the table and sat there, swinging my legs. Down in the paddock I could hear Jo singing and the sound of hammer strokes as Hin drove in the tent poles. It was sunset. There is no twilight to our New Zealand days, but a curious half-hour when everything appears grotesque – it frightens – as though the savage spirit of the country walked abroad and sneered at what it saw. Sitting alone in the hideous room I grew afraid. The woman next door was a long time finding that stuff. What was she doing in there? Once I thought I heard her bang her hands down on the counter, and once she half moaned, turning it into a cough and clearing her throat. I wanted to shout 'Buck up,' but I kept silent.

'Good Lord, what a life!' I thought. 'Imagine being here day in, day out, with that rat of a child and a mangy dog. Imagine bothering about ironing – *mad*, of course she's mad! Wonder how long she's been here – wonder if I could get her to talk.'

At that moment she poked her head round the door.

'Wot was it yer wanted,' she asked.

'Embrocation.'

'Oh, I forgot. I got it, it was in front of the pickle jars.' She handed me the bottle.

'My, you do look tired, you do! Shall I knock yer up a few scones for supper? There's some tongue in the store, too, and I'll cook yer a cabbage if you fancy it.'

'Right-o.' I smiled at her. 'Come down to the paddock and bring the kid for tea.'

She shook her head, pursing up her mouth.

'Oh no. I don't fancy it. I'll send the kid down with the things and a billy of milk. Shall I knock up a few extry scones to take with you ter-morrow?'

'Thanks.'

She came and stood by the door.

'How old is the kid?'

'Six – come next Christmas. I 'ad a bit of trouble with 'er one way an' another. I 'adn't any milk till a month after she was born and she sickened like a cow.'

'She's not like you – takes after her father?' Just as the woman had shouted her refusal at us before, she shouted at me then.

'No, she don't; she's the dead spit of me. Any fool could see that. Come on in now, Els, you stop messing in the dirt.'

I met Jo climbing over the paddock fence.

'What's the old bitch got in the store?' he asked.

'Don't know – didn't look.'

'Well, of all the fools. Hin's slanging you. What have you been doing all the time?'

'She couldn't find this stuff. Oh, my shakes, you are smart!'

Jo had washed, combed his wet hair in a line across his forehead, and buttoned a coat over his shirt. He grinned.

Hin snatched the embrocation from me. I went to the end of the paddock where the willows grew and bathed in the creek. The water was clear and soft as oil. Along the edges held by the grass and rushes, white foam tumbled and bubbled. I lay in the water and looked up at the trees that were still a moment, then quivered lightly, and again were

still. The air smelt of rain. I forgot about the woman and the kid until I came back to the tent. Hin lay by the fire, watching the billy boil.

I asked where Jo was and if the kid had brought our supper.

'Pooh,' said Hin, rolling over and looking up at the sky. 'Didn't you see how Jo had been tittivating – he said to me before he went up to the whare, "Dang it! she'll look better by night light – at any rate, my buck, she's female flesh!"'

'You had Jo about her looks – you had me, too.'

'No – look here. I can't make it out. It's four years since I came past this way, and I stopped here two days. The husband was a pal of mine once, down the West Coast – a fine, big chap, with a voice on him like a trombone. She'd been barmaid down the Coast – as pretty as a wax doll. The coach used to come this way then once a fortnight, that was before they opened the railway up Napier way, and she had no end of time! Told me once in a confidential moment that she knew one hundred and twenty-five different ways of kissing!'

'Oh, go on, Hin! She isn't the same woman!'

'Course she is. . . . I can't make it out. What I think is the old man's cleared out and left her: that's all my eye about shearing. Sweet life! The only people who come through now are Maoris and sundowners!'

Through the dark we saw the gleam of the kid's pinafore. She trailed over to us with a basket in her hand, the milk billy in the other. I unpacked the basket, the child standing by.

'Come over here,' said Hin, snapping his fingers at her.

She went, the lamp from the inside of the tent cast a bright light over her. A mean, undersized brat, with whitish hair, and weak eyes. She stood, legs apart and her stomach protruding.

'What do you do all day?' asked Hin.

She scraped out one ear with her little finger, looked at the result and said – 'Draw.'

'Huh! What do you draw? – leave your ears alone.'

'Pictures.'

'What on?'

'Bits of butter paper an' a pencil of my Mumma's.'

'Boh! What a lot of words at one time!' Hin rolled his eyes at her. 'Baa-lambs and moo-cows?'

'No, everything. I'll draw all of you when you're gone, and your horses and the tent, and that one' – she pointed to me – 'with no clothes on in the creek. I looked at her where she wouldn't see me from.'

'Thanks very much! How ripping of you,' said Hin. 'Where's Dad?'

The kid pouted. 'I won't tell you because I don't like yer face!' She started operations on the other ear.

'Here,' I said. 'Take the basket, get along home and tell the other man supper's ready.'

'I don't want to.'

'I'll give you a box on the ear if you don't,' said Hin, savagely.

'Hie! I'll tell Mumma. I'll tell Mumma' – the kid fled.

We ate until we were full and had arrived at the smoke stage before Jo came back, very flushed and jaunty, a whisky bottle in his hand.

''Ave a drink – you two!' he shouted, carrying off matters with a high hand. ''Ere, shove along the cups.'

'One hundred and twenty-five different ways,' I murmured to Hin.

'What's that? Oh! stow it!' said Jo. 'Why 'ave you always got your knife into me. You gas like a kid at a Sunday School

beano. She wants us to go up there to-night, and have a comfortable chat. I' – he waved his hand airily – 'I got 'er round.'

'Trust you for that,' laughed Hin. 'But did she tell you where the old man's got to?'

Jo looked up. 'Shearing! You 'eard 'er, you fool!'

The woman had fixed up the room, even to a light bouquet of sweet-williams on the table. She and I sat one side of the table, Jo and Hin the other. An oil lamp was set between us, the whisky bottle and glasses, and a jug of water. The kid knelt against one of the forms, drawing on butter paper. I wondered, grimly, if she was attempting the creek episode. But Jo had been right about night time. The woman's hair was tumbled – two red spots burned in her cheeks – her eyes shone – and we knew that they were kissing feet under the table. She had changed the blue pinafore for a white calico dressing jacket and a black skirt – the kid was decorated to the extent of a blue sateen hair ribbon. In the stifling room with the flies buzzing against the ceiling and dropping on to the table – we got slowly drunk.

'Now listen to me,' shouted the woman, banging her fist on the table. 'It's six years since I was married, and four miscarriages. I says to 'im, I says, what do you think I'm doin' up 'ere? If you was back at the Coast, I'd 'ave you lynched for child murder. Over and over I tells 'im – you've broken my spirit and spoiled my looks, and wot for – that's wot I'm driving at.' She clutched her head with her hands and stared round at us. Speaking rapidly, 'Oh, some days – an' months of them I 'ear them two words knockin' inside me all the time – "Wot for," but sometimes I'll be cooking the spuds an' I lifts the lid off to give 'em a prong and I 'ears, quite sudden again, "Wot for." Oh! I don't mean only the

spuds and the kid – I mean – I mean,' she hiccoughed – 'you know what I mean, Mr Jo.'

'I know,' said Jo, scratching his head.

'Trouble with me is,' she leaned across the table, 'he left me too much alone. When the coach stopped coming, sometimes he'd go away days, sometimes he'd go away weeks, and leave me ter look after the store. Back 'e'd come – pleased as Punch. "Oh, 'allo," 'e'd say. "Ow are you gettin' on. Come and give us a kiss." Sometimes I'd turn a bit nasty, and then 'e'd go off again, and if I took it all right, 'e'd wait till 'e could twist me round 'is finger, then 'e'd say, "Well, so long, I'm off," and do you think I could keep 'im? – not me!'

'Mumma,' bleated the kid, 'I made a picture of them on the 'ill, an' you an' me, an' the dog down below.'

'Shut your mouth,' said the woman.

A vivid flash of lightning played over the room – we heard the mutter of thunder.

'Good thing that's broke loose,' said Jo. 'I've 'ad it in me 'ead for three days.'

'Where's your old man now?' asked Hin slowly.

The woman blubbered and dropped her head on to the table. 'Hin, 'e's gone shearin' and left me alone again,' she wailed.

''Ere, look out for the glasses,' said Jo. 'Cheer-o, 'ave another drop. No good cryin' over spilt 'usbands! You Hin, you blasted cuckoo!'

'Mr Jo,' said the woman, drying her eyes on her jacket frill, 'you're a gent, an' if I was a secret woman, I'd place any confidence in your 'ands. I don't mind if I do 'ave a glass on that.'

Every moment the lightning grew more vivid and the thunder sounded nearer. Hin and I were silent – the kid

never moved from her bench. She poked her tongue out and blew on it as she drew.

'It's the loneliness,' said the woman, addressing Jo – he made sheep's eyes at her – 'and bein' shut up 'ere like a broody 'en.' He reached his hand across the table and held hers, and though the position looked most uncomfortable when they wanted to pass the water and whisky, their hands stuck together as though glued. I pushed back my chair and went over to the kid, who immediately sat flat down on her artistic achievements and made a face at me.

'You're not to look,' said she.

'Oh, come on, don't be so nasty!' Hin came over to us, and we were just drunk enough to wheedle the kid into showing us. And those drawings of hers were extraordinary and repulsively vulgar. The creations of a lunatic with a lunatic's cleverness. There was no doubt about it, the kid's mind was diseased. While she showed them to us, she worked herself up into a mad excitement, laughing and trembling, and shooting out her arms.

'Mumma,' she yelled. 'Now I'm going to draw them what you told me I never was to – now I am.'

The woman rushed from the table and beat the child's head with the flat of her hand.

'I'll smack you with yer clothes turned up if yer dare say that again,' she bawled.

Jo was too drunk to notice, but Hin caught her by the arm. The kid did not utter a cry. She drifted over to the window and began picking flies from the treacle paper.

We returned to the table – Hin and I sitting one side, the woman and Jo, touching shoulders, the other. We listened to the thunder, saying stupidly. 'That was a near one,' 'There it goes again,' and Jo, with a heavy hit, 'Now we're off,' 'Steady

on the brake,' until rain began to fall, sharp as cannon shot on the iron roof.

'You'd better doss here for the night,' said the woman.

'That's right,' assented Jo, evidently in the know about this move.

'Bring up yer things from the tent. You two can doss in the store along with the kid – she's used to sleep in there and won't mind you.'

'O, Mumma, I never did,' interrupted the kid.

'Shut yer lies! An' Mr Jo can 'ave this room.'

It sounded a ridiculous arrangement, but it was useless to attempt to cross them, they were too far gone. While the woman sketched the plan of action, Jo sat, abnormally solemn and red, his eyes bulging, and pulled at his moustache.

'Give us a lantern,' said Hin. 'I'll go down to the paddock.' We two went together. Rain whipped in our faces, the land was as light as though a bush fire was raging – we behaved like two children let loose in the thick of an adventure – laughed and shouted to each other, and came back to the whare to find the kid already bedded in the counter of the store. The woman brought us a lamp. Jo took his bundle from Hin, the door was shut.

'Good-night all,' shouted Jo.

Hin and I sat on two sacks of potatoes. For the life of us we could not stop laughing. Strings of onions and half-hams dangled from the ceiling – wherever we looked there were advertisements for 'Camp Coffee' and tinned meats. We pointed at them, tried to read them aloud – overcome with laughter and hiccoughs. The kid in the counter stared at us. She threw off her blanet and scrambled to the floor where she stood in her grey flannel night gown, rubbing one leg against the other. We paid no attention to her.

'Wot are you laughing at,' she said, uneasily.

'You!' shouted Hin, 'the red tribe of you, my child.'

She flew into a rage and beat herself with her hands. 'I won't be laughed at, you curs – you.' He swooped down upon the child and swung her on to the counter.

'Go to sleep, Miss Smarty – or make a drawing – here's a pencil – you can use Mumma's account book.'

Through the rain we heard Jo creak over the boarding of the next room – the sound of a door being opened – then shut to.

'It's the loneliness,' whispered Hin.

'One hundred and twenty-five different ways – alas! my poor brother!'

The kid tore out a page and flung it at me.

'There you are,' she said. 'Now I done it ter spite Mumma for shutting me up 'ere with you two. I done the one she told me I never ought to. I done the one she told me she'd shoot me if I did. Don't care! Don't care!'

The kid had drawn the picture of the woman shooting at a man with a rook rifle and then digging a hole to bury him in.

She jumped off the counter and squirmed about on the floor biting her nails.

Hin and I sat till dawn with the drawing beside us. The rain ceased, the little kid fell asleep, breathing loudly. We got up, stole out of the whare, down into the paddock. White clouds floated over a pink sky – a chill wind blew; the air smelled of wet grass. Just as we swung into the saddle, Jo came out of the whare – he motioned to us to ride on.

'I'll pick you up later,' he shouted.

A bend in the road, and the whole place disappeared.

Prelude

I

There was not an inch of room for Lottie and Kezia in the buggy. When Pat swung them on top of the luggage they wobbled; the grandmother's lap was full and Linda Burnell could not possibly have held a lump of a child on hers for any distance. Isabel, very superior, was perched beside the new handy-man on the driver's seat. Hold-alls, bags and boxes were piled upon the floor. 'These are absolute necessities that I will not let out of my sight for one instant,' said Linda Burnell, her voice trembling with fatigue and excitement.

Lottie and Kezia stood on the patch of lawn just inside the gate all ready for the fray in their coats with brass anchor buttons and little round caps with battleship ribbons. Hand in hand, they stared with round solemn eyes first at the absolute necessities and then at their mother.

'We shall simply have to leave them. That is all. We shall simply have to cast them off,' said Linda Burnell. A strange little laugh flew from her lips; she leaned back against the buttoned leather cushions and shut her eyes, her lips trembling with laughter. Happily at that moment Mrs Samuel Josephs, who had been watching the scene from behind her drawing-room blind, waddled down the garden path.

'Why nod leave the chudren with be for the afterdoon, Brs Burnell? They could go on the dray with the storeban when he comes in the eveding. Those thigs on the path have to go, dod't they?'

'Yes, everything outside the house is supposed to go,' said Linda Burnell, and she waved a white hand at the tables and chairs standing on their heads on the front lawn. How absurd they looked! Either they ought to be the other way up, or Lottie and Kezia ought to stand on their heads, too. And she longed to say: 'Stand on your heads, children, and wait for the storeman.' It seemed to her that would be so exquisitely funny that she could not attend to Mrs Samuel Josephs.

The fat creaking body leaned across the gate, and the big jelly of a face smiled. 'Dod't you worry, Brs Burnell. Loddie and Kezia can have tea with by chudren in the dursery, and I'll see theb on the dray afterwards.'

The grandmother considered. 'Yes, it really is quite the best plan. We are very obliged to you, Mrs Samuel Josephs. Children, say "thank you" to Mrs Samuel Josephs.'

Two subdued chirrups: 'Thank you, Mrs Samuel Josephs.'

'And be good little girls, and – come closer –' they advanced, 'don't forget to tell Mrs Samuel Josephs when you want to. . . .'

'No, granma.'

'Dod't worry, Brs Burnell.'

At the last moment Kezia let go Lottie's hand and darted towards the buggy.

'I want to kiss my granma good-bye again.'

But she was too late. The buggy rolled off up the road, Isabel bursting with pride, her nose turned up at all the world, Linda Burnell prostrated, and the grandmother rummaging among the very curious oddments she had put in her black silk reticule at the last moment, for something to give her daughter. The buggy twinkled away in the sunlight and fine golden dust up the hill and over. Kezia bit her lip, but Lottie, carefully finding her handkerchief first, set up a wail.

'Mother! Granma!'

Mrs Samuel Josephs, like a huge warm black silk tea cosy, enveloped her.

'It's all right, by dear. Be a brave child. You come and blay in the dursery!'

She put her arm around weeping Lottie and led her away. Kezia followed, making a face at Mrs Samuel Josephs' placket, which was undone as usual, with two long pink corset laces hanging out of it. . . .

Lottie's weeping died down as she mounted the stairs, but the sight of her at the nursery door with swollen eyes and a blob of a nose gave great satisfaction to the S. J.'s, who sat on two benches before a long table covered with American cloth and set out with immense plates of bread and dripping and two brown jugs that faintly steamed.

'Hullo! You've been crying!'

'Ooh! Your eyes have gone right in.'

'Doesn't her nose look funny.'

'You're all red-and-patchy.'

Lottie was quite a success. She felt it and swelled, smiling timidly.

'Go and sit by Zaidee, ducky,' said Mrs Samuel Josephs, 'and Kezia, you sid ad the end by Boses.'

Moses grinned and gave her a nip as she sat down; but she pretended not to notice. She did hate boys.

'Which will you have?' asked Stanley, leaning across the table very politely, and smiling at her. 'Which will you have to begin with – strawberries and cream or bread and dripping?'

'Strawberries and cream, please,' said she.

'Ah-h-h-h.' How they all laughed and beat the table with their teaspoons. Wasn't that a take in! Wasn't it now! Didn't he fox her? Good old Stan!

'Ma! She thought it was real.'

Even Mrs Samuel Josephs, pouring out the milk and water, could not help smiling. 'You busn't teast theb on their last day,' she wheezed.

But Kezia bit a big piece out of her bread and dripping, and then stood the piece up on her plate. With the bit out it made a dear little sort of gate. Pooh! She didn't care! A tear rolled down her cheek, but she wasn't crying. She couldn't have cried in front of those awful Samuel Josephs. She sat with her head bent, and as the tear dripped slowly down, she caught it with a neat little whisk of her tongue and ate it before any of them had seen.

II

After tea Kezia wandered back to their own house. Slowly she walked up the back steps, and through the scullery into the kitchen. Nothing was left in it but a lump of gritty yellow soap in one corner of the kitchen window sill and a piece of flannel stained with a blue bag in another. The fireplace was choked up with rubbish. She poked among it but found nothing except a hair-tidy with a heart painted on it that had belonged to the servant girl. Even that she left lying, and she trailed through the narrow passage into the drawing-room. The Venetian blind was pulled down but not drawn close. Long pencil rays of sunlight shone through and the wavy shadow of a bush outside danced on the gold lines. Now it was still, now it began to flutter again, and now it came almost as far as her feet. Zoom! Zoom! a blue-bottle knocked against the ceiling; the carpet-tacks had little bits of red fluff sticking to them.

The dining-room window had a square of coloured glass at each corner. One was blue and one was yellow. Kezia

bent down to have one more look at a blue lawn with blue arum lilies growing at the gate, and then at a yellow lawn with yellow lilies and a yellow fence. As she looked a little Chinese Lottie came out on to the lawn and began to dust the tables and chairs with a corner of her pinafore. Was that really Lottie? Kezia was not quite sure until she had looked through the ordinary window.

Upstairs in her father's and mother's room she found a pill box black and shiny outside and red in, holding a blob of cotton wool.

'I could keep a bird's egg in that,' she decided.

In the servant girl's room there was a stay-button stuck in a crack of the floor, and in another crack some beads and a long needle. She knew there was nothing in her grandmother's room; she had watched her pack. She went over to the window and leaned against it, pressing her hands against the pane.

Kezia liked to stand so before the window. She liked the feeling of the cold shining glass against her hot palms, and she liked to watch the funny white tops that came on her fingers when she pressed them hard against the pane. As she stood there, the day flickered out and dark came. With the dark crept the wind snuffling and howling. The windows of the empty house shook, a creaking came from the walls and floors, a piece of loose iron on the roof banged forlornly. Kezia was suddenly quite, quite still, with wide open eyes and knees pressed together. She was frightened. She wanted to call Lottie and to go on calling all the while she ran downstairs and out of the house. But IT was just behind her, waiting at the door, at the head of the stairs, at the bottom of the stairs, hiding in the passage, ready to dart out at the back door. But Lottie was at the back door, too.

'Kezia!' she called cheerfully. 'The storeman's here.

Everything is on the dray and three horses, Kezia. Mrs Samuel Josephs has given us a big shawl to wear around us, and she says to button up your coat. She won't come out because of asthma.'

Lottie was very important.

'Now then, you kids,' called the storeman. He hooked his big thumbs under their arms and up they swung. Lottie arranged the shawl 'most beautifully' and the storeman tucked up their feet in a piece of old blanket.

'Lift up. Easy does it.'

They might have been a couple of young ponies. The storeman felt over the cords holding his load, unhooked the brakechain from the wheel, and whistling, he swung up beside them.

'Keep close to me,' said Lottie, 'because otherwise you pull the shawl away from my side, Kezia.'

But Kezia edged up to the storeman. He towered beside her big as a giant and he smelled of nuts and new wooden boxes.

III

It was the first time that Lottie and Kezia had ever been out so late. Everything looked different – the painted wooden houses far smaller than they did by day, the gardens far bigger and wilder. Bright stars speckled the sky and the moon hung over the harbour dabbling the waves with gold. They could see the lighthouse shining on Quarantine Island, and the green lights on the old coal hulks.

'There comes the Picton boat,' said the storeman, pointing to a little steamer all hung with bright beads.

But when they reached the top of the hill and began to go down the other side the harbour disappeared, and although

they were still in the town they were quite lost. Other carts rattled past. Everybody knew the storeman.

'Night, Fred.'

'Night O,' he shouted.

Kezia liked very much to hear him. Whenever a cart appeared in the distance she looked up and waited for his voice. He was an old friend; and she and her grandmother had often been to his place to buy grapes. The storeman lived alone in a cottage that had a glasshouse against one wall built by himself. All the glasshouse was spanned and arched over with one beautiful vine. He took her brown basket from her, lined it with three large leaves, and then he felt in his belt for a little horn knife, reached up and snapped off a big blue cluster and laid it on the leaves so tenderly that Kezia held her breath to watch. He was a very big man. He wore brown velvet trousers, and he had a long brown beard. But he never wore a collar, not even on Sunday. The back of his neck was burnt bright red.

'Where are we now?' Every few minutes one of the children asked him the question.

'Why, this is Hawk Street, or Charlotte Crescent.'

'Of course it is,' Lottie pricked up her ears at the last name; she always felt that Charlotte Crescent belonged specially to her. Very few people had streets with the same name as theirs.

'Look, Kezia, there is Charlotte Crescent. Doesn't it look different?' Now everything familiar was left behind. Now the big dray rattled into unknown country, along new roads with high clay banks on either side, up steep, steep hills, down into bushy valleys, through wide shallow rivers. Further and further. Lottie's head wagged; she drooped, she slipped half into Kezia's lap and lay there. But Kezia could

not open her eyes wide enough. The wind blew and she shivered; but her cheeks and ears burned.

'Do stars ever blow about?' she asked.

'Not to notice,' said the storeman.

'We've got a nuncle and a naunt living near our new house,' said Kezia. 'They have got two children, Pip, the eldest is called, and the youngest's name is Rags. He's got a ram. He has to feed it with a nenamuel teapot and a glove top over the spout. He's going to show us. What is the difference between a ram and a sheep?'

'Well, a ram has horns and runs for you.'

Kezia considered. 'I don't want to see it frightfully,' she said. 'I hate rushing animals like dogs and parrots. I often dream that animals rush at me – even camels – and while they are rushing, their heads swell e-enormous.'

The storeman said nothing. Kezia peered up at him, screwing up her eyes. Then she put her finger out and stroked his sleeve; it felt hairy. 'Are we near?' she asked.

'Not far off, now,' answered the storeman. 'Getting tired?'

'Well, I'm not an atom bit sleepy,' said Kezia. 'But my eyes keep curling up in such a funny sort of way.' She gave a long sigh, and to stop her eyes from curling she shut them. . . . When she opened them again they were clanking through a drive that cut through the garden like a whip lash, looping suddenly an island of green, and behind the island, but out of sight until you came upon it, was the house. It was long and low built, with a pillared verandah and balcony all the way round. The soft white bulk of it lay stretched upon the green garden like a sleeping beast. And now one and now another of the windows leaped into light. Someone was walking through the empty rooms carrying a lamp. From a window downstairs the light of a fire flickered. A strange beautiful excitement seemed

to stream from the house in quivering ripples.

'Where are we?' said Lottie, sitting up. Her reefer cap was all on one side and on her cheek there was the print of an anchor button she had pressed against while sleeping. Tenderly the storeman lifted her, set her cap straight, and pulled down her crumpled clothes. She stood blinking on the lowest verandah step watching Kezia who seemed to come flying through the air to her feet.

'Ooh!' cried Kezia, flinging up her arms. The grandmother came out of the dark hall carrying a little lamp. She was smiling.

'You found your way in the dark?' said she.

'Perfectly well.'

But Lottie staggered on the lowest verandah step like a bird fallen out of the nest. If she stood still for a moment she fell asleep, if she leaned against anything her eyes closed. She could not walk another step.

'Kezia,' said her grandmother, 'can I trust you to carry the lamp?'

'Yes, my granma.'

The old woman bent down and gave the bright breathing thing into her hands and then she caught up drunken Lottie. 'This way.'

Through a square hall filled with bales and hundreds of parrots (but the parrots were only on the wall-paper) down a narrow passage where the parrots persisted in flying past Kezia with her lamp.

'Be very quiet,' warned the grandmother, putting down Lottie and opening the dining-room door. 'Poor little mother has got such a headache.'

Linda Burnell, in a long cane chair, with her feet on a hassock, and a plaid over her knees, lay before a crackling

fire. Burnell and Beryl sat at the table in the middle of the room eating a dish of fried chops and drinking tea out of a brown china teapot. Over the back of her mother's chair leaned Isabel. She had a comb in her fingers and in a gentle absorbed fashion she was combing the curls from her mother's forehead. Outside the pool of lamp and firelight the room stretched dark and bare to the hollow windows.

'Are those the children?' But Linda did not really care; she did not even open her eyes to see.

'Put down the lamp, Kezia,' said Aunt Beryl, 'or we shall have the house on fire before we are out of the packing cases. More tea, Stanley?'

'Well, you might just give me five-eighths of a cup,' said Burnell, leaning across the table. 'Have another chop, Beryl. Tip-top meat, isn't it? Not too lean and not too fat.' He turned to his wife. 'You're sure you won't change your mind, Linda darling?'

'The very thought of it is enough.' She raised one eyebrow in the way she had. The grandmother brought the children bread and milk and they sat up to the table, flushed and sleepy behind the wavy steam.

'I had meat for my supper,' said Isabel, still combing gently.

'I had a whole chop for my supper, the bone and all and Worcester Sauce. Didn't I, father?'

'Oh, don't boast, Isabel,' said Aunt Beryl.

Isabel looked astounded. 'I wasn't boasting, was I, Mummy? I never thought of boasting. I thought they would like to know. I only meant to tell them.'

'Very well. That's enough,' said Burnell. He pushed back his plate, took a tooth-pick out of his pocket and began picking his strong white teeth.

'You might see that Fred has a bit of something in the kitchen before he goes, will you, mother?'

'Yes, Stanley.' The old woman turned to go.

'Oh, hold on half a jiffy. I suppose nobody knows where my slippers were put? I suppose I shall not be able to get at them for a month or two – what?'

'Yes,' came from Linda. 'In the top of the canvas hold-all marked "urgent necessities".'

'Well you might get them for me will you, mother?'

'Yes, Stanley.'

Burnell got up, stretched himself, and going over to the fire he turned his back to it and lifted up his coat tails.

'By Jove, this is a pretty pickle. Eh, Beryl?'

Beryl, sipping tea, her elbows on the table, smiled over the cup at him. She wore an unfamiliar pink pinafore; the sleeves of her blouse were rolled up to her shoulders showing her lovely freckled arms, and she had let her hair fall down her back in a long pig-tail.

'How long do you think it will take to get straight – couple of weeks – eh?' he chaffed.

'Good heavens, no,' said Beryl airily. 'The worst is over already. The servant girl and I have simply slaved all day, and ever since mother came she has worked like a horse, too. We have never sat down for a moment. We have had a day.'

Stanley scented a rebuke.

'Well, I suppose you did not expect me to rush away from the office and nail carpets – did you?'

'Certainly not,' laughed Beryl. She put down her cup and ran out of the dining-room.

'What the hell does she expect us to do?' asked Stanley. 'Sit down and fan herself with a palm leaf fan while I have a gang of professionals to do the job? By Jove, if she can't do a

hand's turn occasionally without shouting about it in return for . . .'

And he gloomed as the chops began to fight the tea in his sensitive stomach. But Linda put up a hand and dragged him down to the side of her long chair.

'This is a wretched time for you, old boy,' she said. Her cheeks were very white but she smiled and curled her fingers into the big red hand she held. Burnell became quiet. Suddenly he began to whistle 'Pure as a lily, joyous and free' – a good sign.

'Think you're going to like it?' he asked.

'I don't want to tell you, but I think I ought to, mother,' said Isabel. 'Kezia is drinking tea out of Aunt Beryl's cup.'

IV

They were taken off to bed by the grandmother. She went first with a candle; the stairs rang to their climbing feet. Isabel and Lottie lay in a room to themselves, Kezia curled in her grandmother's soft bed.

'Aren't there going to be any sheets, my granma?'

'No, not to-night.'

'It's tickly,' said Kezia, 'but it's like Indians.' She dragged her grandmother down to her and kissed her under the chin. 'Come to bed soon and be my Indian brave.'

'What a silly you are,' said the old woman, tucking her in as she loved to be tucked.

'Aren't you going to leave me a candle?'

'No. Sh-h. Go to sleep.'

'Well, can I have the door left open?'

She rolled herself up into a round but she did not go to sleep. From all over the house came the sound of steps. The house itself creaked and popped. Loud whispering voices

came from downstairs. Once she heard Aunt Beryl's rush of high laughter, and once she heard a loud trumpeting from Burnell blowing his nose. Outside the window hundreds of black cats with yellow eyes sat in the sky watching her – but she was not frightened. Lottie was saying to Isabel:

'I'm going to say my prayers in bed to-night.'

'No you can't, Lottie.' Isabel was very firm. 'God only excuses you saying your prayers in bed if you've got a temperature.' So Lottie yielded:

Gentle Jesus meek anmile,
Look pon a little chile.
Pity me, simple Lizzie
Suffer me to come to thee.

And then they lay down back to back, their little behinds just touching, and fell asleep.

Standing in a pool of moonlight Beryl Fairfield undressed herself. She was tired, but she pretended to be more tired than she really was – letting her clothes fall, pushing back with a languid gesture her warm, heavy hair.

'O, how tired I am – very tired.'

She shut her eyes a moment, but her lips smiled. Her breath rose and fell in her breast like two fanning wings. The window was wide open; it was warm, and somewhere out there in the garden a young man, dark and slender, with mocking eyes, tip-toed among the bushes, and gathered the flowers into a big bouquet, and slipped under her window and held it up to her. She saw herself bending forward. He thrust his head among the bright waxy flowers, sly and laughing. 'No, no,' said Beryl. She turned from the window

and dropped her nightgown over her head.

'How frightfully unreasonable Stanley is sometimes,' she thought, buttoning. And then, as she lay down, there came the old thought, the cruel thought – ah, if only she had money of her own.

A young man, immensely rich, had just arrived from England. He meets her quite by chance. . . . The new governor is unmarried. . . . There is a ball at Government house. . . . Who is that exquisite creature in *eau de nil* satin? Beryl Fairfield. . . .

'The thing that pleases me,' said Stanley, leaning against the side of the bed and giving himself a good scratch on his shoulders and back before turning in, 'is that I've got the place dirt cheap, Linda. I was talking about it to little Wally Bell to-day and he said he simply could not understand why they had accepted my figure. You see land about here is bound to become more and more valuable . . . in about ten years' time . . . of course we shall have to go very slow and cut down expenses as fine as possible. Not asleep – are you?'

'No, dear, I've heard every word,' said Linda. He sprang into bed, leaned over her and blew out the candle.

'Good night, Mr Business Man,' said she, and she took hold of his head by the ears and gave him a quick kiss. Her faint far-away voice seemed to come from a deep well.

'Good night, darling.' He slipped his arm under her neck and drew her to him.

'Yes, clasp me,' said the faint voice from the deep well.

Pat the handy man sprawled in his little room behind the kitchen. His sponge-bag, coat and trousers hung from the door-peg like a hanged man. From the edge of the blanket

his twisted toes protruded, and on the floor beside him was an empty cane bird-cage. He looked like a comic picture.

'Honk, honk,' came from the servant girl. She had adenoids.

Last to go to bed was the grandmother.

'What. Not asleep yet?'

'No, I'm waiting for you,' said Kezia. The old woman sighed and lay down beside her. Kezia thrust her head under the grandmother's arm and gave a little squeak. But the old woman only pressed her faintly, and sighed again, took out her teeth, and put them in a glass of water beside her on the floor.

In the garden some tiny owls, perched on the branches of a lace-bark tree, called: 'More pork; more pork.' And far away in the bush there sounded a harsh rapid chatter: 'Ha-ha-ha . . . Ha-ha-ha.'

V

Dawn came sharp and chill with red clouds on a faint green sky and drops of water on every leaf and blade. A breeze blew over the garden, dropping dew and dropping petals, shivered over the drenched paddocks, and was lost in the sombre bush. In the sky some tiny stars floated for a moment and then they were gone – they were dissolved like bubbles. And plain to be heard in the early quiet was the sound of the creek in the paddock running over the brown stones, running in and out of the sandy hollows, hiding under clumps of dark berry bushes, spilling into a swamp of yellow water flowers and cresses.

And then at the first beam of sun the birds began. Big cheeky birds, starlings and mynahs, whistled on the lawns, the little birds, the goldfinches and linnets and fantails flicked from bough to bough. A lovely kingfisher perched

on the paddock fence preening his rich beauty, and a *tui* sang his three notes and laughed and sang them again.

'How loud the birds are,' said Linda in her dream. She was walking with her father through a green paddock sprinkled with daisies. Suddenly he bent down and parted the grasses and showed her a tiny ball of fluff just at her feet. 'Oh, Papa, the darling.' She made a cup of her hands and caught the tiny bird and stroked its head with her finger. It was quite tame. But a funny thing happened. As she stroked it began to swell, it ruffled and pouched, it grew bigger and bigger and its round eyes seemed to smile knowingly at her. Now her arms were hardly wide enough to hold it and she dropped it into her apron. It had become a baby with a big naked head and a gaping bird-mouth, opening and shutting. Her father broke into a loud clattering laugh and she work to see Burnell standing by the windows rattling the Venetian blind up to the very top.

'Hullo,' he said. 'Didn't wake you, did I? Nothing much wrong with the weather this morning.'

He was enormously pleased. Weather like this set a final seal on his bargain. He felt, somehow, that he had bought the lovely day, too – got it chucked in dirt cheap with the house and ground. He dashed off to his bath and Linda turned over and raised herself on one elbow to see the room by daylight. All the furniture had found a place – all the old paraphernalia – as she expressed it. Even the photographs were on the mantelpiece and the medicine bottles on the shelf above the wash-stand. Her clothes lay across a chair – her outdoor things, a purple cape and a round hat with a plume in it. Looking at them she wished that she was going away from this house, too. And she saw herself driving away from them all in a little buggy, driving away from everybody and not even waving.

Back came Stanley girt with a towel, glowing and slapping his thighs. He pitched the wet towel on top of her hat and cape, and standing firm in the exact centre of a square of sunlight he began to do his exercises. Deep breathing, bending and squatting like a frog and shooting out his legs. He was so delighted with his firm, obedient body that he hit himself on the chest and gave a loud 'Ah.' But this amazing vigour seemed to set him worlds away from Linda. She lay on the white tumbled bed and watched him as if from the clouds.

'Oh, damn! Oh, blast!' said Stanley, who had butted into a crisp white shirt only to find that some idiot had fastened the neck-band and he was caught. He stalked over to Linda waving his arms.

'You look like a big fat turkey,' said she.

'Fat. I like that,' said Stanley. 'I haven't a square inch of fat on me. Feel that.'

'It's rock – it's iron,' mocked she.

'You'd be surprised,' said Stanley, as though this were intensely interesting, 'at the number of chaps at the club who have got a corporation. Young chaps, you know – men of my age.' He began parting his bushy ginger hair, his blue eyes fixed and round in the glass, his knees bent, because the dressing table was always – confound it – a bit too low for him. 'Little Wally Bell, for instance,' and he straightened, describing upon himself an enormous curve with the hairbrush. 'I must say I've a perfect horror. . . .'

'My dear, don't worry. You'll never be fat. You are far too energetic.'

'Yes, yes, I suppose that's true,' said he, comforted for the hundredth time, and taking a pearl pen-knife out of his pocket he began to pare his nails.

'Breakfast, Stanley.' Beryl was at the door. 'Oh, Linda, mother says you are not to get up yet.' She popped her head in at the door. She had a big piece of syringa stuck through her hair.

'Everything we left on the verandah last night is simply sopping this morning. You should see poor dear mother wringing out the tables and the chairs. However, there is no harm done –' this with the faintest glance at Stanley.

'Have you told Pat to have the buggy round in time? It's a good six and a half miles to the office.'

'I can imagine what this early start for the office will be like,' thought Linda. 'It will be very high pressure indeed.'

'Pat, Pat.' She heard the servant girl calling. But Pat was evidently hard to find; the silly voice went baa-baaing through the garden.

Linda did not rest again until the final slam of the front door told her that Stanley was really gone.

Later she heard her children playing in the garden. Lottie's stolid, compact little voice cried: 'Ke–zia. Isa–bel.' She was always getting lost or losing people only to find them again, to her great surprise, round the next tree or the next corner. 'Oh, there you are after all.' They had been turned out after breakfast and told not to come back to the house until they were called. Isabel wheeled a neat pramload of prim dolls and Lottie was allowed for a great treat to walk beside her holding the doll's parasol over the face of the wax one.

'Where are you going to, Kezia?' asked Isabel, who longed to find some light and menial duty that Kezia might perform and so be roped in under her government.

'Oh, just away,' said Kezia. . . .

Then she did not hear them any more. What a glare there was in the room. She hated blinds pulled up to the top at

any time, but in the morning it was intolerable. She turned over to the wall and idly, with one finger, she traced a poppy on the wall-paper and a leaf and a stem and a fat bursting bud. In the quiet, and under her tracing finger, the poppy seemed to come alive. She could feel the sticky, silky petals, the stem, hairy like a gooseberry skin, the rough leaf and the tight glazed bud. Things had a habit of coming alive like that. Not only large substantial things like furniture but curtains and the patterns of stuffs and the fringes of quilts and cushions. How often she had seen the tassel fringe of her quilt change into a funny procession of dancers with priests attending. . . . For there were some tassels that did not dance at all but walked stately, bent forward as if praying or chanting. How often the medicine bottles had turned into a row of little men with brown top-hats on; and the washstand jug had a way of sitting in the basin like a fat bird in a round nest.

'I dreamed about birds last night,' thought Linda. What was it? She had forgotten. But the strangest part of this coming alive of things was what they did. They listened, they seemed to swell out with some mysterious important content, and when they were full she felt that they smiled. But it was not for her, only, their sly secret smile; they were members of a secret society and they smiled among themselves. Sometimes, when she had fallen asleep in the daytime, she woke and could not lift a finger, could not even turn her eyes to left or right because THEY were there; sometimes when she went out of a room and left it empty, she knew as she clicked the door to that THEY were filling it. And there were times in the evenings when she was upstairs, perhaps, and everybody else was down, when she could hardly escape from them. Then she could not hurry, she

could not hum a tune; if she tried to say ever so carelessly – 'Bother that old thimble' – THEY were not deceived, THEY knew how frightened she was; THEY saw how she turned her head away as she passed the mirror. What Linda always felt was that THEY wanted something of her, and she knew that if she gave herself up and was quiet, more than quiet, silent, motionless, something would really happen.

'It's very quiet now,' she thought. She opened her eyes wide, and she heard the silence spinning its soft endless web. How lightly she breathed; she scarcely had to breathe at all.

Yes, everything had come alive down to the minutest, tiniest particle, and she did not feel her bed, she floated, held up in the air. Only she seemed to be listening with her wide open watchful eyes, waiting for someone to come who just did not come, watching for something to happen that just did not happen.

VI

In the kitchen at the long deal table under the two windows old Mrs Fairfield was washing the breakfast dishes. The kitchen window looked out on to a big grass patch that led down to the vegetable garden and the rhubarb beds. On one side the grass patch was bordered by the scullery and wash-house and over this whitewashed lean-to there grew a knotted vine. She had noticed yesterday that a few tiny corkscrew tendrils had come right through some cracks in the scullery ceiling and all the windows of the lean-to had a thick frill of ruffled green.

'I am very fond of a grape vine,' declared Mrs Fairfield, 'but I do not think that the grapes will ripen here. It takes Australian sun.' And she remembered how Beryl when she was a baby had been picking some white grapes from the vine

on the back verandah of their Tasmanian house and she had been stung on the leg by a huge red ant. She saw Beryl in a little plaid dress with red ribbon tie-ups on the shoulders screaming so dreadfully that half the street rushed in. And how the child's leg had swelled! 'T–t–t–t!' Mrs Fairfield caught her breath remembering. 'Poor child, how terrifying it was.' And she set her lips tight and went over to the stove for some more hot water. The water frothed in the big soapy bowl with pink and blue bubbles on top of the foam. Old Mrs Fairfield's arms were bare to the elbow and stained a bright pink. She wore a grey foulard dress patterned with large purple pansies, a white linen apron and a high cap shaped like a jelly mould of white muslin. At her throat there was a silver crescent moon with five little owls seated on it, and round her neck she wore a watch-guard made of black beads.

It was hard to believe that she had not been in that kitchen for years; she was so much a part of it. She put the crocks away with a sure, precise touch, moving leisurely and ample from the stove to the dresser, looking into the pantry and the larder as though there were not an unfamiliar corner. When she had finished, everything in the kitchen had become part of a series of patterns. She stood in the middle of the room wiping her hands on a check cloth; a smile beamed on her lips; she thought it looked very nice, very satisfactory.

'Mother! Mother! Are you there?' called Beryl.

'Yes, dear. Do you want me?'

'No. I'm coming,' and Beryl rushed in, very flushed, dragging with her two big pictures.

'Mother, whatever can I do with these awful hideous Chinese paintings that Chung Wah gave Stanley went he went bankrupt? It's absurd to say that they are valuable, because they were hanging in Chung Wah's fruit shop for

months before. I can't make out why Stanley wants them kept. I'm sure he thinks them just as hideous as we do, but it's because of the frames,' she said spitefully. 'I suppose he thinks the frames might fetch something some day or other.'

'Why don't you hang them in the passage?' suggested Mrs Fairfield; 'they would not be much seen there.'

'I can't. There is no room. I've hung all the photographs of his office there before and after building, and the signed photos of his business friends, and that awful enlargement of Isabel lying on the mat in her singlet.' Her angry glance swept the placid kitchen. 'I know what I'll do. I'll hang them here. I will tell Stanley they got a little damp in the moving so I have put them in here for the time being.'

She dragged a chair forward, jumped on it, took a hammer and a big nail out of her pinafore pocket and banged away.

'There! That's enough! Hand me the picture, mother.'

'One moment, child.' Her mother was wiping over the carved ebony frame.

'Oh, mother, really you need not dust them. It would take years to dust all those little holes.' And she frowned at the top of her mother's head and bit her lip with impatience. Mother's deliberate way of doing things was simply maddening. It was old age, she supposed, loftily.

At last the two pictures were hung side by side. She jumped off the chair, stowing away the little hammer.

'They don't look so bad there, do they?' said she. 'And at any rate nobody need gaze at them except Pat and the servant girl – have I got a spider's web on my face, mother? I've been poking into that cupboard under the stairs and now something keeps tickling my nose.'

But before Mrs Fairfield had time to look Beryl had turned away. Someone tapped on the window: Linda was

there, nodding and smiling. They heard the latch of the scullery door lift and she came in. She had no hat on; her hair stood up on her head in curling rings and she was wrapped up in an old cashmere shawl.

'I'm so hungry,' said Linda: 'where can I get something to eat, mother? This is the first time I've been in the kitchen. It says "mother" all over; everything is in pairs.'

'I will make you some tea,' said Mrs Fairfield, spreading a clean napkin over a corner of the table, 'and Beryl can have a cup with you.'

'Beryl, do you want half my gingerbread?' Linda waved the knife at her. 'Beryl, do you like the house now that we are here?'

'Oh yes, I like the house immensely and the garden is beautiful, but it feels very far away from everything to me. I can't imagine people coming out from town to see us in that dreadful jolting bus, and I am sure there is not anyone here to come and call. Of course it does not matter to you because –'

'But there's the buggy,' said Linda. 'Pat can drive you into town whenever you like.'

That was a consolation, certainly, but there was something at the back of Beryl's mind, something she did not even put into words for herself.

'Oh, well, at any rate it won't kill us,' she said dryly, putting down her empty cup and standing up and stretching. 'I am going to hang curtains.' And she ran away singing:

How many thousand birds I see
That sing aloud from every tree . . .

'. . . birds I see That sing aloud from every tree. . . .' But when she reached the dining-room she stopped singing, her

face changed; it became gloomy and sullen.

'One may as well rot here as anywhere else,' she muttered savagely, digging the stiff brass safety-pins into the red serge curtains.

The two left in the kitchen were quiet for a little. Linda leaned her cheek on her fingers and watched her mother. She thought her mother looked wonderfully beautiful with her back to the leafy window. There was something comforting in the sight of her that Linda felt she could never do without. She needed the sweet smell of her flesh, and the soft feel of her cheeks and her arms and shoulders still softer. She loved the way her hair curled, silver at her forehead, lighter at her neck, and bright brown still in the big coil under the muslin cap. Exquisite were her mother's hands, and the two rings she wore seemed to melt into her creamy skin. And she was always so fresh, so delicious. The old woman could bear nothing but linen next to her body and she bathed in cold water winter and summer.

'Isn't there anything for me to do?' asked Linda.

'No, darling. I wish you would go into the garden and give an eye to your children; but that I know you will not do.'

'Of course I will, but you know Isabel is much more grown up than any of us.'

'Yes, but Kezia is not,' said Mrs Fairfield.

'Oh, Kezia has been tossed by a bull hours ago,' said Linda, winding herself up in her shawl again.

But no, Kezia had seen a bull through a hole in a knot of wood in the paling that separated the tennis lawn from the paddock. But she had not liked the bull frightfully, so she had walked away back through the orchard, up the grassy slope, along the path by the lace bark tree and so into the spread tangled garden. She did not believe that she would

ever not get lost in this garden. Twice she had found her way back to the big iron gates they had driven through the night before, and then had turned to walk up the drive that led to the house, but there were so many little paths on either side. On one side they all led into a tangle of tall dark trees and strange bushes with flat velvet leaves and feathery cream flowers that buzzed with flies when you shook them – this was the frightening side, and no garden at all. The little paths here were wet and clayey with tree roots spanned across them like the marks of big fowls' feet.

But on the other side of the drive there was a high box border and the paths had box edges and all of them led into a deeper and deeper tangle of flowers. The camellias were in bloom, white and crimson and pink and white striped with flashing leaves. You could not see a leaf on the syringa bushes for the white clusters. The roses were in flower – gentlemen's button-hole roses, little white ones, but far too full of insects to hold under anyone's nose, pink monthly roses with a ring of fallen petals round the bushes, cabbage roses on thick stalks, moss roses, always in bud, pink smooth beauties opening curl on curl, red ones so dark they seemed to turn black as they fell, and a certain exquisite cream kind with a slender red stem and bright scarlet leaves.

There were clumps of fairy bells, and all kinds of geraniums, and there were little trees of verbena and bluish lavender bushes and a bed of pelargoniums with velvet eyes and leaves like moths' wings. There was a bed of nothing but mignonette and another of nothing but pansies – borders of double and single daisies and all kinds of little tufty plants she had never seen before.

The red-hot pokers were taller than she; the Japanese sunflowers grew in a tiny jungle. She sat down on one of

the box borders. By pressing hard at first it made a nice seat. But how dusty it was inside! Kezia bent down to look and sneezed and rubbed her nose.

And then she found herself at the top of the rolling grassy slope that led down to the orchard. . . . She looked down at the slope a moment; then she lay down on her back, gave a squeak and rolled over and over into the thick flowery orchard grass. As she lay waiting for things to stop spinning, she decided to go up to the house and ask the servant girl for an empty match-box. She wanted to make a surprise for the grandmother. . . . First she would put a leaf inside with a big violet lying on it, then she would put a very small white picotee, perhaps, on each side of the violet, and then she would sprinkle some lavender on the top, but not to cover their heads.

She often made these surprises for her grandmother, and they were always most successful.

'Do you want a match, my granny?'

'Why, yes, child, I believe a match is just what I'm looking for.'

The grandmother slowly opened the box and came upon the picture inside.

'Good gracious, child! How you astonished me!'

'I can make her one every day here,' she thought, scrambling up the grass on her slippery shoes.

But on her way back to the house she came to that island that lay in the middle of the drive, dividing the drive into two arms that met in front of the house. The island was made of grass banked up high. Nothing grew on the top except one huge plant with thick, grey-green, thorny leaves, and out of the middle there sprang up a tall stout stem. Some of the leaves of the plant were so old that they curled

up in the air no longer; they turned back, they were split and broken; some of them lay flat and withered in the ground.

Whatever could it be? She had never seen anything like it before. She stood and stared. And then she saw her mother coming down the path.

'Mother, what is it?' asked Kezia.

Linda looking up at the fat swelling plant with its cruel leaves and fleshy stem. High above them, as though becalmed in the air, and yet holding so fast to the earth it grew from, it might have had claws instead of roots. The curving leaves seemed to be hiding something; the blind stem cut into the air as if no wind could ever shake it.

'That is an aloe, Kezia,' said her mother.

'Does it ever have any flowers?'

'Yes, Kezia,' and Linda smiled down at her, and half shut her eyes. 'Once every hundred years.'

VII

On his way home from the office Stanley Burnell stopped the buggy at the Bodega, got out and bought a large bottle of oysters. At the Chinaman's shop next door he bought a pineapple in the pink of condition, and noticing a basket of fresh black cherries he told John to put him a pound of those as well. The oysters and the pine he stowed away in the box under the seat, but the cherries he kept in his hand.

Pat, the handy-man, leapt off the box and tucked him up again in the brown rug.

'Lift yer feet, Mr Burnell, while I give yer a fold under,' said he.

'Right! Right! First-rate!' said Stanley. 'You can make straight for home now.'

Pat gave the grey mare a touch and the buggy sprang forward.

'I believe this man is a first-rate chap,' thought Stanley. He liked the look of him sitting up there in his neat brown coat and brown bowler. He liked the way Pat had tucked him in, and liked his eyes. There was nothing servile about him – and if there was one thing he hated more than another it was servility. And he looked as if he was pleased with his job happy and contented already.

The grey mare went very well; Burnell was impatient to be out of the town. He wanted to be home. Ah, it was splendid to live in the country – to get right out of that hole of a town once the office was closed; and this drive in the fresh warm air, knowing all the while that his own house was at the other end, with its garden and paddocks, its three tip-top cows and enough fowls and ducks to keep them in poultry, was splendid too.

As they left the town finally and bowled away up the deserted road his heart beat hard for joy. He rooted in the bag and began to eat the cherries, three or four at a time, chucking the stones over the side of the buggy. They were delicious, so plump and cold, without a spot or a bruise on them.

Look at those two, now – black one side and white the other – perfect! A perfect little pair of Siamese twins. And he stuck them in his button-hole. . . . By Jove, he wouldn't mind giving that chap up there a handful – but no, better not. Better wait until he had been with him a bit longer.

He began to plan what he would do with his Saturday afternoons and his Sundays. He wouldn't go to the club for lunch on Saturday. No, cut away from the office as soon as possible and get them to give him a couple of slices of cold meat and half a lettuce when he got home. And then he'd get

a few chaps out from town to play tennis in the afternoon. Not too many – three at most. Beryl was a good player, too. . . . He stretched out his right arm and slowly bent it, feeling the muscle. . . . A bath, a good rub-down, a cigar on the verandah after dinner. . . .

On Sunday morning they would go to church – the children and all. Which reminded him that he must hire a pew, in the sun if possible and well forward so as to be out of the draught of the door. In fancy he heard himself intoning extremely well: 'When thou did overcome the *Sharpness* of Death Thou didst open the *King*dom of Heaven to *all* Believers.' And he saw the neat brass-edged card on the corner of the pew – Mr Stanley Burnell and family. . . . The rest of the day he'd loaf about with Linda. . . . Now they were walking about the garden; she was on his arm, and he was explaining to her at length what he intended doing at the office the week following. He heard her saying:

'My dear, I think that is most wise.' . . . Talking things over with Linda was a wonderful help even though they were apt to drift away from the point.

Hang it all! They weren't getting along very fast. Pat had put the brake on again. Ugh! What a brute of a thing it was. He could feel it in the pit of his stomach.

A sort of panic overtook Burnell whenever he approached near home. Before he was well inside the gate he would shout to anyone within sight: 'Is everything all right?' And then he did not believe it was until he heard Linda say: 'Hullo! Are you home again?' That was the worst of living in the country – it took the deuce of a long time to get back. . . . But now they weren't far off. They were on the top of the last hill; it was a gentle slope all the way now and not more than half a mile.

Pat trailed the whip over the mare's back and he coaxed

her: 'Goop now. Goop now.'

It wanted a few minutes to sunset. Everything stood motionless bathed in bright, metallic light and from the paddocks on either side there streamed the milky scent of ripe grass. The iron gates were open. They dashed through and up the drive and round the island, stopping at the exact middle of the verandah.

'Did she satisfy yer, Sir?' said Pat, getting off the box and grinning at his master.

'Very well indeed, Pat,' said Stanley.

Linda came out of the glass door; her voice rang in the shadowy quiet. 'Hullo! Are you home again?'

At the sound of her his heart beat so hard that he could hardly stop himself dashing up the steps and catching her in his arms.

'Yes, I'm home again. Is everything all right?'

Pat began to lead the buggy round to the side gate that opened into the courtyard.

'Here, half a moment,' said Burnell. 'Hand me those two parcels.' And he said to Linda, 'I've brought you back a bottle of oysters and a pineapple,' as though he had brought her back all the harvest of the earth.

They went into the hall; Linda carried the oysters in one hand and the pineapple in the other. Burnell shut the glass door, threw his hat down, put his arms round her and strained her to him, kissing the top of her head, her ears, her lips, her eyes.

'Oh, dear! Oh, dear!' said she. 'Wait a moment. Let me put down these silly things,' and she put the bottle of oysters and the pine on a little carved chair. 'What have you got in your buttonhole – cherries?' She took them out and hung them over his ear.

'Don't do that, darling. They are for you.'

So she took them off his ear again. 'You don't mind if I save them. They'd spoil my appetite for dinner. Come and see your children. They are having tea.'

The lamp was lighted on the nursery table. Mrs Fairfield was cutting and spreading bread and butter. The three little girls sat up to table wearing large bibs embroidered with their names. They wiped their mouths as their father came in ready to be kissed. The windows were open; a jar of wild flowers stood on the mantelpiece, and the lamp made a big soft bubble of light on the ceiling.

'You seem pretty snug, mother,' said Burnell, blinking at the light. Isabel and Lottie sat one on either side of the table, Kezia at the bottom – the place at the top was empty.

'That's where my boy ought to sit,' thought Stanley. He tightened his arm round Linda's shoulder. By God, he was a perfect fool to feel as happy as this!

'We are, Stanley. We are very snug,' said Mrs Fairfield, cutting Kezia's bread into fingers.

'Like it better than town – eh, children?' asked Burnell.

'Oh, yes,' said the three little girls, and Isabel added as an after-thought: 'Thank you very much indeed, father dear.'

'Come upstairs,' said Linda. 'I'll bring your slippers.'

But the stairs were too narrow for them to go up arm in arm. It was quite dark in the room. He heard her ring tapping on the marble mantelpiece as she felt for the matches.

'I've got some, darling. I'll light the candles.'

But instead he came up behind her and again he put his arms round her and pressed her head into his shoulder.

'I'm so confoundedly happy,' he said.

'Are you?' She turned and put her hands on his breast and looked up at him.

'I don't know what has come over me,' he protested.

It was quite dark outside now and heavy dew was falling. When Linda shut the window the cold dew touched her finger tips. Far away a dog barked. 'I believe there is going to be a moon,' she said.

At the words, and with the cold wet dew on her fingers, she felt as though the moon had risen – that she was being strangely discovered in a flood of cold light. She shivered; she came away from the window and sat down upon the box ottoman beside Stanley.

* * *

In the dining-room, by the flicker of a wood fire, Beryl sat on a hassock playing the guitar. She had bathed and changed all her clothes. Now she wore a white muslin dress with black spots on it and in her hair she had pinned a black silk rose.

> Nature has gone to her rest, love,
>   See, we are alone.
> Give me your hand to press, love,
>   Lightly within my own.

She played and sang half to herself, for she was watching herself playing and singing. The firelight gleamed on her shoes, on the ruddy belly of the guitar, and on her white fingers. . . .

'If I were outside the window and looked in and saw myself I really would be rather struck,' thought she. Still more softly she played the accompaniment – not singing now but listening.

. . . 'The first time that I ever saw you, little girl – oh, you had no idea that you were not alone – you were sitting with

your little feet upon a hassock, playing the guitar. God, I can never forget. . . .' Beryl flung up her head and began to sing again:

Even the moon is aweary . . .

But there came a loud bang at the door. The servant girl's crimson face popped through.

'Please, Miss Beryl, I've got to come and lay.'

'Certainly, Alice,' said Beryl, in a voice of ice. She put the guitar in a corner. Alice lunged in with a heavy black iron tray.

'Well, I have had a job with that oving,' said she. 'I can't get nothing to brown.'

'Really!' said Beryl.

But no, she could not stand that fool of a girl. She ran into the dark drawing-room and began walking up and down. . . . Oh, she was restless, restless. There was a mirror over the mantel. She leaned her arms along and looked at her pale shadow in it. How beautiful she looked, but there was nobody to see, nobody.

'Why must you suffer so?' said the face in the mirror. 'You were not made for suffering. . . . Smile!'

Beryl smiled, and really her smile *was* so adorable that she smiled again – but this time because she could not help it.

VIII

'Good morning, Mrs Jones.'

'Oh, good morning, Mrs Smith. I'm so glad to see you. Have you brought your children?'

'Yes, I've brought both my twins. I have had another baby since I saw you last, but she came so suddenly that I haven't had time to make her any clothes, yet. So I left her. . . . How is your husband?'

'Oh, he is very well, thank you. At least he had a nawful cold but Queen Victoria – she's my godmother, you know – sent him a case of pineapples and that cured it im-mediately. Is that your new servant?'

'Yes, her name's Gwen. I've only had her two days. Oh, Gwen, this is my friend Mrs Smith.'

'Good morning, Mrs Smith. Dinner won't be ready for about ten minutes.'

'I don't think you ought to introduce me to the servant. I think I ought to just begin talking to her.'

'Well, she's more of a lady-help than a servant and you do introduce lady-helps, I know, because Mrs Samuel Josephs had one.'

'Oh, well, it doesn't matter,' said the servant, carelessly, beating up a chocolate custard with half a broken clothes peg. The dinner was baking beautifully on a concrete step. She began to lay the cloth on a pink garden seat. In front of each person she put two geranium leaf plates, a pine needle fork and a twig knife. There were three daisy heads on a laurel leaf for poached eggs, some slices of fuchsia petal cold beef, some lovely little rissoles made of earth and water and dandelion seeds, and the chocolate custard which she had decided to serve in the pawa shell she had cooked it in.

'You needn't trouble about my children,' said Mrs Smith graciously. 'If you'll just take this bottle and fill it at the tap – I mean at the dairy.'

'Oh, all right,' said Gwen, and she whispered to Mrs Jones: 'Shall I go and ask Alice for a little bit of real milk?'

But someone called from the front of the house and the luncheon party melted away, leaving the charming table, leaving the rissoles and the poached eggs to the ants and to an old snail who pushed his quivering horns over the edge of the garden seat and began to nibble a geranium plate.

'Come round to the front, children. Pip and Rags have come.'

The Trout boys were the cousins Kezia had mentioned to the storeman. They lived about a mile away in a house called Monkey Tree Cottage. Pip was tall for his age, with lank black hair and a white face, but Rags was very small and so thin that when he was undressed his shoulder blades stuck out like two little wings. They had a mongrel dog with pale blue eyes and a long tail turned up at the end who followed them everywhere; he was called Snooker. They spent half their time combing and brushing Snooker and dosing him with various awful mixtures concocted by Pip, and kept secretly by him in a broken jug covered with an old kettle lid. Even faithful little Rags was not allowed to know the full secret of these mixtures. . . . Take some carbolic tooth powder and a pinch of sulphur powdered up fine, and perhaps a bit of starch to stiffen up Snooker's cat. . . . But that was not all; Rags privately thought that the rest was gun-powder. . . . And he never was allowed to help with the mixing because of the danger. . . . 'Why if a spot of this flew in your eye, you would be blinded for life,' Pip would say, stirring the mixture with an iron spoon. 'And there's always the chance – just the chance, mind you – of it exploding if you whack it hard enough. . . . Two spoons of this in a kerosene tin will be enough to kill thousands of fleas.' But Snooker spent all his spare time biting and snuffling, and he stank abominably.

'It's because he is such a grand fighting dog,' Pip would say. 'All fighting dogs smell.'

The Trout boys had often spent the day with the Burnells in town, but now that they lived in this fine house and boncer garden they were inclined to be very friendly. Besides, both of them liked playing with girls – Pip, because he could fox them so, and because Lottie was so easily frightened, and Rags for a shameful reason. He adored dolls. How he would look at a doll as it lay asleep, speaking in a whisper and smiling timidly, and what a treat it was to him to be allowed to hold one. . . .

'Curve your arms around her. Don't keep them stiff like that. You'll drop her,' Isabel would say sternly.

Now they were standing on the verandah and holding back Snooker who wanted to go into the house but wasn't allowed to because Aunt Linda hated decent dogs.

'We came over in the bus with Mum,' they said, 'and we're going to spend the afternoon with you. We brought over a batch of our gingerbread for Aunt Linda. Our Minnie made it. It's all over nuts.'

'I skinned the almonds,' said Pip. 'I just stuck my hand into a saucepan of boiling water and grabbed them out and gave them a kind of pinch and the nuts flew out of the skins, some of them as high as the ceiling. Didn't they, Rags?'

Rags nodded. 'When they make cakes at our place,' said Pip, 'we always stay in the kitchen, Rags and me, and I get the bowl and he gets the spoon and the egg beater. Sponge cake's best. It's all frothy stuff, then.'

He ran down the verandah steps to the lawn, planted his hands on the grass, bent forward, and just did not stand on his head.

'That lawn's all bumpy,' he said. 'You have to have a flat place for standing on your head. I can walk round the

monkey tree on my head at our place. Can't I, Rags?'

'Nearly,' said Rags faintly.

'Stand on your head on the verandah. That's quite flat,' said Kezia.

'No, smarty,' said Pip. 'You have to do it on something soft. Because if you give a jerk and fall over, something in your neck goes click, and it breaks off. Dad told me.'

'Oh, do let's play something,' said Kezia.

'Very well,' said Isabel quickly, 'we'll play hospitals. I will be the nurse and Pip can be the doctor and you and Lottie and Rags can be the sick people.'

Lottie didn't want to play that, because last time Pip had squeezed something down her throat and it hurt awfully.

'Pooh,' scoffed Pip. 'It was only the juice out of a bit of mandarin peel.'

'Well, let's play ladies,' said Isabel. 'Pip can be the father and you can be all our dear little children.'

'I hate playing ladies,' said Kezia. 'You always make us go to church hand in hand and come home and go to bed.'

Suddenly Pip took a filthy handkerchief out of his pocket. 'Snooker! Here, sir,' he called. But Snooker, as usual, tried to sneak away, his tail between his legs. Pip leapt on top of him, and pressed him between his knees.

'Keep his head firm, Rags,' he said, and he tied the handkerchief round Snooker's head with a funny knot sticking up at the top.

'Whatever is that for?' asked Lottie.

'It's to train his ears to grow more close to his head – see?' said Pip. 'All fighting dogs have ears that lie back. But Snooker's ears are a bit too soft.'

'I know,' said Kezia. 'They are always turning inside out. I hate that.'

Snooker lay down, made one feeble effort with his paw to get the handkerchief off, but finding he could not, trailed after the children, shivering with misery.

IX

Pat came swinging along; in his hand he held a little tomahawk that winked in the sun.

'Come with me,' he said to the children, 'and I'll show you how the kings of Ireland chop the head off a duck.'

They drew back – they didn't believe him, and besides, the Trout boys had never seen Pat before.

'Come on now,' he coaxed, smiling and holding out his hand to Kezia.

'Is it a real duck's head? One from the paddock?'

'It is,' said Pat. She put her hand in his hard dry one, and he stuck the tomahawk in his belt and held out the other to Rags. He loved little children.

'I'd better keep hold of Snooker's head if there's going to be any blood about,' said Pip, 'because the sight of blood makes him awfully wild.' He ran ahead dragging Snooker by the handkerchief.

'Do you think we ought to go?' whispered Isabel. 'We haven't asked or anything. Have we?'

At the bottom of the orchard a gate was set in the paling fence. On the other side a steep bank led down to a bridge that spanned the creek, and once up the bank on the other side you were on the fringe of the paddocks. A little old stable in the first paddock had been turned into a fowl house. The fowls had strayed far away across the paddock down to a dumping ground, in a hollow, but the ducks kept close to that part of the creek that flowed under the bridge.

Tall bushes overhung the stream with red leaves and yellow

flowers and clusters of blackberries. At some places the stream was wide and shallow, but at others it tumbled into deep little pools with foam at the edges and quivering bubbles. It was in these pools that the big white ducks had made themselves at home, swimming and guzzling along the weedy banks.

Up and down they swam, preening their dazzling breasts, and other ducks with the same dazzling breasts and yellow bills swam upside down with them.

'There is the little Irish navy,' said Pat, and look at the old admiral there with the green neck and the grand little flagstaff on his tail.'

He pulled a handful of grain from his pocket and began to walk towards the fowl-house, lazy, his straw hat with the broken crown pulled over his eyes.

'Lid. Lid – lid – lid – lid –' he called.

'Qua. Qua – qua – qua – qua –' answered the ducks, making for land, and flapping and scrambling up the bank they streamed after him in a long waddling line. He coaxed them, pretending to throw the grain, shaking it in his hands and calling to them until they swept round him in a white ring.

From far away the fowls heard the clamour and they too came running across the paddock, their heads thrust forward, their wings spread, turning in their feet in the silly way fowls run and scolding as they came.

Then Pat scattered the grain and the greedy ducks began to gobble. Quickly he stooped, seized two, one under each arm, and strode across to the children. Their darting heads and round eyes frightened the children – all except Pip.

'Come on, sillies,' he cried, 'they can't bite. They haven't any teeth. They've only got those two little holes in their beaks for breathing through.'

'Will you hold one while I finish with the other?' asked Pat. Pip let go of Snooker. 'Won't I? Won't I? Give us one. I don't mind how much he kicks.'

He nearly sobbed with delight when Pat gave the white lump into his arms.

There was an old stump beside the door of the fowl-house. Pat grabbed the duck by the legs, laid it flat across the stump, and almost at the same moment down came the little tomahawk and the duck's head flew off the stump. Up the blood spurted over the white feathers and over his hand.

When the children saw the blood they were frightened no longer. They crowded round him and began to scream. Even Isabel leaped about crying: 'The blood! The blood!' Pip forgot all about his duck. He simply threw it away from him and shouted, 'I saw it. I saw it,' and jumped round the wood block.

Rags, with cheeks as white as paper, ran up to the little head, put out a finger as if he wanted to touch it, shrank back again and then again put out a finger. He was shivering all over.

Even Lottie, frightened little Lottie, began to laugh and pointed at the duck and shrieked: 'Look, Kezia, look.'

'Watch it!' shouted Pat. He put down the body and it began to waddle – with only a long spurt of blood where the head had been; it began to pad away without a sound towards the steep bank that led to the stream. . . . That was the crowning wonder.

'Do you see that? Do you see that?' yelled Pip. He ran among the little girls tugging at their pinafores.

'It's like a little engine. It's like a funny little railway engine,' squealed Isabel.

But Kezia suddenly rushed at Pat and flung her arms round his legs and butted her head as hard as she could

against his knees.

'Put head back! Put head back!' she screamed.

When he stooped to move her she would not let go or take her head away. She held on as hard as she could and sobbed: 'Head back! Head back!' until it sounded like a loud strange hiccup.

'It's stopped . It's tumbled over. It's dead,' said Pip.

Pat dragged Kezia up into his arms. Her sun-bonnet had fallen back, but she would not let him look at her face. No, she pressed her face into a bone in his shoulder and clasped her arms round his neck.

The children stopped screaming as suddenly as they had begun. They stood round the dead duck. Rags was not frightened of the head any more. He knelt down and stroked it, now.

'I don't think the head is quite dead yet,' he said. 'Do you think it would keep alive if I gave it something to drink?'

But Pip got very cross: 'Bah! You baby.' He whistled to Snooker and went off.

When Isabel went up to Lottie, Lottie snatched away.

'What are you always touching me for, Isabel?'

'There now,' said Pat to Kezia. 'There's the grand little girl.'

She put up her hands and touched his ears. She felt something. Slowly she raised her quivering face and looked. Pat wore little round gold ear-rings. She never knew that men wore ear-rings. She was very much surprised.

'Do they come on and off?' she asked huskily.

X

Up in the house, in the warm tidy kitchen, Alice, the servant girl, was getting the afternoon tea. She was 'dressed'. She had on a black stuff dress that smelt under the arms, a white

apron like a large sheet of paper, and a lace bow pinned on to her hair with two jetty pins. Also her comfortable carpet slippers were changed for a pair of black leather ones that pinched her corn on her little toe something dreadful. . . .

It was warm in the kitchen. A blow-fly buzzed, a fan of whity steam came out of the kettle, and the lid kept up a rattling jig as the water bubbled. The clock ticked in the warm air, slow and deliberate, like the click of an old woman's knitting needle, and sometimes – for no reason at all, for there wasn't any breeze – the blind swung out and back, tapping the window.

Alice was making water-cress sandwiches. She had a lump of butter on the table, a barracouta loaf, and the cresses tumbled in a white cloth.

But propped against the butter dish there was a dirty, greasy little book, half unstitched, with curled edges, and while she mashed the butter she read:

'To dream of black-beetles drawing a hearse is bad. Signifies death of one you hold near or dear, either father, husband, brother, son, or intended. If beetles crawl backwards as you watch them it means death from fire or from great height such as flight of stairs, scaffolding, etc.

'Spiders. To dream of spiders creeping over you is good. Signifies large sum of money in near future. Should party be in family way an easy confinement may be expected. But care should be taken in sixth month to avoid eating of probable present of shell fish. . . .'

How many thousand birds I see.

Oh, life. There was Miss Beryl. Alice dropped the knife and slipped the *Dream Book* under the butter dish. But she

hadn't time to hide it quite, for Beryl ran into the kitchen and up to the table, and the first thing her eye lighted on were those greasy edges. Alice saw Miss Beryl's meaning little smile and the way she raised her eyebrows and screwed up her eyes as though she were not quite sure what that could be. She decided to answer if Miss Beryl should ask her: 'Nothing as belongs to you, Miss.' But she knew Miss Beryl would not ask her.

Alice was a mild creature in reality, but she had the most marvellous retorts ready for questions that she knew would never be put to her. The composing of them and the turning of them over and over in her mind comforted her just as much as if they'd been expressed. Really, they kept her alive in places where she'd been that chivvied she'd been afraid to go to bed at night with a box of matches on the chair in case she bit the tops off in her sleep, as you might say.

'Oh, Alice,' said Miss Beryl. 'There's one extra to tea, so heat a plate of yesterday's scones, please. And put on the Victoria sandwich as well as the coffee cake. And don't forget to put little doyleys under the plates – will you? You did yesterday, you know, and the tea looked so ugly and common. And, Alice, don't put that dreadful old pink and green cosy on the afternoon teapot again. That is only for the mornings. Really, I think it ought to be kept for the kitchen – it's so shabby, and quite smelly. Put on the Japanese one. You quite understand, don't you?'

Miss Beryl had finished.

That sing aloud from every tree . . .

she sang as she left the kitchen, very pleased with her firm handling of Alice.

Oh, Alice was wild. She wasn't one to mind being told, but there was something in the way Miss Beryl had of speaking to her that she couldn't stand. Oh, that she couldn't. It made her curl up inside, as you might say, and she fair trembled. But what Alice really hated Miss Beryl for was that she made her feel low. She talked to Alice in a special voice as though she wasn't quite all there; and she never lost her temper with her – never. Even when Alice dropped anything or forgot anything important Miss Beryl seemed to have expected it to happen.

'If you please, Mrs Burnell,' said an imaginary Alice, as she buttered the scones, 'I'd rather not take my orders from Miss Beryl. I may be only a common servant girl as doesn't know how to play the guitar, but. . . .'

This last thrust pleased her so much that she quite recovered her temper.

'The only thing to do,' she heard, as she opened the dining-room door, 'is to cut the sleeves out entirely and just have a broad band of black velvet over the shoulders instead. . . .'

XI

The white duck did not look as if it had ever had a head when Alice placed it in front of Stanley Burnell that night. It lay, in beautifully basted resignation, on a blue dish – its legs tied together with a piece of string and a wreath of little balls of stuffing round it.

It was hard to say which of the two, Alice or the duck, looked the better basted; they were both such a rich colour and they both had the same air of gloss and strain. But Alice was fiery and the duck a Spanish mahogany.

Burnell ran his eye along the edge of the carving knife. He prided himself very much upon his carving, upon making

a first-class job of it. He hated seeing a woman carve; they were always too slow and they never seemed to care what the meat looked like afterwards. Now he did; he took a real pride in cutting delicate shaves of cold beef, little wads of mutton, just the right thickness, and in dividing a chicken or a duck with nice precision. . . .

'Is this the first of the home products?' he asked, knowing perfectly well that it was.

'Yes, the butcher did not come. We have found out that he only calls twice a week.'

But there was no need to apologise. It was a superb bird. It wasn't meat at all, but a kind of superior jelly. 'My father would say,' said Burnell, 'this must have been one of those birds whose mother played to it in infancy upon the German flute. And the sweet strains of the dulcet instrument acted with such effect upon the infant mind. . . . Have some more, Beryl? You and I are the only ones in this house with a real feeling for food. I'm perfectly willing to state, in a court of law, if necessary, that I love good food.'

Tea was served in the drawing-room, and Beryl, who for some reason had been very charming to Stanley ever since he came home, suggested a game of crib. They sat at a little table near one of the open windows. Mrs Fairfield disappeared, and Linda lay in a rocking-chair, her arms above her head, rocking to and fro.

'You don't want the light – do you, Linda?' said Beryl. She moved the tall lamp so that she sat under its soft light.

How remote they looked, those two, from where Linda sat and rocked. The green table, the polished cards, Stanley's big hands and Beryl's tiny ones, all seemed to be part of one mysterious movement. Stanley himself, big and solid, in his dark suit, took his ease, and Beryl tossed her bright head

and pouted. Round her throat she wore an unfamiliar velvet ribbon. It changed her, somehow – altered the shape of her face – but it was charming, Linda decided. The room smelled of lilies; there were two big jars of arums in the fire-place.

'Fifteen two – fifteen four – and a pair is six and a run of three is nine,' said Stanley, so deliberately, he might have been counting sheep.

'I've nothing but two pairs,' said Beryl, exaggerating her woe because she knew how he loved winning.

The cribbage pegs were like two little people going up the road together, turning round the sharp corner, and coming down the road again. They were pursuing each other. They did not so much want to get ahead as to keep near enough to talk – to keep near, perhaps that was all.

But no, there was always one who was impatient and hopped away as the other came up, and would not listen. Perhaps the white peg was frightened of the red one, or perhaps he was cruel and would not give the red one a chance to speak. . . .

In the front of her dress Beryl wore a bunch of pansies, and once when the little pegs were side by side, she bent over and the pansies dropped out and covered them.

'What a shame,' said she, picking up the pansies. 'Just as they had a chance to fly into each other's arms.'

'Farewell, my girl,' laughed Stanley, and away the red peg hopped.

The drawing-room was long and narrow with glass doors that gave on to the verandah. It had a cream paper with a pattern of gilt roses, and the furniture, which had belonged to old Mrs Fairfield, was dark and plain. A little piano stood against the wall with yellow pleated silk let into the carved front. Above it hung an oil painting by Beryl of a large

cluster of surprised looking clematis. Each flower was the size of a small saucer, with a centre like an astonished eye fringed in black. But the room was not finished yet. Stanley had set his heart on a Chesterfield and two decent chairs. Linda liked it best as it was. . . .

Two big moths flew in through the window and round and round the circle of lamplight.

'Fly away before it is too late. Fly out again.'

Round and round they flew; they seemed to bring the silence and the moonlight in with them on their silent wings. . . .

'I've two kings,' said Stanley. 'Any good?'

'Quite good,' said Beryl.

Linda stopped rocking and got up. Stanley looked across. 'Anything the matter, darling?'

'No, nothing. I'm going to find mother.'

She went out of the room and standing at the foot of the stairs she called, but her mother's voice answered her from the verandah.

The moon that Lottie and Kezia had seen from the storeman's wagon was full, and the house, the garden, the old woman and Linda – all were bathed in dazzling light.

'I have been looking at the aloe,' said Mrs Fairfield. 'I believe it is going to flower this year. Look at the top there. Are those buds, or is it only an effect of light?'

As they stood on the steps, the high grassy bank on which the aloe rested rose up like a wave, and the aloe seemed to ride upon it like a ship with the oars lifted. Bright moonlight hung upon the lifted oars like water, and on the green wave glittered the dew.

'Do you feel it, too,' said Linda, and she spoke to her mother with the special voice that women use at night to

each other as though they spoke in their sleep or from some hollow cave – 'Don't you feel that it is coming towards us?'

She dreamed that she was caught up out of the cold water into the ship with the lifted oars and the budding mast. Now the oars fell striking quickly, quickly. They rowed far away over the top of the garden trees, the paddocks and the dark bush beyond. Ah, she heard herself cry: 'Faster! Faster!' to those who were rowing.

How much more real this dream was than that they should go back to the house where the sleeping children lay and where Stanley and Beryl played cribbage.

'I believe those are buds,' she said. 'Let us go down into the garden, mother. I like that aloe. I like it more than anything here. And I am sure I shall remember it long after I've forgotten all the other things.'

She put her hand on her mother's arm and they walked down the steps, round the island and on to the main drive that led to the front gates.

Looking at it from below she could see the long sharp thorns that edged the aloe leaves, and at the sight of them her heart grew hard. . . . She particularly liked the long sharp thorns. . . . Nobody would dare to come near the ship or to follow after.

'Not even my Newfoundland dog,' thought she, 'that I'm so fond of in the daytime.'

For she really was fond of him; she loved and admired and respected him tremendously. Oh, better than anyone else in the world. She knew him through and through. He was the soul of truth and decency, and for all his practical experience he was awfully simple, easily pleased and easily hurt. . . .

If only he wouldn't jump at her so, and bark so loudly, and watch her with such eager, loving eyes. He was too

strong for her; she had always hated things that rush at her, from a child. There were times when he was frightening – really frightening. When she just had not screamed at the top of her voice: 'You are killing me.' And at those times she had longed to say the most coarse, hateful things. . . .

'You know I'm very delicate. You know as well as I do that my heart is affected, and the doctor has told you I may die any moment. I have had three great lumps of children already. . . .'

Yes, yes, it was true. Linda snatched her hand from mother's arm. For all her love and respect and admiration she hated him. And how tender he always was after times like those, how submissive, how thoughtful. He would do anything for her; he longed to serve her. . . . Linda heard herself saying in a weak voice:

'Stanley, would you light a candle?'

And she heard his joyful voice answer: 'Of course I will, my darling,' and he leapt out of bed as though he were going to leap at the moon for her.

It had never been so plain to her as it was at this moment. There were all her feelings for him, sharp and defined, one as true as the other. And there was this other, this hatred, just as real as the rest. She could have done her feelings up in little packets and given them to Stanley. She longed to hand him that last one, for a surprise. She could see his eyes as he opened that. . . .

She hugged her folded arms and began to laugh silently. How absurd life was – it was laughable, simply laughable. And why this mania of hers to keep alive at all? For it really was a mania, she thought, mocking and laughing.

'What am I guarding myself for so preciously? I shall go on having children and Stanley will go on making money

and the children and the gardens will grow bigger and bigger, with whole fleets of aloes in them for me to choose from.'

She had been walking with her head bent, looking at nothing. Now she looked up and about her. They were standing by the red and white camellia trees. Beautiful were the rich dark leaves spangled with light and the round flowers that perch among them like red and white birds. Linda pulled a piece of verbena and crumpled it, and held her hands to her mother.

'Delicious,' said the old woman. 'Are you cold, child? Are you trembling? Yes, your hands are cold. We had better go back to the house.'

'What have you been thinking about?' said Linda. 'Tell me.'

'I haven't really been thinking of anything. I wondered as we passed the orchard what the fruit trees were like and whether we should be able to make much jam this autumn. There are splendid healthy currant bushes in the vegetable garden. I noticed them to-day. I should like to see those pantry shelves thoroughly well stocked with our own jam. . . .'

XII

'My Darling Nan,

Don't think me a piggy wig because I haven't written before. I haven't had a moment, dear, and even now I feel so exhausted that I can hardly hold a pen.

Well, the dreadful deed is done. We have actually left the giddy whirl of town, and I can't see how we shall ever go back again, for my brother-in-law has bought this house "lock, stock and barrel", to use his own words.

In a way, of course, it is an awful relief, for he has been threatening to take a place in the country ever since I've

lived with them – and I must say the house and garden are awfully nice – a million times better than that awful cubby-hole in town.

But buried, my dear. Buried isn't the word.

We have got neighbours, but they are only farmers – big louts of boys who seem to be milking all day, and two dreadful females with rabbit teeth who brought us some scones when we were moving and said they would be pleased to help. But my sister who lives a mile away doesn't know a soul here, so I am sure we never shall. It's pretty certain nobody will ever come out from town to see us, because though there is a bus it's an awful old rattling thing with black leather sides that any decent person would rather die than ride in for six miles.

Such is life. It's a sad ending for poor little B. I'll get to be a most awful frump in a year or two and come and see you in a mackintosh and a sailor hat tied on with a white china silk motor veil. So pretty.

Stanley says that now we are settled – for after the most awful week of my life we really are settled – he is going to bring out a couple of men from the club on Saturday afternoons for tennis. In fact, two are promised as a great treat to-day. But, my dear, if you could see Stanley's men from the club . . . rather fattish, the type who look frightfully indecent without waistcoats – always with toes that turn in rather – so conspicuous when you are walking about a court in white shoes. And they are pulling up their trousers every minute – don't you know – and whacking at imaginary things with their rackets.

I used to play with them at the club last summer, and I am sure you will know the type when I tell you that after I'd been there about three times they all called me Miss Beryl. It's

a weary world. Of course mother simply loves the place, but then I suppose when I am mother's age I shall be content to sit in the sun and shell peas into a basin. But I'm not–not–not.

What Linda thinks about the whole affair, per usual, I haven't the slightest idea. Mysterious as ever. . . .

My dear, you know that white satin dress of mine. I have taken the sleeves out entirely, put bands of black velvet across the shoulders and two big red poppies off my dear sister's *chapeau.* It is a great success, though when I shall wear it I do not know.'

Beryl sat writing this letter at a little table in her room. In a way, of course, it was all perfectly true, but in another way it was all the greatest rubbish and she didn't believe a word of it. No, that wasn't true. She felt all those things, but she didn't really feel them like that.

It was her other self who had written that letter. It not only bored, it rather disgusted her real self.

'Flippant and silly,' said her real self. Yet she knew that she'd send it and she'd always write that kind of twaddle to Nan Pym. In fact, it was a very mild example of the kind of letter she generally wrote.

Beryl leaned her elbows on the table and read it through again. The voice of the letter seemed to come up to her from the page. It was faint already, like a voice heard over the telephone, high, gushing, with something bitter in the sound. Oh, she detested it to-day.

'You've always got so much animation,' said Nan Pym. 'That's why men are so keen on you.' And she had added, rather mournfully, for men were not at all keen on Nan, who was a solid kind of girl, with fat hips and a high colour – 'I can't understand how you can keep it up. But it is your nature, I suppose.'

What rot. What nonsense. It wasn't her nature at all. Good heavens, if she had ever been her real self with Nan Pym, Nannie would have jumped out of the window with surprise. . . . My dear, you know that white satin of mine. . . . Beryl slammed the letter-case to.

She jumped up and half unconsciously, half consciously she drifted over to the looking-glass.

There stood a slim girl in white – a white serge skirt, a white silk blouse, and a leather belt drawn in very tightly at her tiny waist.

Her face was heart-shaped, wide at the brows and with a pointed chin – but not too pointed. Her eyes, her eyes were perhaps her best feature; they were such a strange uncommon colour – greeny blue with little gold points in them.

She had fine black eyebrows and long lashes – so long, that when they lay on her cheeks you positively caught the light in them, someone or other had told her.

Her mouth was rather large. Too large? No, not really. Her underlip protruded a little; she had a way of sucking it in that somebody else had told her was awfully fascinating.

Her nose was her least satisfactory feature. Not that it was really ugly. But it was not half as fine as Linda's. Linda really had a perfect little nose. Hers spread rather – not badly. And in all probability she exaggerated the spreadiness of it just because it was her nose, and she was so awfully critical of herself. She pinched it with a thumb and first finger and made a little face. . . .

Lovely, lovely hair. And such a mass of it. It had the colour of fresh fallen leaves, brown and red with a glint of yellow. When she did it in a long plait she felt it on her backbone like a long snake. She loved to feel the weight of it dragging

her head back, and she loved to feel it loose, covering her bare arms. 'Yes, my dear, there is no doubt about it, you really are a lovely little thing.'

At the words her bosom lifted; she took a long breath of delight, half closing her eyes.

But even as she looked the smile faded from her lips and eyes. Oh God, there she was, back again, playing the same old game. False – false as ever. False as when she'd written to Nan Pym. False even when she was alone with herself, now.

What had that creature in the glass to do with her, and why was she staring? She dropped down to one side of her bed and buried her face in her arms.

'Oh,' she cried, 'I am so miserable – so frightfully miserable. I know that I'm silly and spiteful and vain; I'm always acting a part. I'm never my real self for a moment.' And plainly, plainly, she saw her false self running up and down the stairs, laughing a special trilling laugh if they had visitors, standing under the lamp if a man came to dinner, so that he should see the light on her hair, pouting and pretending to be a little girl when she was asked to play the guitar. Why? She even kept it up for Stanley's benefit. Only last night when he was reading the paper her false self had stood beside him and leaned against his shoulder on purpose. Hadn't she put her hand over his, pointing out something so that he should see how white her hand was beside his brown one.

How despicable! Despicable! Her heart was cold with rage. 'It's marvellous how you keep it up,' said she to the false self. But then it was only because she was so miserable – so miserable. If she had been happy and leading her own life, her false life would cease to be. She saw the real Beryl – a shadow . . . a shadow. Faint and unsubstantial she shone.

What was there of her except the radiance? And for what tiny moments she was really she. Beryl could almost remember every one of them. At those times she had felt: 'Life is rich and mysterious and good, and I am rich and mysterious and good, too.' Shall I ever be that Beryl for ever? Shall I? How can I? And was there ever a time when I did not have a false self? . . . But just as she had got that far she heard the sound of little steps running along the passage; the door handle rattled. Kezia came in.

'Aunt Beryl, mother says will you please come down? Father is home with a man and lunch is ready.'

Botheration! How she had crumpled her skirt, kneeling in that idiotic way.

'Very well, Kezia.' She went over to the dressing table and powdered her nose.

Kezia crossed too, and unscrewed a little pot of cream and sniffed it. Under her arm she carried a very dirty calico cat.

When Aunt Beryl ran out of the room she sat the cat up on the dressing table, and stuck the top of the cream jar over its ear.

'Now look at yourself,' said she sternly.

The calico cat was so overcome by the sight that it toppled over backwards and bumped and bumped on to the floor. And the top of the cream jar flew through the air and rolled like a penny in a round on the linoleum – and did not break.

But for Kezia it had broken the moment it flew through the air, and she picked it up, hot all over, and put it back on the dressing table.

Then she tip-toed away, far too quickly and airily. . . .

The Daughters of the Late Colonel

I

The week after was one of the busiest weeks of their lives. Even when they went to bed it was only their bodies that lay down and rested; their minds went on, thinking things out, talking things over, wondering, deciding, trying to remember where. . . .

Constantia lay like a statue, her hands by her sides, her feet just overlapping each other, the sheet up to her chin. She stared at the ceiling.

'Do you think father would mind if we gave his top-hat to the porter?'

'The porter?' snapped Josephine. 'Why ever the porter? What a very extraordinary idea!'

Because,' said Constantia slowly, 'he must often have to go to funerals. And I noticed at – at the cemetery that he only had a bowler.' She paused. 'I thought then how very much he'd appreciate a top-hat. We ought to give him a present, too. He was always very nice to father.'

'But,' cried Josephine, flouncing on her pillow and staring across the dark at Constantia, 'father's head!' And suddenly, for one awful moment, she nearly giggled. Not, of course, that she felt in the least like giggling. It must have been habit. Years ago, when they had stayed awake at night talking, their beds had simply heaved. And now the porter's head, disappearing, popped out, like a candle, under father's hat. . . . The giggle mounted, mounted; she clenched her hands; she fought it down; she frowned fiercely at the dark

and said 'Remember' terribly sternly.

'We can decide to-morrow,' she said.

Constantia had noticed nothing; she sighed.

'Do you think we ought to have our dressing-gowns dyed as well?'

'Black?' almost shrieked Josephine.

'Well, what else?' said Constantia. 'I was thinking – it doesn't seem quite sincere, in a way, to wear black out of doors and when we're fully dressed, and then when we're at home –'

'But nobody sees us,' said Josephine. She gave the bedclothes such a twitch that both her feet came uncovered, and she had to creep up the pillows to get them well under again.

'Kate does,' said Constantia. 'And the postman very well might.'

Josephine thought of her dark-red slippers, which matched her dressing-gown, and of Constantia's favourite indefinite green ones which went with hers. Black! Two black dressing-gowns and two pairs of black woolly slippers, creeping off to the bath-room like black cats.

'I don't think it's absolutely necessary,' said she.

Silence. Then Constantia said, 'We shall have to post the papers with the notice in them to-morrow to catch the Ceylon mail. . . . How many letters have we had up till now?'

'Twenty-three.'

Josephine had replied to them all, and twenty-three times when she came to 'We miss our dear father so much' she had broken down and had to use her handkerchief, and on some of them even to soak up a very light-blue tear with an edge of blotting-paper. Strange! She couldn't have put it on – but twenty-three times. Even now, though, when she said over

to herself sadly 'We miss our dear father *so* much,' she could have cried if she'd wanted to.

'Have you got enough stamps?' came from Constantia.

'Oh, how can I tell?' said Josephine crossly. 'What's the good of asking me that now?'

'I was just wondering,' said Constantia mildly.

Silence again. There came a little rustle, a scurry, a hop.

'A mouse,' said Constantia.

'It can't be a mouse because there aren't any crumbs,' said Josephine.

'But it doesn't know there aren't,' said Constantia.

A spasm of pity squeezed her heart. Poor little thing! She wished she'd left a tiny piece of biscuit on the dressing-table. It was awful to think of it not finding anything. What would it do?

'I can't think how they manage to live at all,' she said slowly.

'Who?' demanded Josephine.

And Constantia said more loudly than she meant to, 'Mice.'

Josephine was furious. 'Oh, what nonsense, Con!' she said. 'What have mice got to do with it? You're asleep.'

'I don't think I am,' said Constantia. She shut her eyes to make sure. She was.

Josephine arched her spine, pulled up her knees, folded her arms so that her fists came under her ears, and pressed her cheek hard against the pillow.

II

Another thing which complicated matters was they had Nurse Andrews staying on with them that week. It was their own fault; they had asked her. It was Josephine's idea. On

the morning – well, on the last morning, when the doctor had gone, Josephine had said to Constantia, 'Don't you think it would be rather nice if we asked Nurse Andrews to stay on for a week as our guest?'

'Very nice,' said Constantia.

'I thought,' went on Josephine quickly, 'I should just say this afternoon, after I've paid her, "My sister and I would be very pleased, after all you've done for us, Nurse Andrews, if you would stay on for a week as our guest." I'd have to put that in about being our guest in case –'

'Oh, but she could hardly expect to be paid!' cried Constantia.

'One never knows,' said Josephine sagely.

Nurse Andrews had, of course, jumped at the idea. But it was a bother. It meant they had to have regular sit-down meals at the proper times, whereas if they'd been alone they could just have asked Kate if she wouldn't have minded bringing them a tray wherever they were. And meal-times now that the strain was over were rather a trial.

Nurse Andrews was simply fearful about butter. Really they couldn't help feeling that about butter, at least, she took advantage of their kindness. And she had that maddening habit of asking for just an inch more bread to finish what she had on her plate, and then, at the last mouthful, absent-mindedly – of course it wasn't absent-mindedly – taking another helping. Josephine got very red when this happened, and she fastened her small, bead-like eyes on the tablecloth as if she saw a minute strange insect creeping through the web of it. But Constantia's long, pale face lengthened and set, and she gazed away – away – far over the desert, to where that line of camels unwound like a thread of wool. . . .

'When I was with Lady Tukes,' said Nurse Andrews, 'she

had such a dainty little contray-vance for the buttah. It was a silvah Cupid balanced on the – on the bordah of a glass dish, holding a tayny fork. And when you wanted some buttah you simply pressed his foot and he bent down and speared you a piece. It was quite a gayme.'

Josephine could hardly bear that. But 'I think those things are very extravagant' was all she said.

'But whey?' asked Nurse Andrews, beaming through her eyeglasses. 'No one, surely, would take more buttah than one wanted – would one?'

'Ring, Con,' cried Josephine. She couldn't trust herself to reply.

And proud young Kate, the enchanted princess, came in to see what the old tabbies wanted now. She snatched away their plates of mock something or other and slapped down a white, terrified blancmange.

'Jam, please, Kate,' said Josephine kindly.

Kate knelt and burst open the sideboard, lifted the lid of the jampot, saw it was empty, put it on the table, and stalked off.

'I'm afraid,' said Nurse Andrews a moment later, 'there isn't any.'

'Oh, what a bother!' said Josephine. She bit her lip. 'What had we better do?'

Constantia looked dubious. 'We can't disturb Kate again,' she said softly.

Nurse Andrews waited, smiling at them both. Her eyes wandered, spying at everything behind her eyeglasses. Constantia in despair went back to her camels. Josephine frowned heavily – concentrated. If it hadn't been for this idiotic woman she and Con would, of course, have eaten their blancmange without. Suddenly the idea came.

'I know,' she said. 'Marmalade. There's some marmalade in the sideboard. Get it, Con.'

'I hope,' laughed Nurse Andrews, and her laugh was like a spoon tinkling against a medicine-glass – 'I hope it's not very bittah marmalayde.'

III

But, after all, it was not long now, and then she'd be gone for good. And there was no getting over the fact that she had been very kind to father. She had nursed him day and night at the end. Indeed, both Constantia and Josephine felt privately she had rather overdone the not leaving him at the very last. For when they had gone in to say good-bye Nurse Andrews had sat beside his bed the whole time, holding his wrist and pretending to look at her watch. It couldn't have been necessary. It was so tactless, too. Supposing father had wanted to say something – something private to them. Not that he had. Oh, far from it! He lay there, purple, a dark, angry purple in the face, and never even looked at them when they came in. Then, as they were standing there, wondering what to do, he had suddenly opened one eye. Oh, what a difference it would have made, what a difference to their memory of him, how much easier to tell people about it, if he had only opened both! But no – one eye only. It glared at them a moment and then . . . went out.

IV

It had made it very awkward for them when Mr Farolles, of St John's, called the same afternoon.

'The end was quite peaceful, I trust?' were the first words he said as he glided towards them through the dark drawing-room.

'Quite,' said Josephine faintly. They both hung their heads. Both of them felt certain that eye wasn't at all a peaceful eye.

'Won't you sit down?' said Josephine.

'Thank you, Miss Pinner,' said Mr Farolles gratefully. He folded his coat-tails and began to lower himself into father's arm-chair, but just as he touched it he almost sprang up and slid into the next chair instead.

He coughed. Josephine clasped her hands; Constantia looked vague.

'I want you to feel, Miss Pinner,' said Mr Farolles, 'and you, Miss Constantia, that I'm trying to be helpful. I want to be helpful to you both, if you will let me. These are the times,' said Mr Farolles, very simply and earnestly, 'when God means us to be helpful to one another.'

'Thank you very much, Mr Farolles,' said Josephine and Constantia.

'Not at all,' said Mr Farolles gently. He drew his kid gloves through his fingers and leaned forward. 'And if either of you would like a little Communion, either or both of you, here *and* now, you have only to tell me. A little Communion is often very help – a great comfort,' he added tenderly.

But the idea of a little Communion terrified them. What! In the drawing-room by themselves – with no – no altar or anything! The piano would be much too high, thought Constantia, and Mr Farolles could not possibly lean over it with the chalice. And Kate would be sure to come bursting in and interrupt them, thought Josephine. And supposing the bell rang in the middle? It might be somebody important – about their mourning. Would they get up reverently and go out, or would they have to wait . . . in torture?

'Perhaps you will send round a note by your good Kate if you would care for it later,' said Mr Farolles.

'Oh yes, thank you very much!' they both said.

Mr Farolles got up and took his black straw hat from the round table.

'And about the funeral,' he said softly. 'I may arrange that – as your dear father's old friend and yours, Miss Pinner – and Miss Constantia?'

Josephine and Constantia got up too.

'I should like it to be quite simple,' said Josephine firmly, 'and not too expensive. At the same time, I should like –'

'A good one that will last,' thought dreamy Constantia, as if Josephine were buying a nightgown. But of course Josephine didn't say that. 'One suitable to our father's position.' She was very nervous.

'I'll run round to our good friend Mr Knight,' said Mr Farolles soothingly. 'I will ask him to come and see you. I am sure you will find him very helpful indeed.'

V

Well, at any rate, all that part of it was over, though neither of them could possibly believe that father was never coming back. Josephine had had a moment of absolute terror at the cemetery, while the coffin was lowered, to think that she and Constantia had done this thing without asking his permission. What would father say when he found out? For he was bound to find out sooner or later. He always did. 'Buried. You two girls had me *buried*!' She heard his stick thumping. Oh, what would they say? What possible excuse could they make? It sounded such an appallingly heartless thing to do. Such a wicked advantage to take of a person because he happened to be helpless at the moment. The other people seemed to treat it all as a matter of course. They were strangers; they couldn't be expected to understand that father was the very last person

for such a thing to happen to. No, the entire blame for it all would fall on her and Constantia. And the expense, she thought, stepping into the tight-buttoned cab. When she had to show him the bills. What would he say then?

She heard him absolutely roaring, 'And do you expect me to pay for this gimcrack excursion of yours?'

'Oh,' groaned poor Josephine aloud, 'we shouldn't have done it, Con!'

And Constantia, pale as a lemon in all that blackness, said in a frightened whisper, 'Done what, Jug?'

'Let them bu-bury father like that,' said Josephine, breaking down and crying into her new, queer-smelling mourning handkerchief.

'But what else could we have done?' asked Constantia wonderingly. 'We couldn't have kept him, Jug – we couldn't have kept him unburied. At any rate, not in a flat that size.'

Josephine blew her nose; the cab was dreadfully stuffy.

'I don't know,' she said forlornly. 'It is all so dreadful. I feel we ought to have tried to, just for a time at least. To make perfectly sure. One thing's certain' – and her tears sprang out again – 'father will never forgive us for this – never!'

VI

Father would never forgive them. That was what they felt more than ever when, two mornings later, they went into his room to go through his things. They had discussed it quite calmly. It was even down on Josephine's list of things to be done. *Go through father's things and settle about them.* But that was a very different matter from saying after breakfast:

'Well, are you ready, Con?'

'Yes, Jug – when you are.'

'Then I think we'd better get it over.'

It was dark in the hall. It had been a rule for years never to disturb father in the morning, whatever happened. And now they were going to open the door without knocking even. . . . Constantia's eyes were enormous at the idea; Josephine felt weak in the knees.

'You – you go first,' she gasped, pushing Constantia.

But Constantia said, as she always had said on those occasions, 'No, Jug, that's not fair. You're eldest.'

Josephine was just going to say – what at other times she wouldn't have owned to for the world – what she kept for her very last weapon, 'But you're tallest,' when they noticed that the kitchen door was open, and there stood Kate. . . .

'Very stiff,' said Josephine, grasping the door-handle and doing her best to turn it. As if anything ever deceived Kate!

It couldn't be helped. That girl was. . . . Then the door was shut behind them, but – but they weren't in father's room at all. They might have suddenly walked through the wall by mistake into a different flat altogether. Was the door just behind them? They were too frightened to look. Josephine knew that if it was it was holding itself tight shut; Constantia felt that, like the doors in dreams, it hadn't any handle at all. It was the coldness which made it so awful. Or the whiteness – which? Everything was covered. The blinds were down, a cloth hung over the mirror, a sheet hid the bed; a huge fan of white paper filled the fire-place. Constantia timidly put out her hand; she almost expected a snowflake to fall. Josephine felt a queer tingling in her nose, as if her nose was freezing. Then a cab klop-klopped over the cobbles below, and the quiet seemed to shake into little pieces.

'I had better pull up a blind,' said Josephine bravely.

'Yes, it might be a good idea,' whispered Constantia.

They only gave the blind a touch, but it flew up and the

cord flew after, rolling round the blind-stick, and the little tassel tapped as if trying to get free. That was too much for Constantia.

'Don't you think – don't you think we might put it off for another day?' she whispered.

'Why?' snapped Josephine, feeling, as usual, much better now that she knew for certain that Constantia was terrified. 'It's got to be done. But I do wish you wouldn't whisper, Con.'

'I didn't know I was whispering,' whispered Constantia.

'And why do you keep on staring at the bed?' said Josephine, raising her voice almost defiantly. 'There's nothing *on* the bed.'

'Oh, Jug, don't say so!' said poor Connie. 'At any rate, not so loudly.'

Josephine felt herself that she had gone too far. She took a wide swerve over to the chest of drawers, put out her hand, but quickly drew it back again.

'Connie!' she gasped, and she wheeled round and leaned with her back against the chest of drawers.

'Oh, Jug – what?'

Josephine could only glare. She had the most extraordinary feeling that she had just escaped something simply awful. But how could she explain to Constantia that father was in the chest of drawers? He was in the top drawer with his handkerchiefs and neck-ties, or in the next with his shirts and pyjamas, or in the lowest of all with his suits. He was watching there, hidden away – just behind the door-handle – ready to spring.

She pulled a funny old-fashioned face at Constantia, just as she used to in the old days when she was going to cry.

'I can't open,' she nearly wailed.

'No, don't, Jug,' whispered Constantia earnestly. 'It's

much better not to. Don't let's open anything. At any rate, not for a long time.'

'But – but it seems so weak,' said Josephine, breaking down.

'But why not be weak for once, Jug?' argued Constantia, whispering quite fiercely. 'If it is weak.' And her pale stare flew from the locked writing-table – so safe – to the huge glittering wardrobe, and she began to breathe in a queer, panting way. 'Why shouldn't we be weak for once in our lives, Jug? It's quite excusable. Let's be weak – be weak, Jug. It's much nicer to be weak than to be strong.'

And then she did one of those amazingly bold things that she'd done about twice before in their lives; she marched over to the wardrobe, turned the key, and took it out of the lock. Took it out of the lock and held it up to Josephine, showing Josephine by her extraordinary smile that she knew what she'd done, she'd risked deliberately father being in there among his overcoats.

If the huge wardrobe had lurched forward, had crashed down on Constantia, Josephine wouldn't have been surprised. On the contrary, she would have thought it the only suitable thing to happen. But nothing happened. Only the room seemed quieter than ever, and bigger flakes of cold air fell on Josephine's shoulders and knees. She began to shiver.

'Come, Jug,' said Constantia, still with that awful callous smile, and Josephine followed just as she had that last time, when Constantia had pushed Benny into the Round Pond.

VII

But the strain told on them when they were back in the dining-room. They sat down, very shaky, and looked at each other.

'I don't feel I can settle to anything,' said Josephine, 'until I've had something. Do you think we could ask Kate for two cups of hot water?'

'I really don't see why we shouldn't,' said Constantia carefully. She was quite normal again. 'I won't ring. I'll go to the kitchen door and ask her.'

'Yes, do,' said Josephine, sinking down into a chair. 'Tell her, just two cups, Con, nothing else – on a tray.'

'She needn't even put the jug on, need she?' said Constantia, as though Kate might very well complain if the jug had been there.

'Oh no, certainly not! The jug's not at all necessary. She can pour it direct out of the kettle,' cried Josephine, feeling that would be a labour-saving indeed.

Their cold lips quivered at the greenish brims. Josephine curved her small red hands round the cup; Constantia sat up and blew on the wavy steam, making it flutter from one side to the other.

'Speaking of Benny,' said Josephine.

And though Benny hadn't been mentioned Constantia immediately looked as though he had.

'He'll expect us to send him something of father's, of course. But it's so difficult to know what to send to Ceylon.'

'You mean things get unstuck so on the voyage,' murmured Constantia.

'No, lost,' said Josephine sharply. 'You know there's no post. Only runners.'

Both paused to watch a black man in white linen drawers running through the pale fields for dear life, with a large brown-paper parcel in his hands. Josephine's black man was tiny; he scurried along glistening like an ant. But there was something blind and tireless about Constantia's tall, thin

fellow, which made him, she decided, a very unpleasant person indeed. . . . On the verandah, dressed all in white and wearing a cork helmet, stood Benny. His right hand shook up and down, as father's did when he was impatient. And behind him, not in the least interested, sat Hilda, the unknown sister-in-law. She swung in a cane rocker and flicked over the leaves of the *Tatler.*

'I think his watch would be the most suitable present,' said Josephine.

Constantia looked up; she seemed surprised.

'Oh, would you trust a gold watch to a native?'

'But of course I'd disguise it,' said Josephine. 'No one would know it was a watch.' She liked the idea of having to make a parcel such a curious shape that no one could possibly guess what it was. She even thought for a moment of hiding the watch in a narrow cardboard corset-box that she'd kept by her for a long time, waiting for it to come in for something. It was such beautiful firm cardboard. But, no, it wouldn't be appropriate for this occasion. It had lettering on it: *Medium Women's 28. Extra Firm Busks.* It would be almost too much of a surprise for Benny to open that and find father's watch inside.

'And of course it isn't as though it would be going – ticking, I mean,' said Constantia, who was still thinking of the native love of jewellery. 'At least,' she added, 'it would be very strange if after all that time it was.'

VIII

Josephine made no reply. She had flown off on one of her tangents. She had suddenly thought of Cyril. Wasn't it more usual for the only grandson to have the watch? And then dear Cyril was so appreciative, and a gold watch meant so much

to a young man. Benny, in all probability, had quite got out of the habit of watches; men so seldom wore waistcoats in those hot climates. Whereas Cyril in London wore them from year's end to year's end. And it would be so nice for her and Constantia, when he came to tea, to know it was there. 'I see you've got on grandfather's watch, Cyril.' It would be somehow so satisfactory.

Dear boy! What a blow his sweet, sympathetic little note had been! Of course they quite understood; but it was most unfortunate.

'It would have been such a point, having him,' said Josephine.

'And he would have enjoyed it so,' said Constantia, not thinking what she was saying.

However, as soon as he got back he was coming to tea with his aunties. Cyril to tea was one of their rare treats.

'Now, Cyril, you mustn't be frightened of our cakes. Your Auntie Con and I bought them at Buszard's this morning. We know what a man's appetite is. So don't be ashamed of making a good tea.'

Josephine cut recklessly into the rich dark cake that stood for her winter gloves or the soling and heeling of Constantia's only respectable shoes. But Cyril was most unmanlike in appetite.

'I say, Aunt Josephine, I simply can't. I've only just had lunch, you know.'

'Oh, Cyril, that can't be true? It's after four,' cried Josephine. Constantia sat with her knife poised over the chocolate-roll.

'It is, all the same,' said Cyril. 'I had to meet a man at Victoria, and he kept me hanging about till . . . there was only time to get lunch and to come on here. And he gave

me – phew' – Cyril put his hand to his forehead – 'a terrific blow-out,' he said.

It was disappointing – today of all days. But still he couldn't be expected to know.

'But you'll have a meringue, won't you, Cyril?' said Aunt Josephine. 'These meringues were bought specially for you. Your dear father was so fond of them. We were sure you are, too.'

'I *am*, Aunt Josephine,' cried Cyril ardently. 'Do you mind if I take half to begin with?'

'Not at all, dear boy; but we mustn't let you off with that.'

'Is your dear father still so fond of meringues?' asked Auntie Con gently. She winced faintly as she broke through the shell of hers.

'Well, I don't quite know, Auntie Con,' said Cyril breezily.

At that they both looked up.

'Don't know?' almost snapped Josephine. 'Don't know a thing like that about your own father, Cyril?'

'Surely,' said Auntie Con softly.

Cyril tried to laugh it off. 'Oh, well,' he said, 'it's such a long time since –' He faltered. He stopped. Their faces were too much for him.

'Even *so*,' said Josephine.

And Auntie Con looked.

Cyril put down his teacup. 'Wait a bit,' he cried. 'Wait a bit, Aunt Josephine. What am I thinking of?'

He looked up. They were beginning to brighten. Cyril slapped his knee.

'Of course,' he said, 'it was meringues. How could I have forgotten? Yes, Aunt Josephine, you're perfectly right. Father's most frightfully keen on meringues.'

They didn't only beam. Aunt Josephine went scarlet with

pleasure; Auntie Con gave a deep, deep sigh.

'And now, Cyril, you must come and see father,' said Josephine. 'He knows you were coming to-day.'

'Right,' said Cyril, very firmly and heartily. He got up from his chair; suddenly he glanced at the clock.

'I say, Auntie Con, isn't your clock a bit slow? I've got to meet a man at – at Paddington just after five. I'm afraid I shan't be able to stay very long with grandfather.'

'Oh, he won't expect you to stay *very* long!' said Aunt Josepine.

Constantia was still gazing at the clock. She couldn't make up her mind if it was fast or slow. It was one or the other, she felt amost certain of that. At any rate, it had been.

Cyril still lingered. 'Aren't you coming along, Auntie Con?'

'Of course,' said Josphine, 'we shall all go. Come on, Con.'

IX

They knocked at the door, and Cyril followed his aunts into grandfather's hot, sweetish room.

'Come on,' said Grandfather Pinner. 'Don't hang about. What is it? What've you been up to?'

He was sitting in front of a roaring fire, clasping his stick. He had a thick rug over his knees. On his lap there lay a beautiful pale yellow silk handkerchief.

'It's Cyril, father,' said Josephine shyly. And she took Cyril's hand and led him forward.

'Good afternoon, grandfather,' said Cyril, trying to take his hand out of Aunt Josephine's. Grandfather Pinner shot his eyes at Cyril in the way he was famous for. Where was Auntie Con? She stood on the other side of Aunt Josephine;

her long arms hung down in front of her; her hands were clasped. She never took her eyes off grandfather.

'Well,' said Grandfather Pinner, beginning to thump, 'What have you got to tell me?'

What had he, what had he got to tell him? Cyril felt himself smiling like a perfect imbecile. The room was stifling, too.

But Aunt Josephine came to his rescue. She cried brightly, 'Cyril says his father is still very fond of meringues, father dear.'

'Eh?' said Grandfather Pinner, curving his hand like a purple meringue-shell over one ear.

Josephine repeated, 'Cyril says his father is still very fond of meringues.'

'Can't hear,' said old Colonel Pinner. And he waved Josephine away with his stick, then pointed with his stick to Cyril. 'Tell me what she's trying to say,' he said.

(My God!) 'Must I?' said Cyril, blushing and staring at Aunt Josephine.

'Do, dear,' she smiled. 'It will please him so much.'

'Come on, out with it!' cried Colonel Pinner testily, beginning to thump again.

And Cyril leaned forward and yelled, 'Father's still very fond of meringues.'

At that Grandfather Pinner jumped as though he had been shot.

'Don't shout!' he cried. 'What the matter with the boy? *Meringues*! What about 'em?'

'Oh, Aunt Josephine, must we go on?' groaned Cyril desperately.

'It's quite all right, dear boy,' said Aunt Josephine, as though he and she were at the dentist's together. 'He'll

understand in a minute.' And she whispered to Cyril, 'He's getting a bit deaf, you know.' Then she leaned forward and really bawled at Grandfather Pinner, 'Cyril only wanted to tell you, father dear, that *his* father is still very fond of meringues.'

Colonel Pinner heard that time, heard and brooded, looking Cyril up and down.

'What an esstrordinary thing!' said old Grandfather Pinner. 'What an esstrodinary thing to come all this way here to tell me!'

And Cyril felt it *was*.

'Yes, I shall send Cyril the watch,' said Josephine.

'That would be very nice,' said Constantia. 'I seem to remember last time he came there was some little trouble about the time.'

X

They were interrupted by Kate bursting through the door in her usual fashion, as though she had discovered some secret panel in the wall.

'Fried or boiled?' asked the bold voice.

Fried or boiled? Josephine and Constantia were quite bewildered for the moment. They could hardly take it in.

'Fried or boiled what, Kate?' asked Josephine, trying to begin to concentrate.

Kate gave a loud sniff. 'Fish.'

'Well, why didn't you say so immediately?' Josephine reproached her gently. 'How could you expect us to understand, Kate? There are a great many things in this world, you know, which are fried or boiled.' And after such a display of courage she said quite brightly to Constantia,

'Which do you prefer, Con?'

'I think it might be nice to have it fried,' said Constantia. 'On the other hand, of course boiled fish is very nice. I think I prefer both equally well. . . . Unless you. . . . In that case –'

'I shall fry it,' said Kate, and she bounced back, leaving their door open and slamming the door of her kitchen.

Josephine gazed at Constantia; she raised her pale eyebrows until they rippled away into her pale hair. She got up. She said in a very lofty, imposing way, 'Do you mind following me into the drawing-room, Constantia? I've something of great importance to discuss with you.'

For it was always to the drawing-room they retired when they wanted to talk over Kate.

Josephine closed the door meaningly. 'Sit down, Constantia,' she said, still very grand. She might have been receiving Constantia for the first time. And Con looked round vaguely for a chair, as though she felt indeed quite a stranger.

'Now the question is,' said Josephine, bending forward, 'whether we shall keep her or not.'

'That is the question,' agreed Constantia.

'And this time,' said Josephine firmly, 'we must come to a definite decision.'

Constantia looked a moment as though she might begin going over all the other times, but she pulled herself together and said, 'Yes, Jug.'

'You see, Con,' explained Josephine, 'everything is so changed now.' Constantia looked up quickly. 'I mean,' went on Josephine, 'we're not dependent on Kate as we were.' And she blushed faintly. 'There's not father to cook for.'

'That is perfectly true,' agreed Constantia. 'Father certainly doesn't want any cooking now whatever else –'

Josephine broke in sharply, 'You're not sleepy, are you, Con?'

'Sleepy, Jug?' Constantia was wide-eyed.

'Well, concentrate more,' said Josephine sharply, and she returned to the subject. 'What it comes to is, if we did' – and this she barely breathed, glancing at the door – 'give Kate notice' – she raised her voice again – 'we could manage our own food.'

'Why not?' cried Constantia. She couldn't help smiling. The idea was so exciting. She clasped her hands. 'What should we live on, Jug?'

'Oh, eggs in various forms!' said Jug, lofty again. 'And, besides, there are all the cooked foods.'

'But I've always heard,' said Constantia, 'they are considered so very expensive.'

'Not if one buys them in moderation,' said Josephine. But she tore herself away from this fascinating bypath and dragged Constantia after her.

'What we've got to decide now, however, is whether we really do trust Kate or not.'

Constantia leaned back. Her flat little laugh flew from her lips.

'Isn't it curious, Jug,' said she, 'that just on this one subject I've never been able to quite make up my mind?'

XI

She never had. The whole difficulty was to prove anything. How did one prove things, how could one? Suppose Kate had stood in front of her and deliberately made a face. Mightn't she very well have been in pain? Wasn't it impossible, at any rate, to ask Kate if she was making a face at her? If Kate answered 'No' – and of course she would say 'No' –

what a position! How undignified! Then again Constantia suspected, she was almost certain that Kate went to her chest of drawers when she and Josephine were out, not to take things but to spy. Many times she had come back to find her amethyst cross in the most unlikely places, under her lace ties or on top of her evening Bertha. More than once she had laid a trap for Kate. She had arranged things in a special order and then called Josephine to witness.

'You see, Jug?'

'Quite, Con.'

'Now we shall be able to tell.'

But, oh dear, when she did go to look, she was as far off from a proof as ever! If anything was displaced, it might so very well have happened as she closed the drawer; a jolt might have done it so easily.

'You come, Jug, and decide. I really can't. It's too difficult.'

But after a pause and a long glare Josephine would sigh, 'Now you've put the doubt into my mind, Con, I'm sure I can't tell myself.'

'Well, we can't postpone it again,' said Josephine. 'If we postpone it this time –'

XII

But at that moment in the street below a barrel-organ struck up. Josephine and Constantia sprang to their feet together.

'Run, Con,' said Jospehine. 'Run quickly. There's sixpence on the –'

Then they remembered. It didn't matter. They would never have to stop the organ-grinder again. Never again would she and Constantia be told to make that monkey take his noise somewhere else. Never would sound that loud, strange bellow when father thought they were not hurrying

enough. The organ-grinder might play there all day and the slick would not thump.

It never will thump again,
It never will thump again,

played the barrel-organ.

What was Constantia thinking? She had such a strange smile; she looked different. She couldn't be going to cry.

'Jug, Jug,' said Constantia softly, pressing her hands together. 'Do you know what day it is? It's Saturday. It's a week to-day, a whole week.'

A week since father died,
A week since father died,

cried the barrel-organ. And Josephine, too, forgot to be practical and sensible; she smiled faintly, strangely. On the Indian carpet there fell a square of sunlight, pale red; it came and went and came – and stayed, deepened – until it shone almost golden.

'The sun's out,' said Josephine, as though it really mattered.

A perfect fountain of bubbling notes shook from the barrel-organ, round, bright notes, carelessly scattered.

Constantia lifted her big, cold hands as if to catch them, and then her hands fell again. She walked over to the mantelpiece to her favourite Buddha. And the stone and gilt image, whose smile always gave her such a queer feeling, almost a pain and yet a pleasant pain, seemed to-day to be more than smiling. He knew something; he had a secret. 'I know something that you don't,' said her Buddha. Oh, what

was it, what could it be? And yet she had always felt there was . . . something.

The sunlight pressed through the windows, thieved its way in, flashed its light over the furniture and the photographs. Josephine watched it. When it came to mother's photograph, the enlargement over the piano, it lingered as though puzzled to find so little remained of mother, except the ear-rings shaped like tiny pagodas and a black feather boa. Why did the photographs of dead people always fade so? wondered Josephine. As soon as a person was dead their photograph died too. But, of course, this one of mother was very old. It was thirty-five years old. Josephine remembered standing on a chair and pointing out that feather boa to Constantia and telling her that it was a snake that had killed their mother in Ceylon. . . . Would everything have been different if mother hadn't died? She didn't see why. Aunt Florence had lived with them until they had left school, and they had moved three times and had their yearly holiday and . . . and there'd been changes of servants, of course.

Some little sparrows, young sparrows they sounded, chirped on the window-ledge. *Yeep – eyeep – yeep.* But Josephine felt they were not sparrows, not on the window-ledge. It was inside her, that queer little crying noise. *Yeep – eyeep – yeep.* Ah, what was it crying, so weak and forlorn?

If mother had lived, might they have married? But there had been nobody for them to marry. There had been father's Anglo-Indian friends before he quarrelled with them. But after that she and Constantia never met a single man except clergymen. How did one meet men? Or even if they'd met them, how could they have got to know men well enough to be more than strangers? One read of people having adventures, being followed, and so on. But nobody had

ever followed Constantia and her. Oh yes, there had been one year at Eastbourne a mysterious man at their boarding-house who had put a note on the jug of hot water outside their bedroom door! But by the time Connie had found it the steam had made the writing too faint to read; they couldn't even make out to which of them it was addressed. And he had left next day. And that was all. The rest had been looking after father and at the same time keeping out of father's way. But now? But now? The thieving sun touched Josephine gently. She lifted her face. She was drawn over to the window by gentle beams. . . .

Until the barrel-organ stopped playing Constantia stayed before the Buddha, wondering, but not as usual, not vaguely. This time her wonder was like longing. She remembered the times she had come in here, crept out of bed in her nightgown when the moon was full, and lain on the floor with her arms outstretched, as though she was crucified. Why? The big, pale moon had made her do it. The horrible dancing figures on the carved screen had leered at her and she hadn't minded. She remembered too how, whenever they were at the seaside, she had gone off by herself and got as close to the sea as she could, and sung something, something she had made up, while she gazed all over that restless water. There had been this other life, running out, bringing things home in bags, getting things on approval, discussing them with Jug, and taking them back to get more things on approval, and arranging father's trays and trying not to annoy father. But it all seemed to have happened in a kind of tunnel. It wasn't real. It was only when she came out of the tunnel into the moonlight or by the sea or into a thunderstorm that she really felt herself. What did it mean? What was it she was always wanting? What did it all lead to? Now? Now?

She turned away from the Buddha with one of her vague gestures. She went over to where Josephine was standing. She wanted to say something to Josephine, something frightfully important, about – about the future and what. . . .

'Don't you think perhaps –' she began.

But Josephine interrupted her. 'I was wondering if now –' she murmured. They stopped; they waited for each other.

'Go on, Con,' said Josephine.

'No, no, Jug; after you,' said Constantia.

'No, say what you were going to say. You began,' said Josephine.

'I . . . I'd rather hear what you were going to say first,' said Constantia.

'Don't be absurd, Con.'

'Really, Jug.'

'Connie!'

'Oh, *Jug*!'

A pause. Then Constantia said faintly, 'I can't say what I was going to say, Jug, because I've forgotten what it was . . . that I was going to say.'

Josephine was silent for a moment. She stared at a big cloud where the sun had been. Then she replied shortly, 'I've forgotten too.'

Her First Ball

Exactly when the ball began Leila would have found it hard to say. Perhaps her first real partner was the cab. It did not matter that she shared the cab with the Sheridan girls and their brother. She sat back in her own little corner of it, and the bolster on which her hand rested felt like the sleeve of an unknown young man's dress suit; and away they bowled, past waltzing lamp-posts and houses and fences and trees.

'Have you really never been to a ball before, Leila? But, my child, how too weird' – cried the Sheridan girls.

'Our nearest neighbour was fifteen miles,' said Leila softly, gently opening and shutting her fan.

Oh, dear, how hard it was to be indifferent like the others! She tried not to smile too much; she tried not to care. But every single thing was so new and exciting. . . . Meg's tuberoses, Jose's long loop of amber, Laura's little dark head, pushing above her white fur like a flower through snow. She would remember for ever. It even gave her a pang to see her cousin Laurie throw away the wisps of tissue paper he pulled from the fastenings of his new gloves. She would like to have kept those wisps as a keepsake, as a remembrance. Laurie leaned forward and put his hand on Laura's knee.

'Look here, darling,' he said. 'The third and the ninth as usual. Twig?'

Oh, how marvellous to have a brother! In her excitement Leila felt that if there had been time, if it hadn't been impossible, she couldn't have helped crying because she was an only child, and no brother had ever said 'Twig?' to her,

no sister would ever say, as Meg said to Jose that moment, 'I've never known your hair go up more successfully than it has to-night!'

But, of course, there was no time. They were at the drill hall already; there were cabs in front of them and cabs behind. The road was bright on either side with moving fan-like lights, and on the pavement gay couples seemed to float through the air; little satin shoes chased each other like birds.

'Hold on to me, Leila; you'll get lost,' said Laura.

'Come on girls, let's make a dash for it,' said Laurie.

Leila put two fingers on Laura's pink velvet cloak, and they were somehow lifted past the big golden lantern, carried along the passage, and pushed into the little room marked 'Ladies'. Here the crowd was so great there was hardly space to take off their things; the noise was deafening. Two benches on either side were stacked high with wraps. Two old women in white aprons ran up and down tossing fresh armfuls. And everybody was pressing forward trying to get at the little dressing-table and mirror at the far end.

A great quivering jet of gas lighted the ladies' room. It couldn't wait; it was dancing already. When the door opened again and there came a burst of tuning from the drill hall, it leaped almost to the ceiling.

Dark girls, fair girls were patting their hair, tying ribbons again, tucking handkerchiefs down the fronts of their bodices, smoothing marble-white gloves. And because they were all laughing it seemed to Leila that they were all lovely.

'Aren't there any invisible hair-pins?' cried a voice. 'How most extraordinary! I can't see a single invisible hair-pin.'

'Powder my back, there's a darling,' cried someone else.

'But I must have a needle and cotton. I've torn simply miles and miles of the frill,' wailed a third.

Then, 'Pass them along, pass them along!' The straw basket of programmes was tossed from arm to arm. Darling little pink-and-silver programmes, with pink pencils and fluffy tassels. Leila's fingers shook as she took one out of the basket. She wanted to ask some one, 'Am I meant to have one too?' but she had just time to read: 'Waltz 3. *Two, Two in a Canoe.* Polka 4. *Making the Feathers Fly*,' when Meg cried, 'Ready, Leila?' and they pressed their way through the crush in the passage towards the big double doors of the drill hall.

Dancing had not begun yet, but the band had stopped tuning, and the noise was so great it seemed that when it did begin to play it would never be heard. Leila, pressing close to Meg, looking over Meg's shoulder, felt that even the little quivering coloured flags strung across the ceiling were talking. She quite forgot to be shy; she forgot how in the middle of dressing she had sat down on the bed with one shoe off and one shoe on and begged her mother to ring up her cousins and say she couldn't go after all. And the rush of longing she had had to be sitting on the verandah of their forsaken up-country home, listening to the baby owls crying 'More pork' in the moonlight, was changed to a rush of joy so sweet that it was hard to bear alone. She clutched her fan, and, gazing at the gleaming, golden floor, the azaleas, the lanterns, the stage at one end with its red carpet and gilt chairs and the band in a corner, she thought breathlessly, 'How heavenly; how simply heavenly!'

All the girls stood grouped together at one side of the door, the men at the other, and the chaperones in dark dresses, smiling rather foolishly, walked with little careful steps over the polished floor towards the stage.

'This is my little country cousin Leila. Be nice to her.

Find her partners; she's under my wing,' said Meg, going up to one girl after another.

Strange faces smiled at Leila – sweetly, vaguely. Strange voices answered, 'Of course, my dear.' But Leila felt the girls didn't really see her. They were looking towards the men. Why didn't the men begin? What were they waiting for? There they stood, smoothing their gloves, patting their glossy hair and smiling among themselves. Then, quite suddenly, as if they had only just made up their minds that that was what they had to do, the men came gliding over the parquet. There was a joyful flutter among the girls. A tall, fair man flew up to Meg, seized her programme, scribbled something; Meg passed him on to Leila. 'May I have the pleasure?' He ducked and smiled. There came a dark man wearing an eyeglass, then cousin Laurie with a friend, and Laura with a little freckled fellow whose tie was crooked. Then quite an old man – fat, with a big bald patch on his head – took her programme and murmured, 'Let me see, let me see!' And he was a long time comparing his programme, which looked black with names, with hers. It seemed to give him so much trouble that Leila was ashamed. 'Oh, please don't bother,' she said eagerly. But instead of replying the fat man wrote something, glanced at her again. 'Do I remember this bright little face?' he said softly. 'Is it known to me of yore?' At that moment the band began playing; the fat man disappeared. He was tossed away on a great wave of music that came flying over the gleaming floor, breaking the groups up into couples, scattering them, sending them spinning. . . .

Leila had learned to dance at boarding school. Every Saturday afternoon the boarders were hurried off to a little corrugated iron mission hall where Miss Eccles (of London) held her 'select' classes. But the difference between that

dusty-smelling hall – with calico texts on the walls, the poor terrified little woman in a brown velvet toque with rabbit's ears thumping the cold piano, Miss Eccles poking the girls' feet with her long white wand – and this was so tremendous that Leila was sure if her partner didn't come and she had to listen to that marvellous music and to watch the others sliding, gliding over the golden floor, she would die at least, or faint, or lift her arms and fly out of one of those dark windows that showed the stars.

'Ours, I think –' Some one bowed, smiled, and offered her his arm; she hadn't to die after all. Some one's hand pressed her waist, and she floated away like a flower that is tossed into a pool.

'Quite a good floor, isn't it?' drawled a faint voice close to her ear.

'I think it's most beautifully slippery,' said Leila.

'Pardon!' The faint voice sounded surprised. Leila said it again. And there was a tiny pause before the voice echoed, 'Oh, quite!' and she was swung round again.

He steered so beautifully. That was the great difference between dancing with girls and men, Leila decided. Girls banged into each other, and stamped on each other's feet; the girl who was the gentleman always clutched you so.

The azaleas were separate flowers no longer; they were pink and white flags streaming by.

'Were you at the Bells' last week?' the voice came again. It sounded tired. Leila wondered whether she ought to ask him if he would like to stop.

'No, this is my first dance,' she said.

Her partner gave a little gasping laugh. 'Oh, I say,' he protested.

'Yes, it is really the first dance I've ever been to,' Leila was

most fervent. It was such a relief to be able to tell somebody. 'You see, I've lived in the country all my life up till now. . . .'

At that moment the music stopped, and they went to sit on two chairs against the wall. Leila tucked her pink satin feet under and fanned herself, while she blissfully watched the other couples passing and disappearing through the swing doors.

'Enjoying yourself, Leila?' asked Jose, nodding her golden head.

Laura passed and gave her the faintest little wink; it made Leila wonder for a moment whether she was quite grown up after all. Certainly her partner did not say very much. He coughed, tucked his handkerchief away, pulled down his waistcoat, took a minute thread off his sleeve. But it didn't matter. Almost immediately the band started, and her second partner seemed to spring from the ceiling.

'Floor's not bad,' said the new voice. Did one always begin with the floor? And then, 'Were you at the Neaves' on Tuesday?' And again Leila explained. Perhaps it was a little strange that her partners were not more interested. For it was thrilling. Her first ball! She was only at the beginning of everything. It seemed to her that she had never known what the night was like before. Up till now it had been dark, silent, beautiful very often – oh, yes – but mournful somehow. Solemn. And now it would never be like that again – it had opened dazzling bright.

'Care for an ice?' said her partner. And they went through the swing doors, down the passage, to the supper room. Her cheeks burned, she was fearfully thirsty. How sweet the ices looked on little glass plates, and how cold the frosted spoon was, iced too! And when they came back to the hall there was the fat man waiting for her by the door. It gave her quite

a shock again to see how old he was; he ought to have been on the stage with the fathers and mothers. And when Leila compared him with her other partners he looked shabby. His waistcoat was creased, there was a button off his glove, his coat looked as if it was dusty with French chalk.

'Come along, little lady,' said the fat man. He scarcely troubled to clasp her, and they moved away so gently, it was more like walking than dancing. But he said not a word about the floor. 'Your first dance, isn't it?' he murmured.

'How *did* you know?'

'Ah,' said the fat man, 'that's what it is to be old!' He wheezed faintly as he steered her past an awkward couple. 'You see, I've been doing this kind of thing for the last thirty years.'

'Thirty years?' cried Leila. Twelve years before she was born!

'It hardly bears thinking about, does it?' said the fat man gloomily. Leila looked at his bald head, and she felt quite sorry for him.

'I think it's marvellous to be still going on,' she said kindly.

'Kind little lady,' said the fat man, and he pressed her a little closer, and hummed a bar of the waltz. 'Of course,' he said, 'you can't hope to last anything like as long as that. No-o,' said the fat man, 'long before that you'll be sitting up there on the stage, looking on, in your nice black velvet. And these pretty arms will have turned into little short fat ones, and you'll beat time with such a different kind of fan – a black bony one.' The fat man seemed to shudder. 'And you'll smile away like the poor old dears up there, and point to your daughter, and tell the elderly lady next to you how some dreadful man tried to kiss her at the club ball. And

your heart will ache, ache' – the fat man squeezed her closer still, as if he really was sorry for that poor heart – 'because no one wants to kiss you now. And you'll say how unpleasant these polished floors are to walk on, how dangerous they are. Eh, Mademoiselle Twinkletoes?' said the fat man softly.

Leila gave a light little laugh, but she did not feel like laughing. Was it – could it all be true? It sounded terribly true. Was this first ball only the beginning of her last ball after all? At that the music seemed to change; it sounded sad, sad; it rose upon a great sigh. Oh, how quickly things changed! Why didn't happiness last for ever? For ever wasn't a bit too long.

'I want to stop,' she said in a breathless voice. The fat man led her to the door.

'No,' she said, 'I won't go outside. I won't sit down. I'll just stand here, thank you.' She leaned against the wall, tapping with her foot, pulling up her gloves and trying to smile. But deep inside her a little girl threw her pinafore over her head and sobbed. Why had he spoiled it all?

'I say, you know,' said the fat man, 'you mustn't take me seriously, little lady.'

'As if I should!' said Leila, tossing her small dark head and sucking her underlip. . . .

Again the couples paraded. The swing doors opened and shut. Now new music was given out by the bandmaster. But Leila didn't want to dance any more. She wanted to be home, or sitting on the verandah listening to those baby owls. When she looked through the dark windows at the stars, they had long beams like wings. . . .

But presently a soft, melting, ravishing tune began, and a young man with curly hair bowed before her. She would have to dance, out of politeness, until she could find Meg.

Very stiffly she walked into the middle; very haughtily she put her hand on his sleeve. But in one minute, in one turn, her feet glided, glided. The lights, the azaleas, the dresses, the pink faces, the velvet chairs, all became one beautiful flying wheel. And when her next partner bumped her into the fat man and he said, 'Par*don*,' she smiled at him more radiantly than ever. She didn't even recognize him again.

The Voyage

The Picton boat was due to leave at half-past eleven. It was a beautiful night, mild, starry, only when they got out of the cab and started to walk down the Old Wharf that jutted out into the harbour, a faint wind blowing off the water ruffled under Fenella's hat, and she put up her hand to keep it on. It was dark on the Old Wharf, very dark; the wool sheds, the cattle trucks, the cranes standing up so high, the little squat railway engine, all seemed carved out of solid darkness. Here and there on a rounded wood-pile, that was like the stalk of a huge black mushroom, there hung a lantern, but it seemed afraid to unfurl its timid, quivering light in all that blackness; it burned softly, as if for itself.

Fenella's father pushed on with quick, nervous strides. Beside him her grandma bustled along in her crackling black ulster; they went so fast that she had now and again to give an undignified little skip to keep up with them. As well as her luggage strapped into a neat sausage, Fenella carried clasped to her her grandma's umbrella, and the handle, which was a swan's head, kept giving her shoulder a sharp little peck as if it too wanted her to hurry. . . . Men, their caps pulled down, their collars turned up, swung by; a few women all muffled scurried along; and one tiny boy, only his little black arms and legs showing out of a white woolly shawl, was jerked along angrily between his father and mother; he looked like a baby fly that had fallen into the cream.

Then suddenly, so suddenly that Fenella and her grandma both leapt, there sounded from behind the largest wool shed,

that had a trail of smoke hanging over it, *Mia-oo-oo-O-O!*

'First whistle,' said her father briefly, and at that moment they came in sight of the Picton boat. Lying beside the dark wharf, all strung, all beaded with round golden lights, the Picton boat looked as if she was more ready to sail among stars than out into the cold sea. People pressed along the gangway. First went her grandma, then her father, then Fenella. There was a high step down on to the deck, and an old sailor in a jersey standing by gave her his dry, hard hand. They were there; they stepped out of the way of the hurrying people, and standing under a little iron stairway that led to the upper deck they began to say good-bye.

'There, mother, there's your luggage!' said Fenella's father, giving grandma another strapped-up sausage.

'Thank you, Frank.'

'And you've got your cabin tickets safe?'

'Yes, dear.'

'And your other tickets?'

Grandma felt for them inside her glove and showed him the tips.

'That's right.'

He sounded stern, but Fenella, eagerly watching him, saw that he looked tired and sad. *Mia-oo-oo-O-O!* The second whistle blared just above their heads, and a voice like a cry sounded, 'Any more for the gangway?'

'You'll give my love to father,' Fenella saw her father's lips say. And her grandma, very agitated, answered. 'Of course I will, dear. Go now. You'll be left. Go now, Frank. Go now.'

'It's all right, mother. I've got another three minutes.' To her surprise Fenella saw her father take off his hat. He clasped grandma in his arms and pressed her to him. 'God bless you, mother!' she heard him say.

And grandma put her hand, with the black thread glove that was worn through on her ring finger, against his cheek, and she sobbed, 'God bless you, my own brave son!'

This was so awful that Fenella quickly turned her back on them, swallowed once, twice, and frowned terribly at a little green star on a mast head. But she had to turn round again; her father was going.

'Good-bye, Fenella. Be a good girl.' His cold, wet moustache brushed her cheek. But Fenella caught hold of the lapels of his coat.

'How long am I going to stay?' she whispered anxiously. He wouldn't look at her. He shook her off gently, and gently said, 'We'll see about that. Here! Where's your hand?' He pressed something into her palm. 'Here's a shilling in case you should need it.'

A shilling! She must be going away for ever! 'Father!' cried Fenella. But he was gone. He was the last off the ship. The sailors put their shoulders to the gangway. A huge coil of dark rope went flying through the air and fell 'thump' on the wharf. A bell rang; a whistle shrilled. Silently the dark wharf began to slip, to slide, to edge away from them. Now there was a rush of water between. Fenella strained to see with all her might. 'Was that father turning round?' – or waving? – or standing alone? – or walking off by himself? The strip of water grew broader, darker. Now the Picton boat began to swing round steady, pointing out to sea. It was no good looking any longer. There was nothing to be seen but a few lights, the face of the town clock hanging in the air, and more lights, little patches of them, on the dark hills.

The freshening wind tugged at Fenella's skirts; she went back to her grandma. To her relief grandma seemed no longer sad. She had put the two sausages of luggage one

on top of the other, and she was sitting on them, her hands folded, her head a little on one side. There was an intent, bright look on her face. Then Fenella saw that her lips were moving and guessed that she was praying. But the old woman gave her a bright nod as if to say the prayer was nearly over. She unclasped her hands, sighed, clasped them again, bent forward, and at last gave herself a soft shake.

'And now, child,' she said fingering the bow of her bonnet-strings, 'I think we ought to see about our cabins. Keep close to me, and mind you don't slip.'

'Yes, grandma!'

'And be careful the umbrellas aren't caught in the stair rail. I saw a beautiful umbrella broken in half like that on my way over.'

'Yes, grandma.'

Dark figures of men lounged against the rails. In the glow of their pipes a nose shone out, or the peak of a cap, or a pair of surprised-looking eyebrows. Fenella glanced up. High in the air, a little figure, his hands thrust in his short jacket pockets, stood staring out to sea. The ship rocked ever so little, and she thought the stars rocked too. And now a pale steward in a linen coat, holding a tray high in the palm of his hand, stepped out of a lighted doorway and skimmed past them. They went through that doorway. Carefully over the high brass-bound step on to the rubber mat and then down such a terribly steep flight of stairs that grandma had to put both feet on each step, and Fenella clutched the clammy brass rail and forgot all about the swan-necked umbrella.

At the bottom grandma stopped; Fenella was rather afraid she was going to pray again. But no, it was only to get out the cabin tickets. They were in the saloon. It was glaring bright and stifling; the air smelled of paint and burnt chop-bones

and indiarubber. Fenella wished her grandma would go on, but the old woman was not to be hurried. An immense basket of ham sandwiches caught her eye. She went up to them and touched the top one delicately with her finger.

'How much are the sandwiches?' she asked.

'Tuppence!' bawled a rude steward, slamming down a knife and fork.

Grandma could hardly believe it.

'Twopence *each*?' she asked.

'That's right,' said the steward, and he winked at his companion.

Grandma made a small, astonished face. Then she whispered primly to Fenella. 'What wickedness!' And they sailed out at the further door and along a passage that had cabins on either side. Such a very nice stewardess came to meet them. She was dressed all in blue, and her collar and cuffs were fastened with large brass buttons. She seemed to know grandma well.

'Well, Mrs Crane,' said she, unlocking their washstand. 'We've got you back again. It's not often you give yourself a cabin.'

'No,' said grandma. 'But this time my dear son's thoughtfulness –'

'I hope –' began the stewardess. Then she turned round and took a long mournful look at grandma's blackness and at Fenella's black coat and skirt, black blouse, and hat with a crêpe rose.

Grandma nodded. 'It was God's will,' said she.

The stewardess shut her lips and, taking a deep breath, she seemed to expand.

'What I always say is,' she said, as though it was her own discovery, 'sooner or later each of us has to go, and that's a

certingty.' She paused. 'Now, can I bring you anything, Mrs Crane? A cup of tea? I know it's no good offering you a little something to keep the cold out.'

Grandma shook her head. 'Nothing, thank you. We've got a few wine biscuits, and Fenella has a very nice banana.'

'Then I'll give you a look later on,' said the stewardess, and she went out, shutting the door.

What a very small cabin it was! It was like being shut up in a box with grandma. The dark round eye above the washstand gleamed at them dully. Fenella felt shy. She stood against the door, still clasping her luggage and the umbrella. Were they going to get undressed in here? Already her grandma had taken off her bonnet, and, rolling up the strings, she fixed each with a pin to the lining before she hung the bonnet up. Her white hair shone like silk; the little bun at the back was covered with a black net. Fenella hardly ever saw her grandma with her head uncovered; she looked strange.

'I shall put on the woollen fascinator your dear mother crocheted for me,' said grandma, and, unstrapping the sausage, she took it out and wound it round her head; the fringe of grey bobbles danced at her eyebrows as she smiled tenderly and mournfully at Fenella. Then she undid her bodice, and something under that, and something else under that. Then there seemed a short, sharp tussle, and grandma flushed faintly. Snip! Snap! She had undone her stays. She breathed a sigh of relief, and sitting on the plush couch, she slowly and carefully pulled off her elastic-sided boots and stood them side by side.

By the time Fenella had taken off her coat and skirt and put on her flannel dressing-gown grandma was quite ready.

'Must I take off my boots, grandma? They're lace.'

Grandma gave them a moment's consideration. 'You'd feel a great deal more comfortable if you did, child,' said she. She kissed Fenella. 'Don't forget to say your prayers. Our dear Lord is with us when we are at sea even more than when we are on dry land. And because I am an experienced traveller,' said grandma briskly, 'I shall take the upper berth.'

'But, grandma, however will you get up there?'

Three little spider-like steps were all Fenella saw. The old woman gave a small silent laugh before she mounted them nimbly, and she peered over the high bunk at the astonished Fenella.

'You didn't think your grandma could do that, did you?' said she. And as she sank back Fenella heard her light laugh again.

The hard square of brown soap would not lather, and the water in the bottle was like a kind of blue jelly. How hard it was, too, to turn down those stiff sheets; you simply had to tear your way in. If everything had been different, Fenella might have got the giggles. . . . At last she was inside, and while she lay there panting, there sounded from above a long, soft whispering, as though some one was gently, gently rustling among tissue paper to find something. It was grandma saying her prayers. . . .

A long time passed. Then the stewardess came in; she trod softly and leaned her hand on grandma's bunk.

'We're just entering the Straits,' she said.

'Oh!'

'It's a fine night, but we're rather empty. We may pitch a little.'

And indeed at that moment the Picton boat rose and rose and hung in the air just long enough to give a shiver

before she swung down again, and there was the sound of heavy water slapping against her sides. Fenella remembered she had left that swan-necked umbrella standing up on the little couch. If it fell over, would it break? But grandma remembered too, at the same time.

'I wonder if you'd mind, stewardess, laying down my umbrella,' she whispered.

'Not at all, Mrs Crane.' And the stewardess, coming back to grandma breathed, 'Your little granddaughter's in such a beautiful sleep.'

'God be praised for that!' said grandma.

'Poor little motherless mite!' said the stewardess. And grandma was still telling the stewardess all about what had happened when Fenella fell asleep.

But she hadn't been asleep long enough to dream before she woke up again to see something waving in the air above her head. What was it? What could it be? It was a small grey foot. Now another joined it. They seemed to be feeling about for something; there came a sigh.

'I'm awake, grandma,' said Fenella.

'Oh, dear, am I near the ladder?' asked grandma. 'I thought it was this end.'

'No, grandma, it's the other. I'll put your foot on it. Are we there?' asked Fenella.

'In the harbour,' said grandma. 'We must get up, child. You'd better have a biscuit to steady yourself before you move.'

But Fenella had hopped out of her bunk. The lamp was still burning, but night was over, and it was cold. Peering through that round eye, she could see far off some rocks. Now they were scattered over with foam; now a gull flipped by; and now there came a long piece of real land.

'It's land, grandma,' said Fenella, wonderingly, as though they had been at sea for weeks together. She hugged herself; she stood on one leg and rubbed it with the toes of the other foot; she was trembling. Oh, it had all been so sad lately. Was it going to change? But all her grandma said was, 'Make haste, child. I should leave your nice banana for the stewardess as you haven't eaten it.' And Fenella put on her black clothes again, and a button sprang off one of her gloves and rolled to where she couldn't reach it. They went up on deck.

But if it had been cold in the cabin, on deck it was like ice. The sun was not up yet, but the stars were dim, and the cold pale sky was the same colour as the cold pale sea. On the land a white mist rose and fell. Now they could see quite plainly dark bush. Even the shapes of the umbrella ferns showed, and those strange silvery withered trees that are like skeletons. . . . Now they could see the landing-stage and some little houses, pale too, clustered together, like shells on the lid of a box. The other passengers tramped up and down, but more slowly than they had the night before, and they looked gloomy.

And now the landing-stage came out to meet them. Slowly it swam towards the Picton boat, and a man holding a coil of rope, and a cart with a small drooping horse and another man sitting on the step, came too.

'It's Mr Penreddy, Fenella, come for us,' said grandma. She sounded pleased. Her white waxen cheeks were blue with cold, her chin trembled, and she had to keep wiping her eyes and her little pink nose.

'You've got my –'

'Yes, grandma.' Fenella showed it to her.

The rope came flying through the air, and 'smack' it fell on the deck. The gangway was lowered. Again Fenella

followed her grandma on to the wharf over to the little cart, and a moment later they were bowling away. The hooves of the little horse drummed over the wooden piles, then sank softly into the sandy road. Not a soul was to be seen; there was not even a feather of smoke. The mist rose and fell, and the sea still sounded asleep as slowly it turned on the beach.

'I seen Mr Crane yestiddy,' said Mr Penreddy. 'He looked himself then. Missus knocked him up a batch of scones last week.'

And now the little horse pulled up before one of the shell-like houses. They got down. Fenella put her hand on the gate, and the big, trembling dew-drops soaked through her glove-tips. Up a little path of round white pebbles they went, with drenched sleeping flowers on either side. Grandma's delicate white picotees were so heavy with dew that they were fallen, but their sweet smell was part of the cold morning. The blinds were down in the little house; they mounted the steps on to the verandah. A pair of old bluchers was on one side of the door, and a large red watering-can on the other.

'Tut! tut! Your grandpa,' said grandma. She turned the handle. Not a sound. She called, 'Walter!' And immediately a deep voice that sounded half stifled called back, 'Is that you, Mary?'

'Wait, dear,' said grandma. 'Go in there.' She pushed Fenella gently into a small dusky sitting-room.

On the table a white cat, that had been folded up like a camel, rose, stretched itself, yawned, and then sprang on to the tips of its toes. Fenella buried one cold little hand in the white, warm fur, and smiled timidly while she stroked and listened to grandma's gentle voice and the rolling tones of grandpa.

A door creaked. 'Come in, dear.' The old woman beckoned, Fenella followed. There, lying to one side of an immense bed, lay grandpa. Just his head with a white tuft, and his rosy face and long silver beard showed over the quilt. He was like a very old wide-awake bird.

'Well, my girl!' said grandpa. 'Give us a kiss!' Fenella kissed him. 'Ugh!' said grandpa. 'Her little nose is as cold as a button. What's that she's holding? Her grandma's umbrella?'

Fenella smiled again, and crooked the swan neck over the bed-rail. Above the bed there was a big text in a deep-black frame:

Lost! One Golden Hour
Set with Sixty Diamond Minutes.
No *Reward Is Offered*
For It Is GONE FOR EVER!

'Yer grandma painted that,' said grandpa. And he ruffled his white tuft and looked at Fenella so merrily she almost thought he winked at her.

The Garden Party

And after all the weather was ideal. They could not have had a more perfect day for a garden party if they had ordered it. Windless, warm, the sky without a cloud. Only the blue was veiled with a haze of light gold, as it is sometimes in early summer. The gardener had been up since dawn, mowing the lawns and sweeping them, until the grass and the dark flat rosettes where the daisy plants had been seemed to shine. As for the roses, you could not help feeling they understood that roses are the only flowers that impress people at garden parties; the only flowers that everybody is certain of knowing. Hundreds, yes, literally hundreds, had come out in a single night; the green bushes bowed down as though they had been visited by archangels.

Breakfast was not yet over before the men came to put up the marquee.

'Where do you want the marquee put, mother?'

'My dear child, it's no use asking me. I'm determined to leave everything to you children this year. Forget I am your mother. Treat me as an honoured guest.'

But Meg could not possibly go and supervise the men. She had washed her hair before breakfast, and she sat drinking her coffee in a green turban, with a dark wet curl stamped on each cheek. Jose, the butterfly, always came down in a silk petticoat and a kimono jacket.

'You'll have to go, Laura, you're the artistic one.'

Away Laura flew, still holding her piece of bread-and-butter. It's so delicious to have an excuse for eating out of

doors, and besides, she loved having to arrange things; she always felt she could do it so much better than anybody else.

Four men in their shirt-sleeves stood grouped together on the garden path. They carried staves covered with rolls of canvas, and they had big tool-bags slung on their backs. They looked impressive. Laura wished now that she was not holding that piece of bread-and-butter, but there was nowhere to put it, and she couldn't possibly throw it away. She blushed and tried to look severe and even a little bit short-sighted as she came up to them.

'Good morning,' she said, copying her mother's voice. But that sounded so fearfully affected that she was ashamed, and stammered like a little girl. 'Oh – er – have you come – is it about the marquee?'

'That's right, miss,' said the tallest of the men, a lanky, freckled fellow, and he shifted his tool-bag, knocked back his straw hat and smiled down at her. 'That's about it.'

His smile was so easy, so friendly, that Laura recovered. What nice eyes he had, small, but such a dark blue! And now she looked at the others, they were smiling too. 'Cheer up, we won't bite,' their smile seemed to say. How very nice workmen were! And what a beautiful morning! She mustn't mention the morning; she must be business-like. The marquee.

'Well, what about the lily-lawn? Would that do?'

And she pointed to the lily-lawn with the hand that didn't hold the bread-and-butter. They turned, they stared in the direction. A little fat chap thrust out his under-lip, and the tall fellow frowned.

'I don't fancy it,' said he. 'Not conspicuous enough. You see, with a thing like a marquee,' and he turned to Laura in his easy way, 'you want to put it somewhere where it'll give you a bang slap in the eye, if you follow me.'

Laura's upbringing made her wonder for a moment whether it was quite respectful of a workman to talk to her of bangs slap in the eye. But she did quite follow him.

'A corner of the tennis-court,' she suggested. 'But the band's going to be in one corner.'

'H'm, going to have a band, are you?' said another of the workmen. He was pale. He had a haggard look as his dark eyes scanned the tennis-court. What was he thinking?'

'Only a very small band,' said Laura gently. Perhaps he wouldn't mind so much if the band was quite small. But the tall fellow interrupted.

'Look here, miss, that's the place. Against those trees. Over there. That'll do fine.'

Against the karakas. Then the karaka trees would be hidden. And they were so lovely, with their broad, gleaming leaves, and their clusters of yellow fruit. They were like trees you imagined growing on a desert island, proud, solitary, lifting their leaves and fruits to the sun in a kind of silent splendour. Must they be hidden by a marquee?

They must. Already the men had shouldered their staves and were making for the place. Only the tall fellow was left. He bent down, pinched a sprig of lavender, put his thumb and forefinger to his nose and snuffed up the smell. When Laura saw the gesture she forgot all about the karakas in her wonder at him caring for things like that – caring for the smell of lavender. How many men that she knew would have done such a thing. Oh, how extraordinarily nice workmen were, she thought. Why couldn't she have workmen for friends rather than the silly boys she danced with and who came to Sunday night supper? She would get on much better with men like these.

It's all the fault, she decided, as the tall fellow drew

something on the back of an envelope, something that was to be looped up or left to hang, of these absurd class distinctions. Well, for her part, she didn't feel them. Not a bit, not an atom. . . . And now there came the chock-chock of wooden hammers. Some one whistled, some one sang out, 'Are you right there, matey?' 'Matey!' The friendliness of it, the – the – Just to prove how happy she was, just to show the tall fellow how at home she felt, and how she despised stupid conventions, Laura took a big bite of her bread-and-butter as she stared at the little drawing. She felt just like a work-girl.

'Laura, Laura, where are you? Telephone, Laura!' a voice cried from the house.

'Coming!' Away she skimmed, over the lawn, up the path, up the steps, across the verandah, and into the porch. In the hall her father and Laurie were brushing their hats ready to go to the office.

'I say, Laura,' said Laurie very fast, 'you might just give a squiz at my coat before this afternoon. See if it wants pressing.'

I will,' said she. Suddenly she couldn't stop herself. She ran at Laurie and gave him a small, quick squeeze. 'Oh, I do love parties, don't you?' gasped Laura.

'Ra-ther,' said Laurie's warm, boyish voice, and he squeezed his sister too, and gave her a gentle push. 'Dash off to the telephone, old girl.'

The telephone. 'Yes, yes; oh yes. Kitty? Good morning, dear. Come to lunch? Do, dear. Delighted of course. It will only be a very scratch meal – just the sandwich crusts and broken meringue-shells and what's left over. Yes, isn't it a perfect morning? Your white? Oh, I certainly should. One moment – hole! the line. Mother's calling.' And Laura sat back. 'What, mother? Can't hear.'

Mrs Sheridan's voice floated down the stairs. 'Tell her to wear that sweet hat she had on last Sunday.'

'Mother says you're to wear that *sweet* hat you had on last Sunday. Good. One o'clock. Bye-bye.'

Laura put back the receiver, flung her arms over her head, took a deep breath, stretched and let them fall. 'Huh,' she sighed, and the moment after the sigh she sat up quickly. She was still, listening. All the doors in the house seemed to be open. The house was alive with soft, quick steps and running voices. The green baize door that led to the kitchen regions swung open and shut with a muffled thud. And now there came a long, chuckling absurd sound. It was the heavy piano being moved on its stiff castors. But the air! If you stopped to notice, was the air always like this? Little faint winds were playing chase in at the tops of the windows, out at the doors. And there were two tiny spots of sun, one on the inkpot, one on a silver photograph frame, playing too. Darling little spots. Especially the one on the inkpot lid. It was quite warm. A warm little silver star. She could have kissed it.

The front door bell pealed, and there sounded the rustle of Sadie's print skirt on the stairs. A man's voice murmured; Sadie answered, careless, 'I'm sure I don't know. Wait. I'll ask Mrs Sheridan.'

'What is it, Sadie?' Laura came into the hall.

'It's the florist, Miss Laura.'

It was, indeed. There, just inside the door, stood a wide, shallow tray full of pots of pink lilies. No other kind. Nothing but lilies – canna lilies, big pink flowers, wide open, radiant, almost frighteningly alive on bright crimson stems.

'O-oh, Sadie!' said Laura, and the sound was like a little moan. She crouched down as if to warm herself at the blaze

of lilies; she felt they were in her fingers, on her lips, growing in her breast.

'It's some mistake,' she said faintly. 'Nobody ever ordered so many. Sadie, go and find mother.'

But at that moment Mrs Sheridan joined them.

'It's quite right,' she said calmly. 'Yes, I ordered them. Aren't they lovely?' She pressed Laura's arm. 'I was passing the shop yesterday, and I saw them in the window. And I suddenly thought for once in my life I shall have enough canna lilies. The garden party will be a good excuse.'

'But I thought you said you didn't mean to interfere,' said Laura. Sadie had gone. The florist's man was still outside at his van. She put her arm round her mother's neck and gently, very gently, she bit her mother's ear.

'My darling child, you wouldn't like a logical mother, would you? Don't do that. Here's the man.'

He carried more lilies still, another whole tray.

'Bank them up just inside the door, on both sides of the porch, please,' said Mrs Sheridan. 'Don't you agree, Laura?'

'Oh, I *do,* mother.'

In the drawing-room Meg, Jose and good little Hans had at last succeeded in moving the piano.

'Now, if we put this chesterfield against the wall and move everything out of the room except the chairs, don't you think?'

'Quite.'

'Hans, move these tables into the smoking-room, and bring a sweeper to take these marks off the carpet and – one moment, Hans –' Jose loved giving orders to the servants, and they loved obeying her. She always made them feel they were taking part in some drama. 'Tell mother and Miss Laura to come here at once.'

'Very good, Miss Jose.'

She turned to Meg. 'I want to hear what the piano sounds like, just in case I'm asked to sing this afternoon. Let's try over "This life is Weary".'

Pom! Ta-ta-ta *Tee-ta!* The piano burst out so passionately that Jose's face changed. She clasped her hands. She looked mournfully and enigmatically at her mother and Laura as they came in.

> This Life is *Wee*-ary,
> A Tear – a Sigh.
> A Love that *Chan*-ges,
> This Life is *Wee*-ary,
> A Tear – a Sigh.
> A Love that *Chan*-ges,
> And then . . . Good-bye!

But at the word 'Good-bye', and although the piano sounded more desperate than ever, her face broke into a brilliant, dreadfully unsympathetic smile.

'Aren't I in good voice, mummy?' she beamed.

> This Life is *Wee*-ary,
> Hope comes to Die.
> A Dream – a *Wa*-kening.

But now Sadie interrupted them. 'What is it, Sadie?'

'If you please, m'm, cook says have you got the flags for the sandwiches?'

'The flags for the sandwiches, Sadie?' echoed Mrs Sheridan dreamily. And the children knew by her face that she hadn't got them. 'Let me see.' And she said to Sadie firmly, 'Tell cook I'll let her have them in ten minutes.'

Sadie went out.

'Now, Laura,' said her mother quickly, 'come with me into the smoking-room. I've got the names somewhere on the back of an envelope. You'll have to write them out for me. Meg, go upstairs this minute and take that wet thing off your head. Jose, run and finish dressing this instant. Do you hear me, children, or shall I have to tell your father when he comes home to-night? And – and, Jose, pacify the cook if you do go into the kitchen, will you? I'm terrified of her this morning.'

The envelope was found at last behind the dining-room clock, though how it had got there Mrs Sheridan could not imagine.

'One of you children must have stolen it out of my bag, because I remember vividly – cream-cheese and lemon-curd. Have you done that?'

'Yes.'

'Egg and –' Mrs Sheridan held the envelope away from her. 'It looks like mice. It can't be mice, can it?'

'Olive, pet,' said Laura, looking over her shoulder.

'Yes, of course, olive. What a horrible combination it sounds. Egg and olive.'

They were finished at last, and Laura took them off to the kitchen. She found Jose there pacifying the cook, who did not look at all terrifying.

'I have never seen such exquisite sandwiches,' said Jose's rapturous voice. 'How many kinds did you say there were, cook? Fifteen?'

'Fifteen, Miss Jose.'

'Well, cook, I congratulate you.'

Cook swept up crusts with the long sandwich knife, and smiled broadly.

'Godber's has come,' announced Sadie, issuing out of the pantry. She had seen the man pass the window.

That meant the cream puffs had come. Godber's were famous for their cream puffs. Nobody ever thought of making them at home.

'Bring them in and put them on the table, my girl,' ordered cook.

Sadie brought them in and went back to the door. Of course Laura and Jose were far too grown-up to really care about such things. All the same, they couldn't help agreeing that the puffs looked very attractive. Very. Cook began arranging them, shaking off the extra icing sugar.

'Don't they carry one back to all one's parties?' said Laura.

'I suppose they do,' said practical Jose, who never liked to be carried back. 'They look beautifully light and feathery, I must say.'

'Have one each, my dears,' said cook in her comfortable voice. 'Yer ma won't know.'

Oh, impossible. Fancy cream puffs so soon after breakfast. The very idea made one shudder. All the same, two minutes later Jose and Laura were licking their fingers with that absorbed inward look that only comes from whipped cream.

'Let's go into the garden, out by the back way,' suggested Laura. 'I want to see how the men are getting on with the marquee. They're such awfully nice men.'

But the back door was blocked by cook, Sadie, Godber's man and Hans.

Something had happened.

'Tuk-tuk-tuk,' clucked cook like an agitated hen. Sadie had her hand clapped to her cheek as though she had toothache. Han's face was screwed up in the effort to understand. Only Godber's man seemed to be enjoying himself; it was his story.

'What's the matter? What's happened?'

'There's been a horrible accident,' said cook. 'A man killed.'

'A man killed! Where? How? When?'

But Godber's man wasn't going to have his story snatched from under his very nose.

'Know those little cottages just below here, miss?' Know them? Of course, she knew them. 'Well, there's a young chap living there, name of Scott, a carter. His horse shied at a traction-engine, corner of Hawke Street this morning, and he was thrown out on the back of his head. Killed.'

'Dead!' Laura stared at Godber's man.

'Dead when they picked him up,' said Godber's man with relish. 'They were taking the body home as I come up here.' And he said to the cook, 'He's left a wife and five little ones.'

'Jose, come here.' Laura caught hold of her sister's sleeve and dragged her through the kitchen to the other side of the green baize door. There she paused and leaned against it. 'Jose!' she said, horrified, 'however are we going to stop everything?'

'Stop everything, Laura!' cried Jose in astonishment. 'What do you mean?'

'Stop the garden party, of course.' Why did Jose pretend?

But Jose was still more amazed. 'Stop the garden party? My dear Laura, don't be so absurd. Of course we can't do anything of the kind. Nobody expects us to. Don't be so extravagant.'

'But we can't possibly have a garden party with a man dead just outside the front gate.'

That really was extravagant, for the little cottages were in a lane to themselves at the very bottom of a steep rise that led up to the house. A broad road ran between. True, they

were far too near. They were the greatest possible eyesore, and they had no right to be in that neighbourhood at all. They were little mean dwellings painted a chocolate brown. In the garden patches there was nothing but cabbage stalks, sick hens and tomato cans. The very smoke coming out of their chimneys was poverty-stricken. Little rags and shreds of smoke, so unlike the great silvery plumes that uncurled from the Sheridans' chimneys. Washer-women lived in the lane and sweeps and a cobbler, and a man whose house-front was studded all over with minute bird-cages. Children swarmed. When the Sheridans were little they were forbidden to set foot there because of the revolting language and of what they might catch. But since they were grown up, Laura and Laurie on their prowls sometimes walked through. It was disgusting and sordid. They came out with a shudder. But still one must go everywhere; one must see everything. So through they went.

'And just think of what the band would sound like to that poor woman,' said Laura.

'Oh, Laura!' Jose began to be seriously annoyed. 'If you're going to stop a band playing every time someone has an accident, you'll lead a very strenuous life. I'm every bit as sorry about it as you. I feel just as sympathetic.' Her eyes hardened. She looked at her sister just as she used to when they were little and fighting together. 'You won't bring a drunken workman back to life by being sentimental,' she said softly.

'Drunk! Who said he was drunk?' Laura turned furiously on Jose. She said just as they had used to say on those occasions, 'I'm going straight up to tell mother.'

'Do, dear,' cooed Jose.

'Mother, can I come into your room?' Laura turned the big glass door-knob.

'Of course, child. Why, what's the matter? What's given you such a colour?' And Mrs Sheridan turned round from her dressing-table. She was trying on a new hat.

'Mother, a man's been killed,' began Laura.

'*Not* in the garden?' interrupted her mother.

'No, no!'

'Oh, what a fright you gave me!' Mrs Sheridan sighed with relief, and took off the big hat and held it on her knees.

'But listen, mother,' said Laura. Breathless, half-choking, she told the dreadful story. 'Of course, we can't have our party, can we?' she pleaded. 'The band and everybody arriving. They'd hear us, mother; they're nearly neighbours.'

To Laura's astonishment her mother behaved just like Jose; it was harder to bear because she seemed amused. She refused to take Laura seriously.

'But, my dear child, use your common sense. It's only by accident we've heard of it. If some one had died there normally – and I can't understand how they keep alive in those poky little holes – we should still be having our party, shouldn't we?'

Laura had to say 'yes' to that, but she felt it was all wrong. She sat down on her mother's sofa and pinched the cushion frill.

'Mother, isn't it really terribly heartless of us?' she asked.

'Darling!' Mrs Sheridan got up and came over to her, carrying the hat. Before Laura could stop her she had popped it on. 'My child!' said her mother, 'the hat is yours. It's made for you. It's much too young for me. I have never seen you look such a picture. Look at yourself!' And she held up her hand-mirror.

'But, mother,' Laura began again. She couldn't look at herself; she turned aside.

This time Mrs Sheridan lost patience just as Jose had done.

'You are being very absurd, Laura,' she said coldly. 'People like that don't expect sacrifices from us. And it's not very sympathetic to spoil everybody's enjoyment as you're doing now.'

'I don't understand,' said Laura, and she walked quickly out of the room into her own bedroom. There, quite by chance, the first thing she saw was this charming girl in the mirror, in her black hat trimmed with gold daisies, and a long black velvet ribbon. Never had she imagined she could look like that. Is mother right? she thought. And now she hoped her mother was right. Am I being extravagant? Perhaps it was extravagant. Just for a moment she had another glimpse of that poor woman and those little children, and the body being carried into the house. But it all seemed blurred, unreal, like a picture in the newspaper. I'll remember it again after the party's over, she decided. And somehow that seemed quite the best plan. . . .

Lunch was over by half-past one. By half-past two they were all ready for the fray. The green-coated band had arrived and was established in a corner of the tennis-court.

'My dear!' trilled Kitty Maitland, 'aren't they too like frogs for words? You ought to have arranged them round the pond with the conductor in the middle on a leaf.'

Laurie arrived and hailed them on his way to dress. At the sight of him Laura remembered the accident again. She wanted to tell him. If Laurie agreed with the others, then it was bound to be all right. And she followed him into the hall.

'Laurie!'

'Hallo!' He was half-way upstairs, but when he turned round and saw Laura he suddenly puffed out his cheeks

and goggled his eyes at her. 'My word, Laura! You do look stunning,' said Laurie. 'What an absolutely topping hat!'

Laura said faintly 'Is it?' and smiled up at Laurie, and didn't tell him after all.

Soon after that people began coming in streams. The band struck up; the hired waiters ran from the house to the marquee. Wherever you looked there were couples strolling, bending to the flowers, greeting, moving on over the lawn. They were like bright birds that had alighted in the Sheridans' garden for this one afternoon, on their way to – where? Ah, what happiness it is to be with people who all are happy, to press hands, press cheeks, smile into eyes.

'Darling Laura, how well you look!'

'What a becoming hat, child!'

'Laura, you look quite Spanish. I've never seen you look so striking.'

And Laura, glowing, answered softly, 'Have you had tea? Won't you have an ice? The passion-fruit ices really are rather special.' She ran to her father and begged him. 'Daddy darling, can't the band have something to drink?'

And the perfect afternoon slowly ripened, slowly faded, slowly its petals closed.

'Never a more delightful garden party. . . .' 'The greatest success. . . .' 'Quite the most. . . .'

Laura helped her mother with the good-byes. They stood side by side in the porch till it was all over.

'All over, all over, thank heaven,' said Mrs Sheridan. 'Round up the others, Laura. Let's go and have some fresh coffee. I'm exhausted. Yes, it's been very successful. But oh, these parties, these parties! Why will you children insist on giving parties!' And they all of them sat down in the deserted marquee.

'Have a sandwich, daddy dear. I wrote the flag.'

'Thanks.' Mr Sheridan took a bite and the sandwich was gone. He took another. 'I suppose you didn't hear of a beastly accident that happened to-day?' he said.

'My dear,' said Mrs Sheridan, holding up her hand, 'we did. It nearly ruined the party. Laura insisted we should put it off.'

'Oh, mother!' Laura didn't want to be teased about it.

'It was a horrible affair all the same,' said Mr Sheridan. 'The chap was married too. Lived just below in the lane, and leaves a wife and half a dozen kiddies, so they say.'

An awkward little silence fell. Mrs Sheridan fidgeted with her cup. Really, it was very tactless of father. . . .

Suddenly she looked up. There on the table were all those sandwiches, cakes, puffs, all un-eaten, all going to be wasted. She had one of her brilliant ideas.

'I know,' she said. 'Let's make up a basket. Let's send that poor creature some of this perfectly good food. At any rate, it will be the greatest treat for the children. Don't you agree? And she's sure to have neighbours calling in and so on. What a point to have it all ready prepared. Laura!' She jumped up. 'Get me the big basket out of the stairs cupboard.'

'But, mother, do you really think it's a good idea?' said Laura.

Again, how curious, she seemed to be different from them all. To take scraps from their party. Would the poor woman really like that?

'Of course! What's the matter with you to-day? An hour or two ago you were insisting on us being sympathetic, and now '

Oh well! Laura ran for the basket. It was filled, it was heaped by her mother.

'Take it yourself, darling,' she said. 'Run down just as you are. No, wait, take the arum lilies too. People of that class are so impressed by arum lilies.'

'The stems will ruin her lace frock,' said practical Jose.

So they would. Just in time. 'Only the basket, then. And, Laura!' – her mother followed her out of the marquee – 'don't on any account –'

'What mother?'

No, better not put such ideas into the child's head! 'Nothing! Run along.'

It was just growing dusky as Laura shut their garden gates. A big dog ran by like a shadow. The road gleamed white, and down below in the hollow the little cottages were in deep shade. How quiet it seemed after the afternoon. Here she was going down the hill to somewhere where a man lay dead, and she couldn't realize it. Why couldn't she? She stopped a minute. And it seemed to her that kisses, voices, tinkling spoons, laughter, the smell of crushed grass were somehow inside her. She had no room for anything else. How strange! She looked up at the pale sky, and all she thought was, 'Yes, it was the most successful party.'

Now the broad road was crossed. The lane began, smoky and dark. Women in shawls and men's tweed caps hurried by. Men hung over the palings; the children played in the doorways. A low hum came from the mean little cottages. In some of them there was a flicker of light, and a shadow, crab-like, moved across the window. Laura bent her head and hurried on. She wished now she had put on a coat. How her frock shone! And the big hat with the velvet streamer – if only it was another hat! Were the people looking at her? They must be. It was a mistake to have come; she knew all along it was a mistake. Should she go back even now?

No, too late. This was the house. It must be. A dark knot of people stood outside. Beside the gate an old, old woman with a crutch sat in a chair, watching. She had her feet on a newspaper. The voices stopped as Laura drew near. The group parted. It was as though she was expected, as though they had known she was coming here.

Laura was terribly nervous. Tossing the velvet ribbon over her shoulder, she said to a woman standing by, 'Is this Mrs Scott's house?' and the woman, smiling queerly, said, 'It is, my lass.'

Oh, to be away from this! She actually said, 'Help me, God,' as she walked up the tiny path and knocked. To be away from those staring eyes, or to be covered up in anything, one of those women's shawls even. I'll just leave the basket and go, she decided. I shan't even wait for it to be emptied.

Then the door opened. A little woman in black showed in the gloom.

Laura said, 'Are you Mrs Scott?' But to her horror the woman answered, 'Walk in, please, miss,' and she was shut in the passage.

'No,' said Laura, 'I don't want to come in. I only want to leave this basket. Mother sent –'

The little woman in the gloomy passage seemed not to have heard her. 'Step this way, please, miss,' she said in an oily voice, and Laura followed her.

She found herself in a wretched little low kitchen, lighted by a smoky lamp. There was a woman sitting before the fire.

'Em,' said the little creature who had let her in. 'Em! It's a young lady.' She turned to Laura. She said meaningly, 'I'm 'er sister, miss. You'll excuse 'er, won't you?'

'Oh, but of course!' said Laura. 'Please, please don't disturb her. I – I only want to leave –'

But at that moment the woman at the fire turned round. Her face, puffed up, red, with swollen eyes and swollen lips, looked terrible. She seemed as though she couldn't understand why Laura was there. What did it mean? Why was this stranger standing in the kitchen with a basket? What was it all about? And the poor face puckered up again.

'All right, my dear,' said the other. 'I'll thank the young lady.'

And again she began, 'You'll excuse her, miss, I'm sure,' and her face, swollen too, tried an oily smile.

Laura only wanted to get out, to get away. She was back in the passage. The door opened. She walked straight through into the bedroom where the dead man was lying.

'You'd like a look at 'im, wouldn't you?' said Em's sister, and she brushed past Laura over to the bed. 'Don't be afraid, my lass,' – and now her voice sounded fond and sly, and fondly she drew down the sheet – ''e looks a picture. There's nothing to show. Come along, my dear.'

Laura came.

There lay a young man, fast asleep – sleeping so soundly, so deeply, that he was far, far away from them both. Oh, so remote, so peaceful. He was dreaming. Never wake him up again. His head was sunk in the pillow, his eyes were closed; they were blind under the closed eyelids. He was given up to his dream. What did garden parties and baskets and lace frocks matter to him? He was far from all those things. He was wonderful, beautiful. While they were laughing and while the band was playing, this marvel had come to the lane. Happy . . . happy. . . . All is well, said that sleeping face. This is just as it should be. I am content.

But all the same you had to cry, and she couldn't go out

of the room without saying something to him. Laura gave a loud childish sob.

'Forgive my hat,' she said.

And this time she didn't wait for Em's sister. She found her way out the door, down the path, past all those dark people. At the corner of the lane she met Laurie.

He stepped out of the shadow. 'Is that you, Laura?'

'Yes.'

'Mother was getting anxious. Was it all right?'

'Yes, quite. Oh, Laurie!' She took his arm, she pressed up against him.

'I say, you're not crying, are you?' asked her brother.

Laura shook her head. She was.

Laurie put his arm round her shoulder. 'Don't cry,' he said in his warm, loving voice. 'Was it awful?'

'No,' sobbed Laura. 'It was simply marvellous. But, Laurie –' She stopped, she looked at her brother. 'Isn't life,' she stammered, 'isn't life –' But what life was she couldn't explain. No matter. He quite understood.

'*Isn't* it, darling?' said Laurie.

FRANK SARGESON

Conversation with My Uncle

My uncle wears a hard knocker. His wife put him up to it. She says it's the thing for a man in his position, and my uncle's position is pretty good. He's a partner in one of those big firms. He grumbles a bit but who doesn't grumble a bit? I admit that these days his trousers are a bit shiny but people don't look at his trousers. They look at his hard knocker.

It's difficult to have a talk with my uncle. You can walk under his nose in the street and he won't see you, and if you sit next to him on a tramcar he'll find out you're there just as soon as you tell him. It chills you a bit if you're a sensitive person. It's because he's got a lot to occupy his mind. He's often told me that. You see he's on the City Council and one of those Boards, the sort you get paid for being on. Once he stood for Parliament but he didn't get in.

It's very difficult to have a talk with my uncle. It doesn't interest him to listen to what you've got to say any more than it interests him to look into people's faces in the street. But he likes to get going himself. He loves the sound of his own voice and he's all the time waiting for you to finish so that he can get going himself. I know we're all like that a bit, but all of us aren't as commonplace as my uncle. Oh Lord! I hope not. He never reads a book – well, just a murder story now and then.

I've tried talking about lots of things with my uncle but it's too difficult. Once I asked him, suppose he went to a picnic and there was only one banana each, would he try to get two bananas for himself, or three or more? He said he

never went to picnics. Now you might think my uncle was trying to be funny. He wasn't. He can't suppose. So I said, say anyone went to a picnic they wouldn't try to monopolise the bananas, would they? Not if they were decent? He said, no, of course not. Then I asked him, what about the social picnic? Social picnic? He repeated the words. He didn't understand and I had to leave it at that. He was so puzzled I felt sorry for him.

Once or twice I've tried talking to my uncle about risky subjects. Just out of devilment. He's an ascetic, my uncle is. He eats only a few mouthfuls of food a day. He's very thin, very cold to shake hands with. His wife says his hard knocker is the thing for a man in his position. I say it's the thing for a man with his asceticism too. He dislikes me when I bring up a risky subject. He says, Change the subject. A decent man doesn't let his mind dwell on those things. He looks very serious, very responsible.

Oh Lord! it's a good job everybody isn't like my uncle. We don't want a world full of dead men walking about in hard knockers.

An Affair of the Heart

At Christmastime our family always went to the beach. In those days there weren't the roads along the Gulf that there are now, so father would get a carrier to take our luggage down to the launch steps. And as my brother and I would always ride on the cart, that was the real beginning of our holidays.

It was a little bay a good distance out of the harbour that we'd go to, and of course the launch trip would be even more exciting than the ride on the carrier's cart. We'd always scare mother beforehand by telling her it was sure to be rough. Each year we rented the same bach and we'd stay right until our school holidays were up. All except father who used to have only a few days' holiday at Christmas. He'd give my brother and me a lecture about behaving ourselves and not giving mother any trouble, then he'd go back home. Of course we'd spend nearly all our time on the beach, and mother'd have no more trouble with us than most mothers are quite used to having.

Well, it's all a long time ago. It's hard now to understand why the things that we occupied our time over should have given us so much happiness. But they did. As I'll tell you, I was back in that bay not along ago, and for all that I'm well on in years I was innocent enough to think that to be there again would be to experience something of that same happiness. Of course I didn't experience anything of the kind. And because I didn't I had some reflections instead that gave me the very reverse of happiness. But this is by the

way. I haven't set out to philosophize. I've set out to tell you about a woman who lived in a bach not far beyond that bay of ours, and who, an old woman now, lives there to this day.

As you can understand, we children didn't spend all our time on our own little beach. When the tide was out we'd go for walks round the rocks, and sometimes we'd get mother to go with us. My brother and I would be one on each side of her, holding her hands, dragging her this way and that. We'd show her the wonders we'd found, some place where there were sea-eggs underneath a ledge, or a pool where the sea-anemones grew thick.

It was one of these times when we had mother with us that we walked further round the rocks than we had ever been before. We came to a place where there was a fair-sized beach, and there, down near low-water mark, was the woman I've spoken about. She was digging for pipis, and her children were all round her scratching the sand up too. Every now and then they'd pick up handfuls of pipis and run over near their mother, and drop the pipis into a flax kit.

Well, we went over to look. We liked pipis ourselves, but there weren't many on our own beach. The woman hardly took any notice of us, and we could have laughed at the way she was dressed. She had on a man's old hat and coat, and the children were sketches too. There were four of them, three girls and a boy; and the boy, besides being the smallest and skinniest, looked the worst of all because he was so badly in need of a hair-cut.

The woman asked mother if she'd like some pipis to take home. She said she sold pipis and mussels. They made good soup, she said. Mother didn't buy any but she said she would some other day, so the woman slung the kit on her shoulder, and off she went towards a tumble-down bach that stood a

little way back from the beach. The children ran about all round her, and the sight made you think of a hen that was out with her chickens.

Of course going back round the rocks we talked about the woman and her children. I remember we poked a bit of fun at the way they were dressed, and we wondered why the woman wanted to sell us pipis and mussels when we could have easily got some for ourselves.

Perhaps they're poor, mother said.

That made us leave off poking fun. We didn't know what it was to be poor. Father had only his wages, and sometimes when we complained about not getting enough money to spend, he asked what we thought would happen to us if he got the sack. We took it as a joke. But this time there was something in what mother said that made us feel a little frightened.

Well, later on my brother and I made lots of excursions as far as that beach, and gradually we got to know the woman and her children, and saw inside their bach. We'd go home in great excitement to tell mother the things we'd found out. The woman was Mrs Crawley. She lived there all the year round, and the children had miles to walk to school. They didn't have any father, and Mrs Crawley collected pipis and mussels and sold them, and as there were lots of pine trees along the cliffs she gathered pine cones into sugar bags and sold them too. Another way she had of getting money was to pick up the kauri gum that you found among the sea-weed at high-tide mark, and sell that. But it was little enough she got all told. There was a road not very far back from the beach, and about once a week she'd collect there the things she had to sell, and a man who ran a cream lorry would give her a lift into town. And the money she got she'd spend on things

like flour and sugar, and clothes that she bought in second-hand shops. Mostly, though, all there was to eat was the soup from the pipis and mussels, and vegetables out of the garden. There was a sandy bit of garden close by the bach. It was ringed round with tea-tree brush to keep out the wind, and Mrs Crawley grew kumaras and tomatoes, drumhead cabbages and runner beans. But most of the runner beans she'd let go to seed, and shell for the winter.

It was all very interesting and romantic to me and my brother. We were always down in the dumps when our holidays were over. We'd have liked to camp at our bach all the year round, so we thought the young Crawleys were luckier then we were. Certainly they were poor, and lived in a tumble-down bach with sacking nailed on to the walls to keep the wind out, and slept on heaps of fern sewn into sacking. But we couldn't see anything wrong with that. We'd have done it ourselves any day. But we could see that mother was upset over the things we used to tell her.

Such things shouldn't be said, she'd say. She'd never come to visit the Crawleys, but she was always giving us something or other that we didn't need in our bach to take round to them. But Mrs Crawley never liked taking the things that mother sent. She'd rather be independent, she said. And she told us there were busybodies in the world who'd do people harm if they could.

One thing we noticed right from the start. It was that Mrs Crawley's boy Joe was her favourite. One time mother gave us a big piece of Christmas cake to take round, and the children didn't happen to be about when we got there, so Mrs Crawley put the cake away in a tin. Later on my brother let the cat out of the bag. He asked one of the girls how she liked the cake. Well, she didn't know anything about

it, but you could tell by the way Joe looked that he did. Mrs Crawley spoilt him, sure enough. She'd bring him back little things from town when she never brought anything back for the girls. He didn't have to do as much work as any of the girls either, and his mother was always saying, Come here Joe, and let me nurse you. It made us feel a bit uncomfortable. In our family we never showed our feelings much.

Well, year after year we took the launch to our bay, and we always looked forward to seeing the Crawleys. The children shot up the same as we did. The food they had kept them growing at any rate. And when Joe was a lanky boy of fifteen his mother was spoiling him worse than ever. She'd let him off work more and more, even though she never left off working herself for a second. And she was looking old and worn out by that time. Her back was getting bent with so much digging and picking up pine cones, and her face looked old and tired too. Her teeth were gone and her mouth was sucked in. It made her chin stick out until you thought of the toe of a boot. But it was queer the way she never looked old when Joe was there. Her face seemed to go young again, and she never took her eyes off him. He was nothing much to look at we thought, but although my brother and I never spoke about it we both somehow understood how she felt about him. Every day she spent digging in her garden or digging up pipis, pulling up mussels from the reefs or picking up pine cones; and compared to our mother she didn't seem to have much of a life. But it was all for Joe, and so long as she had Joe what did it matter? She never told us that, but we knew all the same. I don't know how much my brother understood about it, because as I've said we never said anything to each other. But I felt a little bit frightened. It was perhaps the first time

I understood what deep things there could be in life. It was easy to see how mad over Joe Mrs Crawley was, and evidently when you went mad over a person like that you didn't take much account of their being nothing much to look at. And perhaps I felt frightened because there was a feeling in me that going mad over a person in that way could turn out to be quite a terrible thing.

Anyhow, the next thing was our family left off going to the bay. My brother and I were old enough to go away camping somewhere with our cobbers, and father and mother were sick of the bother of going down to the bay. It certainly made us a bit sorry to think that we wouldn't be seeing the Crawley's that summer, but I don't think we lost much sleep over it. I remember that we talked about sending them a letter. But it never got beyond talk.

What I'm going to tell you about happened last Christmas. It was twenty odd years since I'd been to the bay and I happened to be passing near.

I may as well tell you that I've not been what people call a success in life. Unlike my brother who's a successful business man, with a wife and a car and a few other ties that successful men have, I've never been able to settle down. Perhaps the way I'd seen the Crawleys live had an upsetting influence on me. It's always seemed a bit comic to me to see people stay in one place all their lives and work at one job. I like meeting different people and tackling all sorts of jobs, and if I've saved up a few pounds it's always come natural to me to throw up my job and travel about a bit. It gets you nowhere, as people say, and it's a sore point with my mother and father who've just about ceased to own me. But there are lots of compensations.

Well, last Christmas Day I was heading up North after a job I'd heard was going on a fruit-farm, and as I was short of money at the time I was hoofing it. I got the idea that I'd turn off the road and have a look at the bay. I did, and had a good look. But it was a mistake. As I've said the kick that I got was the opposite to what I was expecting, and I came away in a hurry. It's my belief that only the very toughest sort of people should ever go back to places where they've been happy.

Then I thought of the Crawleys. I couldn't believe it possible they'd be living on their beach still, but I felt like having a look. (You can see why I've never been a success in life. I never learn from my mistakes, even when I've just made them.)

I found that the place on the road where Mrs Crawley used to wait for a lift into town had been made into a bus terminus, and there was a little shelter shed and a store. All the way down to the beach baches had been built, and lots of young people were about in shorts. And I really got the shock of my life when I saw the Crawley's bach still standing there; but there it was, and except for a fresh coat of Stockholm tar it didn't look any different.

Mrs Crawley was in the garden. I hardly recognised her. She'd shrivelled up to nothing, and she was fixed in such a bend that above the waist she walked parallel to the ground. Her mouth had been sucked right inside her head, so her chin stuck out like the toe of a boot more than ever. Naturally she didn't know me, I had to shout to make her hear, and her eyes were bad too. When I'd told her I was Freddy Coleman, and she'd remembered who Freddy Coleman was, she ran her hands over my face as though to help her know whether or not I was telling the truth.

Fancy you coming, she said, and after I'd admired the garden and asked her how many times she'd put up a fresh ring of tea-tree brush, she asked me inside.

The bach was much the same. The sacking was still nailed up over the places where the wind came in, but only two of the fern beds were left. One was Mrs Crawley's and the other was Joe's, and both were made up. The table was set too, but covered over with tea-towels. I didn't know what to say. It was all too much for me. Mrs Crawley sat and watched me, her head stuck forward, and I didn't know where to look.

It's a good job you came early, she said. If you'd come late you'd have given me a turn.

Oh, I said.

Yes, she said. He always comes late. Not till the last bus.

Oh, I said, I suppose you mean Joe.

Yes, Joe, she said. He never comes until the last bus.

I asked her what had become of the girls, but she took no notice. She went on talking about Joe and I couldn't follow her, so I got up to leave. She offered me a cup of tea, but I said no thank you. I wanted to get away.

You've got Joe's Christmas dinner ready for him, I said, and I touched the table.

Yes, she said, I've got him everything that he likes. And she took away the tea-towels. It was some spread. Ham, fruit, cake, nuts, everything you can think of for Christmas. It was a shock after the old days. Joe was evidently making good money, and I felt a bit envious of him.

He'll enjoy that, I said. What line's he in, by the way?

He'll come, she said. I've got him everything that he likes. He'll come.

It was hopeless, so I went.

Then, walking back to the road I didn't feel quite so bad. It all came back to me about how fond of Joe Mrs Crawley had been. She hadn't lost him at anyrate. I thought of the bach all tidied up, and the Christmas spread, and it put me in quite a glow. I hadn't made a success of my life, and the world was in a mess, but here was something you could admire and feel thankful for. Mrs Crawley still had her Joe. And I couldn't help wondering what sort of a fellow Joe Crawley had turned out.

Well, when I was back on the road again a bus hadn't long come in, and the driver was eating a sandwich. So I went up to him.

Good-day, I said. Can you tell me what sort of a fellow Joe Crawley is?

Joe Crawley, he said, I've never seen him.

Oh, I said. Been driving out here long?

He told me about five years, so I jerked my thumb over towards the beach.

Do you know Mrs Crawley? I asked him.

Do I what! he said. She's sat in that shed waiting for the last bus every night that I can remember.

He told me all he knew. Long ago, people said, Joe would come several times a year, then he'd come just at Christmas. When he did come it would be always on the last bus, and he'd be off again first thing in the morning. But for years now he hadn't come at all. No one knew for sure what he used to do. There were yarns about him being a bookmaker, some said he'd gone to gaol, others that he'd cleared off to America. As for the girls they'd married and got scattered, though one was supposed to write now and then. Anyhow, wet or fine, summer or winter, Mrs Crawley never missed a night sitting in that shelter shed waiting to see if Joe'd turn

up on the last bus. She still collected pine cones to sell, and would drag the bags for miles; and several times, pulling up mussels out on the reefs she'd been knocked over by the sea, and nearly drowned. Of course she got the pension, but people said she saved every penny of it and lived on the smell of an oil-rag. And whenever she did buy anything she always explained that she was buying it for Joe.

Well, I heard him out. Then I took to the road. I felt small. All the affairs of the heart that I had had in my life, and all that I had seen in other people, seemed petty and mean compared to this one of Mrs Crawley's. I looked at the smart young people about in their shorts with a sort of contempt. I thought of Mrs Crawley waiting down there in the bach with her wonderful Christmas spread, the bach swept out and tidied, and Joe's bed with clean sheets on all made up ready and waiting. And I thought of her all those years digging in the garden, digging for pipis, pulling up mussels and picking up cones, bending her body until it couldn't be straightened out again, until she looked like a new sort of human being. All for Joe. For Joe who'd never been anything much to look at, and who, if he was alive now, stayed away while his mother sat night after night waiting for him in a bus shelter shed. I knew how he'd been spoilt, and I remembered how as a boy I'd sort of understood the way Mrs Crawley felt towards him might turn out to be quite a terrible thing. And sure enough, it had. But I never understood until last Christmas Day, when I was walking northwards to a job on a fruit-farm, how anything in the world that was such a terrible thing, could at the same time be so beautiful.

The Making of a New Zealander

When I called at that farm they promised me a job for two months so I took it on, but it turned out to be tough going. The boss was all right, I didn't mind him at all, and most days he'd just settle down by the fire and get busy with his crochet. It was real nice to see him looking happy and contented as he sat there with his ball of wool.

But this story is not about a cocky who used to sit in front of the fire and do crochet. I'm not saying I haven't got a story about him, but I'll have to be getting round to it another time.

Yes, the boss was all right, it was his missis that was the trouble. Some people say, never work for a woman, women'll never listen to reason. But that's not my experience. Use your block and in no time you'll be unlucky if you don't have them eating out of your hand.

But this time I was unlucky. This Mrs Crump was a real tough one. She and the boss ran a market garden besides the cows. She'd tie a flour-bag over her head, get into gumboots, and not counting the time she put in in the house, she'd do about twelve hours a day, and she had me doing the same. Not that I minded all that much. The best of working on the land is that you're not always wishing it was time to knock off. Nor thinking of pay-day, either, particularly if there isn't a pub handy. I'm not going to explain. If you don't believe me, try it yourself and see.

But twelve hours a day, every day. I'll admit I used to get tired. Mrs Crump would see I was done in and tell me to

stop working, and that was just what I was waiting for her to do. But there'd be a look in her eye. She'd say that I wasn't built for hard work, but she wasn't surprised because she'd never met a man she couldn't work to a standstill. Well, after she'd said that I'd just go on working, and if I was feeling cheeky I'd tell her I didn't mind giving her a run for her money. And before those two months were up I was feeling cheeky pretty often. Once she got going about my wages and everything else she had to pay out. She couldn't keep the wolf from the door, she said. Well then, I said, if you can't you'll just have to keep the door shut.

Now I'm running on ahead so I'd better break off again, because this isn't just a no-account story about how I began to get cheeky and put wisecracks across Mrs Crump. It's not about Mrs Crump, she only comes into it. I'm not saying I haven't got a story about her too, but it's another one I'll be getting round to another time.

What I want to tell is about how I sat on a hillside one evening and talked with a man. That's all, just a summer evening and a talk with a man on a hillside. Maybe there's nothing in it and maybe there is.

The man was one of two young Dallies who ran an orchard up at the back of Mrs Crump's place. These two had come out from Dalmatia and put some money down on the land, not much, just enough to give them the chance to start working the land. They were still paying off and would be for a good many years. There was a shed where they could live, and to begin with they took it in turns to go out and work for the money they needed to live and buy trees.

All that was some years before I turned up. The Dallies had worked hard, but it wasn't all plain sailing. They had about twenty-five acres, but it sloped away from the sun.

They'd planted pines for shelter, but your shelter has to make a lot of growth before it's any use on land with a good slope to the south. And it was poor land, just an inch or two of dark soil on top of clay. You could tell it was poor from the tea-tree, which made no growth after it was a few feet high. Apples do best on land like that, so it was apple-trees the Dallies had mainly gone in for.

Of course Mrs Crump gossiped to me about all this. When I was there the Dallies weren't keeping a cow, so she was letting them have milk at half the town price. She didn't mind doing that much for them, she said, they worked so hard. And my last job each day was to take a billy up to the back fence. I'd collect an empty billy that'd be hanging on a hook, and I'd always consider going on and having a yarn with the Dallies. It wasn't far across to their shed but it would be getting dark, I'd be feeling like my tea so I'd tell myself I'd go over another time.

Then one evening the billy wasn't on the hook and I went on over, but the door was shut and there was no one about. The dog went for me but he never had a show. He'd had distemper, he couldn't move his hind legs and just had to pull himself along. I had a look round but there wasn't much to see, just two flannels and a towel hanging on the line, and a few empty barrels splashed with bluestone. Close to the shed there were grape vines growing on wires, then the trees began. They were carrying a lot of fruit and looked fine and healthy, but just a bit too healthy I thought. You could tell from the growth that the Dallies had put on a lot of fertilizer. For a while I waited about, kidding to the dog until he wagged his tail, then I went back.

The next day one of the Dallies brought the billy over but I didn't see him. When we were milking Mrs Crump told

me. He was the one called Nick, and the evening before he'd had to take his mate into hospital. He'd had a spill off his bike and broken some ribs and his collar-bone. Mrs Crump thought perhaps there'd been some drinking, she said they made wine. Anyhow Nick was upset. If his mate died, he said, he would die too. He'd have nothing left, nothing. And how could he work and live there by himself when his mate was lying all broken up in the hospital? Every afternoon he would leave off working and ride into town to see his mate.

There's a pal for you, Mrs Crump said.

Well, up at the fence the billy would always be on the hook, but if Nick was in town seeing his cobber I'd think it would be no use going over. Then one evening he was just coming across with the billy so I went over to meet him. We greeted each other, and I think we both felt a bit shy. He was small and dark, almost black, and his flannel and denims were pretty far gone the same as mine were. I gave him my tin and told him to roll a cigarette, and when he lit up he went cross-eyed. I noticed that, and I saw too that there was a sort of sadness on his face.

I asked him how his cobber was, and he said he was good.

In two days he will be here, he said. You could see he was excited about it and his face didn't look so sad. In two weeks, he said, it will be just as if it never happened.

That's great, I said, and we sat down and smoked.

How's the dog? I said.

He is getting better too, Nick said.

He whistled, and the dog pulled himself over to us by his front paws and put his chin on Nick's leg, and somehow with the dog there it was easier to talk.

I asked Nick about his trees and he said they were all right, but there were too many diseases.

Too much quick manure, I said.

He said yes, but what could they do? It would take a long time to make the soil deep and sweet like it was in the part of Dalmatia he came from. Out here everybody wanted money quick, so they put on the manure. It was money, money, all the time. But he and his mate never had any. Everything they got they had to pay out, and if the black-spot got among the apples they had to pay out more than they got. Then one of them had to go out and try for a job.

It's the manure that gives you the black-spot, I said.

Sometimes I think it is God, Nick said.

Well, maybe you're right, I said, but what about the grapes?

Oh no, Nick said, they grow, yes. But they are not sweet. To make wine we must put in sugar. In Dalmatia it is not done. Never.

Yes, I said, but you don't go back to Dalmatia.

Oh, he said, now I am a New Zealander.

No, I said, but your children will be.

I have no children and I will never marry, Nick said.

No? I said, then your cobber will.

He will never marry either, Nick said.

Why? I said, there are plenty of Dalmatian girls out here. I bet you could get New Zealand girls too.

But Nick only said no no no no no.

If you were in Dalmatia I bet you'd be married, I said.

But I am not in Dalmatia, Nick said, now I am a New Zealander. In New Zealand everybody says they cannot afford to get married.

Yes, I said, that's what they say. But it's all wrong.

Yes, Nick said, it is all wrong. Because it is all wrong I am a Communist.

Good, I said. Well, I thought, spoil a good peasant and you might as well go the whole hog.

I bet you don't tell Mrs Crump you're a Communist, I said.

Oh no, Nick said, she would never be a Communist.

No fear, I said.

I will tell you about Mrs Crump, Nick said. She should go to Dalmatia. In Dalmatia our women wear bags on their heads just like her, and she would be happy there.

Yes, I said, I believe you're right. But Nick, I said, I thought you'd be a Catholic.

No, Nick said. It is all lies. In Dalmatia they say that Christ was born when there was snow on the ground in Palestine. But now I have read in a book there is no snow in Palestine. So now I know that they tell lies.

So you're a Communist instead, I said.

Yes, I am a Communist, Nick said. But what is the good of that? I am born too soon, eh? What do you think?

Maybe, I said.

You too, Nick said. You think that you and me are born too soon? What do you think?

He said it over and over, and I couldn't look him in the face. It had too much of that sadness . . . I mightn't have put it the way Nick had, I mightn't have said I was born too soon, but Nick knew what he was talking about. Nick and I were sitting on the hillside and Nick was saying he was a New Zealander, but he knew he wasn't a New Zealander. And he knew he wasn't a Dalmatian any more.

He knew he wasn't anything any more.

Listen, Nick said, do you drink wine?

Yes, I said.

Then to-morrow night you come up here and we will drink wine, Nick said.

Yes, I said, that's O.K. with me.

There is only to-morrow night, Nick said, then my mate will be here. We will drink a lot of wine, I have plenty and we will get very, very drunk. Oh, heaps drunk.

Yes, I said. Sure thing.

To-morrow night, he said.

He got up and I got up, he just waved his hand at me and walked off. He picked the dog up under his arm and walked off, and I just stood there and watched him go.

But it turned out I never went up to Nick's place. When I was having my tea that evening Mrs Crump told me about how a woman she knew had worked too hard and dropped dead with heart failure. But there's nothing wrong with my heart, she said.

No, I said, except that maybe it's not in the right place.

Of course it must have sounded like one of my wisecracks, but I was thinking of Dalmatia.

Anyhow Mrs Crump said she'd stood enough from me, so when I'd finished my tea I could go.

I wasn't sorry. I stood on the road and wondered if I'd go up to Nick's place, but instead I walked into town, and for a few days I never left off drinking.

I wanted to get Nick out of my mind. He knew what he was talking about, but maybe it's best for a man to hang on.

The Hole That Jack Dug

Jack had got a pretty considerable hole dug in the backyard before I knew anything about it. I went round one scorching hot Saturday afternoon, and Jack was in the hole with nothing on except his boots and his little tight pair of shorts. Jack is a big specimen of a bloke, he's very powerfully developed, and seeing he's worked in the quarry for years in just that rigout, he's browned a darker colour than you'd ever believe possible on a white man. And that afternoon he was sweating so much he had a shine on as well.

Hello Jack, I said, doing a spot of work?

And Jack leaned on his shovel and grinned up at me. The trouble with Jack's grin is that it shows too many teeth. It's easy to pick they're not the real thing, and I've always thought they somehow don't fit in with the rest of him. Also his eyes are sky-blue, and it almost scares you to see them staring out of all that sunburn. I don't say *they* don't fit in though. They always have a bit of a crazy look about them, and even though Jack is my closest cobber I will say that he'll do some crazy things.

Yes Tom, he said, I'm doing a job.

But it's hot work, I said.

I've said it was scorching hot and it was. We'd been having a good summer, the first one after the war broke out. You'd hear folks say what lovely days we were having, and you'd be somehow always telling yourself you just couldn't believe there was any war on, when everything round about you looked so fine and dandy. But anyhow, I was just going

to ask Jack if he wanted a hand, when his missis opened the back door and asked if I'd go in and have a cup of tea.

No thanks, Mrs Parker, I said, I've only just had one.

She didn't ask Jack, but he said he could do with one, so we both went inside and his missis had several of her friends there. She always has stacks of friends, and most times you'll find them around. But I'm Jack's friend, about the only one he has that goes to the house. I first ran across Jack in camp during the last war, though I only got to be cobbers with him a fair while after, when we lived at the same boardinghouse and worked at the same job, shovelling cement. In those days he hadn't started to trot the sheila he eventually married, though later on when he did I heard all about it. It knocked Jack over properly. He was always telling me about how she was far too good for him, a girl with her brains and refinement. Before she came out from England she'd been a governess, and I remember how Jack said she'd read more than ten books by an author called Hugh Walpole. Anyhow Jack was knocked over properly, and I reckon she must have been too. Or why did she marry him? As for me, I reckon it was because she did have the brains to tell a real man when she saw one, and hook on to him when she got the chance. But all that must be well over twenty years ago now, and it's always a wonder to me the way Jack still thinks his missis is the greatest kid that ever was, even though she couldn't make it plainer than she does, without a word said, that she's changed her mind about him. Not that you can altogether blame her of course. Just about any man, I should say, would find it awfully trying to be a woman married to Jack. But for a cobber you couldn't pick on a finer bloke.

One thing Mrs Parker's always had against Jack is that he's stayed working in the quarry year after year, instead of

trying to get himself a better job. Meaning by a better job one that brings in more pay, without it mattering if it's only senseless and stupid sort of work you have to do. Of course, Jack knows that to run the house, with the snooks growing up fast, his missis could have always done with considerably more money than he's able to let her have. He lets her have the lot anyway, he never would smoke or drink or put money on a horse. But he isn't the sort that's got much show of ever being in the big money, and any case it would need to be pretty big, because his missis is always coming to light with some big ideas. Not to mention a car, one thing she's always on about is a refrigerator. It would save money in the long run is what she reckons, and maybe she's right, but it's always seemed too much of a hurdle to Jack.

Do you know dear, I heard him say once, when I was a little boy, and my mother opened the safe, and there was a blowfly buzzing about, it sometimes wouldn't even bother to fly inside.

And Mrs Parker said, What's a blowfly (or your mother for that matter) got to do with us having a refrigerator? And Jack went on grinning until she got cross and said, Well, why *wouldn't* it fly inside?

Because dear, Jack said, it knew it was no good flying inside.

And you could tell it annoyed his missis because she still couldn't work it out, but she wasn't going to let on by asking Jack to explain.

But I was telling about that Saturday afternoon when we went inside, and Jack had his cup of tea and I wouldn't have one.

Well, do sit down, Mrs Parker said to me, but I stayed standing. It sounds dirty I know, but I've had years of

experience behind me. I've only got a sort of polite interest in Jack's missis and those friends of hers. They're always talking about books and writers, but never any I know anything about. Henry Lawson now, that would be different. Though I've always remembered that name Hugh Walpole, and once I started one of his, I forget the name, but I never got past the first chapter. I only go there because I'm Jack's cobber, but Mrs Parker is a mighty good-looking woman, so I suppose she's always naturally expected everybody of the male sex to be more interested in her than in her old man. Everybody is anyhow, except me. But still she's never seemed satisfied. And with things that way I've usually always picked on fine weekends to go round and see Jack, because then the pair of us can work in the garden, and I don't have to listen to his missis all the time nipping at him. And times when it comes on wet I've usually shoved off, though sometimes we've gone and sat yarning on the camp stretcher in the little room off the back verandah where Jack sleeps. Jack mightn't have the brains that his missis has but he isn't dumb, and I've always liked to hear him talk. He's such a good-natured cuss, always wanting everything in the garden to be lovely for everybody that walks the earth, and he'll spout little pieces of poetry to show what he means. Years before the war broke out I was listening to him talking about the way things were going with the world, and saying what he thought was going to happen. After all, the pair of us had been in the last war, and I agreed when Jack said he could see it all coming again. And he had more to worry about than I had, because his eldest one was a colt. (I say was, because later on it was rotten to get the news from Italy about him.)

Anyhow, one reason I stayed standing when Mrs Parker asked me to sit down, was because I thought I'd get Jack back

into the garden sooner if I didn't sit down. And although he grinned round at the company, looking awfully hairy and sweaty though not too naked on account of his dark colour, and even spouted one of his pieces of poetry (which his missis several times tried to interrupt), he was all the time gulping several cups of tea down hot, and I reckoned he had that hole he was digging on his mind, which as it turned out he had.

That hole!

It was right up against the wash-house wall, and we went out and looked at it, and Jack said it would take a lot of work but never mind. He said he hadn't thought about me giving him a hand, but never mind that either. We could widen it another four feet so the pair of us could work there together. And he went and got the spade, and I began by taking the turf off the extra four feet, while Jack got down below again with the shovel.

Now I've known Jack a longer time than his missis has, so maybe that's the reason why I know it's never any good pestering him with straightout questions, because if you do you only get an answer back like the one I'd heard his missis get over the refrigerator. Only seeing Jack knows me pretty thoroughly, he'll probably make it a lot more difficult to work out than that one was. So if he wanted to dig a hole that was all right with me, and I thought if I just kept my mouth shut I'd find out in plenty of good time what he was digging it *for*. To begin with though, I don't know that I thought about it much at all. It was Jack's concern, and he didn't have to tell me.

But I admit it wasn't long before I began wondering. You see, when we finished up that Saturday afternoon Jack said we'd done a good job of work, but how about if I came round

and we carried on one night during the week? And that was all right, I said for one night I could cut out taking a few bob off the lads that were learning to play billiards along at the room, and I'd make it Wednesday. And Wednesday after work I had my wash but didn't change out of my working clothes, and after dinner I got on my bike and went round to Jack's place and found him hard at it. Also it was easy to tell this wasn't the only night he'd been working because already by now it was a whopping great hole he was working in. Anyhow we had our usual yarn, then the pair of us got to work and kept on until it was too dark to see any more. And just about then Jack's missis came round the corner of the wash-house.

Whatever are you two boys doing? she wanted to know.

We've been working Mrs Parker, I said.

Yes, she said, but what are you digging that hole for?

You see dear, Jack said, some people say they don't like work, but what would we ever have if we didn't work? And now the war's on we've all got to do our share. Think of the soldier-boys. Fighting's hard work, and Tom and me want to do our bit as well.

But before he'd finished Mrs Parker had gone inside again. I was putting my bicycle clips on my trousers, but Jack was still down the hole, and he asked if I'd mind handing him down a box with a candle and matches that I'd see in the wash-house. I watched while he lit up and fixed the box so the light shone where he wanted to work. And for a few minutes I stayed watching, the shovel going in deep each time under his weight, the candle-light showing up the hollows and curves made by his big muscles, and the sweat making him look as if he was all covered with oil. I left him to it, but said I'd be round again Saturday afternoon, and

going home I thought perhaps it was a septic tank he was putting in. Or was it an asparagus bed? Or was he going to set a grape vine. It was evidently going to be a proper job any way, whatever it was.

Well. The job went on for weeks. As far as I could make out Jack must have come home and worked at it every night until late. He didn't like taking time off to shift away the spoil from the edge, so that was the job I took on, and I must have shifted tons of the stuff down to the bottom of the garden in the wheelbarrow. Nor would Jack let me go down the hole any more, he said it was too dangerous, and it certainly looked like it. Because once he'd got down deep he started to undercut in all directions, particularly on the wash-house side, which seemed pretty crazy to me. Once he struck rock, so brought some gelly home from the quarry and plugged a bit in and set it off, and it brought a lot of earth down on the wash-house side. Then he had to get to work and spend a lot of time rigging up props in case the blocks that were holding the wash-house up came through. I was hanged if I could get a line on what it was all about, and it was beginning to get me worried. His missis didn't ask any more questions, not while I was there anyhow, but I noticed she was getting round with a worried look, and I'd never felt that way before but I did feel a bit sorry for her then. About the only ones that got a kick out of the business were Jack's youngest snooks. The gelly he set off had been a real bit of fun for them, and they and their cobbers were always hanging around in the hope of another explosion. One that would finish off the wash-house, no doubt. Another thing was that for several weeks Jack hadn't done a tap of work in the garden, and one afternoon when Mrs Parker came out with cups of tea for us, she said he must be losing his

eyesight if he couldn't see there was plenty just crying out to be done.

Yes dear, Jack said, in that good-natured sort of loving tone he always uses to her. Things being what they are between them, I can understand how it must make her want to knock him over the head. Yes dear, he said, but just now there are other things for Tom and me to do.

He was sitting on the edge of the hole, and after the strain of a long bout of shovelling his chest was going like a big pair of bellows worked by machinery. The day was another scorcher but blowy as well, and the dust had stuck to him, and run and caked, and stuck again, until about all you could see that was actually him was those eyes of his. And the bloodshot white and pure blue staring out of all that was something you almost couldn't bear to look at.

Yes dear, he repeated, we have other things to do.

And it was just then that half a dozen planes flying down quite low happened to suddenly come over. And of course we all of us stared up at them.

You see dear, Jack went on saying, though you could hardly hear him for the noise of the planes. You see dear, he said, we have more important things to do than those boys flying up there. Or at any rate, he went on, just as important.

But since we were watching the planes we didn't pay much attention to him. And it wasn't until they were nearly out of sight that I realized he'd disappeared down the hole again. You could tell he was there all right. The shovelfuls of spoil were coming flying up over the edge at a tremendous rate. And it was only afterwards, thinking it over, that I remembered what he'd been saying.

Well. This is the end of my yarn about Jack and the hole he dug. Next time I went round he was filling it in again,

and he'd already got a fair bit done. All he said was that if he didn't go ahead and get his winter garden in he'd be having the family short of vegetables. And his missis had told him he'd got to do something about the hole because it was dangerous when there were kids about. So I took over wheeling the stuff up from the bottom of the garden, and Jack rammed it back in so tight that by the time he was up to ground level again there was practically nothing left over.

I must end up with a joke though. It was only a few summers later that we had the Jap scare, and Jack earned a considerable amount of money digging shelters for people who were wanting them put in in a hurry, and weren't so particular how much they paid to get the work done. His missis appreciated the extra money, but she was always on to him to dig one for the family. All her friends agreed it was scandalous, the callous way he didn't seem to care if his own wife and children were all blown to bits!

As for me, I'm ready to stick up for Jack any time. Though I don't say his missis is making a mistake when she says that some day he'll end up in the lunatic asylum.

The Undertaker's Story

A stocky powerful man somewhat gone to seed, he was thrown out of a seaside pub one fine Saturday afternoon when I was sitting on the verandah.

The bar had been too crowded and noisy, too intolerably hot and sticky, and I had taken my beer outside, where the sun would be some time yet before it hit the bench against the front wall. A breeze off the harbour kept the high tide slapping at the sand, which sloped up until it met the concrete verandah flooring, but the glare and glitter was too trying on my eyes and I turned sideways on. The noise from within was a babble and roar, but the moment my ears began to pick out the sounds of a quarrel, it was strange to see how the backs that curved from the wide-open windows began to straighten. As the moment of climax approached they all disappeared.

Spluttering and blowing, his face red unshaved and swollen, he braked with his feet and grabbed at the jamb of the doorway, but so many were pulling and shoving he hadn't a chance. He went limp as they heaved him down the slope, and he lay like something washed up by the tide. It was as though he knew himself to have been defeated beyond all question.

They all turned and went inside again, dusting and straightening their clothes. There was no fuss, no sign of either malice or sympathy. A quarrelsome drunk had been dealt with. The faces at the windows looked the other way, and the backs curved out again.

There were two of us outside now, and while I was trying to work out the problem the incident had presented me with, there appeared in the doorway an elderly undersized man, very tidy in a panama hat a maroon blazer and flat rubber-soled shoes. With his white tooth-brush moustache as well, he looked as though he had by some mistake dropped in instead of going to bowls. He had with him an old felt hat, which he dusted with his handkerchief as he went down the beach, and for quite some time he kept turning it in his hands as he sat beside the heap of discarded humanity. When he began to speak I could not hear what he said, but the heap immediately came to life. The hat was accepted, and soon they were sitting side by side with their backs to the pub as they talked. Or rather, while the older man went on talking.

I was moved, but perhaps my strongest feeling was one of gratitude that my problem hadn't had to be solved.

When they at last stood up and parted, it seemed that the drunk was perhaps not so drunk. Quite steady on his feet, he returned from along the beach for the ceremony of trust and friendship. Hands were gripped and held, placed on shoulders and left there. It was a sort of tableau, or they might have been figures on a frieze. Beyond them the sea's dark blue suggested melancholy, and the unceasing movement seemed not to hold out any promise of permanency for their bond, but at least they stood on sand that was solid and clean after the high tide, and there was the sunlight for an impartial golden blessing.

The elderly man gave me a nod when he re-entered the pub, and I was not surprised when he brought out his own beer.

Ay, he said, quite without any preliminaries as he sat down alongside, ay. It is a sad thing when a man cannot forgive himself for his own failure.

This was direct and intelligent, somewhat unusual. Also, he spoke with a slight Scottish burr, which is often supposed to go with reticence.

I said I thought I understood.

Duncan, he said. I knew him when he was a Highland lad, a sturdy young bull of a lad that lived his days on the hills with the sheep. I remember well I saw few lads of his like when I went on my rounds to those Highland places.

Ay, he said – and it seemed not unlikely that the hills he looked at across the harbour, were re-shaping themselves into something rather different.

You're not a Highland man yourself? I asked.

No. I was a Paisley boy. My people settled from Lancashire, Manchester. I grew up a Lowland Scot, but except for a manner of speaking there's not all that difference. The Lowland Scot is Anglo-Saxon as you may remember from your schoolbooks, and much the same by nature according to the way I figure it out. But there is much to separate him from the Highlander.

You visited the Highlands? I prompted him.

I was a young man travelling with a line of knick-knacks. For the most part it was jewellery, cheapjack stuff. There was money to be had by my boss in Glasgow, but nothing much for a young fellow working on commission. The Highlanders were hard folk to persuade, and if it had not been for the lassies, with their liking to deck themselves out with a bit of finery – well, the order sheets I sent back to my boss would never have added up to much of a turnover.

But this Duncan? I prompted again.

Duncan, he said. I remember well I said to his mother, a Mrs McGowan – I said the land's poor and the season is bad, and I don't forget there is always the landlord, but remember

Mrs McGowan I said, it's the townsman in the big city that's first to go without his supper when times are bad. I said it was goodbye to Scotland, for I was off to New Zealand, where by God's help and good luck I would make my fortune.

It must have been a long time ago, I said. How is it you remember so exactly?

Duncan, he said. It was Duncan. The boy was there in the yard, feeding a handful of grain to his mother's hens while I talked at the doorstep. He heard me say the name of this country.

How could I know, he continued, how could I know that name would never shift from the boy's memory?

So he followed you out here? I questioned, thinking I might cut down some of the story's trimmings.

It would be wrong to say that. He never remembered my face, and I did not recognise him until I heard his name called out and took stock of him. You see, I had not made my fortune after near on twenty years, and I had trouble enough to put thoughts of Scotland far from my mind. It was bad luck I took up with my old line of commercial travelling, although it did not look like bad luck at the time. I was employed by a grocery warehouse, and glad of my opportunity to see the country, but there is temptation for a young man when it is rare for him to sleep in any bed except what he can get at the country pubs. I don't mean to say I went to the bad with the drink, because your Scot is canny as a rule, and he has a great respect for book-learning. Many a night when there was drinking it would be no attraction for me, because I was lying on my bed with a book, and to this day I am a great reader of good books. But there is the temptation of women, and that our Maker has decreed for the population of the world. No man may refrain, as

you a young man will understand. But no great amount of looseness was ever in my nature, and I took my wife from a pub where I was in the habit of staying, a grand girl with a good hand for cooking, and a full bosom where any man might wish to pillow his head for his contentment.

Yes yes, I said, but what about Duncan?

Duncan, he said. If you are not in a hurry there is time to tell you about Duncan – and he was silent a moment while he appeared to gather up his threads.

My wife left me, and she took away the wee boy. I had never settled in this country, do you see? – even though it was ten or twelve years since I landed. I was still on the road, and it was no life for my wife. A woman should not be exposed to temptation when she has a husband to tend her. I tried, but I could not mend my situation, so I swore by God's help I would mend my ways in case I had another opportunity for settling. I thought hard and deep, and I decided to give up the road. I sat and looked at my soft hands, and I remembered about my grandfather. He was a master spinner, and he settled in the North because he hoped to better himself at the fine Paisley work. There was none of that sort of thing in New Zealand, but I remembered my bachelor uncle gave me a cardboard box of carpenter's tools for my birthday when I was ten. It was because I had said I was going to be a carpenter. The tools were toys, which I was proud to bring out to show the visitors, but although there was a book of directions, and my uncle brought me pieces of wood, I was never known to try to use those tools. It all came back to me in my distress, and I decided (when I was near to turning forty, mind you), I decided I would make myself into the carpenter I said I was going to be.

And? I had to prompt.

Did you not see the big sign as you came through the town?

I thought a moment, and replied that apart from the hoardings, the only sign I could remember was the undertaker's.

That's it, he said. Robert Wilson is my name.

But, I was about to say, when he continued.

You see, I was a very determined man and I had made my decision. I learned the carpentry, and I did more by learning the joinery and cabinet-making. I discovered I had nimble hands when a delicate job was called for. I came over to the coast here, and I set myself up in the furniture line of business, but it would be untruthful to say I prospered. I made none of your cheapjack stuff, which the public preferred because of my prices. I remember well a customer said when I showed him a kitchen cupboard – he said I had put in enough work to make it watertight. He said I should have been a boatbuilder. Ah, but it was about that same time my opportunity came to me. There was just one other furniture-maker in the township as it was then, and he was the undertaker. He died, he was undertaken himself as you might say, and I made my arrangements to take over his business. Now wasn't that a strange thing? – it was honest work for living folk I had done, but the public wouldn't have it on account of the prices. I did not prosper until I worked for the dead man that could have no argument about the price, and no say about what I provided.

He paused, but he held up his hand when I opened my mouth to speak.

Duncan, he said. It was about that same time when I began the undertaking. It was unbeknown to me that Duncan was living behind the hills you see eastwards yonder as you

come up the coast. He had taken up a bit of land in a ballot. It was O.R.P. if you understand, occupation with right of purchase, what is reckoned third class land. But alongside of him being hampered for lack of ready money, the floods washed out his fences, and the wind blew a gale that carried away his cowshed, and the lean-to where he lived until he could prosper. I learned the story of his misfortunes one day when I had business at the Court-house, and heard his name called out before the Justices for sheep-stealing. Duncan, I said, when they allowed me to talk with him, before he was taken away to be tried at the Supreme Court – Duncan, I said, do your time as you must if the judgment of the law goes against you, but don't lose heart man. Stand up on your two feet and look folks in the face, for it is in the nature of man to fall according to the law of God. But all may hope to raise themselves by the help of God and man, and if the Almighty does his share so will I too.

You see, I am none of your strict Calvinists in my belief, he broke off to say.

I told Duncan I had not made my fortune, but I stood in a fair way to prosper, and if he would return to the district I would do everything on his behalf that lay in my ability.

And he did return, I said.

Yes. But not before I had lost sight of him for close on ten years. He was not much changed in his appearance, but I never knew a man so reluctant to speak. He scarce spoke a word to me as a boy, and I forced the answers from him that sad day he was brought to the Court, but now he spoke up only one answer when ten might be required. And not to hear his wife answer at all was very aggravating.

You see, he said after a pause, he had taken a wife, and the pair were like foreign immigrants to America that have

not learned to speak the English language. But what was the more strange, it was rare you heard them say a word to each other – no, not even upon an occasion of importance as you will hear.

Now do you see? he went on, I had my doubts about them being married. They were matched like to like if you understand, and in the marriage state it is best for the dark to be set against the fair, and the light and merry against what is more sober. But I did an injustice. Duncan had his bit of money saved up, and wished me to help him on to the land according to the word I had promised. I had prospered and I was willing to honour my bond, and indeed it suited me well, because I had bought up sixteen acres of good dairy country going cheap beyond the town boundary. If Duncan would settle, he and his wife could milk for the town supply, and by delivering to the householder as well the profit would be increased. So we made an arrangment, but first I told Duncan there was just one matter. He was a man with a conviction, but that would never be held against him with me supporting him – and I explained how I now had the honour of sitting as a J.P. But there must be nothing irregular in addition that might cause people to talk, and if he would pardon me for mentioning it I would be favoured if he would show his marriage certificate.

Good Lord! I couldn't help exclaiming. And did he crack you?

I was aware of the risk, he went on. But do you see? – I knew if the marriage lines were shown swiftly, I could fairly reckon it was because they were in the possession of Mrs McGowan, and instead of free choice, I could infer the probability of what the young people nowadays speak of as a shotgun marriage. And in the event, it turned out that

Duncan's wife visited me immediately with the document I wished to see.

But there was no child, I said.

Ah, I'm coming to that. I supposed the child had miscarried, and there I had the explanation of two people, man and woman, bound up together as man and wife for no reason but the child. There was no child, but they were still bound. Duncan, a fine strong handsome man, was bound to a poor creature that carried scarce a hint of feminine flesh anywhere on her bones.

His pause was so long I had to say, And?

And I was deceived. They settled nicely, putting heart and soul and all the strength of their two bodies into the work on the land. But I confess I was very surprised to hear there was to be seen a wee boy running about the place, and sometimes riding on the float when Duncan came to town for the early delivery. I inquired, and I found he had been left with his grandmother, Duncan's mother-in-law, until they were settled. Not that I counted the circumstance against them, but it irked me to be deceived when I was right in my reckoning. And I still could not understand why they did not speak to each other, whatever the wrong that had been done, when they had the boy to compensate them for being bound. He was a merry lad, too young for his schooling, but fine strong and healthy. And he was equally fond of Duncan and his mother. He would run from one to the other, and although his frolics never persuaded either to speak except perhaps a syllable, I marked it one day when Duncan placed his hand on the child's head – because Duncan smiled, and that was a thing I had never known him to do.

Ah, but then it all happened, and it was sudden like the plagues visited on the Egyptians by the God of Israel.

I have no evidence that Duncan was in the habit of taking liquor privately, but occasionally of an afternoon, perhaps one day a fortnight, he would ride into town and drink until closing time. It was never reported to me he drank to excess, and indeed it was complained by the barmen that he was the slowest drinker on record. But it did not matter how much he drank, he would never seek company in the bar. For my own satisfaction I ascertained that his wife did not sit wringing her hands waiting on his return, on the contrary she would have the milking done and everything washed up ready for the morning, so I did not consider I had any grounds for complaint. But so far as I can piece together the happenings, one late winter evening Duncan rode home and heard the cows bellowing on account of not being milked. His wife's excuse was Jock, the laddie – he had been taken ill with a bad stomach pain in the afternoon. He was tossing and delirious with fever, and the wife dared not leave him to walk some considerable distance where she could ring up the doctor. She asked Duncan to go and ring, but he was obstinate and said the boy would be well by the morning. He went to milk the cows, first forbidding his wife to leave the house, and swearing he would have no doctor calling, with authority to poison the boy with his medicines. The poor creature was distracted, but she obeyed her husband, and Duncan delayed returning to the house until the evening was well spent. She thought from the delay he had been for the doctor after all, but it was not so, and immediately he returned she risked disobedience, because although the boy had turned quiet he lay cold in a sweat – and when the doctor came at last, husband and wife were sitting each side of the bed, not speaking, but each clasping upon the boy's hands. And the boy was dead.

He was silent a moment, and the noise from inside the bar seemed suddenly very loud. I did not know what to say and said, I see.

But, he went on, there was more happened that winter night. The doctor got me out of bed to notify me on the phone. I could not sleep after such news, accustomed though I was to notification of the kind, so I dressed myself and drove out to the farm. I shut off the engine to coast down the hill to the gate, and I considered returning to town, because there was no glimmer of light to indicate they were not in their bed. But a light commenced to shine beneath the macrocarpas that separated the garden from the paddocks, so I walked up the track and rounded the house but I went no further. There was toi-toi I could stand behind, and I could see well that Duncan's wife was holding a storm lantern while Duncan dug and chopped at the roots of the biggest tree. I heard him grunt at his work but he never spoke, and he worked hard and fast until there was a big hole tucked well in under the tree. Then I had to hold in my breath as they passed near returning into the house, but immediately they came again, Mrs McGowan still carrying the lantern but Duncan bearing a rough timber box. He placed it well in the hole, and when he had finished throwing back the earth and was stamping it with his feet, then his wife placed the lantern on the ground and returned into the house. Neither had spoke a word, but as for Duncan, when he had finished stamping he picked up the lantern and stood before he returned into the house. And I heard him say, Jock! my Jock.

For quite some time we were both silent, but the spell was broken when he had to respond to greetings from a group which came round the side of the pub to enter by the

front door. It was in any case high time for me to be out on the road, to wait for the bus that would take me further up the coast.

I shouldered my rucksack.

Are they still living together? I asked.

Never. She left him after the inquiry.

And is Duncan still on the farm?

Never, never. He earns his bit of money here and there. He is tipped for marking the scores in the billiard saloon.

Tell me, I said, did you ever marry again?

Ay, he replied. I married my housekeeper. It was in keeping with my position when I was appointed a Justice of the Peace. My wife is a fine figure of a woman.

There was an indefinable something about his eyes – what is called a twinkle, I suppose.

And she has an excellent hand for cooking.

Yes, I said as I raised my hand for a goodbye. I'd expect that.

Just Trespassing, Thanks

Very early one fine summer morning Edward Corrie, a suburban recluse with the tall and distinguished appearance of a retired statesman, discovered from the doorway of his ancient two-roomed cottage, that the stretcher bed on his verandah was occupied. But it was difficult to decide much about the three people who were asleep on their backs in a row, since besides being covered to the chin by the bed-rug they were all wearing dark glasses. It was nonetheless Edward's belief they were unknown to him; it also somewhat troubled him that they had very little room. Most uncomfortable, very hot and sticky at this time of the year. But the thought was distasteful, and he passed on out of doors in his soft slippers. Nothing was clear to him except that his visitors were young, although he could be tolerably certain the one in-between was a young woman.

The large area enclosed by an untidy hedge was known to the inhabitants of the suburb as Corrie's corner; but to Edward it was all that remained of his grandfather's farm, the scene of summertime explorations during school holidays sixty years ago and more. He remembered paddocks with creeks and creekbanks; trees, some of them native; scrub on the hillsides; besides his grandfather's cows there had been an orchard, and one season a crop of wheat. Many abstract forces had been at work since those days, and bulldozers and builders had done all the rest: in every direction variety had been replaced by rolling hillsides covered with tiled roofs. It was not a view for which Edward had any affection

and he preferred as a rule to remain indoors, apart from an early half hour beneath his pine trees before the whosh of an occasional car along the motorway had multiplied into the commuting roar. If the wind was in the wrong direction there would be a smell of fumes. Eye ear and nose offended – what was the world coming to! It had been his habit to walk late at night, stirring with his feet the smell of pine needles in the damp air; but along with the motorway had come strings of powerful lights – to remind him that to hang up lamps had been in his day a signal for the freedom of gaiety and laughter. Except for the flying cars the motorway was empty: it was seldom that anyone strolled on the concrete of the adjacent streets: the lights promised joy only to reveal there was nothing human there.

When he returned to the cottage, it pleased him to discover that his visitors had departed. The rug required straightening, and he looked briefly for signs that his spare bed had been used for purposes additional to repose. It was satisfactory not to discover any. But on the table indoors he immediately noticed a pair of dark glasses alongside his loaf of bread – which had diminished by several slices; and after crossing to his bedroom doorway he remained transfixed, with his eyes upon the bedside table from which some odd pieces of change had disappeared – until he began to tremble as he became abruptly aware that a figure completely enveloped by the bedclothes was occupying his bed. To step across and reach an unsteady hand to investigate was to reveal a young man with freckles and a head of ruddy-gold hair, who appeared promptly to wake and answer his stare with the friendliest of smiles from a pair of blue eyes and a row of unblemished teeth. But without a word spoken his young visitor again enveloped

himself in the bedclothes and rolled over to resume his sleep.

All that day Edward was about his usual occupations. Attending to his needs he tidied himself and his living room, and he sparingly ate. Much of the time his long frame, a structure which appeared to be composed exclusively of skin and bone, was accommodated by his easy chair while he engaged his attention upon a book of Latin grammar. He had lately occupied himself with problems of syntax; and once again the thought passed in his head that all boiled down to a question of the best means of communication. In the heat of the afternoon, when his attention flagged and wandered to the curtain hung across his bedroom doorway; it occurred to him that all day he had not heard one sound from his sleeping visitor. Before he abandoned the book he idly turned over the pages from syntax to prosody. Ruricolae, sylvarum numina, Fauni / et Satyri fratres. . . . While he was putting his feet up he glanced out the window, where countryside had been replaced by cement and tarmac: wilderness was perhaps the appropriate name for what had once been woodland – and hardly the right kind of breeding-ground for a race of deities. It occurred to him that he could make use of the dark glasses, and he adjusted them across his eyes against the light. As he settled to sleep the defensive asceticism of his superior features was slowly dissolved; it perhaps disconcerted a little that he was revealed as vulnerable.

There was nothing furtive about the movements of the young man who emerged from behind the curtain despite the silence of his bare feet; nothing about his glance at Edward to suggest that he was in any way glad to have

discovered him at a disadvantage. The emphasis of his glance about his surroundings suggested that he would be held by the titles on the bookshelves, but he settled instead for a showy soft cover which he drew from his hip pocket. The protective gloss had failed to preserve the inside pages from being reduced to disgraceful rags, and it was not until he had fingered among them that he could focus his attention. While he sat facing Edward with his legs extended from the edge of a stiff-backed chair, his lips began a rapid motion as he mouthed the words he read; nor did he desist when it became apparent that Edward was awake (the lines of his face betrayed him as his defences were reconstituted, a knowledge which was perhaps too difficult for him to come by).

From behind the dark glasses Edward was busy with the preparation of a judgment. Cheek, cool cheek – and yet there was something remarkably open. In presenting himself before his judge the young man had had the wisdom to bring only his naked humanity except for a rag of shirt – and a pair of trousers so remarkable that they almost destroyed Edward's serious thoughts about the judgment he would presently deliver. Fancy material stove-pipe cut and front pockets, the fashionable kind of thing he had been accustomed to among the young rips of his own day. But a well set-up young man – measured out on a small scale perhaps, but neatly put together. It was unfortunate that his vivid colouring of hair and countenance was destroyed by the dark glasses; but Edward removed them not to restore to his visitor his colour, rather it piqued his curiosity not to be able to decipher the title of the dreadful book. A Deadwood Dick no doubt, an illiterate young man despite the qualities which recommended him.

But the book's title and the young man's reaction to his coming alive were a double astonishment.

Listen to this, Mr Corrie, he began. And after a gesture which sought to impose silence with authority he read from Matthew Arnold; concluding the passage with, He too upon the wintry clime / Had fallen – on this iron time / Of doubts, disputes, distractions, fears.

Now sir, he went on, don't you reckon? . . .

While he referred the poet's words to time past and time present, Edward's attention was for the most part taken by recollections of gown and mortar-board worn by the women, and one man – who had also dared sometimes to seat himself with his book on the college steps, an exhibit for passers-by; he too had read poetry aloud and argued about it afterwards. But the mockery had been severe, and it had been a relief in the end to retreat into disputes about free trade and protection. Yet away in some remote corner of himself he could still blush. Perhaps in those days and circumstances cap and gown had been an extravagant badge to wear, but poetry had moved him and his retreat had been cowardly, a shameful denial which had persisted until the dogged recovery of these latter days: the dead stick had flowered.

It struck him as a very curious experience to listen as his own voice said, Matthew Arnold wrote a number of very fine things.

He had intended to enumerate, but the young man again employed his gesture and read from *Switzerland*, from *Empedocles*. . . . And again Edward failed to halt his wandering attention. If he was put to it he too could quote from Arnold, and from memory . . . though long wanderings intervene / They recognise a former scene. . . . His personal history was

repeating itself, he had acquired the ability to observe himself as a young man. It did not greatly matter that the locale was not the same, that the badge had been replaced by stovepipe trousers – the potent essence remained: poetry. But if he was obliged to name the force that had proved itself even more powerful he would say, Social Resistance! And that, he told himself with a dismaying sense of transposition, was now located in himself. Despite his late flowering he remained more or less identical with the environment which had first defeated and then digested him: from this young man's point of view he would be, without any doubt at all, an environmental fact.

It was with a flooding sense of anguish that he reacted from those thoughts to discover himself again in his character as judge. Poetry was all very well, but intruders in the beds of other people must be resisted: the young man together with his vanished companions (and unless the world had returned overnight to its condition of pristine innocence one of the three was the doxy of the other two), must be called smartly to account.

Do you expect me? he began – and he was aware of his barbarism: he was interrupting verses which compellingly rendered the frustration which the poet had experienced as a monstrous agony. And yet he continued, Am I expected to accept you without question as a lodger in my bed and a boarder at my table?

I was born in there, Mr Corrie, the young man replied. And while he employed his smile he pointed in the direction of the bedroom. Then he obliged Edward by supplying some elucidation of words which might have been either profound mad or just plain silly. That's what my grandmother told me, sir. She used to keep house for your grandfather, Mr Corrie.

And having put to Edward's thoughts the match which exploded them in all directions, he returned his attention to Matthew Arnold. His gesture remained poised, as though held in reserve until he alighted upon the passage which would again demand to be read aloud.

From appearances it might have been supposed that Edward, with his eyes closed and his long fingers crossed against his hollowed chest, was depicting a man relaxed as he recovered after sustaining an injury. But in fact it had not been wholly disagreeable to be reminded of the young man's grandmother, who without much doubt would be identical with the young woman he had familiarly known as Fanny. Also, it satisfied the mature moralist in him to recollect that he had not impaired the young person's virtue – although there had indeed been an occasion when, underneath a row of pine trees long since cut from beyond the motorway, he had pressed matters strongly enough to induce what he had at the time been misled into believing was 'a fainting fit'. By his ignorance or by his timidity, perhaps even by Fanny herself (though from later experience he judged that to be unlikely), he had been denied Fanny. And although he had no regrets he nursed a resentment, for it was on account of Fanny that he had afterwards come to expect all such kindred occasions to be accompanied by the redolence of pine needles. They never had been, and he had arrived at the climax of his disappointment in his marriage. In all his years of bedroom relations he had never been rid of a sense of suffocation until (his son established overseas as a botanist, and his sons-in-law having assumed responsibility for his daughters), he had welcomed the day when his wife intimated that she had never been rid of a sense of having made a mistake in preferring him to the man she had not married. It had been remarkably easy

to say to her with an easy conscience, My dear, I have no such reciprocal confession to make, but I do have a sense of regret over devoting many good years of my life to managing the local affairs of an oil company. I would like in my last years to revive interests not much connected with the marketing of petroleum derivatives, and I would prefer in this matter not to be hampered by any further experience of matrimony. In short. . . .

And with a surprising absence of fuss it had all been arranged. He had been glad to provide generously for his wife so long as he might retire undisturbed to the cottage which had remained intact from the days when it had housed his grandfather's share-milker. It had been his folly not to reckon upon the growth of the suburb and the coming of the motorway, but his complaints were trifling apart from his regret that he had never encountered anyone who might have seriously shared his interests; and indeed, unless he was mistaken, there was nobody of his acquaintance who even respected them. In any case, regrets were not for people of his age: his contemporaries who were not already dead must certainly be preparing to be – that was to say, he would permit himself the hope that a sense of preparation was active, although it was no proper concern of his by what way other people made their approach to final dissolution: it might be drink, or debauchery, or prayer, or whatsoever; no doubt all had their uses, and perhaps also their wisdom. . . . By some unusual good chance even this strange young man appeared to have discovered his own wisdom.

While his eyes remained closed he said, I congratulate you upon your appreciation of poetry.

Just a kind of second nature wouldn't you reckon, Mr Corrie? You mightn't remember but I used to deliver the

newspaper right to your door if the weather was wet. I used to step inside and borrow a book if there was nobody about – thinking you wouldn't mind, Mr Corrie.

Edward opened his eyes to stare, and he smiled.

It was you helped to start me off, Mr Corrie. Then I went to the university but I didn't stay. Everybody went for the ticket. It only takes a few years and you see them everywhere. They sit in buses and talk to you out of the newspaper. The forty hour week and all that crap, I didn't want to have it on.

It was with a strong sense of having aimed at saying something quite different that Edward said, What were you doing in my bed?

We're hot, Mr Corrie.

In his slovenly speech he had said something which sounded like an abbreviated, We were hot; but Edward couldn't be sure. He shifted his glance to the window, wondering whether any such young man would be spawned under a tiled roof. Or was the story alleged by his grandmother to be believed?

I daresay, he said.

But it was time now for the young man to stand up and return *All the Poems of Matthew Arnold* to his back pocket; and then, without any sign of self-consciousness or uncertainty to go to the cupboard for the loaf and butter the slices he cut.

I presume you have an occupation of some kind, Edward said; and he declined the slice of bread that was offered him.

The young man was cramming his mouth so he vigorously shook his head – for the first time it was even evident that he was displeased.

No, Mr Corrie, I told you. I'm not going to have it on. I never used to deliver the bread when I had to write my

poetry. People complained. There might be a password in any bit of poetry, Mr Corrie. It'll send you. Nobody wants to stay always what they are. All right, okay, call it crap, call it what you like. So what?

As he finished the bread and butter he said, By God, I'm *never* going to have it on!

And Edward was deprived of the exegesis which all this difficult language appeared to demand by the arrival of the young man's ex-bedmates. Or so he might presume them to be – not to mention concede them to be a handsome couple if allowance were made for the show of eccentricity from which all surprise had been emptied by the events of the day. The young woman in her crash helmet, and wearing over tight trousers a kind of leather armour (though evidently not, he told himself, for defence of her chastity), might have arrived from that region which was increasingly mentioned in the newspapers as Space, and which would always demand from Edward such a mental exercise: it was by no means easy at his time of life to replace a nebulous kind of Nowhere with a positive and even precise Somewhere. But he could without difficulty recognize the Space creature's companion as belonging to Earth. Of a height which exceeded his own, and of probably Polynesian extraction if one judged from hair authentic tint of skin and carving of feature, he wore what had always been known in bygone years as dungarees. He was burdened by a large carton which shortly turned out to contain a great quantity of food in tins, and he appeared to be possessed of a grinning good nature which radiated a comprehensive warmth. Edward was involuntarily moved by his own inclusion, and astonished that within himself an area might have been pin-pointed which glowed in return: but all this was not to say that any of them paid him more

than passing attention, and indeed, after his tin-opener had been located, they were much too busy consuming vast amounts of mixed food at a speed which Edward judged to be ruinous to the human digestion. He was not however excluded from the banquet, for in quick succession he was offered baked beans, apricots in syrup, Japanese caviare, sausages in spaghetti, processed cream, asparagus tips, fruit salad, Californian tuna; on each occasion from an opened tin with a spoon standing upright as though urgently at attention to serve the cause of human nourishment.

Such unceremonious untidy eating might well have tried Edward's patience if it had gone unaccompanied by the interest of their conversation. (Although the Space woman had nothing to say: she ate certainly, and voraciously, but her only additional function was to select and hand up tins from the carton as she sat on the floor.) Edward was reminded of distant parts of the earth's surface he had visited on oil company business: his ears were constantly registering sounds from which he might reasonably infer that he was listening to a language composed of English words; but at that point all clear understanding of the matter ended, for many words were apparently unrelated to meanings which it had long been his habit to take for granted; and he was sharp enough to be aware that questions far beyond restricted matters of etymology were implied. It was a case in point that, despite the present satisfaction of appetite, his young visitors were much preoccupied with talk of food; and although he could be certain that animal and vegetable matter suitable for the sustenance of human life was signified, it was also strongly implied that this matter was primarily to be thought of as deriving from tins: he was in addition greatly puzzled to gather that nobody with

any brains would ever make the mistake of reckoning these tins to be items of commerce. Prominent among other words which appeared to have been subjected to related mutations of meaning were car gas tyre and girl. And yet it astonished Edward's puzzled wits that the most prominent of all words was poetry. It was even a transcendent marvel that the word's meaning had not greatly altered, and might be investigated in language well within his range of habit and understanding. Each time the two young men swapped their quotations he was conscious that he possessed a sense of hearing which had been unaccountably sharpened. It was as though he was determined to miss nothing. And yet he was prompted not to believe his ears when he at least gathered that the quotations read from scraps of lavatory paper discovered in the depths of their pockets were in fact verses of their own composition. Of softest substance, cassia and rain / Thy body is composed, my love: the dark-skinned young man pronounced the lines to be acceptable, although a Parnassian flavour was to be regretted: but presently a contribution of his own (Shatter the ice-casked heart / Send me the avalanching thunder), was held to be of some merit if it was possible to overlook its corny rhetoric.

It was now that Edward felt himself powerfully impelled to intervene. The young people were licking their fingers as they put empty tins together in a convenient heap. Poetry was dropped from their conversation in favour of remarks about getting cracking taking off and shooting through. Several times it was insisted, All right, remember we're hot. There were calculations to do with time speed and distance. But Edward, although he continued to register the words, was much too preoccupied to persist in his attempts at penetrating their meaning. The glowing area within

himself which might previously have been pin-pointed had expanded, seeming now to lodge in his throat and prompt him to speech. He felt strongly that if he spoke he would speak with the tongue of an angel, and that what he spoke would be poetry: dredged up from among his memories and held suspended now in his mind were some verses of his own, things not nearly so good and beautiful as these young people were apparently capable of, but which might perhaps contribute worthily to the events of a strange day. All these events appeared now to have united to create a country of the imagination, a transfigured region illuminated by shafts of light which had their origin in poetry: it was a region that was permanent although entirely without substance, and inviolate even though readily accessible. Had not the young man spoken of a password? . . .

The young people were waving him goodbye as they crowded at the doorway. They were leaving him what remained of the tinned food, they said. Edward felt in his pocket and they declared, No, no, Mr Corrie, you have them. They were gone, and he recollected that unless he was greatly mistaken they already had his loose change. He discovered himself to be exhausted and profoundly satisfied, a satisfaction which he had previously experienced only after carnal union on very rare occasions. To look out the window and discover the tiled roofs were still there was a surprise. Sylvarum numina. Perhaps the day had arrived for Ovid to be rewritten. It was not difficult to understand that deities would expect to be paid token money: but they on their part could hardly be expected to pay their regards to worldly morality.

MAURICE DUGGAN

A Small Story

(for F.S.)

The fairhaired boy and the fairhaired girl swung on the gate.

They stood with their feet thrust between the wooden rungs and pushed the gate back and rode on it as it swung forward. They had been forbidden to ride on the gate but that was another time; each day had its own rules.

The sun shone. The dust on the pavement stirred.

They were waiting for the postman.

The concrete road that ran past the house shimmered in the heat. On the opposite side of the street a gate like the one on which they swung had written on it, Sans Souci, No Hawkers. For the boy and the girl it was an exotic name. They did not puzzle over it. Their own gate had no name. There was a number on the gatepost.

The postman cycled along the footpath. He stopped at the gate.

'We're a bit late, today,' he said. He was sweating.

The girl took the letters. The postman said, 'Goodbye, and don't go losing them,' and rode off. He bumped his pushbike across the kerb and crossed the road to Sans Souci.

The girl looked at the letters. The letter on top was addressed to Mrs Lenihan.

'It's to Missus Lenihan,' she told the boy.

His long face smiled at her.

'That was mother's name,' the girl said.

The boy pushed back the gate and let it go. It swung forward and banged shut.

'Whee,' the boy said.

'People don't write to dead people,' the girl said.

A sparrow flew into the hedge. They heard the noise it made but could not see it. A bus went by on the road and they both waved. The girl waved the letter. The bus windows winked back.

'Is Dad coming?' the boy asked.

'Not till next week,' the girl said.

'Is the maid coming?' he asked.

'You shouldn't call her the maid. Call her Aunt Grace.'

'Is she coming?'

'I don't know,' the girl said. 'Perhaps next week.'

The boy got the gate back and gave a push with his foot and it slammed shut and they both jumped off.

'You hurt my stomach,' the girl said.

The boy looked at her.

'They're married,' the girl said. 'I knew it all the time. I guessed it when they went away. She's Missus Lenihan.'

'Who is?'

'Who do you think? Aunt Grace, of course.'

'Are they coming back?' the boy asked.

'I don't know,' the girl said.

She climbed on to the gate. She began to swing it on her own.

'You're too rough,' she said. 'They might be gone for good.'

They ran through the house to the front door and when they opened it there was their father standing there. They had seen his shadow through the glass panel. He picked them up, one on each arm, and kissed them, the girl first then the

boy. Over his shoulder they saw a taxi in the road and the driver mounting the steps carrying a suitcase in each hand.

'Put them anywhere,' Mr Lenihan said, putting the boy and the girl down. 'Uh, you're ton weights. What's the damage?' he asked the driver.

He rattled the change in his pocket and put two coins in the driver's hand. The driver looked at it.

'That's right,' the driver said, and went down the steps.

Mrs Lenihan was on her way up.

'It's a stiff climb,' the driver said to the new Mrs Lenihan.

Mr and Mrs Lenihan and the boy and girl went into the house. Mr Lenihan put the bags down outside the bedroom door.

'Hadn't we better tell them and get it over?' Mrs Lenihan said.

'Perhaps we'd better,' Mr Lenihan said.

The children followed them into the large bedroom. The blinds were pulled down in an even row over three-quarters the length of each window. The sun shone through small pin-sized holes in the blind. The curtain flared in the draught. On the dark polished table the cut glass bottles of a toilet set were spaced out on lacework mats.

Mrs Lenihan unpinned her hat before the mirror and ran her hands through her hair. She sat on the edge of the bed. In the bed's centre, flounced, sat a kewpie doll.

'I can't use her things,' Mrs Lenihan said to her husband. She nodded at the cut glass bottles.

'Just as you like,' Mr Lenihan said.

'Well, can I?' Mrs Lenihan said.

'No. I suppose not,' Mr Lenihan said. 'We'll put them out of the way somewhere. But now . . .' and his eyes slipped to the children.

They stood just inside the door. Mrs Lenihan held out her hands to them, and smiled.

'I've got a surprise for you,' Mr Lenihan said.

He had rehearsed the next sentence all the way back from the train, in the taxi, and now it failed him. 'After all, I've no idea how they see things,' he had said to his wife. And, 'Oh bosh,' Mrs Lenihan had abruptly said.

'This is your new mother,' Mr Lenihan said.

Mrs Lenihan widened her smile. Her great bosom swelled; her rouge flushed face went darker; her blue eyes, protruding, blinked. She was animated with fond feelings.

The children looked and looked.

'We'll have to decide what you're to call your mother,' Mr Lenihan said. 'Is it to be mother or mum or mummy, or what? I'm not too keen on mummy,' he said. 'But whatever you think.'

'Grace,' the girl said.

'Grace,' the boy echoed.

'That won't do,' Mr Lenihan said. 'She's not Aunt Grace any more, you know that. She's your mother now. Can't you call her mother?'

'That's right, don't mind me,' Mrs Lenihan said. 'Just make out I'm not here.'

'I'm sorry, dear,' Mr Lenihan said. He patted her shoulder.

'We called our mother, mother,' the girl said.

Mr and Mrs Lenihan looked briefly at one another and seemed in unison, impatiently, to sigh.

'What do you say, young Harry?' Mr Lenihan said.

'I don't know,' the boy said.

'Why won't Aunt Grace do?' the girl said.

'We'll call you the maid,' the boy said.

'You will not,' Mrs Lenihan said. 'For that's what I'm not.

I'm not to be your maid, and that's clear. I hope you can all get that into your head. I'm to be nobody's maid. I suppose Miss Margaret put you up to that one.'

'I did not,' the girl said. 'And I'm not Miss Margaret, I'm Margaret.'

Mrs Lenihan stirred on the bed and stood up. She had kicked off her shoes. She thudded across to the children and stood over them. She smelled strongly of perfume and lightly of sweat. She wore an engagement ring and a wedding ring and on the other hand a ring with a red stone shone in the light.

'Come along,' she said. 'After all you'll have to call me something, won't you now? Or what say you think about it? There's no hurry is there? Your father and I have a lot to do and you can come back and tell us later.'

'That's the idea,' Mr Lenihan said. 'Run along and think it over, and we'll come out and see you later on.'

'Give us a kiss first,' Mrs Lenihan said.

Harry, pushed forward by his father's hand, was folded to her sweet smelling laced bosom and firmly kissed. Margaret took her kiss on the crown of her head, through her fair hair. They went out of the room.

While the door closed, and while they were still near enough to hear, Mr Lenihan laughed. Margaret bent her head to the door and listened. Her hair fell forward over her eyes.

'You've taken on a handful there,' Mr Lenihan said.

'Nonsense,' Mrs Lenihan said. 'The boy will come round soon enough. I've always managed with boys.'

They laughed together.

'Things are probably strange,' Mr Lenihan said.

'Oh don't worry about them now,' Mrs Lenihan said.

'We'll manage.' And she held out to her new husband her great arms, looking just beyond him at the kewpie on the flounced bed.

'You just wait,' Margaret said. 'You'll soon see what she's like. She'll do awful things to you just to get her own way: and she'll shut you in your room in the dark, you see. She'll pinch you till you're black and blue. I heard her say.'

'Did she pinch you?' Harry said.

'Of course not, silly,' Margaret said. 'She wouldn't dare.'

'She smells nice,' Harry said.

His sister caught him by the arm.

'Don't you say that again,' she said. 'If you do I'll do something awful to you. I'll push you right under a bus. I will. She smells horrid. She's put mother's bottles away in the cupboard under the stairs. Mother never smelled like that. Don't you remember?'

'I don't know,' Harry said.

'You don't know anything,' his sister said. 'I could give you a photo you could keep under your pillow, and you could look at it every night. Will you?'

'What if they see?' Harry said.

'They won't see,' Margaret said. 'If they catch you looking you have to put it in your mouth and chew it up.'

'Let's swing on the gate,' Harry said.

'She'd stop us,' Margaret said. 'You see. From now on we won't be allowed to do anything.'

'Let's wait for the postman,' Harry said.

'He's been, silly,' Margaret said.

'What will we do then?' Harry said.

'Nothing. Just nothing,' Margaret said.

She opened the door and went down the steps to the front gate.

'Nothing,' she said. 'If you promise to hate her, I'll tell you something. Do you promise? Promise, go on. Promise Harry. Say I promise to hate her, all the time until we are both dead.'

Harry stared at her. Her eyes were filling with tears. She was going to cry. He didn't understand.

'I promise,' he said. 'Let's swing on the gate.'

They opened the gate which had no name and climbed on to the lower rung and swung back and forth, back and forth, in complete silence.

In Youth is Pleasure

Hopkins had learned the translation by heart: with a pretence of difficulty intended to give listeners the impression that he was translating at sight, he read slowly, filling the long pondering gaps of silence with a rush of words, and pausing again. He stood, huge and uncomfortable, at the edge of his desk and the book lay awkwardly in his hands. His eyes as he recited were fixed not on the lines of print but on the indifferent drawing which, as an aid to vocabulary and a key to the story below, headed the page. His voice, frequently mispronouncing, jerked sporadically forward like a fly trapped in a cobweb, faded a moment into silence and rose again with its suggestion of frenzy and tedium: it was not enough to hide his pretence.

'Stop,' called Brother Mark. 'I say stop.'

And as the recounting drone, telling its rote tale of sentry geese, choked like some stalled motor into silence the small, furtive, inattentive noises of the class died also. One by one the heads came up and one by one they swung about. Brother Mark and Hopkins were at it again: the play was on. As if above that other arena of spectacle and savagery the whole class leaned forward into the familiar drama which, because they were young, jaded them less in its familiarity, in its pattern too often rehearsed than, tiered in the hot imperial amphitheatre, it must have jaded those others.

Brother Mark stepped down into this almost tangible sense of expectation, rested a moment daintily poised on his dancer feet and began to sidle, to mince forward, threatening

down the aisle. Hopkins, now with his mouth fixed as if in silent enunciation of his last word, raised his eyes slowly above the top of the breast-high book: like dancer or boxer, insolent and assured, smiling a very small smile that did not reveal his carious teeth, Brother Mark came on.

'We did not remember,' he lightly mocked, 'so much of the scholar in you.' He made a sly and bitterly amused appeal to the watching boys. 'I confess,' he primly announced, 'I'd be put to it myself to do as nicely.'

Hopkins blushed; the blood climbed over his face into his galleried ears. Brother Mark's eyes, winking and dancing in malicious delight, took him in from head to foot. Hopkins, under that stare, began to squirm: his socks with their striped turn-down of green and white had fallen over the tops of his heavy boots; his serge shorts, ending tightly above his grotesque knees, seemed about to split over his thighs – the tight cloth shone and bulged. Through the open neck of his shirt the hair could be seen, growing high up to the base of his neck, where it had been trimmed in an even line. His ears, dark with embarrassment, stood hugely out.

'Proceed,' said Brother Mark. He rose on the balls of his feet and bending at the knee rocked forward. 'Proceed,' he said.

Hopkins bent again, searching the meaningless page, searching his dumbed memory, pleading with his great slow tender eyes for the print to yield up, in some secret communication, its little mystery. His breathing in the quietened room came slow and heavy. Thirty heads and the eyes of Brother Mark watched and waited, and alone in the arena of that attention Hopkins felt ungainly and afraid. The palms of his hands began to sweat: the lines of print blurred under his eyes.

'Proceed,' said Brother Mark. 'We are waiting.'

The boys, feeling themselves enticed, conspirators and partners to this baiting game, shuffled and giggled: the sound rose abruptly and stilled. Brother Mark, frowning archly, placed himself at Hopkins' shoulder and peered down in enlightened contempt at the elementary page. His forefinger, precisely manicured, with a pale moon gleaming in the pale nail, poked forward and prodded with disdain at the point on the page where the reading had been interrupted: his eyes peered up, quizzical and sure, into the face of the boy who was a full head taller than himself.

'The soldier,' Hopkins bellowed.

'*Of* the soldier, surely,' Brother Mark cut softly in. '*Of* the soldier, wouldn't you agree? The soldier, do you see, possesses something.' And Brother Mark's eyes examined a Hopkins bereft of all possession.

'Of the soldier,' Hopkins parroted, staring down to where the finger rested elegantly on the page. 'Of the soldier,' he muttered, and was silent.

'What?' said Brother Mark. 'What of the soldier?'

'I forget,' Hopkins got out.

'Forget?' Brother Mark exquisitely questioned. 'How forget? Isn't it all down there?' The finger reared and fell. 'It isn't something to remember: come.'

The page on which the finger lightly rapped trembled in the huge hands. The thirty heads watching from all sides offered neither assistance nor sympathy. Brother Mark raised his eyes and gazed about with an air of simulated wonder. His eyes looked out from under jet brows: he leaned forward. Hopkins, struck by that stale breath, drew back: the movement was slight but Brother Mark caught it.

'War,' rapped Brother Mark. 'You see it?'

'War,' cried Hopkins, suddenly safe; and his doubled thumbs erectile and huge rose like twin horns on either side of the cupped book. 'War,' he cried, and caught the thread and bolted on, bellowing through his flawless and cribbed translation, shouting in a meaningless rote while he watched the menacing finger retreat diagonally across the page.

'Enough,' cried Brother Mark. 'Enough.'

Once again the drone fell away: Hopkins' face, red and miserable, swung round.

'We think,' said Brother Mark, 'you are not playing fair. We think,' he menaced, 'that you are cheating.'

'No, Brother,' Hopkins said.

'No?' said Brother Mark. 'Now it would seem that you are lying. Cheating and lying both. You would do well to think of your soul.'

Hopkins was silent.

'Turn back,' Brother Mark said. But without waiting he snatched the book, turned back half-a-dozen pages and thrust it back into the hands that were cupped still, the thumbs dejected, as though they had held it without interruption. 'Try that,' Brother Mark said.

The class stirred again and settled: the summer sun shone into the room and the motes of dust, in inappropriate gaiety, danced before the green board chalked with sums. Through the silence a shout of laughter from a distant class-room mocked and died: Hopkins looked down.

'Regina,' Hopkins read.

'Oh, in English, please,' said Brother Mark.

'The queen,' Hopkins said.

The silence tautened and drew out.

'Last week's lesson,' said Brother Mark.

'The queen,' Hopkins began again.

'The queen; the queen;' shrilled Brother Mark. 'Get on. Get on. What queen: where?' In irate and delightful fancy his eyes, as for that regal one, searched the room and his voice, whinnying in frenzy, rang out: 'Get on.'

But he had shattered the conspiracy; the power relaxed. Faced with something that was not foreseeable or safe the boys' condoning interest flooded back so that once again there remained only that spectacle which, objective and judicious, they continued to watch.

Hopkins, challenged, could not meet it, could not keep up the inconsiderable pretence: the book sank slowly and the mournful face, no longer searching for that assistance once denied, swung slowly across the other glances which, meeting his, fell away or stared back imperious, curious and removed. Brother Mark stepped forward and a floorboard creaked and from a crack between the boards a small volcano of dust erupted among the bright motes, filtering still. The manicured hand reached forward, miming a gesture of plucking at something odious, and nipped, thumb and forefinger, into Hopkins' ear. Under its bite Hopkins shuffled forward with his eyes watering in pain; near the blackboard he was swung about until, clownish and wretchedly benign, he faced the watching class whose eyes like magnetized needles swung to that north, trembled, and stayed. The sun struck full on his great thighs; he was released. The book fell from his hand and at the noise the class shifted again, as if so small a detail brought to the tension some relief, let them off from whatever feelings – censure, sympathy, pleasure, condonation, pain, delight – isolate or complex, rose to their sense.

It was left to some other boy to read the passage: Brother Mark commanded the smallest. He came forward to the

chosen place, so close to the body of Hopkins that he almost touched him and could smell the peculiar smell of sunwarmed cloth. Hopkins overtopped him: the smaller boy was set like something precious and human and compact within the mere animal mass of the greater bulk.

'Go on, Simpson,' Brother Mark said.

Slowly and accurately, in a piping voice that as much as his size seemed to mock the ungainly Hopkins, Simpson read on. The very force of the authority which commanded him released him from blame, released him from any duty to contest it – as though being commanded by a force of grand compulsion should alter the relation between wrong and the doing of wrong. Simpson did not mock: he had been chosen to mock, and there lay all the difference; or so he consoled himself. There was no way out, no other way than to transfer that petty and womanish venom to his own head: he did not care for Hopkins enough for that – no one, it seemed, did care – and he was not brave enough, or foolhardy enough, to venture such a thing on its own account. Even among schoolboys, his actions seemed sturdily to proclaim, there is that sense of aptness; a natural prudence which suits itself to the occasion. This was not the first time Hopkins had been baited nor did anyone think it would be the last. They accepted all that happened as something which, determined beyond them, carried its own air of permanence and order.

The class grew restless under Simpson's unoffending voice: they stirred with the sound the watchers make when – as on the wall of the cave – the flickering pictures fail and the sense rises over them of how they are crammed, only human, into that sudden dark.

'Enough,' called Brother Mark, consumed perhaps with a similar feeling. 'Go back to your place, Simpson.'

Hopkins, doubled forward as though that paining hand nipped still at his ear, bent immobile in effigy of resignation and obscure despair, did not look beyond the heavy toes of his besmirched boots. He feared to find, in the eyes beyond, not the dispassion which he knew would be there, but sympathy which, even mistakenly, he knew he could not meet. He could not have sworn he was being truthful in so standing there: he knew for an instant that he had not done as much as he might have done, as much as, through all his fright, he could have done. Buried far down under his present despair was a bile of slow anger, a record of outrage. They were feelings, no more, but too much present for denial: they bore him along and yet kept him oafishly there, scapegoat to the class, because he had caught, like one glancing dance of light, the almost lost gleam of something there was not time – and never would be, perhaps – to examine. It under rode everything and was to him no more than suspected; and yet it was the reason he would have turned from sympathy: it had no presence and was not more than an ambience, a faint aura of something that, though obscure and lost, yet shone to his dozing mind with its suggestion of guilt and delight. He stayed bent forward and waited the next move: the little flame of anger burned up.

Brother Mark, gay again and smiling, regretting with light impatience that he had run the risk of losing face, of seeming even for an instant to have lost, stepped lightly up on to the teacher's dais.

'There is so little point, Hopkins,' he smiled, 'in denying it. You mustn't think we are all fools. You cheated, you know; you cribbed and you lied to cover it up. That isn't,' and he smiled again, 'the way a grown man is expected to behave.'

Hopkins, finding no relief but only a further threat in

the light, reasonable voice, shuffled one foot over the dusty boards: under his tight shorts the muscles shifted.

'Admit it,' Brother Mark lightly advised. 'Admit you were lying and cheating.'

Hopkins' reply, hollow and averted, was lost.

'It is,' and Brother Mark addressed the class, 'such a waste to put such a fellow to the classics. A convoy, do you see, must take its speed from the slowest ship: we all suffer through such a dunce.'

Brother Mark's shepherding eye went out over his class and returned, light and contemptuous, to the dunce: his palms, turned theatrically upwards, rose as he shrugged and his eyebrows, arch and arched, comically indicated his despair. What could he do, he pleaded in eloquent silence, with such a dunce? How should he deal with such stupid deceit? His smooth voice prodded again at the slumbering bulk of Hopkins who protested no more than by moving his feet. A laugh skittered through the room.

'I am afraid, Hopkins,' sympathized Brother Mark, 'that in our opinion you must be held unsuitable for any but the grosser tasks of this world. We are thirty-two in this room; and yours are the only boots with dung on them.' Brother Mark, struck with this thought, paused, and then went on. 'Your parents would be ill advised to spend any more money on you. There must be country jobs you could do, surely?' He sniffed fastidiously as if those blowing country smells were striking up from Hopkins' boots. 'There is nothing we can do,' Brother Mark said, and his head struck forward and his eyes flared: 'nothing at all for such a massive dishonest lout.'

A small drop of saliva fell from his lips to the back of his wrist: with a gesture of amusing exaggeration Brother Mark drew forth his handkerchief and wiped it away. Not until he

finished and raised his eyes did he see that he had gone too far. He had but a moment to compliment himself that he was a match for any overgrown boy before he retreated an involuntary step and came up against the edge of the reading stand: the handkerchief like some lax signal of premature surrender trailed from his hand. In silence and as one the thirty boys craned forward.

'There is no other way,' the Brother Superior said. 'We will have to let him go.'

'Without an explanation?' Brother Ignatius asked.

'How,' queried the Brother Superior, 'would you propose explaining? Or what?'

'He had been baited,' Brother Ignatius said. 'For a long time, by all accounts. You'll admit there's an end to turning the other cheek.'

The Brother Superior smiled, almost with sadness.

'Not,' he said, 'a Christian end. But that I blame him, don't think that.'

'Has anything been said to Brother Mark?'

'A reprimand, is that what you mean?' the Brother Superior said. 'I have spoken to him. It isn't possible to change a man's nature.'

'The man in question,' Brother Ignatius said, 'might be reminded that it is, on the other hand, possible to lose his soul.'

It drew no rebuke. They sat on either side of a table covered with green baize: a shaded lamp burned between them but left them both in shadow. Hopkins' school reports were spread before them. Brother Ignatius, much older, leaned back into his chair and through some trick of the light his cheekbones seemed to have fallen in and his eyes looked out from their ancient shadow.

'Brother Mark,' the Brother Superior said, 'has, I think, learned a lesson. A painful one, in its way,' he added.

'He has so many lessons to learn,' Brother Ignatius said. 'There hardly seems time for them all. I hope it lasts, that's all.'

'It's left its mark,' the Brother Superior said, and frowned at the unintended pun. 'But why didn't the boy come to me before?'

They looked with a common impulse towards the door; it too was covered in green baize: Brother Superior had a fear of draughts.

'The sanctum sanctorum,' Brother Ignatius mildly joked. 'He was afraid, I suppose. It wouldn't be an easy thing to do, especially for a boy like that: or for anyone. The place has an air.'

'Yes. But it's curious,' and the Brother Superior lightly touched the papers. 'He doesn't get marks in anything but botany and divinity.'

'But?' Brother Ignatius said. 'The world, surely?'

'You know what I mean,' the stern tones rebuked.

'It won't be easy to explain,' Brother Ignatius said. 'What he did was both justified and wrong; right and wrong, so to say. It will seem like splitting hairs, to him.'

'Oh wrong for discipline, wrong for the college, yes. But do you see a way of keeping him on? I'll confess I don't.'

'Brother Mark might go,' Brother Ignatius said.

'That's flippant,' the Brother Superior said. 'You know that isn't possible. You're not being much help.'

'It's not something I like,' Brother Ignatius said.

'He's not stupid: the boy, I mean. But I quite see that there is something in his slowness that could be immensely irritating. Not that I'm making excuses, you know that. The whole thing is unpleasant. I've put him in the infirmary.'

'Him?' said Brother Ignatius. 'We're all turned about, surely?'

'It's the only separate place. But what worries me is how best to go about things. He had no explanation,' the Brother Superior said. 'Except to say he was sorry. And yet if I write to his parents and say that he isn't to blame and then in the same breath I say that I've expelled him, what will they think? What would anyone think? I can't hand them a dilemma like that; to say nothing of how it might reflect on us.'

'Let him go,' Brother Ignatius said, stirring. 'There's nothing else for it. Perhaps God and nature will know what to make of his good marks; perhaps he'll be taken in hand. There's nothing we can do: we aren't organized for such decisions. Right and wrong; it's splitting hairs. And yet, if we look for the evil, where are we then? Right in the mire, I'd say; uncomfortably close to home.'

With great dignity the Brother Superior stood up: his impersonal eye roved over the walls of the room: he brought his unrelenting glance back to Brother Ignatius.

'And do you think,' the Brother Superior said, 'that you have that thought entirely for your own?'

Hopkins sat on the edge of one of the beds in the small two-bed infirmary. The other bed was empty and, on both, the white covers shone with a bleached purity. The room held nothing more: it had a faint smell of damp kapok and disinfectant and common soap. The window was open and the sun was going down: the clear window pane shimmered with light. The afternoon breeze tugged at the austere curtains and blew into the room the shouts of boys out on the playing fields, the sound of a motor-mower tracking

over the summer grass, the smells of dust and summer, of hot bitumen and cooking food. Hopkins' face, patched with freckles and surmounted with a shapeless brush of pale hair, wore an expression of tiredness and gloom: his great spaniel eyes were closed but he was not asleep.

He knew what was coming: could anything be surer? He would be sent home, that was plain enough. His parents would be disappointed and grave but they would not punish him. Their aged faces rose to his mind: he felt himself as bent already under their perplexed and injured eyes, under their dumb reproach. They had sacrificed for him and he had let them down. From the world, those imagined eyes proclaimed, we would expect such things, but not from you. And in the over-furnished room hallowed to such occasions his mother would wait, with a tenderness that was more remorseless than blows, for the moment which would prise from him those assurances, those lies if need be, which would reaffirm her in her belief that he was, in spite of it all, a good boy yet at heart.

'I'm sorry Hoppy,' Simpson said; and Hopkins, who had not heard him come, opened on him eyes framed still in a clown's sorrow and despair. 'I'm sorry,' Simpson said, 'but what could I do?'

The huge head shook and the hair trembled: Hopkins did not speak.

'I've scrounged a biscuit,' Simpson said, and as to something hardly human offered the wholemeal square he had bartered for with a day-boy.

Hopkins took it: he broke it in half and put both halves in his mouth where they stuck a moment before he chewed and swallowed. Both boys were aware of a tension between them.

'Thank you,' Hopkins said formally. He picked a crumb off the hairs on his chest and put it into his mouth.

'He's a bastard,' Simpson said, loudly and with daring. 'Everyone knows that.'

'It doesn't matter,' Hopkins said.

'What will they do?' Simpson said.

'Send me home, I suppose.'

'Expel you, you mean?' Simpson said; and put so bluntly it overcame them both. There was, after all, between them some bond and they looked at one another with an expression near to awe. They had touched on something; they had acknowledged between them that unspoken and even unconscious conspiracy that proclaimed, in the face of everything, their belief in a functioning standard: they were related in a conspiracy which, allowing for the absence of anything as definite as friendship, yet proclaimed, crudely and impermanently perhaps, their belief in some sort of justice. It was unadult, and perhaps between now and maturity they would forget it; but it was impelling and real.

'Will you go?' Simpson asked. But he was not interested in the answer: he knew Hopkins would go; how could he do otherwise? No: what held him there was the feeling that something more was to be done. The precise moment for leaving had not come; and so, between them, Hopkins and he acted it out.

'I'll have to,' Hopkins said.

'Won't your family make a stink?'

'No,' Hopkins said; 'they won't.'

'Won't you even get a hiding?' Simpson curiously asked.

'Not a real one,' Hopkins said.

'I'll write you, if you like,' Simpson said.

'If you want to. It doesn't matter.'

'Are you mad at me?' Simpson asked.

That was the point: they recognized it at once. Simpson hung, waiting for an answer. He wouldn't write; they both knew that. Simpson did not want Hopkins' friendship, and they would not be friends, but that Hopkins should know, should say, that under that force there was nothing else he could have done – that, to Simpson, was important.

Hopkins sat on: under the shouts that blew in, fainter now, through the open window, he stirred; he looked at the white beds; a bird chuckled in a tree. He wanted only to be on his own again and to have it all over, all done with. It had nothing to do with him for, even as they spoke, his sentence, he did not doubt, was being lightly decided behind the green baize door. What did they say? He squeezed his eyes shut as if in this way he might hear, but when he opened them again there was only Simpson waiting still, still to be satisfied. It was, Hopkins realized, out of his hands; it had always been so. Soon enough it would be his mother making a demand that in no way differed from this. He looked at Simpson gravely, lugubriously.

'Are you mad?' Simpson said.

'I don't blame you, if that's what you mean,' Hopkins said. 'Why should I? It hadn't anything to do with you.' He stood up. Who has it to do with? he wondered to himself.

Simpson came round the edge of the bed. Across the white cover, and with all the solemn jesting of those who have found treaty, they touched hands.

'Anyway,' Simpson said, 'it isn't much of a place.' And he was gone.

Hopkins crossed the room, lumbering, and with his huge hands erased the impression of Simpson and himself from the white beds. He went to the window. The bird in the tree

choked on a note and gave up, disgruntled. Two floors down the quadrangle lay, empty except for the Brother Superior walking towards the infirmary. Hopkins waited: the last of the sun shone like pale spears on the stones: the poplars shivered and stood up again into the evening air: in puckish thanksgiving the bird found its song.

The Wits of Willie Graves

The road went in from the coast. The surface was bad, broken into pot-holes and ruts, and Willie was further irritated at being forced to advance so slowly, at being denied the long wild dash and their shock of surprise at his sudden and energetic arrival.

(Truly, these were early days for Willie.) After an hour or so, following the directions so precisely given him by Mrs Rogers, he arrived at the end of the road, let down the Taranaki gate and took the car over the hard dry paddocks, following the wheel tracks. Each further gate, and there were four, gave him the sense of penetrating deeper and deeper into a guarded maze. And remembering Mrs Rogers' warning he was careful to fasten the gates behind him. He thought he would find himself, eventually, as immured within the barbed web as were the scrub cattle and the grey sheep. What lay at the heart of the maze would be what he brought there – a wrangling, an impure rage, a wealth of promises. He had in advance so great a feeling of futility that he was tempted to turn back, now, and to represent his failure as having been due simply to the poverty or absence or intractability or death of Mrs Rogers' debtors. But he went on, following the stream into the valley; trailing, he thought, through a godforsaken country into a very nowhere of a place – as if he had been entering the territory, the actual physical terrain of his most maniacal depressions.

Beyond the last gate, down a scoured slope, the track widened and turned along the fronts of eight or nine

unpainted houses. It gave him an immediate impression of a village abandoned to some approaching, intangible disaster, time or decay; a place ravished by some wholly fatal plague. Willie grimaced, stopped the car and peered about him without getting out.

There wasn't a human being in sight: the road crossed a canted log bridge moored on the upstream side with rusted cables turned around great boulders, and ran into the scrub and was defeated there with stones and fallen logs. The way out was the way back. The doors of the houses were padlocked shut, one of the locks being tied with string where the hasp had come away from the wall. The dry weather-boarding of the houses had taken on a silver patina, a shining polish as though delicately abrased, rubbed up by a dry, stroking and continual wind. A few scurfy hens picked about in the open paddock and a duck shuffled her young, scattering them with her feet, sweeping them with her wing. Willie sat on, not knowing what to do; not knowing, now that he had screwed himself up to wrangle and bully and bluff, just how to accept, how to tone down this empty and complete defeat. The file of unpaid bills lay on the seat beside him; a sheaf of papers, a bundle of names and sums as useless and irrelevant as the scribbled, fading details on a passport to just nowhere at all. He should simply turn the car and get out, for what else was there to do? But he sat on, bemused, depressed.

He had been there almost an hour when he saw a man and four young girls descending the hill in single file, dropping down, hidden, exposed, hidden again, through the dry sharp scrub. When they were almost on the flat Willie climbed from his car and walked towards the bridge; he moved a few steps and stood still. As they advanced across the flat

ground the girls broke out of line and hung back. The man came on, in denims, gumboots, black sleeveless singlet and a dirty undented hat. The youngest girl held her father's belt and moved behind him, screened, as he advanced. All the girls were dressed in cheap sunsuits of printed cotton. The sun burned in an empty sky. The man and the girls having strolled so incredibly out of the scrub and the forest of dead trees came on to the bridge and bore down on Willie. They showed no surprise at seeing him there.

'I hope I'm not trespassing, or anything?' Willie said.

'Not yet, you're not,' the man said. 'It's a public road; or a public disgrace, have it which way you like.' His lips scarcely moved as he spoke.

'I'm looking for the householders,' Willie said. He felt as though he were speaking of ghosts, wraiths, the padlocked dead.

'No harm in looking,' the man said. 'Friend of theirs?'

'Why, no,' Willie said. 'I don't know that I'd recognize them if I saw them.'

'Don't worry, you won't see them. They're off to a hooli somewhere. They're quite a bunch. You knew they were homes I suppose?'

'Yes. I'm from Rogers' store,' Willie said.

'I thought I picked you,' the man said. 'You must be pretty green timber to be chasing pickings out here. Take a look around, why don't you?'

'I'm not selling anything,' Willie said.

'I'll bet you're not. You're not the first to come chasing a few dead bills into the valley. You won't be the first to miss out, either. It takes you a million years to learn a lesson I had pat in the first five minutes – cash on the nail when you're dealing with a kumara.'

'Outstanding accounts,' Willie said smoothly. 'Every business has them, I imagine. There are Maoris who pay and Pakehas who don't: it's a well-balanced scale.' He dropped his butt into the sizzling stream. He smiled a little at the thought that in such an unlikely place he should hear himself repeating the mild, just sentiments of Mrs Rogers. Why should he worry? It was a job like any other. 'If they're not here I'll have a drink and go back.' Willie stood easily before the man's resentment.

'I'll get on with the milking,' the man said. 'Some people have it velvet, eh?'

'You wouldn't care for a drink I suppose?' Willie said.

'Such as what?'

'Whisky,' Willie said.

'Why not?'

Later the man hitched himself off the car seat. 'Cows won't wait,' he said. 'If you're just hanging round you might as well come up to the house and get something to eat. There's only me and the kids; but Beth there is a fair sort of cook, if you're not looking for something fancy. Maybe we could kill that bottle.'

'Why not?' Willie said, having only a moment before decided to get away. 'Could I have a dip while I'm waiting?'

'Up to you. My name's Fisher, by the way. Jack Fisher.'

'Willie. Willie Graves.' Willie had an impulse to laugh: the formality did not belong to this burning underworld.

'Go ahead, Will. The water's free. I don't run the slops into it.'

Willie watched him cuff at the cringing dog and walk away.

That there should be nothing, anywhere, that he must hurry back to, was almost a necessary condition to Willie

Graves; but it could be, he had sometimes thought, a condition that let him down. At this moment he didn't know whether to stay or to go. By being rootless, he thought, you laid yourself open to so much cheap mystery, cheap sentiment: the picture of a man on his own was the picture of a man trying to attach himself to something, someone, then cutting the knot and running off. The tramp, or the man on his own, was a monument to selfishness: the loss outweighed the gain, and he was confident that he knew it. Then Willie looked at the mothering duck. To nowhere, he said to himself, looking at the houses and the dirt road. That's where I've got to – nowhere. And he felt no envy for anything he saw; and he was pleased enough with himself.

He lay on his back in the stream, resting on the flat warm stones. The water laved over him: he gazed, gloomy and vacant, at the vacant sky. Jack Fisher and those motherless girls, what was the story there? The lady couldn't stand it perhaps, this fiery doom of scrub and small cream cheques? Whatever crime it was that Jack Fisher was here paying the price for, in a purgatory of clay and thistle, she wanted no share of perhaps. Or dead? Of boredom, child-bearing, milking and her sulky Jack? Or had he so much imagination and so much hope that he could see it all in pasture, dowering his daughters, running another couple of hundred cows, drained and levelled and purring with profits?

'I wouldn't want to wait for that,' Willie said aloud. 'I wouldn't.'

And what of the kids, he wondered? What could they make of it, this scrub and stone? What sort of caress could they expect from those cuffing horny hands where the cracked flesh gaped as pink as the inside of a fig? What could they . . . ? Willie dozed, lost the thread of his wondering,

and stared up at the blue until dark specks like sandgrains seemed to float down. But Beth – now there was an injustice, a filly in the role of a staid wide-gaited mare.

The girls came skirling down to the bank of the creek. Willie, in his underpants, turned over and slid into the deeper water. He looked up at them where they were ranged on the higher ground. Their bathing suits fitted very badly and Willie wondered why it had not occurred to them to change with one another; surely there would be one good fit among four sizes, for one girl among four? Jack Fisher, sitting in the car with the whisky bottle in his fist, had named them as they played hide-and-seek in the ruined cowshed and stoned the angry drake in the paddock: Shirl, Jannie, Judy and Beth in order of ascending age and size (Shirley, Janet, Judith and Elizabeth). The younger girls were hefty and puppyish, as anonymous as children are to the first glance of a stranger. Beth, the eldest, was drawn out, her face even a little gaunt and ill-tempered.

'Come on in,' Willie called.

The girls jumped one after another into the shallows: the eldest girl remained on the bank. In her ill-fitted bathing suit she had difficulty in keeping her chest covered. She stood with arms folded. Willie floated down-stream: the deeper water was cold. He rounded a bend in the stream, and, out of sight, heaved himself up on to the flat hot boulders and sat in the sun. Up in the scrub a goat bleated, a tufted faun in the ruined countryside: the joyless bleat fell again and again. Willie sat on. When he thought he had given them time enough to get their swim over and go home he walked along the edge of the creek and dressed by the car. The sun had almost dried his shorts. He combed his hair carefully and lit a cigarette: he took the flask from the pocket of the

car and put it in his hip pocket. He looked at the whisky in the bottle, two-thirds full, and reminded himself to recover the cost of it by faking the running expenses of his car. He turned on the car radio and stood before the burned, eroded, unpromising slopes: he walked through the lilting, false tenored air to get a closer look at the empty houses.

Each house had a garden fenced with split palings or slab-wood. Marigolds showed raw colour against the shining green of corn and the dark bloomed green of potato haulms, the withering green of peas and of bean vines. Beyond the gardens the paddocks and scrub were burned and dry. Willie cupped his hands on either side of his face and bent to peer through the windows into the dark rooms of the houses. He couldn't see very clearly: the rooms seemed almost bare. On the splintering verandahs lay a few shards of civilization, the pickings of a crazy and eclectic magpie – the frame of a motor bicycle; holed gumboots; a coil of barbed wire; empty oil and petrol tins; car parts and worn tyres; an axe with a broken handle; a glazed clay demijohn; a saw and a worn shovel. Willie put his hands to the boards of the wall: they were as smooth as the groomed flank of a horse. He stroked them.

The youngest children were playing outside the house when he drove up to it from the creek: they had a giant marmalade cat in an old pram and they ran it round and round the house, hurtling through the long grass and over the cracked path. The cat was still – crouched but quiet with eyes wide open. In the kitchen the eldest girl was preparing a meal; smoke and a smell of frying onions fumed out the open door.

'Your father invited me to a meal,' Willie said. 'Do you mind?'

'Why should I? It's another mouth, that's all.'

'Perhaps I could peel a potato?' Willie said. 'Or even offer you a drink. But no, you're a little young for that.'

'I'm old enough,' the girl said.

'Well, that's always it,' Willie said. He turned his back on the room and gazed down the long funnel of the valley where the sun had not yet gone down. There were hours of daylight to burn yet. 'You're old enough for work but not for drinking. Don't look at me,' Willie said. 'I don't make the rules.'

'I wasn't looking at you.' The girl was contemptuous.

The flanks of the houses shone. On the slope of the hill Willie could see cows penned in a yard. The push and drag of the milking machine was a hissing, light regular noise at this distance. The stillness was broken only by the voices of the children and the crazy clatter of the pram. Willie took a drink from the flask.

'I'll try if you like,' the girl said.

Willie passed it along the bench, looking carefully, casually down the valley. He heard her drink and gasp. After a moment he turned and took up the flask again and moved across the room, past the blast of heat from the wood range. It was a camper's room – everything temporary until death.

'What if my father smells it?'

'He won't,' Willie said. 'He had one or two himself. My name by the way is Willie. And you're Elizabeth?'

'Beth. You're at Rogers' aren't you?'

'Yes,' Willie said. 'I'm at Rogers'.'

'Is it true that Mrs Rogers is going to have a baby?'

'If you've seen me there you must have seen that. There's ample proof.' Willie grinned at his little joke.

'Is Mr Rogers the father?'

'Wait a minute,' Willie said. 'Aren't you a bit young to be

talking like that?'

'I'm old enough. Is he?'

'Why do you ask?'

She peeled a long curling skin from a potato – a wickedly thick skin. She did it most inexpertly, Willie observed, and once it was peeled she seemed to have forgotten what it was she intended for the poor naked thing. She held it and frowned at it and did not answer him.

'Do you mean there's talk?' Willie said.

'We wouldn't hear it, even if there was. We're out of the picture. Dad says he's a cold fish, that's all.'

Willie crossed the room, took the potato from her and dropped it into the pot. 'And you don't like being out of the picture. Is that it?'

'I hate it,' Beth said. 'I'm bored and I hate it. I hate milking and trailing after the kids – oh, they're all right I suppose – and cooking. Do you suppose she likes him still?'

'Who?' Willie said.

'Does Mrs Rogers still like Mr Rogers?'

'Well, I assume so,' Willie said, this time concealing his smile. 'They're together, and there's the baby.'

'I don't mean that. Do you think she loves him, I mean?'

'I've never thought about it,' Willie said in some amazement. 'They've been married a long time, you know.'

'That means she doesn't.'

Willie was peeling the potatoes now while she idly watched, her hip against the bench, her face turned to the grey light from the filmed window. The children screeched by on the path.

'Can I have another drink?'

'You'd better not,' Willie said. 'I was only teasing, you know.'

'You do make the rules, then?'

Willie passed across the flask.

'It must do something wonderful if it tastes so awful,' Beth said. 'I wish I owned a shop and had money to do what I like.'

'What would that be?' Willie said. 'Have I done enough?'

Beth leaned towards the pot. 'I don't know. I suppose so. I'd get out of here, that's all. I'd go to town.'

'And then?' Willie said. He wiped his hands on a teatowel and looked at the girl. She was wearing a faded print dress and sandals: her hair was drawn back tightly from her face, from the wide cheeks and the narrow chin and the indifferent complexion. She was dark skinned. Willie remembered that he had eaten nothing since morning and suddenly thought he might faint from hunger. He crossed the room and sat down and shut his eyes. A mournful, hopeless, faint desire, inappropriate to his years and to his temperament, stirred in him. Cut and run, he whispered to himself. Peddling strong drink to minors isn't your line. He opened his eyes upon the girl crouched to the oven, and raised them, with a little shock as though he had somehow been caught out, to the solid figure of her father standing silently, in his socks, in the kitchen doorway.

'Having a bit of a kip, Will?' Fisher said. Willie saw that the girl too started at the voice. 'God what a life some bastards lead. A permanent smoko. What do you say, Beth?'

He leaned down and smacked his daughter, not gently, on the thin cotton dress stretched tightly over springing buttocks. It made her angry.

'Keep your big hands off of me,' she yelled.

'She's fiery, Will,' Fisher said. 'She'd eat the hand that offered her a lump of sugar, wouldn't you, Beth? Needs a man's hand, don't you Beth?'

'That's what you think,' the girl said and went to the door and called: 'Shirl! Jannie! Judy! You've gotta come in. Shirl-ee! Come on. Bring them in Judy, and hurry up. Dad wants his tea.'

In a cotton print dress, in the farmhouse doorway, calling the names of her sisters, she seemed to Willie's eyes and to his ears to have gathered years about her as if she were already the stout, weary mistress of these gloomy rooms and mother of these hectic grubby children. So that her face, flushed from the fire or from the two small drinks, struck surprise in him as she turned, and without intention he met her eye and the expression of her face which suggested an impatience to have answer to a question he did not know she had asked. It was a moment only and he turned back to the table and poured from the bottle which stood there a liberal whisky for Jack Fisher and a smaller one for himself and took them to the sink and put water into his own. Whisky, thought Willie, was not going to improve Jack Fisher's temper; and he felt uneasy at the thought of the hours before he could leave.

'And then?' he had asked. But she hadn't answered.

Then the three younger children burst into the room as though in flight from something beyond and were silent and still, staring at Willie, staring him down. The marmalade cat sidled round the door and rubbed at Beth's bare calves, then leaped to the arm of a broken couch and settled, adding its round, impersonal stare to the solemn stares of the children. Jack Fisher took off his hat and Willie realized that he hadn't known the man was still wearing it; it seemed to belong. The brown, tough weathered skin of the face stopped at a line on the forehead; above it the skin was white and puffy, as if it had been immersed for days in water. Obviously it did belong; it was never off his head beyond these walls.

'Well, let's get at her,' Jack Fisher said and reached for the bottle. 'See you do him proud, Beth. Any man who's a pal of Johnny Walker is a pal of mine. Eh, Will? That's right, isn't it? Here's looking at you.'

Willie Graves raised his glass and drank. A haze of colour gathered at the foot of the far slope seen beyond the door, and from somewhere behind the house, on high ground, a bull bugled with a sound that almost frightened him.

'I mustn't be too late getting away,' Willie said. 'I don't fancy that road in the dark.'

'Ah, no you don't,' Jack Fisher said. His eyes were quite still, fixed on Willie's face. 'You can't get off that easy. The road's dry this time of the year. There'll be no trouble.' He tipped the bottle. 'Just relax. You don't know how much we appreciate company in here. That right, Beth? Just sit down, Will, and look after your drink. There's always a shake-down if you don't feel up to the road.'

Willie Graves sat down. 'You're right,' he said, and now relaxed and raised his glass again. 'There's nothing to hurry back for after all. Here's how.'

From opposite sides of the table Jack Fisher and Willie Graves watched Beth set out the plates. She did not speak, did not even meet their eyes.

Blues for Miss Laverty

Miss Mary May Laverty drank her bitter and solitary drink (gin and angostura and lemonade, pink as a varnished nail) and looked out from the dark room through dark glass to the floor, the strewn floor of lights four storeys down, and out and away to night mountains and the candy stripes of the harbour lights. Mary May Laverty sighed. She screwed at a dull wisp of hair at her temple and pushed it for the millionth time behind her ear where it uncurled and fell listlessly forward again into the waiting twirl of thumb and forefinger. Light, reflected from somewhere, the sky? the stars?, gleamed faint in the burnished piano dark as a coffin, and on the keys. May Laverty played minor chords. She held the glass in her left hand. The wisp of hair curled forward and stayed.

Down at the street entrance Paul Mooney, aged nine years or ten, in his hand a violin aged not less than seventy years rocking in its case, inspected the faded card in the faded light: Miss Mary May Laverty, Violin and Pianoforte. Please ring. He knew it well. He rang long and listened (he could not hear the bell) then stepped back from the doorway into the street and looked up. A window shrilled, a voice called something lost in air, and something metallic hit the pavement, jangling. Paul Mooney took up the keys, picked out the bronze, opened the door, shut it, ascended the four spiralling flights in faded light and sourceless melody:

I hate to see that evenin' sun . . .

A nameless tenant at the blues.

'Paul Mooney, you're late.'

'Yes, Miss Laverty. Mum said to say sorry but it's the electricity and dinner was late.'

May Laverty sniffed, twisted hair, let the boy advance into the now lighted room and shut the door.

He done left this town . . .

Very very far now and faint as he sprung his case and began tuning while May Laverty stared down on the lost lights dispersed, destroyed by the room's illumination. She moved backwards until she felt a chair behind her and dropped into it. She was more fatigued than drunk, she was sure. Tired to the middle of the marrow of her bones; the yellow bones of the blue Miss Laverty. She let her head settle back. The dark mohair bristled at her nape. She listened without any particular expression of face to the wailing tuning note and felt inside her something tautening in sympathy. (God send that nothing snaps, that's all.)

'Electricity,' she scoffed, sniffing. 'Last week it was the transport system, and the week before that you didn't come at all. No money, no apology, nothing. Who do you Mooneys think you are, that's what I'd like to know?'

'I don't know, Miss Laverty.'

'I've a good mind, Paul Mooney, to call your mother and see are you playing tricks on me.'

'I'm not, Miss Laverty.'

'That's what you say. How am I to tell? It doesn't matter; but don't think I'm to be won with looks of innocence. I

know what they're worth, angelic smiles. Play something, then. I'm not going to give you a full lesson every time you're late. I have to go out.'

'Shall I play the London thing, Miss Laverty?'

'The London thing,' May Laverty said wearily, 'is the Londonderry Air. It has nothing to do with London. Can't you get that clear? No, I'm sick of it. I can't have heard it less than a million times. Play what you like.'

Paul Mooney so clearly gave it thought, without result.

'Then play that thing, what is it, that I keep hearing in my head? It's been badgering me all day.' She hummed it. 'Yes, St Louis Blues. Play that.'

'I think it's what they're playing downstairs. I can't play that, Miss Laverty.'

'No, of course you can't. I was teasing. Give me the fiddle then. And turn off that big light and turn on the piano light. My eyes are burning.'

May Laverty leaned forward, wispy, the angle of her jaw sharpening as if to fury as she strained to hear. She placed the violin and waited with bow poised, inclined to the boy at the angle of an accent acute.

Up through the silent building it rose, tremulous, vague, continuing. May Laverty caught it up in the middle of a bar and thin, melancholy, faintly vibrating, the melody began to fill the room, slow and seeming to expand; seeming to press out to the bare walls and surge back.

'Turn out the light.'

She turned slightly, still playing, and the jewelled floor and beaconed sea glowed from darkness and on the night mountain one light, star or signal, burned and pulsed.

She played a long time, getting the tune sometimes mixed in her mind and straying off into Stormy Weather

and coming back, marking her erratic journey with notes as thick as grief. The boy sat still and wondering in the dark, embarrassed by behaviour he found strange. He wished he might go. He too looked down. And when she stopped he could see her, dark against the dark window. And still there rose, oblivious to the violin, oblivious and constant, the sound like fine drawn wire coiling up:

If I'm feeling tomorrow like I feel today . . .

'Miss Laverty.'

'What is it? You don't like it, is that it?' The figure moved, the light went on. May Laverty had tears on her face, tears black as bruises and black-streaked runnels down either side of her nose. It didn't suggest grief to Paul Mooney.

'Can I go now, Miss Laverty?'

'I'll have to start all over again,' May Laverty said and dabbed at her ruined eyes with toilet tissue. 'Oh damn it; damn everything. I'm sorry. Have you any money for me?'

'Miss Laverty, Mum said there was only a five-pound note and I'm to tell you I'll bring it next time and could you please write it down?'

'Why? I sent the account.'

'I think we lost it.'

May Laverty looked fiercely amused. She threw down the tissue and crossed quickly to the boy. He shrank away slightly as if expecting a blow. 'Only a five-pound note? That's lovely.' She found her purse and took out a card and wrote on the back of it and thrust it into the breast pocket of the boy's shirt. 'It wouldn't occur to your mother, of course, that I have to live too. *Only* a five-pound note – that's rich. Perhaps she fancies I live on air. I have to eat, don't I? Do I look like a canary?'

'No, Miss Laverty.'

'No, and what's more . . . Oh, what's the use? Run along. It's not fair to be slanging you. Make sure you shut the door after you.'

'You said you were going out, Miss Laverty.' The boy slackened strings and clipped shut the female case.

'You don't miss a thing, do you, Paul Mooney? I was going out to dinner on the money your mother didn't have the decency to send.'

'Won't you have dinner, then?'

May Laverty stared a long moment. 'Don't break your heart over that. I'll have dinner all right. Now run along; and shut the door or we'll have the bailiffs in like a draught.' She lit a cigarette and threw the match towards the empty grate, into a trash of cigarette butts and dead matches. She advanced and ruffled the short brush of the boy's hair. 'You've hair like a doormat,' May Laverty said. 'Like a pelt.'

'What's a bailiff, Miss Laverty?'

'That was a joke, Paul. It doesn't matter. Ask your mother.'

She let him out. Insistent, fine, the slow blues rose faint as a far crying through the quiet building. May Laverty went to the stair well and bent over the rail and with her hands cupped about her mouth shouted with a surprising, shrill loudness: 'Shut it off, will you? Shut it off.' There was no more response than the echo which quickly ceased. Then the music welled up in volume, a yellow bar of light showed near the bottom of the shaft, and a voice shouted up, ringing: 'Go mind your own business.' May Laverty cocked a thoughtful miming eyebrow. In the silence, faint again, the melody continued.

'It gives me fits,' May Laverty said reasonably. 'To hear a tune being done to death like that, I mean. You'd think once, or even twice, but . . .'

'Goodbye, Miss Laverty.'

'You've got everything? Down you go then.' She tripped the light and the timing mechanism whirred like a secret beetle in the wall.

Unabashed, persisting, the thread of sound rose to meet the boy as he tip-toed down, fearful of rousing the ire of that rude tenant. May Laverty entered her room and slammed the door behind her: the latch was faulty and she was obliged to slam it a second time before it caught. She made herself another pink gin and turned off the light and sat staring out and down and away. After a little while she began quietly to hum and then to sing:

I hate to see that evenin' sun . . .

Her voice was high, a breathy pipe.

'Oh damn,' she said. 'Damn it to hell.' And taking up her purse she made for the door, stumbling in the dark. She found the light and returned to drain the rest of her drink and went out then, plunging the room into darkness again, not waiting to repair the ravage to her smudged, bruised eyes.

On the landing of the first floor she paused. The music, she had to admit, was not loud enough for complaint; it squeezed out as she stood there, squeezed out with a bar of light under the door of Room 3. May Laverty remembered the force and brevity of that rejoinder and went quietly down. The time switch to the stair light was set mean and she was left in darkness with half a flight to go. In spiteful anger she pressed the switch again before she closed the door. The music which had followed her down was finally imprisoned, beyond hearing, behind that shut door where the light burned wastefully.

*

'Look at this, if you please,' Mrs Mooney said. She dropped May Laverty's card on the newspaper her husband was reading. 'A fine sort of thing.'

Mr Mooney stolidly read: 'Miss Mary May Laverty (lately Music Tutor at Haversham College): Violin and Pianoforte. Tuition for Beginners and Advanced Players. Telephone for appointment.'

'Where's Haversham College?' Mr Mooney asked.

'The other side,' Mrs Mooney said. 'Turn it over: I meant you to look at the other side.'

Mr Mooney turned the card and read: 'No tickee no shirtee. M.M.L.'

'In the matter of impudence,' Mrs Mooney said, 'I've never met anything to match. And from a teacher of music too. You might well ask where Haversham College is: I doubt she's ever been near it. Paul has been there for the last time, I can tell her that.'

'It's direct, certainly,' Mr Mooney said. He glanced at his wife's gaunt and inflamed face. 'I take it we owe her money.'

'After that sort of impudence I doubt that we owe her anything. There's no excuse for that.'

'I'm not suggesting there is. How much do we owe, Ella?'

'How should I know? I don't keep these things in my head. I suppose the account is lying about somewhere. I've had it out with Paul. She didn't even bother to give him a lesson at all tonight. She just sat him in the dark and played him some rubbishy popular song and then pushed him out.'

'In the dark? Is that right, Paul?'

'I think she was angry,' Paul Mooney said. He was distressed by his mother's anger and his sense of being disloyal. 'She said I was late last time, too. And the time

before that I didn't go at all.'

'Is she right about that?'

'There were good reasons,' Mrs Mooney said. 'Her card is unforgivable and I don't see any profit in going into it any further. There's no shortage of music teachers.'

Mr Mooney turned the card. 'But she has the phone, Ella. Did someone ring her to say the boy would be late or that he was unable to come?'

'I don't know,' Paul Mooney said.

'That means no, I suppose. We've been rather inconsiderate too, Ella, by the look of it. I mean if we're going to insist on such a standard . . .'

'We'll see about that,' Mrs Mooney said and snatched the card and went to the telephone. But May Laverty did not reply. It had the effect of short-circuiting Mrs Mooney's anger. For a moment she was nonplussed.

Mr Mooney shook out his paper. 'She has a right to expect payment, Ella. It could be a simple joke, you know.'

'Trust a man to side with a woman,' Mrs Mooney said curtly.

'I think we have to trust to that,' Mr Mooney said, a little amused.

'Just what she's a right to expect, we'll soon decide,' Mrs Mooney said. 'Paul, get your violin, if you please.'

'Now, Ella. You're upsetting yourself unduly. It's a small matter.'

'Robert Mooney, sometimes I just don't understand you. If you think I am going to stand here and be insulted by . . .'

'All right. Have it your way. Get your violin, son. But tune it up before you bring it in here. I can't stand the sound of those things being wound up.'

The house in grief wailed long and uncertainly for Danny

Boy, the violin calling like an aged and faltering tenor.

'Well, that wasn't all that bad,' Mr Mooney said. 'Though I would have preferred some other tune. What was the song this Miss – ah – Laverty played you?'

'I think, Saint Louis Blues.'

'Then what about playing that, now that you're here.'

'Robert Mooney.'

'What's wrong with it, Ella? It's old enough to be respectable, surely? I've always been fond of it.'

'I can't play it,' Paul Mooney said.

'I'm grateful for that, at least,' Mrs Mooney said. 'If you think we're paying out good money for the child to learn that sort of rubbish . . .'

Mr Mooney was again amused. 'But, Ella, surely that's the whole point: we *aren't* paying out good money. That's what got under the woman's skin.'

'I've no patience with you,' Mrs Mooney said.

'Then do what you want, between the two of you,' Mr Mooney said. 'The world isn't losing a Paganini, I suppose.' He took up the card and put it in his pocket and bent to his paper, oblivious to his wife's hard, colouring stare.

Of course, you could rely on it to ring when she was in the bath. Didn't it always? There were times when May Laverty suspected the telephone of being possessed of a malice not usually associated with bits of bakelite and metal or whatever it was. If she had a pound for every time she'd had to get out of the bath to answer the phone . . . She put on a towelling gown, dried her hands carefully (she had read somewhere that you could get a fatal shock if your hands were wet) and padded out. No hope of just letting it ring: she wasn't quite flush enough for that.

It was Mrs Mooney, mother of Paul Mooney, with a voice as chill as a sliding glacier. (Of course, that stupid card!)

Mrs Mooney clearly and coldly could not be expected to treat the matter as a joke. Her voice crackled to May Laverty down the defective wire. Mrs Mooney hardly thought from her son's report that the account could be treated seriously.

'It's serious all right,' May Laverty said, 'I never joke about money.' She managed to get a cigarette out of the packet and to light it with one hand.

Yes, quite; but didn't Miss Laverty see that it could hardly be thought part of the contract, if you called it that, simply to play the boy a hit-parade tune and send him packing.

'It hasn't been on the hit parade since you were a girl, Mrs Mooney.'

Was that intended as an insult? Mrs Mooney hoped that she herself had more dignity than to behave like a fishwife. She would like Miss Laverty to understand that her son would not be returning for further tuition. And, further, she, Mrs Mooney, would make a deduction from the stated amount and send Miss Laverty a cheque. There was one occasion, and Mrs Mooney regretted the lack of notification, when the boy had been unable to attend; and there was last night.

'Mrs Mooney, I'm sorry. I hadn't understood that you were so hard up. If you're as broke as that we'll just forget the whole thing. I'll make you a gift of the lessons.' May Laverty viciously considered the end of her cigarette.

Miss Laverty was being impudent. The telephone went dead.

May Laverty replaced the receiver with infinite gentleness and went back to the bathroom and lay in the lukewarm water and finished her cigarette. She did not enjoy it. Neither did

she enjoy the coffee she made herself when she had dressed. She sat in the high window. There was a fog on the harbour and over the city. May Laverty sat rather glumly above it.

Later she made the four-flight journey down to the mail basket on the street door. The door to Room 3 was shut and the music silenced. There were some things yet that she could be thankful for. And there were two letters in the box. One was a sheet of numbers on pink paper which, searched later for the number of her ticket, showed May Laverty that she had not won the lottery this time either, nor even the most minor prize. The other letter contained a five-pound note from Mr Robert Mooney, pinned to a note asking her to accept this as some reimbursement for the trouble she had been put to over Paul's lateness and non-attendance. Mr Mooney had not yet seen the account, which would be met later. He took the opportunity, in a post-script, of expressing his purely personal preference for the St Louis Blues over and above the Londonderry Air which he referred to as Danny Boy. The letter was on business notepaper: Mooney and Masters, Public Accountants.

'Never say die,' May Laverty said, climbing the gloomy stairs.

In her room she made a note of the telephone number – she had a choice of three – on the scratch pad by the telephone. Mr Mooney must be thanked: the amount was far too much, of course, and May Laverty wondered at it. His tone was, at the least, so different from that of his wife that May Laverty wondered too what this might imply.

May Laverty stood among rings and brooches and wristlet watches in the doorway of the closed jeweller's shop and surveyed the street. There, that was surely him, standing as

if on a hot brick on the corner and flushing red and green as the traffic lights changed. He looked as nervous as she felt, though she had only the back and side of him; but on the whole he was more presentable than she had imagined. Yes, all in all he represented something rather better than she had hoped. Didn't this, though, only serve to widen the gap? Hadn't he, she meant, all the more right if he looked like that, to hope on his side for something a little better than herself? Oh Lord: the long panel of mirroring glass too plainly gave the show away, too clearly told the familiar tale and kept too few secrets. Wasn't she all too raddled, all too much the blown and faded rose? She took up her courage and faced her image, prepared to be stern. (Was it what you called an assignation? No, surely that was too antique a suggestion. A blind date might better describe it. On the corner by the jeweller's in Cannon Street I'll be wearing my tweed, my apricot blouse, flowers, my cracked and batty smile; and my expiring perm. Mary May Laverty. Violin and Pianoforte. Please ring.) It had to be faced; no amount of pressing would take the baggy seat out of this skirt, nor the pouched elbows out of this jacket. She felt positively marsupial. Stand though she might, straight as a tent-pole, head alert and shoulders back, she still appeared to be crouched with elbows bent. Damn. True, her legs weren't bad, though you wouldn't venture more than that. And her face? May Laverty wryly contemplated it. Wide eyes, good forehead: take the best things first. But spreading out from the corners of her eyes, from the corners of her mouth, was a system of lines best to be compared with a railway siding or a shunting yard. Perhaps she exaggerated; but the mirror didn't flatter. Her mouth wasn't young; but then what would she be doing wearing the hopeful rosebud of a young girl?

'Miss Laverty?'

He'd made up his mind to approach. May Laverty took him in. A triangle of pocket handkerchief about the size of a postage stamp in his breast pocket; bald and not trying to conceal it; taller than she was with a kind, even an innocently mischievous expression of face; big, well-kept hands. Dark, groomed, good-humoured and rather at a loss, that was her impression. An Irish mug for all the rich trimmings.

'Mr Mooney, I presume.' She advanced her hand and laughed. The gods be thanked, her teeth were her own. 'Tell me immediately, have you an impulse to turn and run? Please say; now's the time.' She thought she sounded like a revivalist coaxing decisions, or just a little too much as though she hoped he *would* turn and run. The gin gave her confidence, but it was ebbing.

'Have *you* that impulse?' He faced her squarely. The street was empty of all but one or two people dawdling past lighted windows.

'Oh me?' May Laverty said. 'No, I've not.'

'No more have I.'

'Then what . . . ?'

'I wondered, well, I wondered whether you'd be interested in a drink? There's a place I know down here; quite ordinary, of course, but not far to go.'

'An excellent idea,' May Laverty said with some relief.

The bar was noisy and rather crowded. He bought her a large pink gin, and gin and water for himself.

'I was sure you would drink whisky.'

'I'm not much of a drinking man, I'm afraid.'

'Look, there's something I want to say right off. I don't know whether *you're* used to this sort of thing. I mean I don't know what you think. Oh, I'm not pretending to be

innocent. I just want things to be plain, so that we know where we stand.'

Robert Mooney was puzzled. 'I don't think I see. If you mean am I in the habit of, ah, this sort of thing – no, I'm not. I simply thought . . .'

'This is rather awful, isn't it? This place, I mean. I can't hear a word you're saying.'

'Perhaps if I got something to take away. Could we find somewhere, some place . . . ?'

'There's my place,' May Laverty said frankly.

'Yes. Would that be in order?'

'I don't see why not.'

She noticed it immediately, before her hand found the light switch. The St Louis Blues was cascading in considerable volume down the dark stairs.

'No,' May Laverty said. 'It wasn't pre-arranged. We mustn't dawdle or we'll find ourselves in the dark.' The switch snapped and the timing mechanism took over, clicking. They passed Room 3, the crest of the wave, and the volume diminished as they climbed. 'You need a stout heart,' May Laverty said. 'I'm convinced, every now and again, that I'm no longer young enough to live at such a height; but the young ones don't seem to care for it either. So there you are.'

'You do need a stout heart,' Robert Mooney said, and his puffing suggested considerable distress.

The light held until they reached the high landing.

The room smelled a little of damp. Except for the piano it was poorly furnished. May Laverty fetched glasses and made drinks. Through their silent constraint ran the thread of music.

I'm gonna pack up and make my getaway . . .

'It tears at my nerves,' May Laverty said. 'Though I don't mind it at this moment. You find yourself actually holding your breath listening for it; and then you wonder if it hasn't stopped after all and you're imagining you can hear it.'

'No, I can hear it,' Robert Mooney said. He had recovered his breath. 'But I must have misunderstood. I thought Paul said *you* played it to him.'

'Oh that; yes, I did. When it goes on like that it's the first thing and the only thing that comes into your head when you're trying to think of what to play. I've complained; but it won't do any good. It will drive me up the wall if it goes on like that much longer.'

'Who is it?'

'I don't know. It's a man, that's all I know. The others have complained too. But they're scared to do anything because he's drinking in there and they think he might get violent.'

'Have you seen him?'

'No. We had some conversation. I told him to shut up and he told me to mind my own business; if you can call that a conversation. We were shouting up and down the stairs. He's been at it for days: something will have to break soon. Good luck.'

'Good luck,' Robert Mooney looked around. 'You must have a view.'

'Oh, I have,' May Laverty said with excitement. 'I have. It's the whole point. Look.'

She slid the curtains and put out the light and the moment their sight adjusted there, seemingly suspended in dark air, was a liner lighted in tiers and floodlit at funnel and mast, moving slowly across the dark glass, floating as fragile as tinsel

above the broadcast yellow jewels of the city lights. Then the harbour lifted from darkness, striped with beacons and navigation lights, red, orange, yellow and green, and the liner or a tug or some incoming ship (who could know?) gave a long forlorn call. A bladder of a moon, partly deflated, hung over the night mountains; and far up were a few faint stars.

'I hardly understand my impulse,' Robert Mooney said in the dark. 'I don't think I was thinking of anything – ah – very much; to be honest.' He sounded embarrassed.

'But why should you? It was me who phoned.'

'Yes, but I suggested we might meet for a chat.'

'And I accepted, I agreed. What are you trying to say? You wish you hadn't is that it? Is that what you want to say?'

'Well, Miss Laverty, I'm a family man, and . . .'

'Oh look,' May Laverty said. 'The lights are going.'

The lighted liner, suggesting distance, luxury, something mournfully pleasant, sailed slowly out of the darkened pane, into the wall; and where it had been a ruby beacon flashed hard and brief, and after a full minute flashed in darkness again.

'It's all right, Mr Mooney,' May Laverty said. 'You may relax. I'm not after anything, you know; not your money or your life. And I could hardly help knowing you were a family man.'

'Well, I only meant that in a way I've no place to be here.'

'Then why did you come?'

'I don't know, to be truthful. It's pleasant; and you certainly do have a view.'

May Laverty drank and poured. 'You might ask why I let you come.'

'I don't think I . . .'

'I'll tell you, Mr Mooney. I'm not quite what I seem –

picking men off street corners. I'm simply a rather broken-down teacher of music fed up to the teeth on my own company.' She spoke as if the fact were well known and needed no further comment. 'Let me put it another way. I'm not asking for anything more than a little human warmth.'

Robert Mooney stirred. 'Ah, that . . .'

The light came on full. May Laverty drew the curtains. They both winced at the brightness.

'Why? The other was pleasant,' Robert Mooney said.

'Because I've deceived myself too often, in the dark,' May Laverty said. Two coins of high colour burned in her cheeks. Her expression was one of remoteness, grimness. 'I'm like some bird perched over the city on a dark cliff. And that's not what I want to be at all.' She filled the glasses and went to her handbag and took out his five-pound note.

'Take it, please.'

'Why? I thought you'd agreed to accept. You thanked me for it. I don't want it back.'

'Nevertheless, you'll take it,' May Laverty said. 'I thanked you for it, certainly. I don't think I ever intended to keep it. There's no way I could. Take it, please.'

He took it from her fingers. 'I'm sorry about all this. I thought we might chat a little.'

May Laverty shook her head. 'How could we? You're too afraid.'

'Afraid? Of what?'

'Of me, or what you think I am. You're afraid to be here. You suspect complications, scandals, and I don't know what. You said you've no place to be here; no right, I suppose you mean.'

'I wanted things clear. Anyway, the money has nothing to do with it.'

'But it has. It was a gesture I could appreciate even if I couldn't accept. Oh, this pride over money; it's too sordid.'

'Why did we meet then?'

'Curiosity. I don't know. Curiosity is as good a motive as another. Perhaps gratitude on my part. What does it matter?'

'A little human warmth, was that what you said?' It embarrassed him to repeat it.

'Yes,' May Laverty said. 'You'd think it would be easy, wouldn't you? You'd think it would be simple. Sometimes I wonder if there's anything harder.'

He rose and took up his hat and looked at her directly, for a second. She read relief in the steadiness of his gaze.

'You'll be all right?' he said. 'I mean, a straight out loan, if that would help . . .'

'There's too little security,' May Laverty said, and laughed with a high skirl of sound. 'No, I'm not grubbing for banknotes,' she said with some contempt. She went to the door and opened it. 'Goodnight,' she said. 'You'll find it's not so hard on the heart, going down. I'll wait and trip the light a second time in case you miss.'

If it weren't for powder and for store-bought hair . . .

'Goodbye, I'm sorry,' Robert Mooney put on his hat and went down, glancing up to meet her non-committal nod as he turned the first flange of the spiral. He dropped out of sight.

I hate to see that evenin' sun . . .

She tripped the light a second time. It clicked with a sound that echoed on the landing. When it went out she

waited a long time, leaning on the stair rail in the dark, the door of her room swung shut behind her. Clear and full now it rose in the silence like the source and the refrain of all her elderly discontents. Her head was spinning: she felt dizzy. (Nothing. Just a song.)

The record must have ended. There was a break, so brief as hardly to be detected, and it began again.

May Laverty snapped on the light and went down the stairs. She stood at the door of Room 3 and loudly knocked on the painted panelling.

'What do you want?'

She'd expected to confront a violent and unshaven drunk, but if the man in the doorway was drunk he wasn't showing it. He was dressed in sweater and slacks; he was shaved; he was barefooted. The music welled out, beat past him and was magnified in the small walled space of the landing. On a table in the centre of the room May Laverty saw a bottle and a glass and a siphon of soda. An ashtray on the floor spilled cigarette butts. There was no sign of the wild or desperate carousal she had expected: the room was if anything tidier than her own.

'I said, what do you want?'

May Laverty continued to stand in silent indecision.

'Have you come to complain?'

'Would it do any good? To complain, I mean.'

He turned back into the room. The music stopped. He returned holding a record. 'You came at the right moment. Satisfied?'

'No, look,' May Laverty said seriously, frowning. 'I'm not complaining about the music. I admit it isn't even all that loud.'

'Just the one tune, eh?'

'Yes, I'll gladly let you have some records, if you want to go on.'

'No, it's finished. I hope never to hear it again. I've beat it to death.'

'Then what were you doing, punishing yourself or something?' He swayed a little in the bright doorway, looking out at May Laverty. 'Were you wanting something else?'

'Why I . . . no,' May Laverty said. 'But I'm glad it's stopped. It was driving me up the wall.'

'Me too.'

May Laverty greeted it with a surprised and surprising giggle. She was more than a little drunk. Thumb and forefinger found the wayward wisp, twisted, tucked it behind her ear. She peered past him into the room.

'What are you looking for?' He stood there easily, watching May Laverty. He appeared to be amused.

'What was I looking . . . ? I beg your pardon.' May Laverty felt confused.

'It doesn't matter. I wondered what you were looking for, that's all.' He offered the record and she took it. 'Break it in half if you want. It's played to ribbons.'

'A little human warmth,' May Laverty said distinctly.

'What?'

'A little human warmth. I mean, you'd think there'd be nothing simpler, wouldn't you? You wouldn't think it too much to ask, a little human warmth. There was no reason to run; none at all. A little human warmth.'

In the doorway the man straightened. His features, slightly puffed, composed themselves into a frown of wonder. He gently and slowly shook his head and reaching behind him he found the door handle. 'What a hope,' he said. 'Lady, what a hope.'

Then the door shut and May Laverty was on the landing in the dark. She turned and began to climb the three flights to her room, carrying the record, steadying herself with a hand on the banister.

The unfamiliar and persisting sound which filled the stairwell was the sound of May Laverty's laughter: a neighing echo, a falsetto and quavering trumpet. It accompanied her on the steep ascent.

Along Rideout Road That Summer

I'd walked the length of Rideout Road the night before, following the noise of the river in the darkness, tumbling over ruts and stones, my progress, if you'd call it that, challenged by farmers' dogs and observed by the faintly luminous eyes of wandering stock, steers, cows, stud-bulls or milk-white unicorns or, better, a full quartet of apocalyptic horses browsing the marge. In time and darkness I found Puti Hohepa's farmhouse and lugged my fibre suitcase up the verandah, after nearly breaking my leg in a cattle-stop. A journey fruitful of one decision – to flog a torch from somewhere. And of course I didn't. And now my feet hurt; but it was daylight and, from memory, I'd say I was almost happy. Almost. Fortunately I am endowed both by nature and later conditioning with a highly developed sense of the absurd; knowing that you can imagine the pleasure I took in this abrupt translation from shop-counter to tractor seat, from town pavements to back-country farm, with all those miles of river-bottom darkness to mark the transition. In fact, and unfortunately there have to be some facts, even fictional ones, I'd removed myself a mere dozen miles from the parental home. In darkness, as I've said, and with a certain stealth. I didn't consult dad about it, and, needless to say, I didn't tell mum. The moment wasn't propitious; dad was asleep with the *Financial Gazette* threatening to suffocate him and mum was off somewhere moving, as she so often did, that this meeting make public its whole hearted support for the introduction of flogging and public castration for all sex offenders and hanging, drawing

and quartering, for almost everyone else, and as for deliquents (my boy!). . . . Well, put yourself in my shoes, there's no need to go on. Yes, almost happy, though my feet were so tender I winced every time I tripped the clutch.

Almost happy, shouting Kubla Khan, a bookish lad, from the seat of the clattering old Ferguson tractor, doing a steady five miles an hour in a cloud of seagulls, getting to the bit about the damsel with the dulcimer and looking up to see the reputedly wild Hohepa girl perched on the gate, feet hooked in the bars, ribbons fluttering from her ukulele. A perfect moment of recognition, daring rider, in spite of the belch of carbon monoxide from the tincan exhaust up front on the bonnet. Don't, however, misunderstand me: I'd not have you think we are here embarked on the trashy clamour of boy meeting girl. No, the problem you are to understand, was one of connexion. How connect the dulcimer with the ukulele, if you follow. For a boy of my bents this problem of how to cope with the shock of the recognition of a certain discrepancy between the real and the written was rather like watching mum with a shoehorn wedging nines into sevens and suffering merry hell. I'm not blaming old STC for everything, of course. After all, some other imports went wild too; and I've spent too long at the handle of a mattock, a critical function, not to know that. The stench of the exhaust, that's to say, held no redolence of that old hophead's pipe. Let us then be clear and don't for a moment, gentlemen, imagine that I venture the gross unfairness, the patent absurdity, the rank injustice (your turn) of blaming him for spoiling the pasture or fouling the native air. It's just that there was this problem in my mind, this profound, cultural problem affecting dramatically the very nature of my inheritance, nines into sevens in this lovely smiling land.

His was the genius as his was the expression which the vast educational brouhaha invited me to praise and emulate, tranquillizers ingested in maturity, the voice of the ringdove, look up though your feet be in the clay. And read on.

Of course I understood immediately that these were not matters I was destined to debate with Fanny Hohepa. Frankly, I could see that she didn't give a damn; it was part of her attraction. She thought I was singing. She smiled and waved, I waved and smiled, turned, ploughed back through gull-white and coffee loam and fell into a train of thought not entirely free of Fanny and her instrument, pausing to wonder, now and then, what might be the symptoms, the early symptoms, of carbon monoxide poisoning. Drowsiness? Check. Dilation of the pupils? Can't check. Extra cutaneous sensation? My feet. Trembling hands? Vibrato. Down and back, down and back, turning again, Dick and his Ferguson, Fanny from her perch seeming to gather about her the background of green paternal acres, fold on fold. I bore down upon her in all the eager erubescence of youth, with my hair slicked back. She trembled, wavered, fragmented and re-formed in the pungent vapour through which I viewed her. (Oh for an open-air job, eh mate?) She plucked, very picture in jeans and summer shirt of youth and suspicion, and seemed to sing. I couldn't of course hear a note. Behind me the dogleg furrows and the bright ploughshares. Certainly she looked at her ease and, even through the gassed-up atmosphere between us, too deliciously substantial to be creature down on a visit from Mount Abora. I was glad I'd combed my hair. Back, down and back. Considering the size of the paddock this could have gone on for a week. I promptly admitted to myself that her present position, disposition or posture, involving as it did some provocative tautness of cloth, suited me right down to

the ground. I mean to hell with the idea of having her stand knee-deep in the thistle thwanging her dulcimer and plantively chirruping about a pipedream mountain. In fact she was natively engaged in expressing the most profund distillations of her local experience, the gleanings of a life lived in rich contact with a richly understood and native environment: A Slow Boat To China, if memory serves. While I, racked and shaken, composed words for the plaque which would one day stand here to commemorate our deep rapport: *Here played the black lady her dulcimer. Here wept she full miseries. Here rode the knight Fergus' son to her deliverance. Here put he about her ebon and naked shoulders his courtly garment of leather, black, full curiously emblazoned – Hell's Angel.*

When she looked as though my looking were about to make her leave I stopped the machine and pulled out the old tobacco and rolled a smoke, holding the steering wheel in my teeth, though on a good day I could roll with one hand, twist and lick, draw, shoot the head off a pin at a mile and a half, spin, blow down the barrel before you could say:

Gooday. How are yuh?

All right.

I'm Buster O'Leary.

I'm Fanny Hohepa.

Yair, I know.

It's hot.

It's hot right enough.

You can have a swim when you're through.

Mightn't be a bad idea at that.

Over there by the trees.

Yair, I seen it. Like, why don't you join me, eh?

I might.

Go on, you'd love it.

I might.

Goodoh then, see yuh.

A genuine crumpy conversation if ever I heard one, darkly reflective of the Socratic method, rich with echoes of the Kantian imperative, its universal mate, summoning sharply to the minds of each the history of the first trystings of all immortal lovers, the tragic and tangled tale, indeed, of all star-crossed moonings, mum and dad, mister and missus unotoo and all. Enough? I should bloody well hope so.

Of course nothing came of it. Romantic love was surely the invention of a wedded onanist with seven kids. And I don't mean dad. Nothing? Really and truly nothing? Well, I treasure the under-statement; though why I should take such pleasure in maligning the ploughing summer white on loam, river flats, the frivolous ribbons and all the strumming, why I don't know. Xanadu and the jazzy furrows, the wall-eyed bitch packing the cows through the yardgate, the smell of river water . . . Why go on? So few variations to an old, old story. No. But on the jolting tractor I received that extra jolt I mentioned and am actually now making rather too much of, gentlemen: relate Fanny Hohepa and her uke to that mountain thrush singing her black mountain blues.

But of course now, in our decent years, we know such clay questions long broken open or we wouldn't be here, old and somewhat sour, wading up to our battered thighs (forgive me, madam) at the confluence of the great waters, paddling in perfect confidence in the double debouchment of universal river and regional stream, the shallow fast fan of water spreading over the delta, Abyssinia come to Egypt in the rain . . . ah, my country! I speak of cultural problems, in riddles and literary puddles, perform this act of divination with my own entrails: Fanny's dark delta; the nubile and

Nubian sheila with her portable piano anticipating the transistor-set; all gathered into single demesne, O'Leary's orchard. Even this wooden bowl, plucked from the flood, lost from the hand of some anonymous herdsman as he stopped to cup a drink at the river's source. Ah, Buster. Ah, Buster. Buster. Ah, darling. Darling! Love. You recognize it? Could you strum to that? Suppose you gag a little at the sugar coating, it's the same old fundamental toffee, underneath.

No mere cheap cyn. . .sm intended. She took me down to her darkling avid as any college girl for the fruits and sweets of my flowering talents, taking me as I wasn't but might hope one day to be, honest, simple and broke to the wide. The half-baked verbosity and the conceit she must have ignored, or how else could she have borne me? It pains me, gentlemen, to confess that she was too good for me by far. Far. Anything so spontaneous and natural could be guaranteed to be beyond me: granted, I mean, my impeccable upbringing under the white-hot lash of respectability, take that, security, take that, hypocrisy, take that, cant, take that where, does it seem curious?, mum did all the beating flushed pink in ecstasy and righteousness, and that and that and THAT. Darling! How then could I deem Fanny's conduct proper when I carried such weals and scars, top-marks in the lesson on the wickedness of following the heart. Fortunately such a question would not have occurred to Fanny: she was remarkably free from queries of any kind. She would walk past the Home Furnishing Emporium without a glance.

She is too good for you.

It was said clearly enough, offered without threat and as just comment, while I was bent double stripping old Daisy or Pride of the Plains or Rose of Sharon after the cups came

off. I stopped what I was doing, looked sideways until I could see the tops of his gumboots, gazed on *Marathon*, and then turned back, dried off all four tits and let the cow out into the race where, taking the legrope with her, she squittered off wild in the eyes.

She is too good for you.

So I looked at him and he looked back. I lost that game of stare-you-down, too. He walked off. Not a warning, not even a reproach, just something it was as well I should know if I was to have the responsibility of acting in full knowledge – and who the hell wants that? And two stalls down Fanny spanked a cow out through the flaps and looked at me, and giggled. The summer thickened and blazed.

The first response on the part of my parents was silence; which can only be thought of as response in a very general sense. I could say, indeed I will say, stony silence; after all they were my parents. But I knew the silence wouldn't last long. I was an only child (darling, you never guessed?) and that load of woodchopping, lawnmowing, hedgedipping, dishwashing, carwashing, errandrunning, gardenchoring and the rest of it was going to hit them like a folding mortgage pretty soon. I'd like to have been there, to have seen the lank grass grown beyond window height and the uncut hedges shutting out the sun: perpetual night and perpetual mould on Rose Street West. After a few weeks the notes and letters began. The whole gamut, gentlemen, from sweet and sickly to downright abusive. Mostly in mum's masculine hand. A unique set of documents reeking of blood and tripes. I treasured every word, reading between the lines the record of an undying, all-sacrificing love, weeping tears for the idyllic childhood they could not in grief venture to touch

upon, the care lavished, the love squandered upon me. The darlings. Of course I didn't reply. I didn't even wave when they drove past Fanny and me as we were breasting out of the scrub back on to the main road, dishevelled and, yes, almost happy in the daze of summer and Sunday afternoon. I didn't wave. I grinned as brazenly as I could manage with a jaw full of hard boiled egg and took Fanny's arm, brazen, her shirt only casually resumed, while they went by like burnished doom.

Fanny's reaction to all this? An expression of indifference, a downcurving of that bright and wilful mouth, a flirt of her head. So much fuss over so many fossilized ideas, if I may so translate her expression which was, in fact, gentlemen, somewhat more direct and not in any sense exhibiting what mum would have called a due respect for elders and betters. Pouf! Not contempt, no; not disagreement; simply an impatience with what she, Fanny, deemed the irrelevance of so many many words for so light and tumbling a matter. And, for the season at least, I shared the mood, her demon lover in glossy brilliantine.

But as the days ran down the showdown came nearer and finally the stage was set. Low-keyed and sombre notes in the sunlight, the four of us variously disposed on the unpainted Hohepa verandah, Hohepa and O'Leary, the male seniors, and Hohepa and O'Leary, junior representatives, male seventeen, female ready to swear, you understand, that she was sixteen, turning.

Upon the statement that Fanny was too good for me my pappy didn't comment. No one asked him to: no one faced him with the opinion. Wise reticence, mere oversight or a sense of shrieking irrelevance of such a statement, I don't

know. Maori girls, Maori farms, Maori housing: you'd only to hear my father put tongue to any or all of that to know where he stood, solid for intolerance, mac, but solid. Of course, gentlemen, it was phrased differently on his lips, gradual absorption, hmm, perhaps, after, say, a phase of disinfecting. A pillar of our decent, law-abiding community, masonic in his methodism, brother, total abstainer, rotarian and non-smoker, addicted to long volleys of handball, I mean pocket billiards cue and all. Mere nervousness, of course a subconscious habit. Mum would cough and glance down and dad would spring to attention hands behind his back. Such moments of tender rapport are sweet to return to, memories any child might treasure. Then he'd forget again. Straight mate, there were days, especially Sundays, where mum would be hacking away like an advanced case of t.b. Well, you can picture it, there on the verandah. With the finely turned Fanny under his morose eye, you know how it is, hemline hiked and this and that visible from odd angles, he made a straight break of two hundred without one miscue, Daddy! I came in for a couple of remand home stares myself, bread and water and solitary and take that writ on his eyeballs in backhand black while his mouth served out its lying old hohums and there's no reason why matters shouldn't be resolved amicably, etc, black hanging-cap snug over his tonsure and tongue moistening his droopy lip, ready, set, drop. And Puti Hohepa leaving him to it. A dignified dark prince on his ruined acres, old man Hohepa, gravely attending to dad's mumbled slush, winning hands down just by being there and saying nothing, nothing, while Fanny with her fatal incapacity for standing upright unsupported for more than fifteen seconds, we all had a disease of the spine that year, pouted at me as though it were all my fault over

the back of the chair (sic). All my fault being just the pater's monologue, the remarkably imprecise grip of his subject with consequent proliferation of the bromides so typical of all his ilk of elk, all the diversely identical representatives of decency, caution and the colour bar. Of course daddy didn't there and then refer to race, colour creed or uno who. Indeed he firmly believed he believed, if I may recapitulate, gentlemen, that this blessed land was free from such taint, a unique social experiment, two races living happily side by side, respecting each others etc and etc. As a banker he knew the value of discretion, though what was home if not a place to hang up your reticence along with your hat and get stuck into all the hate that was inside you, in the name of justice? Daddy Hohepa said nothing, expressed nothing, may even have been unconscious of the great destinies being played out on his sunlit verandah, or of what fundamental principles of democracy and the freedom of the individual were being here so brilliantly exercised; may have been, in fact, indifferent to daddy's free grating tautologies now, of the need for circumspection in all matters of national moment, all such questions as what shall be done for our dark brothers and sisters, outside the jails? I hope so. After a few minutes Hohepa rangatira trod the boards thoughtfully and with the slowness of a winter bather lowered himself into a pool of sunlight on the wide steps, there to lift his face broad and grave in full dominion of his inheritance and even, perhaps, so little did his expression reveal of his inward reflection, full consciousness of his dispossessions.

What, you may ask, was my daddy saying? Somewhere among the circumlocutions, these habits are catching among the words and sentiments designed to express his grave pondering on the state of the nation and so elicit from his

auditors (not me, I wasn't listening) admission, tacit though it may be, of his tutored opinion, there was centred the suggestion that old man Hohepa and daughter were holding me against my will, ensnaring me with flesh and farm. He had difficulty in getting it out in plain words; some lingering cowardice, perhaps. Which was why daddy Hohepa missed it, perhaps. Or did the view command all his attention?

Rideout Mountain far and purple in the afternoon sun; the jersey cows beginning to move, intermittent and indirect, towards the shed; the dog jangling its chain as it scratched; Fanny falling in slow movement across the end of the old cane lounge chair to lie, an interesting composition of curves and angles, with the air of a junior and rural odalisque. Me? I stood straight, of course, rigid, thumbs along the seams of my jeans, hair at the regulation distance two inches above the right eye, heels together and bare feet at ten to two, or ten past ten, belly flat and chest inflated, chin in, heart out. I mean, can you see me, mac? Dad's grave-suit so richly absorbed the sun that he was forced to retreat into the shadows where his crafty jailer's look was decently camouflaged, blending white with purple blotched with silver wall. Not a bad heart, surely?

As his audience we each displayed differing emotions. Fanny, boredom that visibly bordered on sleep: Puti Hohepa, an inattention expressed in his long examination of the natural scene: Buster O'Leary, a sense of complete bewilderment over what it was the old man thought he could achieve by his harangue and, further, a failure to grasp the relevance of it all for the Hohepas. My reaction, let me say, was mixed with irritation at certain of father's habits. (Described.) With his pockets filled with small change he sounded like the original gypsy orchestra, cymbals and all. I

actually tried mum's old trick of the glance and the cough. No luck. And he went on talking, at me now, going so wide of the mark, for example, as to mention some inconceivable, undocumented and undemonstrated condition, some truly monstrous condition, called your-mother's-love. Plain evidence of his distress, I took it to be, this obscenity uttered in mixed company. I turned my head the better to hear, when it came, the squelchy explosion of his heart. And I rolled a smoke and threw Fanny the packet. It landed neatly on her stomach. She sat up and made herself a smoke then crossed to her old man and, perching beside him in the brilliant pool of light, fire of skin and gleam of hair bronze and blue-black, neatly extracted from his pocket his battered flint lighter. She snorted smoke and passed the leaf to her old man.

Some things, gentlemen, still amaze. To my dying day I have treasured that scene and all its rich implications. In a situation so pregnant of difficulties, in the midst of a debate so fraught with undertones, an exchange (quiet there, at the back) so bitterly fulsome on the one hand and so reserved on the other. I ask you to take special note of this observance of the ritual of the makings, remembering, for the fullest savouring of the nuance, my father's abstention. As those brown fingers moved on the white cylinder, or cone, I was moved almost, to tears, almost, by this companionable and wordless recognition of our common human frailty, father and dark child in silent communion and I too, in some manner not to be explained because inexplicable, sharing their hearts. I mean the insanity, pal. Puti Hohepa and his lass in sunlight on the steps, smoking together, untroubled, natural and patient; and me and daddy glaring at each other in the shades like a couple of evangelists at cross pitch. Love,

thy silver coatings and castings. And thy neighbours! So I went and sat by Fanny and put an arm through hers.

The sun gathered me up, warmed and consoled; the bitter view assumed deeper purples and dark rose; a long way off a shield flashed, the sun striking silver from a water trough. At that moment I didn't care what mad armies marched in my father's voice nor what the clarion was he was trying so strenuously to sound. I didn't care that the fire in his heart was fed by such rank fuel, skeezing envy, malice, revenge, hate and parental power. I sat and smoked and was warm; and the girl's calm flank was against me, her arm through mine. Nothing was so natural as to turn through the little distance between us and kiss her smoky mouth. Ah yes, I could feel, I confess, through my shoulder blades as it were and the back of my head, the crazed rapacity and outrage of my daddy's Irish stare, the blackness and the cold glitter of knives. (Father!) While Puti Hohepa sat on as though turned to glowing stone by the golden light, faced outward to the violent mystery of the natural hour, monumentally content and still.

You will have seen it, known it, guessed that there was between this wild, loamy daughter and me, sunburnt scion of an ignorant, insensitive, puritan and therefore prurient, Irishman (I can't stop) no more than a summer's dalliance, a season's thoughtless sweetness, a boy and a girl and the makings.

In your wisdom, gentlemen, you will doubtless have sensed that something is lacking in this lullaby, some element missing for the articulation of this ranting tale. Right. The key to daddy's impassioned outburst, no less. Not lost in this verbose review, but so far unstated. Point is he'd come to seek

his little son (someone must have been dying because he'd never have come for the opposite reason) and, not being one to baulk at closed doors and drawn shades, wait for it, he'd walked straight in on what he'd always somewhat feverishly imagined and hoped he feared. Fanny took it calmly: I was, naturally, more agitated. Both of us ballocky in the umber light, of course. Still, even though he stayed only long enough to let his eyes adjust and his straining mind take in this historic disposition of flesh, those mantis angles in which for all our horror we must posit our conceivings, it wasn't the greeting he'd expected. It wasn't quite the same, either, between Fanny and me, after he'd backed out, somewhat huffily, on to the verandah. Ah, filthy beasts! He must have been roaring some such expression as that inside his head because his eyeballs were rattling, the very picture of a broken doll, and his face was liver-coloured. I felt sorry for him, for a second, easing backward from the love-starred couch and the moving lovers with his heel hooked through the loop of Fanny's bra, kicking it free like a football hero punting for touch, his dream of reconciliation in ruins.

It wasn't the same. Some rhythms are slow to re-form. And once the old man actually made the sanctuary of the verandah he just had to bawl his loudest for old man Hohepa, Mr Ho-he-pa, Mr Ho-he-pa. It got us into our clothes anyway, Fanny giggling and getting a sneezing fit at the same time, bending forward into the hoof-marked brassiere and blasting off every ten seconds like a burst air hose until I quite lost count on the one-for-sorrow two-for-joy scale and crammed myself sulkily into my jocks.

Meantime dad's labouring to explain certain natural facts and common occurrences to Puti Hohepa, just as though he'd made an original discovery; as perhaps he had

considering what he probably thought of as natural. Puti Hohepa listened, I thought that ominous, then silently deprecated, in a single slow movement of his hand, the wholly inappropriate expression of shock and rage, all the sizzle of my daddy's oratory.

Thus the tableau. We did the only possible thing, ignored him and let him run down, get it off his chest, come to his five battered senses, if he had so many, and get his breath. Brother, how he spilled darkness and sin upon that floor, wilting collar and boiling eyes, the sweat running from his face and, Fanny, shameless, languorous and drowsy, provoking him to further flights. She was young, gentlemen: I have not concealed it. She was too young to have had time to accumulate the history he ascribed to her. She was too tender to endure for long the muscular lash of his tongue and the rake of his eyes. She went over to her dad, as heretofore described, and when my sweet sire, orator general to the dying afternoon, had made his pitch about matters observed and inferences drawn, I went to join her. I sat with my back to him. All our backs were to him, including his own. He emptied himself of wrath and for a moment, a wild and wonderful moment, I thought he was going to join us, bathers in the pool of sun. But no.

Silence. Light lovely and fannygold over the pasture; shreds of mist by the river deepening to rose. My father's hard leather soles rattled harshly on the bare boards like rim-shots. The mad figure of him went black as bug out over the lawn, out over the loamy furrows where the tongue of ploughed field invaded the home paddock, all my doing, spurning in his violence anything less than this direct and abrupt charge towards the waiting car. Fanny's hand touched my arm again and for a moment I was caught in a passion of

sympathy for him, something as solid as grief and love, an impossible pairing of devotion and despair. The landscape flooded with sadness as I watched the scuttling, black, ignominious figure hurdling the fresh earth, the waving arms, seemingly scattering broadcast the white and shying gulls, his head bobbing on his shoulders, as he narrowed into distance.

I wished, gentlemen, with a fervour foreign to my young life, that it had been in company other than that of Puti Hohepa and his brat that we had made our necessary parting. I wished we had been alone. I did not want to see him diminished, made ridiculous and pathetic among strangers, while I so brashly joined the mockers. (Were they mocking?) Impossible notions; for what was there to offer and how could he receive? Nothing. I stroked Fanny's arm. Old man Hohepa got up and unchained the dog and went off to get the cows in. He didn't speak; maybe the chocolate old bastard was dumb, eh? In a minute I would have to go down and start the engine and put the separator together. I stayed to stare at Fanny, thinking of undone things in a naughty world. She giggled, thinking, for all I know, of the same, or of nothing. Love, they sunning trystings and nocturnal daggers. For the first time I admitted my irritation at that girlish, hiccoughing, tenor giggle. But we touched, held, got up and with our arms linked went down the long paddock through the infestation of buttercup, our feet bruising stalk and flower. Suddenly all I wanted and at whatever price was to be able, sometime, somewhere, to make it up to my primitive, violent, ignorant and crazy old man. And I knew I never would. Ah, what a bloody fool. And then the next thing I wanted, a thing far more feasible, was to be back in that room with its shade and smell of hay-dust

and warm flesh, taking up the classic story just where we'd been so rudely forced to discontinue it. Old man Hohepa was bellowing at the dog; the cows rocked up through the paddock gate and into the yard: the air smelled of night. I stopped; and holding Fanny's arm suggested we might run back. Her eyes went wide: she giggled and broke away and I stood there and watched her flying down the paddock, bare feet and a flouncing skirt, her hair shaken loose.

Next afternoon I finished ploughing the river paddock, the nature of Puti Hohepa's husbandry as much a mystery as ever, and ran the old Ferguson into the lean-to shelter behind the cow shed. It was far too late for ploughing: the upper paddocks were hard and dry. But Puti hoped to get a crop of late lettuce off the river flat; just in time, no doubt, for a glutted market, brown rot, wilt and total failure of the heart. He'd have to harrow it first, too; and on his own. Anyway, none of my worry. I walked into the shed. Fanny and her daddy were deep in conversation. She was leaning against the flank of a cow, a picture of rustic grace, a rural study of charmed solemnity. Christ knows what they were saying to each other. For one thing they were speaking in their own language: for another I couldn't hear anything, even that, above the blather and splatter of the bloody cows and the racket of the single cylinder diesel, brand-name Onan out of Edinburgh so help me. They looked up. I grabbed a stool and got on with it, head down to the bore of it all. I'd have preferred to be up on the tractor, poisoning myself straight out, bellowing this and that and the other looney thing to the cynical gulls. Ah, my mountain princess of the golden chords, something was changing. I stripped on, sullenly: I hoped it was me.

We were silent through dinner: we were always silent, through all meals. It made a change from home where all hell lay between soup and sweet, everyone taking advantage of the twenty minutes of enforced attendance to shoot the bile, bicker and accuse, rant and wrangle through the grey disgusting mutton and the two veg. Fanny never chattered much and less than ever in the presence of her pappy: giggled maybe but never said much. Then out of the blue father Hohepa opened up. Buster, you should make peace with your father. I considered it. I tried to touch Fanny's foot under the table and I considered it. A boy shouldn't hate his father: a boy should respect his father. I thought about that too. Then I asked should fathers hate their sons; but I knew the answer. Puti Hohepa didn't say anything, just sat blowing into his tea, looking at his reputedly wild daughter who might have been a beauty for all I could tell, content to be delivered to the truth and so fulfilled. You should do this: a boy shouldn't do that – tune into that, mac. And me thinking proscription and prescription differently ordered in this farm world of crummy acres. I mean I thought I'd left all that crap behind the night I stumbled along Rideout Road following, maybe, the river Alph. I thought old man Hohepa, having been silent for so long, would know better than to pull, of a sudden, all those generalizations with which for seventeen years I'd been beaten dizzy – but not so dizzy as not to be able to look back of the billboards and see the stack of rotting bibles. Gentlemen, I was, even noticeably, subdued. Puti Hohepa clearly didn't intend to add anything more just then. I was too tired to make him an answer. I think I was too tired even for that; and what better indication of the extent of my exhaustion than that? It had been a long summer; how long I was only beginning to discover. It was cold in the kitchen.

Puti Hohepa got up. From the doorway, huge and merging into the night, he spoke again: You must make up your own mind. He went away, leaving behind him the vibration of a gentle sagacity, tolerance, a sense of duty (mine, as usual) pondered over and pronounced upon. The bastard. You must make up your own mind. And for the first time you did that mum had hysterics and dad popped his gut. About what? Made up my mind about what? My black daddy? Fanny? Myself? Life? A country career and agricultural hell? Death? Money? Fornication? (I'd always liked that.) What the hell was he trying to say? What doing but abdicating the soiled throne at the first challenge? Did he think fathers shouldn't hate their sons, or could help it, or would if they could? Am I clear? No matter. He didn't have one of the four he'd sired at home so what the hell sort of story was he trying to peddle? Father with the soft centre. You should, you shouldn't, make up your own mind. Mac, my head was going round. But it was brilliant, I conceded, when I'd given it a bit of thought. My livid daddy himself would have applauded the perfect ambiguity. What a bunch: they keep a dog on a chain for years and years and then let it free on some purely personal impulse and when it goes wild and chases its tail round and round, pissing here and sniffing there in an ecstasy of liberty, a freedom for which it has been denied all training, they shoot it down because it won't come running when they hold up the leash and whistle. (I didn't think you'd go that way, son.) Well, my own green liberty didn't look like so much at that moment; for the first time I got an inkling that life was going to be simply a matter of out of one jail and into another. Oh, they had a lot in common, her dad and mine. I sat there, mildly stupefied, drinking my tea. Then I looked up at Fanny; or, rather, down on Fanny, I've never known

such a collapsible sheila in my life. She was stretched on the kitchen couch, every vertebra having turned to juice in the last minute and a half. I thought maybe she'd have the answer, some comment to offer on the state of disunion. Hell. I was the very last person to let my brew go cold while I pondered the nuance of the incomprehensible, picked at the dubious unsubtlety of thought of a man thirty years my senior who had never, until then, said more than ten words to me. She is too good for you: only six words after all and soon forgotten. Better, yes, if he'd stayed mum, leaving me to deduce from his silence whatever I could, Abora Mountain and the milk of paradise, consent in things natural and a willingness to let simple matters take their simple course.

I was wrong: Fanny offered no interpretation of her father's thought. Exegesis to his cryptic utterance was the one thing she couldn't supply. She lay with her feet up on the end of the couch, brown thighs charmingly bared, mouth open and eyes closed in balmy sleep, displaying in this posture various things but mainly her large unconcern not only for this tragedy of filial responsibility and the parental role but, too, for the diurnal problem of the numerous kitchen articles, pots, pans, plates, the lot. I gazed on her, frowning on her bloom of sleep, the slow inhalation and exhalation accompanied by a gentle flare of nostril, and considered the strength and weakness of our attachment. Helpmeet she was not, thus to leave her lover to his dark ponderings and the chores.

Puti Hohepa sat on the verandah in the dark, hacking over his bowl of shag. One by one, over my second cup of tea, I assessed my feelings, balanced all my futures in the palm of my hand. I crossed to Fanny, crouched beside her, kissed her. I felt embarrassed and, gentlemen, foolish. Her eyes opened wide; then they shut and she turned over.

The dishes engaged my attention not at all, except to remind me, here we go, of my father in apron and rubber gloves at the sink, pearl-diving while mum was off somewhere at a lynching. Poor bastard. Mum had the natural squeeze for the world; they should have changed places. (It's for your own good! Ah, the joyous peal of that as the razor strop came whistling down like tartar's blade.) I joined daddy Hohepa on the verandah. For a moment we shared the crescent moon and the smell of earth damp under dew, Rideout Mountain massed to the west.

I've finished the river paddock.

Yes.

The tractor's going to need a de-coke before long.

Yes.

I guess that about cuts it out.

Yes.

I may as well shoot through.

Buster, is Fanny pregnant?

I don't know. She hasn't said anything to me so I suppose she can't be.

You are going home?

No. Not home. There's work down south. I'd like to have a look down there.

There's work going here if you want it. But you have made up your mind?

I suppose I may as well shoot through.

Yes.

After milking tomorrow if that's okay with you.

Yes.

He hacked on over his pipe. Yes, yes, yes, yes, yes is Fanny pregnant? What if I'd said yes? I didn't know one way or the other. I only hoped, and left the rest to her. Maybe he'd ask

her; and what if she said yes? What then, eh Buster? Maybe I should have said why don't you ask her. A demonstrative, volatile, loquacious old person: a tangible symbol of impartiality, reason unclouded by emotion, his eyes frank in the murk of night and his pipe going bright, dim, bright as he calmly considered the lovely flank of the moon. I was hoping she wasn't, after all. Hoping; it gets to be a habit, a bad habit that does you no good, stunts your growth, sends you insane and makes you, demonstrably, blind. Hope, for Fanny Hohepa.

Later, along the riverbank, Fanny and I groped, gentlemen, for the lost rapport and the parking sign. We were separated by just a little more than an arm's reach. I made note then of the natural scene. Dark water, certainly; dark lush grass underfoot; dark girl; the drifting smell of loam in the night; grant me again as much. Then, by one of those fortuitous accidents not infrequent in our national prosings, our hands met, held, fell away. Darkness. My feet stumbling by the river and my heart going like a tango. Blood pulsed upon blood, undenied and unyoked, as we busied ourselves tenderly at our ancient greetings and farewells. And in the end, beginning my sentence with a happy conjunction, I held her indistinct, dark head. We stayed so for a minute, together and parting as always, with me tumbling down upon her the mute dilemma my mind then pretended to resolve and she offering no restraint, no argument better than the dark oblivion of her face.

Unrecorded the words between us: there can't have been more than six, anyway, it was our fated number. None referred to my departure or to the future or to maculate conceptions. Yet her last touch spoke volumes. (Unsubsidized, gentlemen, without dedication or preamble.) River-damp softened her

hair: her skin smelled of soap: Pan pricking forward to drink at the stream, crushing fennel, exquisitely stooping, bending . . .

And, later again, silent, groping, we ascended in sequence to the paternal porch.

Buster?

Yair?

Goodnight, Buster.

'Night, Fanny. Be seein' yuh.

. . .

Fourteen minute specks of radioactive phosphorus brightened by weak starlight pricked out the hour: one.

In the end I left old STC in the tractor tool box along with the spanner that wouldn't fit any nut I'd ever tried it on and the grease gun without grease and the last letter from mum, hot as radium. I didn't wait for milking. I was packed and gone at the first trembling of light. It was cold along the river-bottom, cold and still. Eels rose to feed: the water was like pewter; old pewter. I felt sick, abandoned, full of self-pity. Everything washed through me, the light, the cold, a sense of what lay behind me and might not lie before, a feeling of exhaustion when I thought of home, a feeling of despair when I thought of Fanny still curled in sleep. Dark. She hadn't giggled: so what? I changed my fibre suitcase to the other hand and trudged along Rideout Road. The light increased; quail with tufted crests crossed the road: I began to feel better. I sat on the suitcase and rolled a smoke. Then the sun caught a high scarp of Rideout Mountain and began to finger down slow and gold. I was so full of relief, suddenly, that I grabbed my bag and ran. Impetuous. I was lucky not to break my ankle. White gulls, loam flesh, dark water, damsel and dome; where would it take you? Where

was there to go, anyway? It just didn't matter; that was the point. I stopped worrying that minute and sat by the cream stand out on the main road. After a while a truck stopped to my thumb and I got in. If I'd waited for the cream truck I'd have had to face old brownstone Hohepa and I wasn't very eager for that. I'd had a fill of piety, of various brands. And I was paid up to date.

I looked back. Rideout Mountain and the peak of ochre red roof, Maori red. That's all it was. I wondered what Fanny and her pappy might be saying at this moment, across the clothes-hanger rumps of cows. The rush of relief went through me again. I looked at the gloomy bastard driving: he had a cigarette stuck to his lip like a growth. I felt almost happy. Almost. I might have hugged him as he drove his hearse through the tail-end of summer.

O'Leary's Orchard

After all the sun was shining. And Miss Bernstein was due at four. Even so a wind of incredible bitterness was blowing from the south west, carrying from grinding ice floes or the circle about the pole perhaps, a few penguin feathers and, from regions less remote, autumnal and rural smells. O'Leary raked up leaves and prunings, working with his back to the icy blast, preparing with a strong anticipation of pleasure another of his seasonal pyres. His plan was not so much one of smoking out the district as of rewarding himself with dense and pungent billows – and only incidentally getting rid of the orchard trash. These great white clouds of smoke were one of O'Leary's addictions: another, at this time, was Miss Bernstein. He called her Isobel: she called him Mr O'Leary, or Gambo when they were alone.

It was as O'Leary, owner of the place, that he started the base fire of newspapers and dry stuff, waiting for the flames to take hold; but it was as Gambo, lively defector, that he began to pile on the debris of a fruitful year. He used a long-handled fork with curved tines. He took his time. Smoke began to rise in pleasing volume, white or dun.

The imminent visit of Miss Bernstein was a trouble at the back of his mind. Without it he would have been free to become totally absorbed in his present mania. Miss Bernstein was fixed in her expectation that he would seduce her: that was the trouble. But where she would limn simplicities or, worse, a casual unimportance, O'Leary's greater age and more diverse experience had him with his foot on the brake.

There were questions of age, discrepancies of May and December. He loved the autumn: she, he fancied, would favour blossom and warmth and downright sun. There were other questions also, among which Mrs Bernstein was notable. She would figure as widow, matron and mother: a sternness could be expected, at the least.

Moodily O'Leary added to the smouldering heap.

Oh he liked her – most immensely he liked her – the lush and lovely Miss Bernstein or Isobel. Better men than O'Leary, or worse, for both were to be found, would sing her praises in their differing keys. He could all but hear the contrapuntal paean. And wiser men, or more foolish, for both again were somewhere about on the unterminating camber of the globe, might find themselves similarly discommoded by Miss Bernstein's headlong rush. She kept her foot down and took the sharpest bends at an undiminishing pace: the passenger seat and its occupant were a mere optional extra. So, at least, O'Leary saw it.

It was unsatisfactory. At first the smoke rose in languid volume and was comforting; but the wind began to gust and fan flames. Soon, where he'd hoped for billows and plumes, an obliteration of white, there was a trembling of fierce heat and no smoke at all. However much he heaped on damp leaves the flames burst through, sending blasts of heat between the fruit trees. The whole orchard trembled. O'Leary sensed danger: this was not his addiction. Even upwind the heat had him sweating. His face was hot while his back gathered a burden, as it felt, of wet snow. He stood back and let the fire burn.

It was three. The sun was only fitful now, but Miss Bernstein was due at four. It would take him that time to shower and shave and change.

He accepted the wind on his face and walked towards the barn.

* * *

Without benefit of hindsight no event could be described as a beginning. Every gesture required a future, looked back on, for significance. O'Leary, at least, could have thought as much.

Faced then with the event O'Leary was forced to remember his own past ambitions, even elements of his own past career.

Acquiescence came easily. Especially with Isobel Bernstein, as spokeswoman for the small group, so encouraging an affirmative, so offering the delightful assurance of gravity and, as far as he could make out in the half-light, charmingly exhibiting a very definite sort of expectation. She did not, that's to say, expect him to refuse; and how, given the circumstances, could he? He had trod for so long that road on which, with an eagerness he could not rebuke, they were now seeking to set foot. If on his side the door was marked 'Exit', on theirs the sign presumably read 'Entrance' in boldest letters. He could resent it as it swung between them, in less of an arc than would be required to reverse their roles or readings. But for her, he saw, he might have been less welcoming; but for her he might have been less accommodating; without Isobel he might have refused.

That, precisely, was what they wanted: accommodation. Room in his great barn to rehearse their play, at a distance from the adverse appraisal and vulgar interference they thought could only be expected from recourse to the usual premises, school or church halls. They knew him to have been,

well, not unconnected with the theatre in his day; although they stumbled a little over the absurdity this represented. His day! O'Leary felt them gather about him, the illustrious dead, Garrick, Kemble, Kean – even the great bard himself – among whom he was held to have been contemporary.

Was he, he wondered, so antic a figure? Did he suggest, so directly, a lifetime of bit parts in provincial and amateur repertory? He supposed he did. The little group were so intimidating in their confidence, their dismissals: they so promised to put, in their very first words on stage, his meagre past to shame. He did not matter: the facilities he could offer did.

They stood before him like executioners, a firing squad: they had nothing against him personally. He could even, they pretended, shut the door in their faces. They watched him as Isobel spoke: O'Leary felt a small tremor of alarm. Equally, he thought, could she have ordered his extinction. The merest gesture would do it: her expression would not change. She would continue to look just so, charming and fresh and young, while he surrendered his last breath. Would it not, therefore, be better to be sensible? To step aside and ask them to come in? O'Leary thought it would. He invited them to enter, and apologized for the poor light. His apology was accepted.

O'Leary lingered at a distance, wanting to interfere. Lights blazed and the stage was set; but the play was incomprehensible to him. Part of the time the players were grotesquely masked. Miss Bernstein took the centre. O'Leary, working hard at his exegesis, supposed her to be representing either lust or carnal temptation – in body tights of sheerest black. He could scarcely as yet cry 'bravo'.

That she had her talents he could immediately concede: though her voice, he thought, rather failed to carry. 'Junoesque' was a word that came rather inevitably to O'Leary's mind: 'absurd' was another, as he tried to decipher the mask she carried before her face. A snout, he made out, pointed ears and a fangy sort of grin or leer. A hyena? He sighed for all dead playwrights spinning in their graves. He was resentful: there was no part for O'Leary here. The players did not welcome him. Yet he had helped them rig extra lights and had taken out extra insurance in the form of a public risk policy; and could expect to foot the bill for both. But there was Miss Bernstein, the only female in the cast.

After the first few nights of rehearsal, O'Leary kept as much as possible to his quarters at the rear of the barn, regretting his acquiescence. It had not been explained to him that his accommodation could be required not for a few nights but for weeks or even months to come. The play was complex: the producer was a perfectionist – these were the reasons given. O'Leary tried to convince himself that it would be nothing, in retrospect. Probably it was sleep he was missing; it seemed a plausible explanation.

Normally he was in bed by ten thirty; but rehearsals continued most nights to a late hour and O'Leary stayed up to see the players out and bolt the door and switch off lights. He was afraid of fire and the producer scattered matches like a man broadcasting seed. Sometimes it was two in the morning before O'Leary got to bed. A routine was necessary to him: he had no routine, now. And it was absurd that he felt he could do no more about it than grumble to himself.

* * *

It was a night O'Leary would remember for reasons other than lack of sleep and the lateness of the hour.

Miss Bernstein fell and opened the flesh of her palm. It was a superficial if bloody wound and O'Leary, emerging to investigate the crash, had offered antiseptic and tape, and recommended a tetanus shot, although it was not on any of his gear she had cut herself. She followed him to his room.

At close quarters her skin-tight garment held its surprises. O'Leary, insofar as conditions permitted, resolutely kept his eyes from undulations and declivities: the flesh was so flawless, the cloth clung so tight, and there was so much youthful hauteur in the extended hand. Miss Bernstein calmly watched trails of blood stain the hot water in the white bowl. O'Leary painted the wound and neatly taped it up. Her finger nails were silver.

He'd made it clear: his quarters were definitely out of bounds: he wanted none of them through here. Therefore the room intrigued Miss Bernstein just that much more. It was bright; it was snug; it was impeccable, if spare. O'Leary, a traveller in his time, watched her finger mementoes of many journeys, the curious objects littering dustless shelves. Her delight was unsimulated: she would never have bothered to pretend. She inspected the equally impeccable kitchen and bathroom. O'Leary, relieved to have her at a distance, wondered did she wear anything at all beneath her extraordinary costume. She was full of questions; but O'Leary was short on answers. She pressed, he felt, too fast; and the others were waiting.

Young she might be, resplendent animal, but the reaches between were great. He needed no looking glass to instruct him in what she saw. He did not pretend to be young, however far he was from the bath chair and the hot cocoa

toddy. He watched Miss Bernstein run a fingernail along the spines of a shelf of books; it could have been a stick rattling along a slat fence. Her friends were calling.

Somehow he urged her out without actually touching her. The last thing he wanted was to have the whole troupe in his room. She took her time in going. Her eyes were quick and no more demure than her impossible garment which she would presumably slough before bedtime, like a snake its skin. O'Leary shuddered on that.

Later that same evening O'Leary put down his book and went out into the barn to close up. The players had gone but the lights still burned.

He enjoyed stalking here in the rich smells of fertilizer and packing straw and sawn timber. The stage and bright lights did not affect him now: he had grown used to them. The young people had commandeered so much of his gear – packing bench, boxes, crates, even a new tarpaulin – that he was sometimes forced to improvise as he worked in the orchard.

They had lost his hammer: the space they occupied forced him to leave the tractor out in the weather: his routine was a joke.

O'Leary took his stand in the centre of the stage and looked on shadows and darkness. Mice or birds made small discontinuous noises above. He tried a phrase or two, softly: he spoke a line or two, loudly. The barn received his voice with a murmur of sound: the acoustics were of medium quality only. O'Leary sang at the top of his voice; it was the prize song from the Mastersingers, for which he invented words. He'd played Shakespeare in his time: Lear when he was too young and Hamlet when he was too old. Neither

performance had inspired the critics: there were references to melodrama, he remembered: 'ham' was a word he winced over. O'Leary shook his fist.

> I'll tell thee. Life and death! I am ashamed
> That thou hast power to shake my manhood thus.

The sad bellow trembled among the small denizens of the roof. He was beginning to enjoy himself. A man could enjoy being ridiculous on his own: he could sing in a moony yell, skipping the high notes: he could spit and leer: he could swagger and strike out, bygod. He stopped, stood stock still, and let himself go upon the emptiness. He was rehearsed.

> You do me wrong to take me out o' the grave;
> Thou art a soul in bliss; but I am bound
> Upon a wheel of fire, that mine own tears
> Do scald like molten lead.

Listening for the dying echoes of the starlings' applause, O'Leary in some amazement heard:

> Sir, do you know me?

Miss Bernstein expressing pity or heartbreak came close with clasped hands: Cordelia in black tights and a cardigan, all tenderness.

> Sir, do you know me?

O'Leary's embarrassment operated as a mnemonic engram: he couldn't remember a bloody thing. He stood in

silence, hunched forward and frowning; it was appropriate.

> Sir, do you know me?

Miss Bernstein insisted, piteously: O'Leary gave a gusty groan.

> You are a spirit I know . . .

Miss Bernstein prompted. O'Leary shifted up a gear and was off, as Miss Bernstein came near, vibrating with filial love. Shamelessly O'Leary quavered, looking with blankest puzzlement into Miss Bernstein's bluest eyes. He reached out a hand. Miss Bernstein was cold to his touch.

> O! look upon me, sir . . .

O'Leary crouched further down and found an old man's falsetto.

> . . . I think this lady
> To be my child Cordelia.

O'Leary agedly peered: Miss Bernstein all but wept.

> And so I am, I am.

Oh wonderful, gently wilting Miss Bernstein. O'Leary's heart was at flood. He leaned upon her as she led him from the stage. He retained his hold as in the dimmer light an active embarrassment grew in him again. He made pointless movements and small coughing sounds and patted Miss

Bernstein unnecessarily.

'Naturally,' he said, 'I had supposed you gone. I shouldn't else have been so free, you understand?'

'I loved it.' Miss Bernstein was intense.

O'Leary supposed she didn't mean his caperings and skirls of purely experimental song. 'Lear?' O'Leary said.

'I played Cordelia, at school.' It was too recent to be forgotten. Miss Bernstein hugged her cardigan across her chest: the barn was cold.

O'Leary congratuled himself on a happy escape: he'd been toying with Romeo as the only other part he was up on. (It was at pruning time he practised, generally, from the top of the ladder.)

'Let's do it again.' Miss Bernstein meant it.

'Good grief,' O'Leary said. He stood full height and placed his palms at the small of his back in the region of the kidneys. 'You're frozen, as it is.'

'I'm not.' Miss Bernstein to prove it removed her cardigan; but it was not convincing to a close observer.

Old and stooped with more than orchard weather O'Leary moved on stage.

> You do me wrong to take me out o' the grave . . .

Miss Bernstein waited with tender eyes, at a slight distance.

Lear wept; and Cordelia dried his eyes. Until it was two or three.

'How will you explain?' O'Leary switched off lights and was tired. 'Won't your family be worried?' Though rehearsals had gone on late before.

'Mummy doesn't worry.' Miss Bernstein had resumed her cardigan and was wearing in addition what appeared to be a

short pelisse of animal skin. Her dark legs emerged beneath: she seemed warmer. 'I'm used to making excuses, anyway.'

O'Leary could believe it. 'I'll see you to the wicket,' he said.

'The wicket?'

'The small door in the big door to save heaving at the vastness.'

It was drizzling at the exit. Miss Bernstein had accepted a shot of whisky and prepared now to brave it to her car. O'Leary felt it would be presumptuous to comment on the weather after what they had just been through. He was, even, masterful in his exhaustion.

'The barge she sat in was a Bentley, eh, or Rolls? You stole it?'

'It's Mummy's.'

'Goodnight, then, Miss Bernstein.'

'Isobel.'

'Goodnight, Isobel. Take the road, at least, with care.'

Isobel Bernstein revealed the tips of delicious teeth in a grateful smile. It was at this point that O'Leary found himself kissing Miss Bernstein in more than farewell, as she stood one step down in the light rain. He desisted, after a minute: Miss Bernstein lingered.

'I'd love to do it again,' Miss Bernstein said, and held her face at a charming cant.

O'Leary's mind had passed into a state of shock. He almost neglected to wave as the spinning wheels flung gravel and the too relaxed turning circle demolished part of his hedge and the car growled sexily out of the drive.

The emptiness of the barn was not its usual comfort as he locked the wicket and walked slowly past the unlighted stage. Miss Bernstein – he preferred to think of her, at the

moment, as that – Miss Bernstein had accepted his kiss. Her mouth had been warm. Had he only imagined a return of pressure? Had Miss Bernstein been kissing him, too? Absurd. Consider the reaches between: May and December; Lear and Cordelia; autumn and spring. But on the whole he had enjoyed himself more than somewhat.

O'Leary's numbness began to pass; and sleep came instantly.

* * *

O'Leary's passion was sleep. He slept stark and hated to rise. For winter he would have chosen hibernation, had there been any way of working it without a programme of continuous sedation and intravenous sustenance. In the hour or two, before getting out of bed became an unavoidable action, under the twin dictates of time and his bladder, it was O'Leary's habit to curl himself as nearly as was possible into the foetal position and give his mind free play in that limbo between sleep and waking. It was not a process of thought: that was to be avoided as fatal to the reverie. First his fantasy; and only then, in the last despairing ten minutes, his plans for the day; only then. Although once up he did not find himself longing to be back in bed.

As O'Leary saw it, it was an experiment. You took someone like Miss Bernstein, like Isobel, and dropped her, a chemical of only partly known elements, into the bubbling alembic – where she might or might not prove to be the universal solvent or alkahest. You waited.

In fact O'Leary's fantasy life was thin and had for some years been unsatisfactory. It was repetitious; it was boring. The process of transmutation by acceleration or modification of

the elements involved evaded him. Sex tended to disappear as money came to the fore. Miss Bernstein was an admixture of which much might be hoped; although he was not insensible, even in a torpid state, to the dangers attendant on his indulgence. Though he might conjure his wraith in so many moods, the danger, of course, would lie in the way this might affect his dealings with the Miss Bernstein of lovely flesh and blood. The important thing was not to infect fact with fantasy, not to follow her every mood so closely nor wear, while shaving, so bemused and soppy a look.

O'Leary began, therefore, to restrain his passion; even to set the clock an hour fast in the (vain) hope of deceiving himself. He began to be stern with himself. He made braver resolutions as he took his morning shower: he sang sadder songs. If his dreamy figurings prepared him to receive a benison of youth, to draw a sustenance and to bask, after all these years, in fresher light, here in the shower box the light was harsher and his very stance a reminder of other roles. Here, too, there was a tap to douse the sybarite cold.

O'Leary braced himself, held his breath, and accepted the discipline. Hadn't the great Jabir or Geber (Abu Musa Jabir ibn Hayyan) himself put it thus: A medicine of the third order, when projected upon an imperfect metal, takes away all corruption and brings the metal to perfection. Or was that Baden-Powell on the subject of self abuse? No matter. Distillation, sublimation, calcination, solution, crystallization and reduction – these were the steps. He could only do his best. What man could or would do more?

Victory over the baser passions being the anticipated outcome of the new regimen, O'Leary next devoted himself to making some provision for the opposite outcome – the untoward victory of the passions themselves. Both the

history of military strategy and the conduct of international diplomacy provided precedent for negative preparedness. With a resolution of spirit and a power of will long supposed by O'Leary to be decrepit in him he embarked on a course of exercises originally developed for personnel of the Royal Canadian Air Force, including combatant units. He omitted neither Saturday nor Sunday and followed faithfully the rate of acceleration recommended for men in the age group just two places lower than his own. At the same time he began to swallow vitamin pills and bought himself a sun lamp.

More than this would have been too resounding an expression of hope, as he followed rehearsals from, as it were, the wings.

The play, to say the least, was bold and curious.

* * *

It was after four.

'Gold,' O'Leary said and lobbed the miniature nugget into her lap. It was the first time he had seen her in a dress and he smiled on what he saw. Blue was her colour and grace her attribute. And he was nervous in the warm room, which was his own.

Isobel gathered it up on its fine chain and cupped it into her palm where it gathered a dull glow: she shook her hand and the chain slithered into coils about the blob of gold.

'Variously described,' O'Leary said. 'A metallic body, citrine, ponderous, mute, fulgid, equally digested in the bowels of the earth and very long washed with mineral water; under the hammer extensible, fusible and sustaining the trial of the cupel and cement. In a word, gold.' He saw

that she had not understood that it was a gift. 'Wear it,' he said. 'It may be lucky.'

'Do you mean I am to have it?' Well-spaced eyes she had, blue in a pretty face.

Isobel slipped the chain over her head and the weight drew it down. The nugget plummeted and was arrested at the base of the loop: O'Leary's token nestled and received a mild warmth. He was grateful for felicities: the day seemed to have drooped. Thoughtfully Isobel thanked him and fingered the unfamiliar chain, the golden thread.

While O'Leary lay back in his chair and wondered was it heart attack or cerebral haemorrhage – as exhaustion flooded him abruptly and darkness drew precipitately down. He tightened his forehead in a feline way and squinted and held on. Until, after a lapse of time whose duration he could not have told the measure of, the world reassembled its white walls and soiled coffee cups – and reality its usual discomforts – all to reinforce his sense of having just missed sinking the long putt, that time at least.

It could only have been a few seconds: Isobel had not moved. She sat sideways in the wicker chair and stared out on the orchard where light was dying.

Flesh, mused O'Leary, logically following up the fright he'd had. Grass. Dust. Isobel Bernstein just so many motes flickering in the barn. Himself, too, miraculously aloft, suspired, a wafting in orchard airs and bosky places, enchoired among angels.

He opened his eyes wide to find his sight wholly restored, with a blessing. From under an aery halo his Isobel was profiled upon the grass environ, thinking him wrapt still, perhaps, in his meditations upon mortality. The low-cut armhole of her dress revealed the beginnings of the youthful

camber of her breast. O'Leary gazed upon it as if upon sculptured perfection, a flawless and formal mounting of a mass, in pure appreciation. These were glimpses that undid the world. All was delicate. He lusted, surely? The armpit itself was naked, axillary fuzz having been, presumably, depilated.

'It must be the smoke I inhaled,' O'Leary said. 'Over the bonfire. I feel somewhat giddy. Should we have a drink? Would you mind?'

'I thought you had fallen asleep.'

'Isobel.' He could find power for that.

It was what enslaved him, he thought, this perfection of bodily beauty. He admired it for what it was, in a spirit of passive and slightly despairing tenderness. Here, indeed, were the reaches between – that perfection and these sore eyes. He could have been content to praise and depart if life, he managed to construe, were ever like that.

She brought him the bottle, and water in a jug. She knelt to pour. She seemed very young, just then. How long to the hour when he must rise?

'They say it's worse than dope,' O'Leary said. 'The psychopath is neither calmed by it nor incapacitated. Which must be hell, for someone.'

But it did the trick. He found his feet and held his young woman in blue: she leaned into his embrace without surprise. O'Leary headily inhaled hair spray and wisps of hair.

'Sir, do you know me?' Isobel was prepared to play; but it was not O'Leary's present mood.

'Do you mind?' O'Leary said. 'Will you, I suppose I mean?'

'Oh Gambo. Of course I don't. Why should I?'

O'Leary could accept absolutes, even so softly delivered.

Geber had no description for these elements, no voice in this arena, no ear for this pounding of blood, as Isobel emerged from blue in truly superb glissades, and then authentic rose.

'I am ashamed,' O'Leary murmured, 'that thou hast power to shake my manhood thus.'

'Ashamed?' It was a moment when Isobel could welcome for her shyness a lightening of the note.

'Enthralled,' said O'Leary, and raised his glass for her to sip.

'I must be careful,' Isobel said. 'I mustn't be too late.'

An appalling thought struck O'Leary.

'Isobel, you aren't by any chance . . . ?'

'No. Of course not.' She was quick to soothe. 'Don't worry. Shall I leave the chain?'

'Ah,' O'Leary said. 'I think not. No, no chains.'

Briskly, noisily a starling was chattering at the apex of the barn. Light lay along dusty beams, remotely. A long way up hard light showed in piercing perforations through the iron. Then afternoon had deepened and rain was falling: falling.

The avidity could not have frightened her, it involved her too much; but the gloom and the lofty birds and the hard pinpricks of light were sources of unease as she resumed white, then blue – the rose Miss Bernstein.

'I'll be late. I must run.'

'Will you take the old brolly?' O'Leary was aware of rained-out fires and charred leaves.

Isobel in her bright rain-hood would have no need of it; it would be an embarrassment. Her face was calm and serious before the luminous mirror whose silvering had blackened.

'I'll see you to the wicket.'

'The little door in the big door to save heaving at the vastness?'

O'Leary allowed it: she was a good mimic. For another thing, she had a memory; it would be a blessing or a curse.

'It sounds like popular theology,' O'Leary said. 'Like who will get God back into the re-entry system.'

The empty stage was merely empty.

Isobel took his arm, swinging the frail charm like a censer.

'It's only a bauble,' O'Leary said. 'Sentimental value, only.'

'I know.'

At the barn door she waited to be kissed, of right. O'Leary bent to her, his sight blackening. The delicate flanges of cheek bone, impatience pulling a tension into her upper lip, the regard that was simply unblinking and unevasive – this was too great a gift to return.

'Look. At any time. This place, whatever . . .' He could not face it out, and even wished it unsaid.

'Sunday,' Isobel said. 'At four.'

The refusal of coyness, the choice of the surest and smallest of smiles, remained with O'Leary long after Miss Bernstein had gone – or Isobel as he preferred, at the moment, to think of her – in red and blue and, as he knew, in white and rose; and gold sustaining trial of the cupel and cement.

It remained with him while he changed into gumboots and went down through the orchard: dark facets, bright cambers and peace of a kind. And blue for a colour, and rose. All animals are sad at such a time.

The gumtree towered and seemed to loom, wheeling across the empty sky. Dark was well and truly down. The fire was not completely extinguished and a few wisps of smoke trailed

through branches. O'Leary was struck with a redolence that evaded, as the cold air smartened his flesh. He felt tired. He scattered grain before the hens in their long coop. Rain dribbled down the mesh of wires. The birds ate quickly with bright concentration, as the wind turned the ends of feathers in ruffs of gold.

Indoors again he righted his room and poured himself a drink. Objects took up their old positions with reluctance: things appeared to be different. The manual cautioned against undue haste: no steps should be omitted.

* * *

O'Leary resented the chill and the hard chairs. Having retained his topcoat he waited for the house lights to dim so that he might resume his gloves: he was delicate in company. There was nothing he could do for his ankles except cross them for companionship and in hope of warmth. The space required for this manoeuvre, however, was greater than the space provided: having crossed his ankles O'Leary found them locked in a position of extreme discomfort, jammed, in fact, through the back of the chair immediately in front of him.

'If you don't mind.' Lacking the warmth, her stare lacked nothing of the colour of burning acetylene.

'Forgive me. A thousand apologies, of course.' He had to use his hands to prise his shins and ankles apart: the attention this attracted was not kind. In a mood of some petulance O'Leary thrust his feet under the rungs of his chair.

The hall was not full but the vicar, from whom it had been rented, occupied a position of prominence before the stage curtain. His profession O'Leary identified from his collar:

his role of custodian was blind surmise. Equally a surmise was O'Leary's identification of a small man with a pointed beard as representative of the fourth estate: a reporter if not a critic. The fellow was scribbling full pelt and the show hadn't even started.

O'Leary could not wait: he drew on his gloves, and placed his hands in his armpits, the left in the right the right in the left, hugging himself without pleasure. The thought of Isobel in nothing more than a body-stocking froze his blood. He sucked a peppermint to disguise the whisky on his breath; it was all too easy to offend.

The programme spared no expense to be elegant; in the chastity of its typography it acknowledged the kindness of Mr G. O'Leary in making premises available for rehearsals and rendered, to Mrs Rebecca Bernstein, those thanks so fully due to one whose generous contribution alone made possible this et cetera and et cetera.

O'Leary deeply regretted it: the reference to himself, set down with such civility, was a disaster. Knowing what was to come he prepared his plea of not guilty, basing it on the argument that as the vicar had also made premises available he, the vicar, should also, in all logic, be charged as party to the commission of a public indecency. Justice demanded it. Mrs Bernstein, on the other hand, whatever she might think of being yoked with O'Leary as an active supporter of the players in this misguided venture, was truly in the gun: with sums great or little, with cash, including the copyright fee presumably, she had actually financed the bloody thing. Her daughter, this innocent girl your honour on my honour, actually played the vicious and debauched heroine of this wholly offensive play in total ignorance, could it be doubted?, of the blasphemy and filth she was

taught to parrot and the obscene actions she was taught to mime. How do you plead, Mrs Bernstein, wherever you are? Remember, before you speak, that it is not denied that this play was translated from the French: any mother anxious for the welfare of her daughter and only child might well have taken that as warning enough.

The vicar, more of a stayer than O'Leary would have believed from knowing nothing about him, left soon after the rise of the curtain on the third act. His departure involved a decidedly noisy shuffle along half the length of one row: his progress up the aisle was magnetic. By the time he reached the door he had a good twenty people in tow. His look threatened action.

Half way through the third act a uniformed sergeant of police climbed up on the stage and stopped the play. The representative of the press approached the sergeant with pad and pencil. The players stood about. Isobel, who after all had not worn a body-stocking, was wrapped in a grubby rug. A fierce argument broke out among a group of young people and a florid gentleman who had been close to the vicar: the young people appeared not to condone the police action. The florid gentleman offered a number of opinions on the class and intellectual competence of the young people, disparaging their appearance as his choler brightened. Several police constables entered the hall and proceeded down the aisles: the audience began to disperse.

O'Leary, who was not sure just what was going on in his mind – it was just now, through some trick of light and difficulty of breathing, a tabula smaragdina – pushed away the empty chair in front of him and crossed his ankles. He placed his hands in his armpits, as before, and lay back as

comfortably as the chair would allow. The police sergeant was speaking to the players. He was a burly man, perfectly cast for his role; and for a moment O'Leary wondered whether this was part of the play. A constable was taking notes, when told to. Of the reporter or critic there was now no sign. The question of refund of the price of admission, in whole or in part, had not been raised by the audience and seemed unlikely to be mentioned by the police. O'Leary calculated that he had received seven-eighths the value of his complimentary ticket.

O'Leary soon became a conspicuous figure: he was the only one seated. Indeed he was the only occupant of the rows of seats. What portion of the audience had remained was gathered at the back of the hall near the door. O'Leary was thus in excellent position to be observed by Isobel – a consideration he had not overlooked. Pale but proud, he thought, she let her eyes rest on him. O'Leary met it with a simultaneous pursing of the mouth and a drawing together of the eyebrows: intended as a grimace or mime whose meaning she should read as reassurance and support, it gave him a vaguely simian look.

O'Leary then withdrew his hands from his armpits and the gloves from his hands. By vigorously opposing his palms he produced a fusillade of applause, a series of rapid and loud reports. He continued this for a full fifteen seconds, sensing the moment when he would pass over into anticlimax or bathos. The sound was arresting. Police and players froze in surprise and the silence to the rear of O'Leary was broken by a babble as of distant geese. O'Leary resumed his gloves. The sergeant spoke to the constable: the stage emptied and the curtain came down.

'I'm afraid I must ask you to leave, sir. The performance has been discontinued.'

'You can say that again,' O'Leary said. 'I'm waiting for someone. The danger is surely past.'

'The danger, sir?'

'Of corruption, contamination, infestation; call it what you will. I am undebauched.'

'Orders are to clear the hall, sir. Now if you wouldn't mind moving.'

'Clear? It would be considered empty, by some.'

O'Leary shuffled sideways along the row, away from and not towards the constable. His passage up the aisle was noble, if less magnetic than that of the vicar: he walked alone. The persons in the porch, which he soon gained, evaded his eye. O'Leary stood among them easily: they were unremarkable: not one, he noted, was slavering with lust or outrage. Beyond the door, across the gravelled drive and the width of footpath, the police sergeant was holding the door of the Bentley as Isobel bundled in still wrapped in her rug. O'Leary thought he could reasonably assume it to be Mrs Bernstein at the wheel. He stepped clear of the porch and waved and, yes, Mrs Bernstein flashed him that acetylene blue stare with, perhaps, just the slightest diminution of confidence, the mildest increase in warmth. Isobel waved in reply; it was a semi-regal acknowledgement, really. She said something to her mother. Mrs Bernstein replied: her lips moved with energy: her plosives would be immense. The car hesitated in its slow forward movement while Mrs Bernstein leaned to look across to O'Leary. The police sergeant also looked. O'Leary continued to stand. It was at such moments that he wished he were a smoker: a cigarette or the action of lighting one could do so much to relieve situations such as this of their rigor. The car resumed its forward movement; its speed increased. O'Leary, in a style totally foreign to him, turned up

his coat collar. He passed before the police sergeant and up the street, giving a curt nod which the sergeant did not return.

He hadn't covered fifty yards, his numb feet paining, when the little man with the pointed beard caught him up.

'Hot foot from the news room?' O'Leary was affable.

'You applauded? I didn't see it, but they said you did.'

'I clapped,' O'Leary said. 'Yes. The intervals between are vital to an assessment of my intention. Slow means one thing; fast, another: you checked on the timing?'

'You were the only one, you know. The consensus of opinion was definitely in the opposite direction.'

O'Leary recognized that his companion was composing his piece as he walked.

'I am not an official,' O'Leary said. 'I don't feel committed to the official view.' It was deeply said and it pleased him.

'Would you like to express an opinion, give your name?'

'For publication?' They had reached the bus stop. O'Leary entered the bleak niche, glancing at his watch.

'Well, I can't promise.'

'I'd hardly meant to elicit a promise,' O'Leary said. 'No I think not: I'd miss my bus. Goodnight. Oh, by the way, it didn't occur to anyone that I might be applauding the action of the police?'

'No. Were you?'

'No. Fast clapping, though.'

O'Leary ascended the steps of the bus. He found his hands were trembling as he deposited coins.

'A cold night,' O'Leary said. 'The wind's bitter.'

The driver found nothing exceptionable in the remark: the bus pulled away.

* * *

The morning paper found a place for it, on the front page. O'Leary settled himself with toast and coffee.

POLICE CLOSE DOWN FIRST PERFORMANCE OF 'THE WOMAN FROM OMSK'
UNPARALLELED DEPRAVITY, SAYS VICAR

Last night's opening performance of 'The Woman from Omsk' came to an unplanned climax when police closed down the play some time before the final curtain.

The Reverend Kindleysides, Vicar of St. Jerome's in whose hall the play was being presented, described the play as unparalleled in its depravity.

It was a shocking comment on the corruption of so many of today's youth, the Vicar said, that such filth, blasphemy and straight-out sexual perversion could be so casually accepted as subjects for dramatic exploitation.

Referring to a golden inheritance from our rich, dramatic past the Reverend Kindleysides said he had been blatantly hoodwinked into believing the play to be unexceptionable, even though cast in the modern idiom.

PLAY TOO OFFENSIVE

Detective Inspector Farrant, speaking for the police, said investigations were proceeding but it was not yet determined whether further action would be taken.

Inspector Farrant denied that the police had acted on a complaint by the vicar. Action had been initiated by a member of the Special Branch who had been a member of the audience. The officer concerned deemed the play too offensive on several grounds and for that reason the play had been stopped. Police

monitoring of doubtful plays was common procedure in most countries, the Inspector remarked.

DRAMA HEAD SPEAKS

Dr Robert Love, Professor of Drama, said last night that although he had not read the text of the play, nor seen the performance in question, he believed the playwright, Vincent de Beauvais, enjoyed a considerable reputation. He was considered one of the foremost exponents of the so-called theatre of cruelty.

Professor Love pointed out that experiment was vital to the theatre. He thought the young people concerned were to be commended for their courage. Given the audience, however, the Professor said, and the venue of the performance, a less controversial play might have been a wiser choice. 'This is definitely not Paris or New York,' the Professor said, 'and we would do well to bear that in mind.'

The university library has no copy of the play.

A MODERN ALLEGORY, SAYS PRODUCER

Prime mover behind the Group, the company responsible for last night's interrupted performance of 'The Woman from Omsk' is Mr Robert Boyle.

Mr Boyle pointed out that the company had no university affiliations.

Miss Isobel Bernstein, who last night played the role of the infamous woman from whom the play takes its title, is a first-year drama student. This was her first appearance with a professional company, though she had previously acted in school plays.

Mr Boyle described the play as a modern allegory that has been acclaimed by critics in Paris and New York. The fact that the play had been banned in

London was hardly relevant, Mr Boyle said.

We live in a century of cruelty and horror, said Mr Boyle, and he hoped the reverend gentleman was not being hoodwinked over that.

Regardless of the outcome of the present 'brouhaha' as he called it, Mr Boyle intends to commence rehearsal, immediately, of another play – *Sister Maybelle*. Our drama critic writes about last night's performance on page 9.

The critic could wait; but the producer's intention of rehearsing another play, under, doubtless, the same difficulties as to premises, had O'Leary hoping. He went out into the barn without clearing away his dishes: he was almost running.

By two in the afternoon the stage had been dismantled and the barn restored to a more usual state of practical disorder. The tractor, jacked up and with the front wheel removed, stood in the space previously occupied by the stage. The stage lights were dismantled and stacked by the door. O'Leary's system of graded exercises stood him in good stead: he panted but was not disqualified by fatigue from finishing the job.

* * *

Time: 4 p.m. Day: Sunday. Weather: south-westerly squalls with hail; thunderstorms intermittent. Temperature: 52 degrees Fahrenheit. Humidity: 70 degrees. Position of Miss Isobel Bernstein on O'Leary's bed: axis NNE SSW, as near as dammit. O'Leary's position: SSW NNE, axis unstable and veering. Lighting up time: not given. Room temperature: 72 degrees Fahrenheit. Miss Bernstein's vital measurements:

34, 26, 36. For O'Leary: 7½ 8½ 10½ 16½; hat, gloves, shoes, shirt – none of which he was wearing.

Isobel Bernstein had been comforted: she felt herself also to have been befriended, to have been loved. She was pleased to be warm, as rain or hail rattled on the roof and the wood-fired stove pulsed. It was perfect weather for being indoors and naked in bed. Earth has no power without the moist.

O'Leary had moved off, to attend to the making of coffee.

Why in hell, it may be asked, was not O'Leary in bed and Isobel brewing up in whatever condition of dress or undress best suited her? O'Leary's answer: life was a calculated risk. He had given for the moment his all: the challenge of a persisting contiguity he knew to be sometimes excessive. It was also, though the relevance could be questioned, O'Leary's birthday: he kept it secret, as he also kept secret the fact that given a choice between water steam and earthly smoke he would have preferred an orchard blaze-up any day to standing around waiting for the bloody coffee to percolate. But, irritation apart, O'Leary enjoyed coffee as only he could make it; and Isobel Bernstein also. It was, in short, a Sunday like many others. Sometimes, some Sundays, the sun shone; at other times, on other Sundays, it rained; occasionally, on yet other Sundays, it was merely overcast. This was the weather of the orchard.

Isobel's distress, after last night's first-and-last-night fiasco, had not been great: her vanity had not been wounded. O'Leary admittedly had dried small tears and prescribed strong drink as a stimulant and, in its exact sense, a depressant. He had assuaged. Hand held and a flawless cheek smoothed – this had occupied a little time. Then with the liberty claimed and the comfort accepted he had bundled his miss into bed, where her eyes were soon dry.

Now they drank coffee together. Isobel sat up in bed and O'Leary, in only moderate comfort, perched on the edge. She was wearing O'Leary's gift, tenderly. The situation was wholly compromising to both, the moreso as the temperature of the room was not such as to require O'Leary's partner to cover herself for warmth.

They had reached, easily enough, just that stage of freedom in each other's company; throughout the protracted rehearsals and since. O'Leary suspected that he was the more enchanted, for the simple reason that Isobel offered enchantments he could scarcely match. As a gentle if somewhat dramatic lover he had done what he could to diminish the years between: he brought her forward while himself moving back. Isobel had developed: she offered the diagnosis herself. And this day O'Leary had felt free to read to youth a strong and silent lesson; free to revenge himself on a day of nativity. He was a little bored with his miss, although Isobel confessedly found the whole thing wonderful to the point of being fabulous.

O'Leary put down his cup and paid homage to splendours, not least his gift of gold on white. The supplicant was honoured and the woman from Omsk exorcised.

All animals are sad at such a time.

The acoustics of the barn, considered by O'Leary as being of medium quality only, tended to magnify all sound other than the human voice. Mice could be loud and starlings thunderous.

The knocking, therefore, separated them as abruptly as if shots had been fired – while they assured each other, in whispers, that all doors were bolted and curtains drawn. O'Leary supposed the plume of smoke might tell a tale but not, surely, of more than a general kind: he could have

slipped out for a minute. Nevertheless they lay quiet. The knocking continued intermittently.

O'Leary, having recently discarded his few garments, crawled on hands and knees to the farthest corner of the room. From here, by bringing his eyes just above the level of the sill, he could see under the curtain. His position commanded a view of the corner of the barn and the driveway, though not of the door itself. He crouched there. The knocking ceased. O'Leary crept back to the bed where Isobel was huddled deep, more in amusement than fright. O'Leary could not see what there was to titter at.

'Didn't you say you came by taxi?'

'Yes, why?'

'There's a Bentley in the drive.'

'Mummy.' Isobel giggled into a wad of bedclothes.

'Could she suspect you were here?'

'No, of course not. It must be something to do with last night. She asked about you in the car.'

'She's probably setting fire to the barn right now.'

'Oh, Gambo. You don't know Mummy. She'd feel she had to talk to someone – someone who understood.'

'Understood?'

'About modern plays.'

'That lets me out. I don't understand a bloody thing.'

'Yes, but you wouldn't be stuffy.'

'Thank you. Would your mother, then, be liberal in her view?'

'She'd try to be, probably. But that's why she came.'

'Let's hope. Fervently.'

O'Leary went more boldly to the curtain. The Bentley was wheeling away. Isobel joined him. They stood there as naked as candles.

'It could be another Bentley,' O'Leary said. 'I believe they make more than one of a model.'

'There'll be a note,' Isobel said. 'Through the flap in the door. Mummy would always come prepared for everything.'

'You frighten me,' O'Leary said. 'I think of a loaded pistol in the glove box: I think of a limpet mine fixed to the wall: I think of canisters of poison gas. Comfort me quick.'

'Let me go and see.'

O'Leary let her go, with all her vital numbers. There seemed to him to be far too much bare flesh about. Comparison could sometimes be too vivid: he put on a robe. Isobel sprinted amazingly back and flung herself into bed.

'Look, I've got goose flesh. It's like an ice-chamber out there. I couldn't find my way: I forgot you'd changed everything back.'

'No time bomb ticking? No trace of poison gas? You should have taken a canary with you.'

Isobel opened the pale blue envelope and extracted the folded note. Her fingers were quick and predatory.

'She wants to see you.'

O'Leary accepted it. Mrs Bernstein wrote upon plain notepaper in a firm hand. She would welcome an opportunity to speak about last night's debacle (accent and circumflex). Isobel had spoken of him, O'Leary, as being a theatrical person. If he, O'Leary, could name a time.

'Will you?' Isobel toyed with the nugget of gold.

'I doubt if we'd see eye to eye,' O'Leary said.

'You could say a word for me. She's mad about the whole thing – about its being me. And all that publicity. She wants me to get right out of drama school altogether. Right out. Or go away, somewhere, to study.'

'Go away?' Did his heart heave and the firmament blacken?

O'Leary considered it. 'The part, you know, was ambitious for a novice. It must be conceded. The critic, as I remember skimming, remarked that an ability to compass a role of that kind could only be actively deplored in an actress of such tender et cetera and et ceteras. He didn't, doubtless, put it so well.' O'Leary was preparing a speech for Mrs Bernstein.

'You're forgetting the physical presence,' Isobel crowed.

'Please,' O'Leary said. 'It was the topless drama bit that did it. Don't arouse the sleeping beast in me. Anyway, I can't speak for you. We have, remember, only the most remote of relationships. I do not, you will notice, smirk; but this would hardly be acceptable to your mum.'

His allusion, not at all obscure, was to intimacies; to a casual scatter of clothing and to distressing jubes of flesh; to obscured windows and locked doors; and to other things he could not entirely forget – discrepancies of the calendar for one.

'I'm merely the proprietor,' O'Leary said, 'of this place and its chattels.'

He was pleased to have said that.

'You are absurd,' Isobel said.

O'Leary accepted the remark as obscure in its reference.

'Gambo, can we have a drink? Can we have a whole lot to drink?'

'Moderation,' O'Leary said. 'The consequences of an excessive ingestion are described in the literature. Many a young woman has been undone down that road. And besides, it would be poor policy, positively unwise, to arrive home loaded at such a time. The air is charged with emotion; and the stuff doesn't encourage reticence.'

Isobel's free laughter, surprisingly mature in its tone, charmed and perplexed him as always. If he thought her a

girl or, at the farthest reach his mind could tolerate, a young woman, her laughter suggested that she had changed under his eyes. The processes of her thought, the way through to her bursts of amusement, were not always open to him: her mirth seemed at times to bear no relation to what he either said or implied. This occasion was not, however, an example of that: he knew what amused her.

O'Leary poured drinks: this was not a medicine of the third order and purification was not to be expected, now. Splendidly Isobel emerged and crossed to the stove to toast herself and turn deeper rose in its glow.

'Alcohol,' O'Leary said. 'A powder for painting the eyes, I believe.' He had found that a little pedantry could sometimes take the place of dangerous endearments; as Isobel simply showed him, in firelight, the perfection of her body and the pride of her youth. 'Junoesque' now seemed to O'Leary, seeing her like this, too solid a word. The gold gathered light. In the orchard it was dark. O'Leary toasted the toasting Isobel. Time: 6.10 p.m.

Superficially, he would have admitted, they seemed interchangeable. That is to say that often enough in his infrequent wanderings at the heart of the city he had picked from the file of flesh so tenderly observed many who matched and not a few who excelled his Isobel. Beauties were rare and Isobel was not such a one; but O'Leary could be bemused by less. In their wake O'Leary had wandered, having forgotten to strap himself to the mast. He had wished for that confidence, if not for that veneer – while their chatter appalled him.

Superficially interchangeable only, then. O'Leary fancied he saw Isobel's grace as glowing at greater depths – as now, when she was not boring him at all. She had for him so many

advantages over all the others: simply expressed this meant that she was, however tenuously, his. Dark facets, bright cambers, rose declivities; and that regard that was simply the most open and calm of looks. Not a pore out of place, bygod.

For himself, as said, he needed no mirror: he wore his personality like a disguise.

'Gambo, what if I became pregnant?'

'Good God,' O'Leary tossed his drink straight off. 'But you told me you took them. Do you mean you don't?'

'It's all right. I do. I was just thinking.'

'Abandon it,' O'Leary said. 'You have a frightening mind.' O'Leary poured a medium shot. 'Please don't indulge it. I'm old enough to be your father.' He could recognize vagueness, inconsequentiality, even obscurity – in himself. And he could wonder why she had raised the question, and be worried.

'You don't have to keep saying that,' Isobel said, turning the long scoop of her back to the warmth. 'What difference does it make?'

(How do you plead, O'Leary?)

'Some girls prefer older men, that's all.' She offered a pout.

'My dear girl, you do have your brevities. That's all, indeed.' He was distracted.

'Don't laugh at me.'

Could a woman be without guile, O'Leary wondered? 'Doesn't it occur to you,' he said, 'that my surely infrequent references to my age might have the purpose not of reminding you of differences but of eliciting your increased respect?'

'What? No.'

'It doesn't to me, either. Doesn't occur, I mean.' O'Leary put down his glass. 'I am a very foolish fond old man,'

O'Leary trembled. 'And skipping the next bit, pray undo me this button.'

'What button?' Isobel said, but moved from the fire.

The great barn magnified all sounds except the human voice; mice were loud and starlings thunderous. A moon showed somewhere. And they laughed.

* * *

The Mappae Clavicula recorded it: On mixing a pure and very strong wine with a third part of salt (xkok cum 111 qbsuf tbmkt – decoded by Berthelot), and heating it in vessels suitable for the purpose, an inflammable water is obtained which on ignition burns away consuming only itself.

O'Leary drank his whisky without ignition.

'You must forgive my hands, Mrs Bernstein.'

O'Leary displayed them. Knuckles were variously abrased and a strip of plaster concealed a wound.

'It's the tractor,' O'Leary said. 'The time of year for overhaul. The sap you see is down.'

'I have remarked, Mr O'Leary, that you alone had opportunity to observe. You alone, therefore, could warn.'

'Another?'

'Thank you. In this weather, without the ice I think.'

'Warned the Reverend XYZ? Kindleysides, it was.'

'Warned me, Mr O'Leary. Thank you.'

'I am here, they are through there.' O'Leary pointed to a wall. 'In my life I have been rather more recipient than donor – of warnings. Have I drowned it?'

'I am enjoying it. But you are a person of the theatre, Mr O'Leary. Or so I am told. This is not true?'

'Of antiquity,' O'Leary said. 'See me as Lear: see me as Bottom; see me as Caliban.'

'A brute,' said Mrs Bernstein.

'Precisely.'

'But the very language, to begin with – you could assess that.'

'Anglo Saxon in places: a translation. A profound history of usage is required to establish an obscenity. Blasphemy, on the other hand, has been described as the obverse of veneration. It too requires a history – a couple of millennia in this case. Correct me if I'm wrong.'

'I do not expect to see, well, breasts bared on stage.'

'With drama, Mrs Bernstein, that is surely of the essence.'

'I am speaking, forgive me, of my daughter's breasts. It is not propriety I am concerned with, Mr O'Leary; it is notoriety. I do not wish to see Isobel confused with the woman from Omsk.'

'In O'Leary's barn . . .' O'Leary said. 'No, let me put it another way: in what I sometimes overlooked but did not supervise – I ask you to remember that – there was no exposure of the person, the upper torso.' O'Leary lowered his eyes, in reverence – or in concealment, should his eyes be shining with the glory of his reminiscence.

'Had Isobel been your daughter, you would have permitted all this?'

'I am old enough to be her father.'

'Are you intending to flatter me, Mr O'Leary? I am her mother.'

'Another?'

'A small one. I am driving.' Mrs Bernstein stood up. She was a tall woman. 'Through there?'

'Yes, to your right.'

'Drinking one night in O'Leary's barn . . .' O'Leary sang soft and poured big drinks. The guest towel she would find immaculate and the soap Imperial Leather.

'Dear Mrs Bernstein, I must warn you. The play in which your daughter intends to perform, publicly, is blasphemous, scurrilous, obscene and indecent. Furthermore it involves exposure of the person. Intimacy is suggested and acts are performed on stage which a decent intelligence could only describe as sadistic, masochistic and phlogistic. Signed, a friend.'

'Isobel has spoken of you, Mr O'Leary.'

'I beg your pardon?' Was he, he wondered, being warned?

'You could have put your signature to it. You could have spoken.'

'Alcohol,' O'Leary said. 'A powder for painting the eyes, I believe.' He considered his glass. 'I am merely the proprietor of this absurdity and its chattels.'

'Have you the time?'

'Early,' O'Leary said. 'Approaching ten. Coffee?'

'Please. Black without sugar.'

'I had no picture of you, Mrs Bernstein. A warning of whatever kind could well have been wholly unacceptable. And on what basis was I to warn? As guardian of the public morality and the tender innocence of the young? Black, without sugar.'

'Oh, innocence.' Mrs Bernstein was impatient. 'Thank you, it smells delicious.'

'I pride myself on it,' O'Leary said. 'But two things are confused. If I could have predicted the unacceptability of the play, to that sort of audience, that is not to be read as a censuring of the play itself. I don't see how I could have spoken nor, reasonably, how you could expect it.'

'The theatre was your profession, Mr O'Leary?'

'Amateur,' O'Leary said. 'Whose derivation is love. Repertory, that was all.'

'Do you see Isobel, Mr O'Leary . . .' She paused. 'Do you see her as having a career in drama? An essential career? From what you know and have seen?'

What he had seen? Gold on white on rose: a nimbus of bright hair: an unction – that was the Isobel he had seen. He could concede the possibility of figmentation: sometimes Isobel looked quite plain.

'How could I comment?' O'Leary said. 'The part, you know, was an ambitious one for a novice to attempt. The critics allowed her a physical presence.'

'Oh I dare say she has that. But haven't a great many others, also? It's not so rare as to be a great distinction, surely?'

'She performed bravely, at best.'

'Boldly, at least. Thank you, only half a cup.'

'Mrs Bernstein, let me be frank. If you consider it an indiscretion, my having allowed the play to be rehearsed here, how am I to consider your having given financial assistance?'

'Call it ignorance, Mr O'Leary. Call it spoiling the child. There was no copy of the play in the library.'

'As financial backer you could have asked the producer to provide you with a copy.'

'It simply didn't occur to me, Mr O'Leary. I was unsuspecting.'

'Then the fact that there was no copy in the library is irrelevant.'

Mrs Bernstein chose to move about, circling O'Leary and the room. She moved with confidence. O'Leary poured

whisky into his coffee and drank; the brew was tepid and distasteful.

'You are a reader, Mr O'Leary. Have you been here long?'

'I bought the place years ago as an investment and made it my hobby, at week-ends and odd times, to bring it back into shape. It was derelict. I moved in, permanently, a few years ago. Happily I have a green thumb: I enjoy it.' He sensed that he was rambling. 'Mrs Bernstein, may I ask what it was you expected from your visit that I am, apparently, unable to provide?'

'I was curious, Mr O'Leary. Isobel prattles, about this place. Perhaps I'd hoped we might put our heads together, to deplore the play and the performance – that sort of thing can be such a luxury. Perhaps I was looking for an ally, an expert to reinforce my opinion and back my argument.'

'Your argument?'

'For getting Isobel out of the whole thing. Mr Bernstein, who had views, died when Isobel was very young. I over-indulge her.'

'I grant you your grounds, as a mother. That the shut-down of the play, the circumstances of it, distressed you, I can believe. That you deplore your daughter's involvement, even her daring, I can understand. I can't however see where I can assist. We deplore different things. Anyway the play is finished.' O'Leary drew breath.

'There's to be another. I have found a text for this one. I am alarmed.'

'You fear that I will provide space, again?'

'Well . . .'

'I am involved with spring,' O'Leary said. 'There isn't an inch of space they could use. If they're determined, however, that won't deter them: they'll find somewhere. So you see I

don't come into it, as one who could prohibit.'

Mrs Bernstein was examining the trinkets on the shelves, moving them slightly without displacing them. She appeared thoughtful, preparing to speak. O'Leary found himself under consideration for long seconds – there too a thin hauteur.

'If you should see Isobel again, Mr O'Leary, I take it you wouldn't support my view? You wouldn't, as a theatrical person, comment on the unsuitability of such parts for a girl of her years and inexperience – without condemning, that is, the plays themselves?'

'My place is not to be used, Mrs Bernstein: you've forgotten that.'

'No, I haven't forgotten.' Mrs Bernstein drew on black gloves. 'But I could suggest she talk it over with you. I could send her, for that.'

O'Leary, on that, could wonder whether he was being rather openly bribed? Impossible, surely?

'I hardly think my view would count,' O'Leary said. 'They see me as fearfully antique, a sort of relic of the splendid, stupid, conventional days. From what position would I speak?'

'You lent them space, Mr O'Leary. You helped them set up their stage. You stayed on, singly, to applaud.' Mrs Bernstein toured along the bookshelf. 'You bandaged Isobel's hand.'

'She wasn't quite bleeding to death.' O'Leary was jocular.

'And you are not a parent: you would speak with another voice.'

'It seems unlikely, Mrs Bernstein.'

'Have you read this play, Mr O'Leary. *Sister Maybelle*, the one they intend to rehearse?'

'I haven't; no.'

'I have. It concerns a rather pretentious strip-tease artist – I think that's the term. Apparently she is convinced that Christianity has staled or become too exclusive: I forget how she puts it. Anyway, she achieves a certain fame by stripping, as she says, for the Lord. Every garment discarded is a small prayer. She is also known as The Heavenly Body. Her G-string is called her God-string; it is composed of rosary beads. I gather that she is required, the actress portraying her is required, to do a strip-tease on stage. The beads are presumably to be shown. The taste is, at the least, questionable: the blasphemy I won't refer to.'

O'Leary laughed, tentatively. 'I'd like to read it. Is it in the library?'

'Oh, read it by all means. I will send you my copy. You'll find it, perhaps, amusing.'

'I take it you didn't?'

'That's not the point, Mr O'Leary. I am not a prude, in that sense.'

'The point is that you fear Isobel may consent to play Sister Maybelle?'

'A point hardly designed to further Mr Boyle's requests, as you may imagine. You still wouldn't be prepared to speak to Isobel?'

'Mrs Bernstein, there must be others better qualified – by family association, friendship and ties of that sort.'

'Those are rather disqualifications, in Isobel's mind, Mr O'Leary.'

'I see.' O'Leary considered it: did he in fact give a damn about Mrs Bernstein's feelings or Isobel's possible strip-tease? On the whole, yes; but he realized that Isobel could be stubborn.

'If I'm not to be put in the ridiculous position of approving

every play she is to act in, I must appeal to her discretion. Or to yours. I realize I have no right to ask for that; but I do. When her mind is mature enough to appreciate the nature of the decisions she makes, the implications, she may act in what she likes. At her present age I feel I have to accept the responsibilities.'

'I can appreciate your feelings – though the danger may not be as great as you fear. The question is whether the notoriety you foresee will be as distasteful to her as to you. She may indeed positively enjoy it. Might not the producer be encouraged, in some way, to take another direction and choose plays less embarrassing? Less embarrassing to you, I mean. Or might not Isobel be encouraged to introduce herself to another producer? Financial backing, forgive me, would be quite a bait.'

'You think she could be encouraged?'

'I? Well of course, how could I possibly know?'

'Will you think it over? The possibility, I mean, of your speaking to her? It's late: I must go. Thank you for the coffee, and the drinks.'

The sky was brilliant and frost was forming. There was nothing Mrs Bernstein could do about that: she would have to accept it on her expensive car, on her, doubtless, barbered lawns. O'Leary held the door as Mrs Bernstein swung creditable legs. It had been an inconclusive evening: the undertones were absurd. Isobel in a G-string of rosary beads?

How brilliant these modern playwrights were.

'I forgot to mention, Mr O'Leary, that I called last Sunday. Sometime around four. The place looked closed up, but there was smoke. I knocked. A discreet retirement seemed suggested.'

'My nap,' O'Leary said. Why was he mumbling? 'It's a routine, of a Sunday.'

'You must allow me to return your hospitality, Mr O'Leary.'

'Sometime, yes,' O'Leary said. 'It would be pleasant. Oh, by the way, I owe you an apology. For bruising you with my clumsy feet.'

'I didn't bruise, Mr O'Leary.' Amusement transfigured her – even her eyes joined in, acetylene blue. O'Leary reappraised the silken knees in the light of the dash lamp. It was natural that a pretty girl should have a handsome mother.

'Goodnight, Mr O'Leary.'

'Goodnight, Mrs Bernstein. Mind the road, it's appalling.'

O stars whose element is ether.

* * *

O'Leary was spraying the orchard. He wore protective clothing and an ugly mask. Great jets sprang out behind the tractor and drifted slowly. The day was still and the hour was almost four. He was not quite finished.

Isobel, who had arrived early, was standing before a tall open cupboard in O'Leary's quarters. The key had been in the lock but the cupboard had not been open when Isobel entered the room. There was nothing furtive in her exploration of the contents.

'I know I'm an awful snoop, but you aren't Mr O'Leary at all, are you?'

'Come out of it, there's a girl.'

Impurely deluged by hazardous elements, O'Leary was hastening into the shower. Total ablution required this state of skin.

'G. A. M. O'Brien M.P.S.' Isobel read.

The day was warmer: the room received natural light, and sunlight on a sill. O'Leary stepped into the shower and meticulously scrubbed. He discouraged Isobel from joining him. Which one of the simple bodies or their natural elements would consume him, he naturally pondered? Would O'Leary stand trial of the cupel and cement?

In slacks and bare chest O'Leary said, 'I am O'Leary.'

'Then all this . . . ?'

'I am O'Leary, by deed poll. Perfectly legal. As O'Brien, as you've fossicked, I was a sometime chemist, dispenser of unguents and pomades, elixirs and panaceas – antibiotics, mostly. Was. Shall we drink something? Gerald Aloysius Martin O'Brien which, with some inversion explains the nickname. My father in his pride had it engraved in gold letters on my first school bag: from then on it was unavoidable. I was not a clever student: O'Brien's pharmacy was a compromise: my father, a man of law, intended me for medicine and the Royal College. His patrimony, he would think, has been mis-spent here.'

'You never stop talking,' Isobel said. 'I don't mean I mind; but don't you ever think something and not say it?'

'My God,' O'Leary said. 'Of what are you accusing me?'

'I thought you were an actor.'

'Amateur,' O'Leary said. 'Whose derivation is love. Repertory, that was all: a passion.'

'Then why?' She showed among other things her confusion and headlong curiosity. 'I always thought there was something, some secret, I don't know why. Mummy said it was odd to find a man like you in a place like this.'

'And a girl like you, she'd doubtless think, too.'

Behind his eyes the years flooded their faded light. His

chest tightened and the room was void for a moment. He refused the past his indulgence.

'It makes no difference,' O'Leary said. 'Close the cupboard on the skeleton. There's actually one in there, I think – disarticulated, of course. And as you're wondering, let me tell you it was a small thing; but large enough, too. I am O'Leary by legal enactment. This isn't a TV serial. I am not a man on the run. I keep a small orchard and a great bloody troublesome barn.' Where mice could be loud and starlings thunderous. 'O'Leary's barn: O'Leary's orchard.'

'Oh Gambo.'

Her eyes were brimming. He did not, could not, relish a superficial impression. These were the tediums of his miss.

'Come here,' O'Leary said. 'Let me tell you about your mother's visit. Or has she told you, already? Lock the cupboard and put the key over there; it was never a secret I worked hard to keep. But I'm not sure I shouldn't smack your bottom, miss, all the same.' He relished the vulgarity, seriously; it was so superb.

'But what did happen, Gambo?' She was close, as requested.

'Decently, my Isobel, a reticence is required. I was somewhat naughty and was magisterially rebuked. I retired amid greenery: there was little else I could do, having had my fill of travel. I regret nothing but would be obliged if you could observe a certain silence for the sake, merely, of convenience. I am happy.'

'I am happy,' Isobel said. 'Gambo, I don't care what you did, I love you.'

'What I did, as you put it, wasn't such as to disqualify me entirely from the world's affection, or your love.' O'Leary was amused, as both overplayed their parts. 'You are a most

sweet and beautiful girl and I am an extremely favoured man. Now lie back and listen: I will tell you how the world is made. Once upon a time . . .'

* * *

The conditions vital to O'Leary's functions were these: A knowledge of the reason for each operation. A full understanding of the instructions. Avoidance of the profitless and impossible. A careful choice of time and season. Seclusion. Trusty friends. Patience and reticence. Perseverance. A determination not to be deceived by appearances into bringing operations to too hasty a conclusion.

But could he run the place or the project on those lines? Doubtful.

Agricola having discovered bismuth, O'Leary took some, with water. The drinking years had given him catarrh of the stomach: he feared for other organs, deeply.

What is witnessed from behind the silverings? O'Leary speculated on this as he shaved, pulling on his life, as he thought of it, like an old Burberry, simply to go down upon the town and revenge himself.

'Before you came,' O'Leary said, 'I lived alone like a hermit in bosky places, philosophically regretting nothing except perhaps the absence of trusty friends, choosing time and season for my operations of, now, a merely vegetable kind. What have you brought me, tell me? Bluebirds? Would the court care to consider my defence? Is it the overt nature of the flower – unfolded and tremulous – that rapes the bee?'

There was no answer: there was no one to answer. O'Leary was addressing his mottled reflection.

'That's my plea,' O'Leary said. 'Even my swan song. Hold still, you devil, you've got me into trouble enough already.'

He was shaving closely for his visit to Mrs Bernstein. His hand was trembling. He thought it natural.

O'Leary saw tumbling sward, pin-oak and pine, burning cannas and a distant gleam of sea. He was spruce in grey flannel of lately unfashionable cut and downright elated on a generous tipple of fine scotch. He stood in the porch and composed himself before ringing the bell. The button was illuminated: he pressed. He was aware of having overdone the aftershave while Isobel, glancing only casually to see that the coast was clear, kissed him on the mouth. She held on like a suction cup, as O'Leary struggled.

O'Leary followed her cheeky haunches and dabbed at his lips. He determined to lave his face at the earliest opportunity. To ask to be shown immediately to the lavatory would be gross. Mrs Bernstein would suspect his prostate, or imagine him to be of a nervous disposition, a diuretic if not an acolyte of the divine sprite herself. What Isobel would think O'Leary could not imagine.

Barometer, yes, falling in polished brass solid and seaworthy. Was the dead husband and father a blue-water man? Did callipygian Isobel take for granted these fathoms of white pile? How happy he was in her wake over wall to wall floors.

'Mummy, Mr O'Leary is here.'

'Good evening, Mr O'Leary. I am pleased you could come.'

'It was kind of you to ask.'

They passed from white to blue, silently: there seemed no end.

'What will you drink, Mr O'Leary?'

'Scotch, if I may. I'd a little for Dutch courage before coming away.' O'Leary was aware that he had probably had enough. He wondered whether he would ever be Gambo to her or she Becky or Rebecca to him. It seemed remote, he to her Hecuba.

'Dutch courage? Mr O'Leary you make us sound a veritable nest of Gorgons.'

It wasn't bad: he must try to match it. The ball was in his court.

'The journey,' O'Leary said. 'I meant, of course, the journey. To tell the truth I go out so little that the operations of the public transport system are as great a mystery to me as the Dead Sea Scrolls.'

Did she get it? Yes. Another subscriber to the Readers' Digest.

'Yes, ice please,' O'Leary said. 'And water.' He was at ease now, accepting the weighty glass. 'Do you know, on a morning's venture recently, intending no further than the public library, I found myself wading waist deep in cows, in dairy country, and dark coming down.' He warned himself to drink slowly: he wasn't as much at ease as all that.

Mrs Bernstein put her head at an angle to receive his foolish banter. Considered décolletage, wide eyes neutral at present (he wasn't kicking), a large mouth painted a dark black-red. Time very properly at bay or riding the billow; and the pressure falling. Effluvium waning? O'Leary secretly sniffed.

'Isobel would happily have called for you, Mr O'Leary.'

'Right round the bay? It's miles.'

'If it's not too far for one purpose, it's not too far for another.'

Aghast, O'Leary struggled to organize a perplexed smile. 'I'm not sure I follow, Mrs Bernstein.'

'Why, if it wasn't too far for rehearsals it can't be too far to fetch a guest.'

O'Leary was not reassured: more than the low table and the tray of drinks lay between them.

'A pleasant room,' O'Leary said. 'There's a distinction in the touch. And you've a prospect.' He just nodded to the windows.

Mrs Bernstein's look went out across the severely formal room. O'Leary, following, took in the dark loom of trees, heard shrill sparrows, saw the final declension of westward light – the prospect through another's eyes.

'Tell me, Mr O'Leary, you've kept up your resolve? Isobel, you may have sherry.'

'My resolve? I'm sorry . . .' Which one, bygod? This woman's ambiguities were unsettling to O'Leary.

'Are you a man of so many resolutions, Mr O'Leary? I meant your decision about rehearsals; about your barn.'

To O'Leary's ear, hypercritical at this time, it bore its suggestion that he lived in squalor and slept among manure and broken crates. Was he too hypercritical? Could he be?

'The seasons dictate,' he said with care. 'The place is increasingly cluttered as we advance into summer. There's simply no room, as I think I said.'

'You did,' Mrs Bernstein said. 'Did you read the play I sent?'

'Yes. Yes, I did. I'd meant to bring it with me: I'll post it back.'

'Don't bother. Isobel could pick it up, sometime when she's out that way. Help yourself, please. What was your opinion?'

'An excellent whisky,' O'Leary said.

Isobel passed the ice bucket: O'Leary kept his head down.

'I was, well, what . . . ?' O'Leary was forcing himself hard upstream. 'Amused? No that's hardly the word. Let's say it was all a bit like the bishop slipping on a banana skin, dignity in absurdity, that sort of thing. Certainly it stones glasshouses; but I can't see it as important. Oh I chuckled, yes. It's brilliantly witty – like a fire in a fireworks factory. Too much so.'

It was tediously said: he had rehearsed it and was pleased to be done.

'Can you conceive of it as being actually playable? Can you see it on the stage?'

O'Leary raised his head then and looked once at the mother and once, more obliquely, at the daughter. He wrinkled the skin of his forehead: he was pondering his answer.

'No,' O'Leary said, and falsely laughed for his conceptions. 'I can't. Not in the ordinary sense. The costume, for one thing. Perhaps a private performance – I can't say.'

'What costume?' Isobel said. 'What play?' Although she knew.

O'Leary returned to the contemplation of his glass.

'A play,' Mrs Bernstein said, 'requiring total nudity on stage, except for a string of beads – rosary beads.'

'Oh, *Sister Maybelle*,' Isobel said.

O'Leary, aware that Isobel had read the play while stretched more nude than Maybelle in the sun of O'Leary's orchard, thought it dangerous ground. Nudity seemed to be all the play contained, for Mrs Bernstein; but he could understand that, given the possibilities.

'I wasn't aware you'd read the play,' Mrs Bernstein said.

'Oh, somewhere,' Isobel said. 'I forget who passed it on.'

'And you can see yourself as Sister Maybelle, on stage in nothing more than a string of beads?'

'What?' Isobel's surprise was explosive. 'Oh Mummy, what an idea.' She pealed merrily.

'Well, thank God for that.' Mrs Bernstein rose sheathed and serious. 'You'll admit there were recently reasons for thinking you might. Mr O'Leary, if you'll excuse me, I must go through to the kitchen for a moment. Isobel will entertain you.'

The door closed behind her. O'Leary sloshed whisky into his glass.

'Phew,' O'Leary said.

'Mummy doesn't like being teased, so I tease her.' Isobel filled and drained her sherry glass twice in quick succession. This left her with an empty glass which she filled and placed on the table. 'What do you think of Mummy?'

'Flabbergasting,' O'Leary said. 'Terrifying, on home ground. We mustn't underestimate her intelligence: she knows more than she's saying.'

'She likes that, to be severe. It's her sense of humour, she says.'

'Has she a sense of humour?' He remembered she had: she didn't bruise.

O'Leary considered a vase of great beauty placed to one side of the mantel: the white porcelain threw a soft bellying shadow on the wall. The belly of the vase itself was reflected in a muted mirror: the lighting was masterful.

'Nevertheless,' O'Leary said, 'sense of humour or no, I think we had better take a little more care.'

'Care, Mr O'Leary? Care of what? I missed it.'

O'Leary experienced the rictus of pure surprise. Mrs Bernstein's moments were precisely calculated.

'Care? Did I say care?' His muscles were slow to relax. 'Oh, care of the parts, of course,' O'Leary said. 'The parts that are chosen. For one, I mean, as an actress, a player. Or that one chooses. Notoriety not being the same thing as a solid reputation. You know the sort of thing I mean.' Was he blind drunk? Was he totally incapacitated by ethyl vapours? He summoned a smile, with God knows what result. Isobel was positively staring at him.

Mrs Bernstein let silence hang as she finished her drink.

'If you are ready, Mr O'Leary, we can go through to dinner. Finish your sherry Isobel.'

'Might I just brush up?' His legs, after all, supported him.

'Of course. Isobel will show you.' She turned to the mantel to make a minute adjustment to the white vase, as though aware his appreciation had sullied it. Her profile was mirrored, her back unrelenting.

In the bathroom another mirror revealed to O'Leary the traces of lipstick his handkerchief had missed. He stared upon it then laved his face. It was unlikely that Mrs Bernstein would assume that he had passionately embraced a woman on the public transport: such encounters were rare, and such assumptions moreso.

O'Leary let the cold water tap run: he had decided on a quick snoop. It was what she smelled of, this soap; it was what her mouth sometimes tasted of, this toothpaste; with this she sprayed her hair.

For what was Mrs Bernstein taking tablets Evipot, Neonacex, Polaramine, Urolucosil, Mycostatin, Floraquin? The syndrome was vast in its inclusions. The packet of oral contraceptives bore no user's name. Mrs Bernstein, surely? Isobel would hardly be so bold. O'Leary continued his evaluation of the weapons for a war that would never be won.

Arrid underarms and Murine eyes, a Selsun scalp, depilatory for legs and thighs. It appeared that both mother and daughter were addicts of every known uncertain cure for established comforts including conception, perception, the process of age and hormonal imbalance. The eye, the ear, the mouth, the nose – all orifices were catered for, a secular do-it-yourself extreme-unction kit. Irritation, inflammation, wakefulness and narcolepsy – all again were catered for: O'Leary searched wildly for the anti-mortality pill. He hoped he was not going to faint – not here of all places. Was this his simple world of gold and beauty? Oil of Ulan. Olé!

Mirrors were clouded and walls just perceptibly moist: someone had recently bathed or showered. It was so intimate a place O'Leary could excuse his slightly lewd curiosity. Who in the world was hooked on Xylocaine viscous?

A latent puritanism was outraged in O'Leary; and time was running short. These were things O'Leary wished not to acknowledge – the imperfections, even of Isobel. Beauty was hard won; and regularity. He felt cold and mournfully considered his broken capillaries. He switched off the merciless tube of light over the mirror (how could they?) and turned off the tap. The rose dimness was consoling. The price of beauty plus the price of the concept of beauty: he would think of that. He was exhausted by his ablutions: he used the towel with care. He emerged in panic.

Isobel was by the door. O'Leary laid his hand flat at the vertex of her belly, the mere hypogastrium, and summoned all his strength. His palm was lifeless, his mind engaged: he said a prayer for Dalton and all his band. He had forgotten too much of what little he knew.

Isobel walked free of his gentle, lifeless hand. She was as cool as paint.

'Why didn't you tell me I'd your precocious war-paint all over my face?' O'Leary whispered it violently. 'She can't have failed to notice.'

'No,' Isobel said. 'She can't, can she? The dining room is through here. Mummy is waiting. You smell nice.'

'I feel awful,' O'Leary said. 'Dying. Something I drank.'

They passed from blue to gold, silently: there seemed no end.

* * *

'What did you do when I went to bed? When I was sent to bed, I mean. I was so mad. Mummy treats me like a schoolgirl.'

'Well, it's only so very recently she's had occasion not to. Come here.'

Could he ask her, he wondered, to dress for him in school uniform? It had long been a fantastic wish; it would entrance him. But how suggest it? This wasn't the moment: she would think him strange.

'What did you talk about?' Being closer she could speak more softly.

'I drank a little brandy for my stomach's sake, and went home. Was driven home. Do you know how your mother drives? Of course, you must. Wrists like iron and no nerves at all, simply daring the poor devils not to give way. Racing changes, heel and toe, good Lord.' He would keep his fantasies in their proper place. 'Did you think we perhaps struggled together in mortal tussle on the blue Wilton or whatever?'

'That's not funny, Gambo. What did you talk about?'

'I was some way past the masterly coherence: I was not

at ease, at first. Where, by the way, do you keep your supply of the pill?'

'In the medicine cabinet, in the bathroom. Did you look?'

'Good God,' O'Leary said. 'You can be that open?'

'Mummy doesn't mind. She says it's reassuring.'

'Pass that glass, do you mind? You're nearest. I feel weak. I'll never understand your mother – perhaps I'll never understand you, either. Do you mean she approves?'

'Of you?'

'God's mouth, I hope not. I mean I hope the question doesn't arise. You haven't by any chance confessed?'

'She might guess,' Isobel said.

'After your lipstick, she might indeed.'

'She knows there's someone. She expected there to be.'

'Behold,' O'Leary said, 'the bemused victim of a mother's expectations. What sort of a world have we put on?'

'I can keep secrets,' Isobel said.

'Are you getting right into bed?' O'Leary was nervous.

'Do you mind?' Isobel was not nervous. 'What did you talk about?'

'The pure filth of modern drama. About which she displayed a tolerance, short of wanting to see you bare on stage. We spoke, too, of girls and their circumstance in this modern age. We touched on the fabric of life, if I remember, its flaws and perforations. Do you want something to drink?'

'All right.'

'We reached, I might say, a profound understanding – while drinking cognac one for one.'

'Thanks. You mean Mummy drank too much? Gambo, come and sit here.'

'Let me finish my paean, first. Your mother, to continue, drank an amount exactly consonant with her capacity to

hold it like a grande dame. I, as is my habit, fairly wallowed.' O'Leary began to wander about the room. 'Then together, windblown and lapped in luxury, we belted through the starlight to O'Leary's O. Where she dumped me.'

O'Leary sat on the bed; it was never a comfortable position and often a distracting one.

'Didn't she come in?' Isobel's mind was quite capable of attending to more than one thing at a time.

'To this anticlimax? Sweet child, for what do you take me? I knelt by the roadside and licked the dust of the district off her tyres. Her condescension demanded it.'

'She isn't condescending.' Isobel was warm. 'She's just rather cold. She takes a long time to get to know people. That's what she says.'

'I may tell you I revolved here an hour in O'Leary's dark navel making my comparisons and my mea culpas. These humble quarters and the four-square castle of the merchant prince, if you follow.'

'This is all right, Gambo. What's wrong with it? You don't need those other things. I love it here. I always have: I always will.'

'Need was never the point. But no, you're right. I haven't really told you what we talked about, you know. She told me you were leaving: she told me you were booked. She's persuaded you to go.'

'Oh, Gambo.' It was a wail. 'Why? I was going to tell you: I just wanted to wait until the right time. I'm sorry. I wanted to tell you myself.'

O'Leary involuntarily yawned. There seemed to be too little air. He crossed to a window and flung it open upon a sweet profusion of blossom, upon the great cadence of the orchard. He felt saddened.

'A matter of weeks, or a month or two at most,' O'Leary said. 'Don't let's consider it now. Come and inspect the glory of my place, the reach of O'Leary's acres. Smell the air? God's mouth,' O'Leary said, 'you're bitter flesh, you young.'

Had fact and fantasy inextricably merged? Dark facets, bright cambers and peace of a kind – could these be enough? O'Leary picked at his watch-strap.

In the simplicity of her flesh Isobel came to the window to inhale the simple mystery. She could smell blossom and damp earth. There were crickets and a felicitous movement of fruitful branches: so much O'Leary knew.

'I'm sorry, Gambo.'

For both it was for more than themselves, this reach of O'Leary's orchard, this place, this melancholy.

'Don't let's consider it now,' O'Leary said. 'There is a time for everything, a time to embrace and a time to refrain from embracing. What time is it, anyway? Are you rushing?'

'No.'

Light thudded and facets brightened: birds came flying under the eaves.

'Then not another word,' O'Leary said, in humour again. 'The password is Rhazes, I imagine.'

'What password?'

'Nothing. I was thinking.'

But behind his smile, in deep self-pity, he sensed frozen tundras and cold northern lights. He would not consider it now. Autumn was behind him; and ahead spring and summer were upon him; then autumn again. It were better to inhale deeply and close the sash; it were better not to consider it now. There were weeks, even months perhaps. She would leave in the summer if things went to plan.

There remained the reaches between them, corners which

neither could invade, subjects not to be broached and silences to be kept: they were not many but they were there. She could move with more freedom in O'Leary's world than he in hers. Her life beyond the orchard was closed to him: questions elicited very little of it; she was not a talkative young woman (he had once been grateful), and how could the great belch of his memory serve her? If he talked more it was to say less: his ribald monologue excused them both from anything approaching a conversation. She tended to the monosyllabic: if she was truthful she didn't care for elucidations and refinements. Impatience, O'Leary wondered? Or a certain intellectual dullness? He wouldn't care to say.

O'Leary had said it once and he'd say it again: he detested sentimentality. He just couldn't handle it. He thought of himself as a man behind a shield. Because the shield was so small he had to be quick in his use of it. Sometimes he was too quick, too suspicious; but that was how it was. Sylphs, salamanders, gnomes and ondines might pray for him; but to whom? Gold was his colour – citrine, ponderous, mute, fulgid – his substance. He wished it were his gift. All the compound bodies are composed of all the simple bodies, he reminded himself. Seek ye knowledge even to China. Every simple body is found specially and most abundantly in its own place.

As a credo it did not help. Least of all with Miss Bernstein, who was calling.

'Gambo, leave the window. It's lovely. No one will come.'

Gambo left the window, after one long look. Time, season and seclusion commanded him. He knew the reason for this operation and appearances did not deceive. He would not be deceived into haste.

* * *

'What would it prove?' O'Leary said. 'That you are stronger? That your youthful vigour is superior to my elderly decrepitude? I concede it, without trial.'

'It would give me a bloody great satisfaction,' Robert Boyle said.

'I thought you'd already enjoyed that, in your conversation with her mother.'

'In blowing the gaff on you? Yes, I took pleasure in that.'

'I can understand it,' O'Leary said. 'But you mustn't be greedy for sensations of that order. How was I to know you'd been thrown over? And what would it have meant, had I known? Doesn't the stage satisfy your instinct for drama?'

'I'm asking you, will you lay off?'

'Discontinue a friendship under threat, do you mean? No, Mr Boyle, I most certainly will not.'

O'Leary found himself on the floor: his Canadian exercises and his vitamin pills had not helped: his reflexes had never been fast. Blood was issuing copiously from his nose. Presently the numbness passed and his nose and face began to pain him. Mr Robert Boyle had gone, taking his satisfaction with him: the open door supported the assumption.

O'Leary, in this position, was succoured by Mrs Bernstein. She entered and bent over him. She had tried the barn door and had come round the path to the back of the barn. Her fashionable shoes were muddy: he was placed to observe it.

'Are you hurt?'

'Not,' O'Leary said, 'as badly as you are perhaps hoping. My nose is bloodied, the claret flows; a lip feels split. Did you, by any chance, order the execution?'

'What would be the reason, Mr O'Leary? Even if I had the power?'

'I think you know,' O'Leary said, keeping his face averted.

'Isobel?'

'In a word, Isobel.'

'Mr O'Leary, if I had been going to act on that I would hardly have waited until now. I have known about it for a long time. Since the night you came to dinner, you might have supposed. In fact, much earlier.'

'Excuse me,' O'Leary said. 'If you would wait a moment.'

Trails of blood stained the water in the white handbasin. Once again he held his face down and held his breath. The bleeding had stopped and the damage to his lip was not great: his nose was swollen or swelling. O'Leary bathed his face and tidied himself.

'It isn't possible,' Mrs Bernstein said, examining the damage, 'it isn't possible, in a place like this, to keep things secret for long. Not, least of all, when the young woman comes in daylight in a rather identifiable car. There were, after all, so many motives the world might have for letting me know; and so many motives I might have, for enquiring. One motive has just been displayed, Mr O'Leary.'

'Oh, vigorously,' O'Leary could look at her now. 'By Mr Robert Boyle who felt jilted. Not an effeminate man: I feel he was vindicating his profession as much as displaying a blunt jealousy.'

'I met him in the driveway,' Mrs Bernstein said. 'It was pure coincidence. He was running. It did cross my mind that he might have murdered you: though that would have been excessive. I knew his interest in Isobel: I also knew yours. I thought it best to see if I could find another entrance. As it turns out, my fears were groundless: you will sting, Mr O'Leary, but you will live.'

'Don't go,' O'Leary said. 'Unless you must. I could use a drink. Have you time to join me?'

'Thank you, yes. I'm in no immediate hurry.'

'You were coming here, anyway, it would seem.'

Remembering his visit to Mrs Bernstein, O'Leary took pains in setting out glass and ice and water; he did not own a decanter.

'I was coming here, yes. But not, I suggest, for the reason you have in mind, Mr O'Leary. Yes, ice please, in this weather. It's charming among your trees at this time.'

'The best is over,' O'Leary said. 'I've never known a more superb blossoming.'

'I don't doubt it, Mr O'Leary.' Mrs Bernstein drew it out: she could be dry.

A toast would have been vulgar: they drank.

'I came, Mr O'Leary, because Isobel's departure is getting close. Specifically I wanted to be sure that you had not been working to discourage that; to be reassured that you will not. With things rather in the open now, I felt it was a question I might ask. Is it?'

'Yes,' O'Leary said. 'All things considered, it is. I have not discouraged: I shall not. Her going is accepted; it isn't thought plans should be, or could be, changed.'

'By her, or by you?'

'If I can speak for her, then by both.'

'I am sure you can speak for her, Mr O'Leary. It was, if you remember, my reason for asking you, earlier, to discourage her from unsuitable parts. I accept the reassurance.' Mrs Bernstein looked out upon the orchard and seemed prepared to be silent.

O'Leary palped the swollen flesh of his nose: the septum felt torn. The whisky stung his lip and he welcomed it for the asepsis that was in it.

'You don't wish to say more?' O'Leary said.

'Do you, Mr O'Leary?'

'If you've suspected, Mrs Bernstein – if you've known all this time . . . ? I wonder would it have been different had I known you knew?'

'Oh, doubtless, Mr O'Leary. It may even have been essential that you should think I didn't. Secrecy contributes its portion, I believe.'

'Then why . . . ?'

'Why consent to, why condone, such an unusual relationship? Except that it isn't all that unusual, surely? For one thing, Mr O'Leary, Isobel is of an age for agreement or consent. However barely. There was no case I could bring, however undesirable I might have thought the whole affair.' She let him see that she could make her own distinctions. 'Not quite so much whisky please. Thank you.'

O'Leary moved to the window but kept his back to the light. Mrs Bernstein swung to face him. He felt no sense of intimidation, no awe. She was a pleasant-looking woman with a generous mouth.

'You thought,' Mrs Bernstein said, 'you even perhaps hoped, at first, that she was under age. When it began, I mean. You know she is not; but it may amuse you to continue the fiction. There are men like that: we live in the world.' She waited but O'Leary did not answer. 'Isobel was a precocious child: she is a precocious young woman. There are reasons, the usual ones, and there's no point in going into them. She will have told you.'

'Something,' O'Leary said. 'Yes, she has told me.' It was a story that did not honour the dead: he could, in such cases, find a tact.

'So I simply saw a choice between the young and possibly irresponsible, and an older man for whom she appeared to

have, forgive me, a strange, even a wayward affection. I did not go so far as to encourage, nor to prohibit. It did occur to me that the choice might not in fact be made – she could have, that's to say, chosen both. But I thought not. My illusions about Isobel are nil: my objectivity might be thought monstrous, by some.'

'I was to be used,' O'Leary said. 'A responsible safety-valve, until you could pack her off. You inferred impermanence, and trusted to a probable discretion?' O'Leary was enjoying it; it was something he missed – conversation.

'Mr O'Leary, I'm going to shock you. At the beginning I had Isobel watched – oh, very discreetly and privately. The hours of rehearsal were extending; and there were other signs. I am a woman as well as a mother. As soon as I had my confirmations, the watching ceased.'

'You had your proof,' O'Leary said. 'And then?'

'Then it was either act, or do not act. There were precedents to assist me: I could consult those. Although I confess I most actively resented your being smeared with her lipstick, in my house.'

'I owe you an apology, Mrs Bernstein. Another?'

'Perhaps not. I am, after all, driving.'

'Nonsense. Your driving that night was impeccable.'

'You are reminding me that I drank more on that occasion? That's not gracious of you, Mr O'Leary. Thank you, then.'

'You spoke of precedents, Mrs Bernstein. I don't follow.'

Their positions were reversed. Mrs Bernstein received sunlight on head and shoulders. O'Leary sat at the table.

'It was my intention simply to ask you for your reassurance, and leave. I didn't anticipate this.'

'Nevertheless,' O'Leary said. 'Since you are here . . .'

'The point is a simple one: I sometimes see myself as mirrored in my daughter. Not in appearance, or not absolutely. I didn't quite have – what shall I call it? – the physical confidence.'

O'Leary murmured: they were sounds, not words.

'I don't wish to embarrass you.' Mrs Bernstein turned away, looking over the orchard. 'I even, you see, at her age had the same problems, if they are problems. Yes, they are. Perhaps we inherit them: perhaps they are passed down, from mother to daughter – especially if there's only one.'

'One mother; or one of each; or one problem for each one?' O'Leary felt need of light relief. If Mrs Bernstein smiled he could not see it: she kept her face from him.

'At least if they are common problems, I couldn't know. I felt mine to be intense. Then I met an older man.'

'Ah,' O'Leary drew it out. 'I begin, at least, to see the boldness.'

'I wonder,' Mrs Bernstein said.

O'Leary wished she would face into the room: he was having difficulty in following her. His hearing, like his reflexes, was not perfect.

'I was just the age Isobel is now.' She granted him his wish. 'I was infatuated: I was flattered.' Mrs Bernstein made a gesture that, given her composure, was almost theatrical. 'Oh, I can't pretend to look back on it with any sort of yearning, please believe that.'

'Surely from where I sit I should prefer that you could.'

'Be reassured, Mr O'Leary: I don't see him as the evil seducer, either. To tell the truth he wasn't at all attractive or even especially intelligent. But he was kind, and tender. And he did care for me without hurting me, without asking for or expecting things in return that I couldn't have given –

things I couldn't have possessed at that age.'

'What things are these then?' O'Leary was alert.

'I'm not sure. Not love, anyway. I was no more ready for that, capable of that, than Isobel is now. I didn't possess that. I was a selfish little bitch, really; and I suppose I used him in the most selfish way.'

'I am following the lesson,' O'Leary said. 'And?'

'It ran its course, and that was that. I wasn't heart-broken. I didn't even particularly mind: there were other things to take its place. I imagine I had regrets of some kind: I can't remember. I missed the flattery, I know.'

'I wonder,' O'Leary said, 'are you discovering similarities or imposing them? The experience was such that you now feel no young girl should be without it? But it depends on the man, surely? Or doesn't that matter?'

'I didn't send her to you, Mr O'Leary. I didn't invent you or the circumstances. The situation had reached a point before I moved to find out just what it was. I even had the poor taste, as you may think it, to find out a little about you.'

'Not quite wanting to deliver your child into the hands of an actual or potential sexual phsychopath?'

'From "O'Brien" to "O'Leary" – you didn't change far. Is one to detect a national loyalty?'

'A national disease. You do indeed take precautions. Isobel, of course, knows this. I didn't tell her; she discovered. I thought my past might have been a burden – all except the amateur dramatics.' O'Leary opened his palms. 'I have my role, then: you've cast me.'

'If it were that simple, Mr O'Leary, I wouldn't be saying all this; it isn't necessary that you know so much. I simply feel that she has experienced something: she is changed. At least I fancy I can see it.'

'You've a sophisticated approach, Mrs Bernstein. I hadn't seen O'Leary's orchard as a finishing school for precocious beauties. Will you mind if I get out of step and have another?' Something was paining O'Leary. His face? His lip? He gently explored.

'You haven't enjoyed it, Mr O'Leary?' The stare was that blue, the mouth sardonic.

'Do you know,' O'Leary said, 'you have shocked me.'

'Ah then . . .'

'And I'm wondering, in purest vanity, how at your age she'll see me? Not particularly attractive or intelligent? Or rather, I'm refusing to wonder. That would be the final irrelevance, for me.'

'He wasn't Mr O'Leary.' An open statement, a droll one.

'And neither will I be, sneaking back from the shadows all those years hence.'

'Regret is a simple thing, Mr O'Leary; it only requires that you indulge it.'

'Suppose she hadn't been willing? Willing to go, I mean?'

Mrs Bernstein shook her head, pleasantly confident.

'You've missed the point, Mr O'Leary. I didn't dictate the move: I merely provided the money. She is genuinely excited at the prospect: she was from the very first. She loves spending money on herself: she loves expensive things, expensive clothes.'

'May and December.' It was O'Leary's turn to be droll. 'An old man's fondness, a young girl's infatuation. We move to the novelette, of course. You wish me not to write?'

Mrs Bernstein shrugged; it was sufficient movement.

'Love and kisses,' O'Leary said. 'X marks my room.'

'I must go,' Mrs Bernstein said. 'What time is it?'

'After four; indeed well after perhaps. My watch has stopped.'

O'Leary walked with Mrs Bernstein to her car: the distance was not great. He held the door: the metal handle was hot.

'You've had your plans,' O'Leary said. 'And your fulfilments.'

'One last thing, Mr O'Leary. I know I shouldn't say it – I've already said far too much – but tell me, what do you see in her? Is it because I am her mother that there are qualities hidden from me? Oh, she's a pretty thing, but well . . . I can't for the life of me see it.'

It would be the wrong moment to reply: a body, an appetite, a charmed and uncritical audience, a mind that could take an impression, a passion.

'Youth and beauty,' O'Leary said. 'Both barrels; it never misses. But I'm pleased for her: I mean that in various ways. You might tell her that.'

'I, Mr O'Leary? Oh I shall tell her nothing. You are the one to speak. Oh no. You see I haven't interfered: I've indulged her. That's all the point. I shan't mention my visit; and Mr Boyle can no doubt be persuaded to be discreet. It's all entirely over to you, Mr O'Leary.'

'To make as pleasant an ending as possible.'

'Mr O'Leary, from what I know, from what I have found out, an ending is the only possibility. I give you credit for having enough intelligence to see that: you would hardly wish to make the same mistake, twice.'

'The cases are different, at least.'

'The girl is older. I don't wish to say any more.'

'I hope we will not completely lose touch, after Isobel is gone.'

'Tell me, Mr O'Leary, shall you mind so much?'

'No,' O'Leary said. 'A little more than she will because I

won't have that immediate distraction – a clever stroke on your part – but not so much. I think I'm not of a deeply emotional nature, not sentimental I mean. Though, like yourself, I fancy I'm capable of certain regrets.'

'I should hope so,' Mrs Bernstein said. She was laughing. 'Goodbye then, Mr O'Leary.'

'Might I phone, sometime?'

'Of course. You'll find me in the phone book.' She paused. 'The woman from Omsk: the real one.' She enjoyed her joke immensely, as she eased away.

O'Leary was not pleased. He had meant to get her opinion on a question that was troubling him.

'Is it, Mrs Bernstein . . . ?' he questioned the air. 'Is it the overt nature of the flower – open, tremulous – that rapes the bee? Would you care to comment? Is that your answer, Mrs Bernstein, this sexy growling and this rattling gravel? Very well, I will say no more.'

O'Leary was tipsy on something: he also felt he was cheating someone. His memory went back a long way – further than Mrs Bernstein's research, by a long way.

* * *

Summer among gravenstein and grannysmith; summer among golden queens and nectarines; avenues of gold, lanes of light, a benediction of leaves.

Isobel was sunbathing naked on a bright towel. The towel itself was spread on the square of mown grass behind the barn: the grass was still green. The gate that gave entry through the board fence enclosing the area was rarely closed; it was locked, now. This privacy O'Leary thought proper for Isobel. For himself he sunbathed in bathing trunks and

a barrel chest: he was in equipoise between Canada and Scotland, between exercise and whisky just holding his own.

The equipoise of Isobel was of a different order: she sunned her front, she sunned her back – a golden spool winding golden light, languidly. Oh doze of hours. O'Leary teased spring of buttock with blade of grass.

'Don't Gambo; it tickles.'

'A metallic body,' O'Leary said. 'Citrine, ponderous, mute, fulgid et cetera.' He reached under her propped arm to weigh the particle as it swung at her throat. At the cost of considerable embarrassment to O'Leary, at the jewellers, the nugget now bore in minute letters the inscription: O'Leary's O. The apostrophe was indiscoverable except with a hand glass; but it was there. Isobel's breasts were squashed against her towel: O'Leary feared for them. He drained the last drops from his glass.

'Gambo, you drink too much. You do.'

'An excess of what's pleasurable is always subject to unfavourable comment: an excess of unpleasantness, say work for instance, is praiseworthy. Why? Don't go out into the world with your mind in that disorder. For what do you think old maids are vulgarly supposed to search under their beds? Their fears are ambiguous. Lost doves, they don't know it. I feel sorry for the world, at times.' There was a thought in it, somewhere.

'What about me?'

'Given the necessary perspective it were even possible to feel sorry for you, my dove.'

'Gambo, don't get drunk on our last day, please.'

'I shan't, don't fear. Stay to supper, our last. My nerves are shot. Don't go, stay. No, I don't mean it; but I'd like to mean it. Are you burning?'

Her upper lip, O'Leary saw, was beaded: along the nodes of her spine, a heartbreaking down. Isobel rolled over, putting her hands under her head with consequent flexion of the pectorals et cetera. It was intolerable. The air was not reaching them in this sheltered, private place. O'Leary was sweating. What did he see in her? In a matter of hours she would cease to be his. It was a day to perform wonders, magic rites. Intolerable cambers, then; impossible light. Ice-floes ground deafeningly in the bright lanes of summer. Then hermetical silence descended. He didn't have Mrs Bernstein's monstrous objectivity.

Isobel sat up. O'Leary was defeated by vibrant bronze. She put her hands upon his chest and pushed. They fell back on the prickling grass.

'Not here, my dove. In case . . .' O'Leary, preferring autumn and its pyres and palls, embraced summer: her flesh was almost too hot to hold.

So time flowed, in sunlight and a movement of leaves, until returning to pluck up the bright towel she gathered in innocence all light to herself upon bosses of flesh, as she stooped then ran.

'Going, going,' O'Leary said, with Isobel under the gavel. 'How soon to be gone?'

'Don't keep reminding me, Gambo.' She could be petulant.

'Or remembering? You're coming in one end as I'm going out the other; it's the cosmic chute.'

There was an artificiality in her mood of sadness: she would confront the unexpected with what was expected of her. But could he match soft words with softer? Could he, he wondered? The grey bleating was not so easily stilled. He lay beside her, summoning strength; it was an exhausting

invocation. The last thing he wanted was to be himself – this day, this night, of all days and nights.

'Change,' O'Leary said in mimic bitterness. 'I see you sigh for it.' Heaving up on one elbow he looked down fathoms to find her, determined if possible to be gay, as she lay graced with dappled light. Nature was against him. 'One more kiss is all it would take, perhaps, to change me into the handsome prince, silver Alvis at the door and a million banknotes crisp in the boot.'

He wasn't managing. Would he miss her so much? Was she asleep? He traced his fingers down her side. 'Jump in my dove,' O'Leary said, 'and off to faery with never a puncture, pleasure without end, amen.'

Most definitely he was not managing. He was surprised to discover that he was, abruptly, bored.

'Don't Gambo. I hate you when you're like this. Please.' She opened her eyes. 'Mummy says your vulgarity is only an act.' Drowsily said, in a voice without expression.

'Mummy does, eh? Bygod, I can hear her saying it, too. And what did you say? Are there any in the world left to defend me?'

'I didn't say anything. I never do. It doesn't matter now.'

Two days running, he remembered, he'd forgotten to feed his fowls; it was a measure of his distress.

'Gambo, will you miss me? Will you write?'

Eyes plainly open and blue; as if she were thinking of something. Chiaroscuro: on the dark bed cover white flesh and the darker brand, the delta. Why if they dyed their hair was this never subject of that cosmetic attention? Purple would be amazing. Tremors of broken light.

'I solemnly promise never to give you another thought.' He teased her: he had better be smiling. 'Never another.'

'Gambo, be serious. Oh, I love it here.'

To him who would not dare seriousness she said it; at a moment when he was bored with the inevitability of himself, wishing this were done. His end of the see-saw was excessively weighted: why else this elevation of his dove, blond against the light? Never another . . . as he eased himself into the background, mere proprietor of this absurdity and its chattels. Is it the overt nature? A lovely thought, mute but ponderous: summer temperature 79 degrees Fahrenheit. Could he let her down gently? He'd long wondered it and now there seemed no need. Oh the see-saw of bee and flower. Fathoms thudded sturdily on O'Leary's heart: he registered certain depths: the blasphemy of beauty, the cost and concept. How do you plead, O'Leary? Unsentimental man?

He was capable of simple regrets over present simplicities on a day where wonders worked. He considered her tears which would not quite come.

'I'm sorry I'm sad,' Isobel said.

'It's heartening to observe a natural phenomenon in this naughty world.'

'No don't, don't Gambo. If I move too close, that's what you say, that's how you say it, in that voice. It's like touching something, something that goes into its shell when you touch.'

Bygod they matured fast – too fast. Or was she infected by her mother? O'Leary, who could treasure girlish nonsense of a kind, fled abruptly from the voice of Mrs Bernstein speaking through her daughter's lips. Had they discussed him, in cold blood?

'A carapace,' O'Leary said in miserable consideration, 'is sometimes necessary.'

'Come here,' Isobel said. 'Come here.' She had found authority.

Predictably O'Leary's vision darkened, his chest heaved.

'Gambo, say you love me.'

'I do, my love.'

'No, say it. Say it this once, please.'

He had never been able to: he never would be. O'Leary, who was immensely fond of Isobel Bernstein, bent above her. There was a great deal to Isobel, really. This much he could keep for a minute or two: this much she could endure, or eagerly accept.

'Please, Gambo.'

She was no longer asking him to speak: he supposed he should compliment himself.

O'Leary stood on the road verge. Isobel sat at the wheel of her mother's car.

'Goodbye, Gambo.'

'I shan't come to the airport, you know.'

'I know. It doesn't matter. Goodbye.'

'Goodbye, Isobel.'

'Gambo, I'll write.'

'Love and kisses. X marks my room.'

They laughed. O'Leary put a hand on her shoulder gaily. He was squinting into the light, the westward haze.

'Take the road slowly,' O'Leary said. 'All roads you travel.'

She put her head out the window and O'Leary bussed her on the cheek – a resounding avuncular farewell as he would have remembered it had she not turned her head and found his mouth. O'Leary gave himself a smart blow on the head as he stepped clear.

'Gambo, look after yourself.'

'Go,' O'Leary said. 'Go now. Goodbye.'

He had to stand clear as she turned, waving with her free hand. It was a perfect evening: she was crying at last, and smiling.

He had lied. He would miss her more than that. His life had been a preparation for a sense of loss. He had missed her often enough already, over the years. It would continue, an indulgence of himself, O'Leary's O of regret, unvoiced. It was what his life was fashioned to contain, this gentle fabrication, this bright figment.

* * *

O'Leary re-entered his oasis slowly, closing the wicket behind him and standing in the dark of the barn. Oasis flooded with smells – lingering, acrid, inexpungeable smells: rotted fruit long dried, sawn boxwood, packing straw, oil, petrol, fertilizer. And over-riding all, the natural full-bodied smell of blood and bone, dominant, pervasive, as pungent as loving.

JANET FRAME

Keel and Kool

Father shook the bidi-bids off the big red and grey rug and then he spread it out again in the grass.

'There you are,' he said. 'Mother here, and Winnie here, and Joan you stay beside Winnie. We'll put the biscuit tin out of the way so it won't come into the photo. Now say cheese.'

He stepped back and cupped his hand over the front of the camera, and then he looked over his shoulder – 'to see if the sun's looking too', he told the children who were saying cheese. And then he clicked the shiny thing at the side of the camera.

'There you are,' he said. 'It's taken. A happy family.'

'Oh,' said Mother. 'Were we all right? Because I want to show the photo to Elsie. It's the first we've taken since Eva – went.'

Mother always said went or passed away or passed beyond when she talked of death. As if it were not death really, only pretend.

'We were good weren't we Dad,' said Winnie. 'And now are you going fishing?'

'Yes,' said Father. 'I'm going fishing. I'll put this in a safe place and then I'm off up the river for salmon.'

He carried the camera over to where the coats were piled, and he stowed it in one of the bags carefully, for photos were precious things.

And then he stooped and fastened the top strap of his gumboots to his belt.

'Cheerio,' he said, kissing Mother. He always kissed everyone when he went away anywhere, even for a little while. And then he kissed Winnie and pulled her hair, and he pulled Joan's hair too but he didn't kiss her because she was the girl over the road and no relation.

'I'll come back with a salmon or I'll go butcher's hook.'

They watched him walking towards the river, a funny clumpy walk because he had his gumboots on. He was leaning to one side, with his right shoulder lower than his left, as if he were trying to dodge a blow that might come from the sky or the trees or the air. They watched him going and going, like someone on the films, who grows smaller and smaller and then The End is printed across the screen, and music plays and the lights go up. He was like a man in a story walking away from them. Winnie hoped he wouldn't go too far away because the river was deep and wild and made a roaring noise that could be heard even above the willow trees and pine trees. It was the greyest river Winnie had ever seen. And the sky was grey too with a tiny dot of sun. The grey of the sky seemed to swim into the grey of the river.

Then Father turned and waved.

Winnie and Joan waved back.

'And now we're going to play by the pine tree Mrs Todd, aren't we Winnie,' said Joan.

'We'll play ladies,' said Winnie.

Mother sighed. The children were such happy little things. They didn't realise. . . .

'All right kiddies,' she said. 'You can run away and play. Don't go near the river and mind the stinging nettle.'

Then she opened her *Woman's Weekly* and put it on her knee. She knew that she would read only as far as Over the Teacups and then she would think all over again about Eva

passing away, her first baby. A sad blow, people said, to lose your first, just when she was growing up to be a help to you. But it's all for the best and you have Wonderful Faith Mrs Todd, she's happier in another sphere, you wouldn't have wished it otherwise, and you've got her photo, it's always nice to have their photos. Bear up Mrs Todd.

Mrs Todd shut her eyes and tried to forget and then she started to read Over the Teacups. It was better to forget and not think about it.

Winnie and Joan raced each other through the grass to the pine tree by the fence, Joan's dark hair bobbing up and down and getting in her eyes. 'Bother,' she said. Winnie stared enviously. She wished her own hair was long enough to hang over her eyes and be brushed away. How nice to say bother, and brush your hair out of your eyes. Eva's hair had been long. It was so funny about Eva, and the flowers and telegrams and Auntie May coming and bringing sugar buns and custard squares. It was so funny at home with Eva's dresses hanging up and her shoes under the wardrobe and no Eva to wear them, and the yellow quilt spread unruffled over her bed, and staying unruffled all night. But it was good wearing Eva's blue pyjamas. They had pink round the bottom of the legs and pink round the neck and sleeves. Winnie liked to walk round the bedroom in them and see herself in the mirror and then get into bed and yawn, stretching her arms above her head like a lady. But it would have been better if Eva were there to see.

And what fun if Eva were there at the picnic!

'Come on,' said Joan. 'We'll play ladies in fur coats. I know because my Mother's got a fur coat.'

'I'm a lady going to bed,' said Winnie. 'I'm wearing some beautiful blue pyjamas and I'm yawning, and my maid's just

brought my coffee to me.' She lay under the pine tree. She could smell the pine and hear the hush-hush of its branches and beyond that the rainy sound of the river, and see the shrivelled-up cones like little brown claws, and the grey sky like a tent with the wind blowing under it and puffing it out. And there was Joan walking up and down in her fur coat, and smiling at all the ladies and gentlemen and saying oh no, I've got heaps of fur coats. Bother, my hair does get in my eyes so.

Joan had been Eva's best friend. She was so beautiful. She was Spanish she said, a little bit anyway. She had secrets with Eva. They used to whisper together and giggle and talk in code.

'I'm tired of wearing my fur coat,' said Joan, suddenly. 'And you can't go on yawning for ever.'

'I can go on yawning for ever if I like,' said Winnie, remembering the giggles and the secrets and the code she couldn't understand. And she yawned and said thank you to the maid for her coffee. And then she yawned again.

'I can do what I like,' she said.

'You can't always,' said Joan. 'Your Mother wouldn't let you. Anyway I'm tired of wearing my fur coat, I want to make something.'

She turned her back on Winnie and sat down in the grass away from the pine tree, and began to pick stalks of feathery grass. Winnie stopped yawning. She heard the rainy-wind sound of the river and she wondered where her Father was. And what was Mother doing? And what was Joan making with the feathery grass?

'What are you making, Joan?'

'I'm making Christmas trees,' answered Joan graciously. 'Eva showed me. Didn't Eva show you?'

And she held up a Christmas tree.

'Yes,' lied Winnie, 'Eva showed me Christmas trees.'

She stared at the tiny tree in Joan's hand. The grass was wet with last night's dew and the tree sparkled, catching the tiny drop of sunlight that fell from the high grey and white air. It was like a fairy tree or like the song they sang at school – Little fir tree neat and green. Winnie had never seen such a lovely thing to make.

'And Eva showed me some new bits to Tinker Tailor,' said Joan, biting off a piece of grass with her teeth. 'Boots, shoes, slippers, clodhoppers, silk, satin, cotton, rags – it's what you're married in.'

'She showed me too,' lied Winnie. 'Eva showed me lots of things.'

'She showed me things too,' said Joan tenaciously.

Winnie didn't say anything to that. She looked up in the sky and watched a seagull flying over. I'm Keel, I'm Keel it seemed to say. Come home Kool come home Kool. Keel Keel. Winnie felt lonely staring up into the sky. Why was the pine tree so big and dark and old? Why was the seagull crying out I'm Keel I'm Keel as if it were calling for somebody who wouldn't come. Keel Keel, come home Kool, come home Kool it cried.

Winnie wished her Mother would call out to them. She wished her Father were back from the river, and they were all sitting on the rug, drinking billy tea and eating water biscuits that crackled in your mouth. She wished Joan were away and there were just Father and Mother and Winnie, and no Joan. She wished she had long hair and could make Christmas trees out of feathery grass. She wished she knew more bits to Tinker Tailor. What was it Joan had said? 'Boots shoes slippers clodhoppers.' Why hadn't Eva told her?

'You're going to sleep,' said Joan suddenly. 'I've made three Christmas trees. Look.'

'I'm not going to sleep. I'm hungry,' said Winnie. 'And I think Joan Mason that some people tell lies.'

Joan flushed. 'I *have* made three Christmas trees.'

'It's not that,' said Winnie, taking up a pine needle and making pine-needle writing in the air.

'I just think that some people tell lies.'

'But I'm not a liar, Winnie,' protested Joan anxiously. 'I'm not honestly.'

'Some people,' Winnie murmured, writing with her pine needle.

'You're not fair Winnie Todd,' quivered Joan throwing down her Christmas trees. 'I know you mean me.'

'Nobody said I did. I just said – some people.'

'Well you looked at me.'

'Did I?'

Winnie crushed her pine needle and smelt it. She wanted to cry. She wished she had never come for a picnic. She was cold too with just her print dress on. She wished she were somewhere far far away from the river and the pine tree and Joan Mason and the Christmas trees, somewhere far far away, she didn't know where.

Perhaps there was no place. Perhaps she would never find anywhere to go. Her Mother would die and her Father would die and Joan Mason would go on flicking the hair from her eyes and saying bother and wearing her fur coat and not knowing what it was like to have a mother and father dead.

'Yes,' said Winnie. 'You're a liar. Eva told me things about you. Your uncle was eaten by cannibals and your father shot an albatross and had a curse put on him and your hair went

green when you went for a swim in Christchurch and you had to be fed on pineapple for three weeks before it turned black again. Eva told me. You're a liar. She didn't believe you either. And take your Christmas trees.' She picked up one of the trees and tore it to pieces.

Joan started to cry.

'Cry baby, liar, so there.'

Winnie reached forward and gave Joan a push, and then she turned to the pine tree and catching hold of the lowest branches, she pulled herself up into the tree. Soon she was over half-way up. The branches rocked up and down, sighing and sighing. Winnie peered down on to the ground and saw Joan running away through the grass, her hair bobbing up and down as she ran. She would be going back to where Winnie's mother was. Perhaps she would tell. Winnie pushed me over and called me names. And then when Winnie got down from the tree and went to join the others her Mother would look at her with a hurt expression in her eyes and say blessed are the peacemakers. And her Father would be sitting there telling them all about the salmon, but he would stop when she came up, hours and hours later, and say sternly I hoped you would behave yourself. And then he would look at Mother, and Winnie would know they were thinking of Eva and the flowers and telegrams and Auntie May saying bear up, you have Wonderful Faith. And then Mother would say have one of these chocolate biscuits, Joan. And Mother and Father and Joan would be together, sharing things.

Winnie's eyes filled with tears of pity for herself. She wished Eva were there. They would both sit up the pine tree with their hands clutching hold of the sticky branches, and they would ride up and down, like two birds on the waves, and then they would turn into princesses and sleep

at night in blue pyjamas with pink round the edges, and in the daytime they would make Christmas trees out of feathery grass and play Tinker Tailor – boots, shoes, slippers, clodhoppers.

'Boots, shoes, slippers, clodhoppers,' whispered Winnie. But there was no one to answer her. Only up in the sky there was a seagull as white as chalk, circling and crying Keel Keel Come home Kool, come home Kool. And Kool would never come, ever.

Solutions

This is a story which belongs in the very room in which I am typing. I am not haunted by it, but I shall tell it to you. It happened once – twice, thrice? – upon a time.

A young man was so bedevilled by the demands of his body that he decided to rid himself of it completely. Now this worry was not a simple matter of occasional annoyance. As soon as the man sat down to work in the morning – he was a private student working all day at this very table with its green plastic cover, drop ends, two protective cork mats – he would be conscious perhaps of an itch in his back which he would be forced to scratch, or he would feel a pain in his arm or shoulder and be unable to rest until he had shaken himself free of pain which would then drop to the carpet and lie there powerless and be sucked into the vacuum cleaner on a Thursday morning when the woman came to clean the house.

Sometimes as the pain lay upon the carpet the man would engage it in conversation; there would be a lively exchange of bitterness and wit, with the man assuring his pain that he felt no ill-will toward it but he wished that its family would cease inhabiting his body just as he was beginning work for the day. But the pain was cunning. It gave no message to its family which returned again and again, and when it was successfully disposed of by the vacuum cleaner and the County Council Dustmen and transported to a County Council grave, another family of pain took its place.

'I must get rid of my body,' the man thought. 'What use is it to me? It interferes with my work, and since my work is

concentrated in my head I think I shall get rid of my body and retain only my head.'

Ah, what freedom then!

There was another difficulty. As soon as the young man wanted to begin his work in the morning, all the feelings which he preferred to inhabit his head to nourish and revive his thoughts, would decide to pack their picnic lunches for the day, and without asking permission, they would set out on the forbidden route to the shady spot between the man's legs where his penis lived in a little house with a red roof, a knocker on the front door, and two gothic columns at the front gate. And there, in the little house in the woods, with the penis as a sometimes thoughtful, sometimes turbulent host, the man's feelings would unwrap their picnic lunch and enjoy a pleasant feast, often sitting outside in the shade of the two gothic columns. And how ardently the sun shone through the trees, through the leaves, in a red haze of burning!

Now you understand that the man became more and more distressed at the way his body demanded so much attention. It had also to be washed, clothed, warmed, cooled, scratched, rubbed, exercised, rested; and should it suffer the slightest harm, pain, like a dragonfly, would alight at the spot with its valise full of instruments of torture which dragonflies used to carry (once, twice, thrice upon a time) when they were the envoys of genuine dragons.

The man grew more and more depressed. He felt himself becoming bankrupt – with his feelings engaged hour after hour in extravagant parties which took no account of the cost, so that bills mounted and could not be paid, and strange authorities intruded to give orders and confuse the situation. And with so little work being done the man did not know where he would find money for rent and food.

Sometimes he was so depressed and alone that he wept. His feelings did not seem to care. Whenever he glanced at the little house in the woods he could see at once that all the lights in the house were blazing; he could hear the boisterous singing at night, and witness the riotous carousing during the day under the melting indiarubber sun.

'What shall I do?' the man cried when he woke one morning feeling tired and discouraged. 'Shall I rid myself of my body?'

He decided to rid himself of his body, to keep only his head which, he was convinced, would work faithfully for him once it was set free.

Therefore, the same morning, feeling lighthearted and singing a gay song, the man sharpened his kitchen knife which he had bought at Woolworths for two and eleven and which had grown blunt from much use as a peeler of vegetables, spreader of marmalade on toast, cutter of string on mysterious packages from foreign countries, whittler of wood on pencils; and, unfolding a copy of the *Guardian*, the man laid it on the kitchen floor, leaned forward, applied the knife to his throat, and in a moment his head had been cut off and the blood was seeping through the Editorial, Letters to the Editor, and the centre news page.

The problem which confronted the man's head now was to get rid of the body, and to clean the blood from the kitchen floor. The head had rolled, its face rather pale with the excitement of its new freedom, as far as the fireplace. Now the man knew of three little mice who lived behind the screen which covered the disused fireplace, and who emerged on expeditions during the night and during the day when they supposed that all the people in the house were at work. The three mice had survived many attempts to kill them.

One of the lodgers from upstairs had shaken three little heaps of poisoned cereal on a strip of hardboard in front of the fireplace and had waited in vain for any sign that the mice had been tempted. She did not know that the young man had warned them. He had been in the kitchen one evening making himself a cup of tea, and he was just about to take a slice of bread from his wrapped sliced white loaf when he saw one of the mice sniffing at the poisoned cereal.

'I wouldn't eat it, if I were you,' the young man said. 'Appearances are deceptive you know. Even I have to be careful with every slice of my wrapped sliced white loaf.'

'Why are you warning me?' the little mouse asked. 'Don't you want to poison me? I thought everybody wanted to poison little mice like me.'

'Don't touch that heap of cereal,' the young man said melodramatically.

The mouse was formal. 'I am grateful sir,' he said, and disappeared.

But naturally the mice were grateful, following the tradition of all rescued animals in fairy stories, and as the young man had indeed been living in a fairy story of despair he had no difficulty now, when he had freed himself from his body, in asking and receiving help from the three mice. They were willing to dispose of the body and to clean the kitchen until the floor was without a trace of blood. In their turn, the mice asked the help of the dustbin downstairs, and because the dustbin had often acted as a gay restaurateur serving delectable suppers to the three mice, and because he did not wish to lose his reputation – for reputations are valuable property and must be stored in a safe place (the dustbin kept his just inside the rim of his grey tin hat) he agreed to come into the house, climb the stairs, remove the body, help to clean away the

mess, and put all the refuse and the information concerning it, beneath his tin hat. And all this he accomplished with swiftness and agility which won praise and applause from the three mice. Also, with a kindly impulse, the dustbin carried the man's head to his room and even gave it lessons in flying, for the dustbin lid was a relative of the flying carpet and knew the secrets of flight, and that was why he had been so agile in climbing the stairs and moving in and out of the kitchen.

How patiently he taught the head to fly! He waited so courteously and sympathetically until the art was mastered, and then bidding the head goodbye returned downstairs (conscious of his new reputation as a hero), out the back door, to his home in the tiny backyard where he lived in the company of a shelf of plant pots and a string bag of clothes pegs which continually quarrelled amongst themselves about who were superior, the plastic clothes pegs or the wooden clothes pegs. These quarrels were all the more bitter because they took place among the older generation of clothes pegs; the younger had forgotten or did not know how to quarrel; they were intermarrying and shared shirt flats on the same clothesline; together they topped the country spaces of blankets, and holidayed near the ski slopes of sheets and pillowcases. . . .

Meanwhile, upstairs, the head was flying rapturously to and fro in the bed-sitting-room, and it continued thus in wild freedom all morning and afternoon.

Once it stopped flying and looked thoughtful. 'Am I a man?' it asked itself.

'Or am I a head? I shall call myself a man, for the most important part of me remains.'

'I'll have one day free,' the man said, 'to think things over, and then I'll start my intellectual work with no dictation or

interference ever again from my presumptuous imperious body. Oh I feel as if I could fly to the sky and circle the moon; thoughts race through me, eager to be set down upon paper and studied by those who have never had the insight or strategy to rid themselves of their cumbersome bodies. My act has made my brain supreme. I shall work day and night without interruption. . . .'

And on and on the man flew, round and round the room in his dizzy delight. Once he flew to the window and looked out, but fortunately no one in the street saw him or there might have been inquiries. Then in the evening, to his surprise, he began to feel tired.

'It seems that sleep is necessary after all,' he said. 'But only a wink or two of sleep, and then I daresay I shall wake refreshed.'

So he lay down beneath the top blanket of his bed, closed his eyes, and slept a deep sleep, and when he woke next morning his first thought almost set him shouting with exhilaration,

'How wonderful to be free!'

That morning the landlady remarked to her husband, 'The man in the upstairs room seems to have gone away. I'm sure he did not come home last night. The room is so quiet. His rent is due this morning, and we need the money. I'll give him a few days' grace, and then if we are not paid we shall have to see about finding a new lodger – for this one dosen't seem to do any work really, does he? I mean any real work where you catch the bus in the morning and come home tired at night with your *Evening News* under your arm, and you are too tired to read it.'

Also that morning the woman lodger remarked to the other lodger who lived in the small room upstairs. 'The man

who shares the kitchen with us has not used his milk – see it's still in the bottle. I was curious and peeped in the door this morning (I was only wondering about the milk, it might go sour, in this heat) and his bed is unruffled, it's not been slept in. Perhaps I should tell the landlady. She likes to know what goes on. He seems to have vanished. There's no sign of him.'

'Ah,' the man was saying at that very moment as he flew about the room, 'I don't need to eat now, yet I am full of vigour and excitement. My former despair has vanished. I will start work as soon as I hear the two lodgers and the landlady and landlord bang on the front door as they go out on their way to work.'

He heard the two lodgers in the kitchen, washing up their breakfast dishes. He heard the landlady putting her clothes through the spin-drier. He heard the landlord go out and start the car.

Then he heard the front door bang, once, twice, three, four times. The house was quiet at last. The man gave a long sigh of content, and prepared to work.

The house was indeed quiet. In the kitchen the three mice emerged from their hiding place to explore and examine the turn of events, for events are like tiny revolving wheels, and mice like to play with them and bowl them along alleyways of yellow light where dustbins glitter and the hats of dustbins shine with pride in their distant relation, the Magic Carpet. . . .

The three mice pattered around the kitchen, and then curious about their friend who had rid himself of his body, they came – one, two, three – into the man's room where they were surprised to observe, on the green plain of the table, the man resting in an attitude of despair.

'Alas,' he was murmuring. 'Where are my fingers to grasp my pen or tap my typewriter, and my hand to reach books

from the shelf? And who will comb my hair and rub the hair tonic into my scalp? Besides, my head itches, there is wax in my ears, I need to keep clearing my throat; how can I blow my nose with dignity? And as for shaving every morning, why, my beard will grow and grow like clematis upon a rotten tree.' Tears trickled from the man's eyes.

The three mice felt very sad. 'We could help you,' they suggested, 'by bringing books to you; but that is all. You need arms, hands, fingers.'

'I need much more,' the man replied. 'Who will listen to my words and love me? And who will want to warm an absent skin or picnic in a deserted house, in darkness, or drink from rivers that have run dry?

'Still,' the man continued, 'my thoughts are free. I have sacrificed these comforts for my thoughts. Yet although I am no longer a slave to my body I am even now subject to irritations. My vanity demands that I rub hair tonic into my scalp to postpone my baldness, for baldness comes early to our family. My need for relief demands that I scratch a spot just above my right ear. My training in hygiene insists that I blow my nose with a square white handkerchief which has my name – Man – embroidered in one corner! Oh if only I could escape from the petty distractions of my head! Then I would indeed do great work, think noble thoughts. Even my head offends me now. If only I did not possess my head, if I could rid myself of it, if I could just keep my brain and the protective shell enclosing it, then surely I could pursue my work in real freedom!'

Then the idea came to him. Why not ask the mice to fetch the knife from the kitchen (they could carry it easily, one taking the blade, the second the handle, the third acting as guide) and remove all parts of my head except the little

walnut which is my brain? It could easily be done. If the mice hurry, the man thought, and set my brain free, no one knows what great work I might accomplish even today before the sun goes down!

So the mice offered to help. They performed the cutting operations and once again the dustbin and the dustbin lid agreed to collect and conceal the remains. Then, when the task was finished the mice laid what was left of the head, upon the table, and silently (for the man could not communicate with them any more) they and the dustbin and the dustbin lid went from the room, the mice to their corner by the fireplace, the dustbin to his place beneath the shelf where the pot plants lived and the older generation of plastic clothes pegs and wooden clothes pegs continued their quarrels in the string bag where they lived.

Blind, speechless, deaf, the man lay upon the table beside his blank writing paper, his books, his typewriter. He did not move. No one could have divined his thoughts; he himself could no longer communicate them.

That night when the lodger returned from work she peered into the room, and seeing no one there, she reported the fact to the landlady who only that afternoon had replied to inquiries for a rented room.

'The man must have flitted,' the landlady said, opening the door and gazing around the room. 'The bed has not been slept in. His luggage is still here. But I think he has flitted because he could not pay his rent. I think he was the type. No regular work. No getting up in the morning to catch the bus and coming home at night with the *Evening News* in his pocket and being too tired to read it.'

Then the landlady gave a slight shiver of anticipation. 'Now I can come into the room and scour it out, wash the

curtains, clean the linoleum and the chair covers, redecorate. I'll move the furniture, too, repair the damages he is sure to have done – look, no castors on the chairs, and the spring of that armchair broken, and the cord hanging from the window, and look at the soot on the window sill!'

Then the landlady glanced at the table and noticed the shrivelled remains of the man.

'Just look!' she exclaimed to the lodger. 'An old prune left lying around. Eating prunes no doubt while he worked; or pretended to work. Such habits only encourage the mice. No wonder they haven't been tempted by the poison I left out for them if they have been living on titbits from this man!' And with an expression of disgust the landlady removed the deaf, blind, speechless, wrinkled man, took him downstairs and threw him into the dustbin, and not even the dustbin recognised him, for he could never any more proclaim his identity – Man; nor could he see that he was lying in a dustbin; nor could he feel anything except a roaring, like the sound in an empty shell which houses only the memory of the tide within its walls.

And the next morning when the three mice were up early and down to the dustbin for breakfast, one saw the shrivelled man, and not recognising him, exclaimed, 'A prune! I've never tasted prunes, but I can always try.' And so the three mice shared the prune, spitting out the hard bits.

'It wasn't bad,' they said. 'It will do for breakfast.'

Then they hurried downstairs to hide while the landlady who was not going to work that day prepared the man's empty room for its new tenant, a clean businessman who would work from nine till five and bring inconvenience upon no one, least of all upon himself.

The Reservoir

It was said to be four or five miles along the gully, past orchards and farms, paddocks filled with cattle, sheep, wheat, gorse, and the squatters of the land who were the rabbits eating like modern sculpture into the hills, though how could we know anything of modern sculpture, we knew nothing but the Warrior in the main street with his wreaths of poppies on Anzac Day, the gnomes weeping in the Gardens because the seagulls perched on their green caps and showed no respect, and how important it was for birds, animals, and people, especially children, to show respect!

And that is why for so long we obeyed the command of the grownups and never walked as far as the forbidden Reservoir, but were content to return 'tired but happy' (as we wrote in our school compositions), answering the question, Where did you walk today? with a suspicion of blackmail, 'Oh, nearly, nearly to the Reservoir!'

The Reservoir was the end of the world; beyond it, you fell; beyond it were paddocks of thorns, strange cattle, strange farms, legendary people whom we would never know or recognise even if they walked among us on a Friday night downtown when we went to follow the boys and listen to the Salvation Army Band and buy a milk shake in the milk bar and then return home to find that everything was all right and safe, that our Mother had not run away and caught the night train to the North Island, that our Father had not shot himself with worry over the bills, but had in fact been downtown himself and had bought the usual

Friday night treat, a bag of liquorice allsorts and a bag of chocolate roughs, from Woolworths.

The Reservoir haunted our lives. We never knew one until we came to this town; we had used pump water. But here, in our new house, the water ran from the taps as soon as we turned them on, and if we were careless and left them on, our Father would shout, as if the affair were his personal concern, 'Do you want the Reservoir to run dry?'

That frightened us. What should we do if the Reservoir ran dry? Would we die of thirst like Burke and Wills in the desert?

'The Reservoir,' our Mother said, 'gives pure water, water safe to drink without boiling it.'

The water was in a different class, then, from the creek which flowed through the gully; yet the creek had its source in the Reservoir. Why had it not received the pampering attention of officialdom which strained weed and earth, cockabullies and trout and eels, from our tap water? Surely the Reservoir was not entirely pure?

'Oh no,' they said, when we inquired. We learned that the water from the Reservoir had been 'treated'. We supposed this to mean that during the night men in light-blue uniforms with sacks over their shoulders crept beyond the circle of pine trees which enclosed the Reservoir, and emptied the contents of the sacks into the water, to dissolve dead bodies and prevent the decay of teeth.

Then, at times, there would be news in the paper, discussed by my Mother with the neighbours over the back fence. Children had been drowned in the Reservoir.

'No child,' the neighbour would say, 'ought to be allowed near the Reservoir.'

'I tell mine to keep strictly away,' my Mother would reply.

And for so long we obeyed our Mother's command, on our favourite walks along the gully simply following the untreated cast-off creek which we loved and which flowed day and night in our heads in all its detail – the wild sweet peas, boiled-lolly pink, and the mint growing along the banks; the exact spot in the water where the latest dead sheep could be found, and the stink of its bloated flesh and floating wool, an allowable earthy stink which we accepted with pleasant revulsion and which did not prompt the 'inky-pinky I smell Stinkie' rhyme which referred to offensive human beings only. We knew where the water was shallow and could be paddled in, where forts could be made from the rocks; we knew the frightening deep places where the eels lurked and the weeds were tangled in gruesome shapes; we knew the jumping places, the mossy stones with their dangers, limitations, and advantages; the sparkling places where the sun trickled beside the water, upon the stones; the bogs made by roaming cattle, trapping some of them to death; their gaunt telltale bones; the little valleys with their new growth of lush grass where the creek had 'changed its course', and no longer flowed.

'The creek has changed its course,' our Mother would say, in a tone which implied terror and a sense of strangeness, as if a tragedy had been enacted.

We knew the moods of the creek, its levels of low-flow, half-high-flow, high-flow which all seemed to relate to interference at its source – the Reservoir. If one morning the water turned the colour of clay and crowds of bubbles were passengers on every suddenly swift wave hurrying by, we would look at one another and remark with the fatality and reverence which attends a visitation or prophecy,

'The creek's going on high-flow. They must be doing something at the Reservoir.'

By afternoon the creek would be on high-flow, turbulent, muddy, unable to be jumped across or paddled in or fished in, concealing beneath a swelling fluid darkness whatever evil which 'they', the authorities, had decided to purge so swiftly and secretly from the Reservoir.

For so long, then, we obeyed our parents, and never walked as far as the Reservoir. Other things concerned us, other curiosities, fears, challenges. The school year ended. I got a prize, a large yellow book the colour of cat's mess. Inside it were editions of newspapers, *The Worms' Weekly*, supposedly written by worms, snails, spiders. For the first part of the holidays we spent the time sitting in the long grass of our front lawn nibbling the stalks of shamrock and reading insect newspapers and relating their items to the lives of those living on our front lawn down among the summer-dry roots of the couch, tinkertailor, daisy, dandelion, shamrock, clover, and ordinary 'grass'. High summer came. The blowsy old red roses shed their petals to the regretful refrain uttered by our Mother year after year at the same time, 'I should have made potpourri, I have a wonderful recipe for potpourri in Dr Chase's Book.'

Our Mother never made the potpourri. She merely quarrelled with our Father over how to pronounce it.

The days became unbearably long and hot. Our Christmas presents were broken or too boring to care about. Celluloid dolls had loose arms and legs and rifts in their bright pink bodies; the invisible ink had poured itself out in secret messages; diaries frustrating in their smallness (two lines to a day) had been filled in for the whole of the coming year. . . . Days at the beach were tedious, with no room in the bathing sheds so that we were forced to undress in the common room downstairs with its floor patched with

wet and trailed with footmarks and sand and its tiny barred window (which made me believe that I was living in the French Revolution).

Rumours circled the burning world. The sea was drying up, soon you could paddle or walk to Australia. Sharks had been seen swimming inside the breakwater; one shark attacked a little boy and bit off his you-know-what.

We swam. We wore bathing togs all day. We gave up cowboys and ranches; and baseball and sledding; and 'those games' where we mimicked grownup life, loving and divorcing each other, kissing and slapping, taking secret paramours when our husband was working out of town. Everything exhausted us. Cracks appeared in the earth; the grass was bled yellow; the ground was littered with beetle shells and snail shells; flies came in from the unofficial rubbish-dump at the back of the house; the twisting flypapers hung from the ceiling; a frantic buzzing filled the room as the flypapers became crowded. Even the cat put out her tiny tongue, panting in the heat.

We realised, and were glad, that school would soon reopen. What was school like? It seemed so long ago, it seemed as if we had never been to school, surely we had forgotten everything we had learned, how frightening, thrilling and strange it would all seem! Where would we go on the first day, who would teach us, what were the names on the new books?

Who would sit beside us, who would be our best friend?

The earth crackled in early-autumn haze and still the February sun dried the world; even at night the rusty sheet of roofing-iron outside by the cellar stayed warm, but with rows of sweat-marks on it; the days were still long, with night face to face with morning and almost nothing in-between

but a snatch of turning sleep with the blankets on the floor and the windows wide open to moths with their bulging lamplit eyes moving through the dark and their grandfather bodies knocking, knocking upon the walls.

Day after day the sun still waited to pounce. We were tired, our skin itched, our sunburn had peeled and peeled again, the skin on our feet was hard, there was dust in our hair, our bodies clung with the salt of sea-bathing and sweat, the towels were harsh with salt.

School soon, we said again, and were glad; for lessons gave shade to rooms and corridors; cloakrooms were cold and sunless. Then, swiftly, suddenly, disease came to the town. Infantile Paralysis. Black headlines in the paper, listing the number of cases, the number of deaths. Children everywhere, out in the country, up north, down south, two streets away.

The schools did not reopen. Our lessons came by post, in smudged print on rough white paper; they seemed makeshift and false, they inspired distrust, they could not compete with the lure of the sun still shining, swelling, the world would go up in cinders, the days were too long, there was nothing to do, there was nothing to do; the lessons were dull; in the front room with the navy-blue blind half down the window and the tiny splits of light showing through, and the lesson papers sometimes covered with unexplained blots of ink as if the machine which had printed them had broken down or rebelled, the lessons were even more dull.

Ancient Egypt and the flooding of the Nile!

The Nile, when we possessed a creek of our own with individual flooding!

'Well let's go along the gully, along by the creek,' we would say, tired with all these.

Then one day when our restlessness was at its height, when the flies buzzed like bees in the flypapers, and the warped wood of the house cracked its knuckles out of boredom, the need for something to do in the heat, we found once again the only solution to our unrest.

Someone said, 'What's the creek on?'

'Half-high flow.'

'Good.'

So we set out, in our bathing suits, and carrying switches of willow.

'Keep your sun hats on!' our mother called.

All right. We knew. Sunstroke when the sun clipped you over the back of the head, striking you flat on the ground. Sunstroke. Lightning. Even tidal waves were threatening us on this southern coast. The world was full of alarm.

'And don't go as far as the Reservoir!'

We dismissed the warning. There was enough to occupy us along the gully without our visiting the Reservoir. First, the couples. We liked to find a courting couple and follow them and when, as we knew they must do because they were tired or for other reasons, they found a place in the grass and lay down together, we liked to make jokes about them, amongst ourselves. 'Just wait for him to kiss her,' we would say. 'Watch. There. A beaut. Smack.'

Often we giggled and lingered even after the couple had observed us. We were waiting for them to do it. Every man and woman did it, we knew that for a fact. We speculated about technical details. Would he wear a frenchie? If he didn't wear a frenchie then she would start having a baby and be forced to get rid of it by drinking gin. Frenchies, by the way, were for sale in Woolworths. Some said they were fingerstalls, but we knew they were frenchies and sometimes

we would go downtown and into Woolworths just to look at the frenchies for sale. We hung around the counter, sniggering. Sometimes we nearly died laughing, it was so funny.

After we tired of spying on the couples we would shout after them as we went our way.

Pound, shillings and pence,
a man fell over the fence,
he fell on a lady
and squashed out a baby,
pound, shillings and pence!

Sometimes a slight fear struck us – what if a man fell on us like that and squashed out a chain of babies?

Our other pastime along the gully was robbing the orchards, but this summer day the apples were small green hard and hidden by leaves. There were no couples either. We had the gully to ourselves. We followed the creek, whacking our sticks, gossiping and singing, but we stopped, immediately silent, when someone – sister or brother – said, 'Let's go to the Reservoir!'

A feeling of dread seized us. We knew, as surely as we knew our names and our address Thirty-three Stour Street Ohau Otago South Island New Zealand Southern Hemisphere The World, that we would some day visit the Reservoir, but the time seemed almost as far away as leaving school, getting a job, marrying.

And then there was the agony of deciding the right time – how did one decide these things?

'We've been told not to, you know,' one of us said timidly.

That was me. Eating bread and syrup for tea had made

my hair red, my skin too, so that I blushed easily, and the grownups guessed if I told a lie.

'It's a long way,' said my little sister.

'Coward!'

But it *was* a long way, and perhaps it would take all day and night, perhaps we would have to sleep there among the pine trees with the owls hooting and the old needle-filled warrens which now reached to the centre of the earth where pools of molten lead bubbled, waiting to seize us if we tripped and then there was the crying sound made by the trees, a sound of speech at its loneliest level where the meaning is felt but never explained, and it goes on and on in a kind of despair, trying to reach a point of understanding.

We knew that pine trees spoke in this way. We were lonely listening to them because we knew we could never help them to say it, whatever they were trying to say, for if the wind who was so close to them could not help them, how could we?

Oh no, we could not spend the night at the Reservoir among the pine trees.

'Billy Whittaker and his gang have been to the Reservoir, Billy Whittaker and the Green Feather gang, one afternoon.'

'Did he say what it was like?'

'No, he never said.'

'He's been in an iron lung.'

That was true. Only a day or two ago our Mother had been reminding us in an ominous voice of the fact which roused our envy just as much as our dread, 'Billy Whittaker was in an iron lung two years ago. Infantile paralysis.'

Some people were lucky. None of us dared to hope that we would ever be surrounded by the glamour of an iron lung; we would have to be content all our lives with paltry flesh lungs.

'Well are we going to the Reservoir or not?'

That was someone trying to sound bossy like our Father, 'Well am I to have salmon sandwiches or not, am I to have lunch at all today or not?'

We struck our sticks in the air. They made a whistling sound. They were supple and young. We had tried to make musical instruments out of them, time after time we hacked at the willow and the elder to make pipes to blow our music, but no sound came but our own voices. And why did two sticks rubbed together not make fire? Why couldn't we ever *make* anything out of the bits of the world lying about us?

An airplane passed in the sky. We craned our necks to read the writing on the underwing, for we collected airplane numbers.

The plane was gone, in a glint of sun.

'Are we?' someone said.

'If there's an eclipse you can't see at all. The birds stop singing and go to bed.'

'Well are we?'

Certainly we were. We had not quelled all our misgivings, but we set out to follow the creek to the Reservoir.

What is it? I wondered. They said it was a lake. I thought it was a bundle of darkness and great wheels which peeled and sliced you like an apple and drew you toward them with demonic force, in the same way that you were drawn beneath the wheels of a train if you stood too near the edge of the platform. That was the terrible danger when the Limited came rushing in and you had to approach to kiss arriving aunts.

We walked on and on, past wild sweet peas, clumps of cutty grass, horse mushrooms, ragwort, gorse, cabbage trees; and then, at the end of the gully, we came to strange territory, fences we did not know, with the barbed wire tearing at our

skin and at our skirts put on over our bathing suits because we felt cold though the sun stayed in the sky.

We passed huge trees that lived with their heads in the sky, with their great arms and joints creaking with age and the burden of being trees, and their mazed and linked roots rubbed bare of earth, like bones with the flesh cleaned from them. There were strange gates to be opened or climbed over, new directions to be argued and plotted, notices which said TRESPASSERS WILL BE PROSECUTED BY ORDER. And there was the remote immovable sun shedding without gentleness its influence of burning upon us and upon the town, looking down from its heavens and considering our infantile-paralysis epidemic, and the children tired of holidays and wanting to go back to school with the new stiff books with their crackling pages, the scrubbed ruler with the sun rising on one side amidst the twelfths, tenths, millimetres, the new pencils to be sharpened with the pencil shavings flying in long pickets and light-brown curls scalloped with red or blue; the brown school, the bare floors, the clump clump in the corridors on wet days!

We came to a strange paddock, a bull-paddock with its occupant planted deep in the long grass, near the gate, a jersey bull polished like a wardrobe, burnished like copper, heavy beams creaking in the wave and flow of the grass.

'Has it got a ring through its nose? Is it a real bull or a steer?'

Its nose was ringed which meant that its savagery was tamed, or so we thought; it could be tethered and led; even so, it had once been savage and it kept its pride, unlike the steers who pranced and huddled together and ran like water through the paddocks, made no impression, quarried no massive shape against the sky.

The bull stood alone.

Had not Mr Bennet been gored by a bull, his own tame bull, and been rushed to Glenham Hospital for thirty-three stitches? Remembering Mr Bennet we crept cautiously close to the paddock fence, ready to escape.

Someone said, 'Look, it's pawing the ground!'

A bull which pawed the ground was preparing for a charge. We escaped quickly through the fence. Then, plucking courage, we skirted the bushes on the far side of the paddock, climbed through the fence, and continued our walk to the Reservoir.

We had lost the creek between deep banks. We saw it now before us, and hailed it with more relief than we felt, for in its hidden course through the bull-paddock it had undergone change, it had adopted the shape, depth, mood of foreign water, foaming in a way we didn't recognise as belonging to our special creek, giving no hint of its depth. It seemed to flow close to its concealed bed, not wishing any more to communicate with us. We realised with dismay that we had suddenly lost posssession of our creek. Who had taken it? Why did it not belong to us any more? We hit our sticks in the air and forgot our dismay. We grew cheerful.

Till someone said that it was getting late, and we reminded one another that during the day the sun doesn't seem to move, it just remains pinned with a drawing pin against the sky, and then, while you are not looking, it suddenly slides down quick as the chopped-off head of a golden eel, into the sea, making everything in the world go dark.

'That's only in the tropics!'

We were not in the tropics. The divisions of the world in the atlas, the different coloured cubicles of latitude and longitude fascinated us.

'The sand freezes in the desert at night. Ladies wear bits of sand. . . .'

'grains . . .'

'grains or bits of sand as necklaces, and the camels . . .'

'with necks like snails . . .'

'with horns, do they have horns?'

'Minnie Stocks goes with boys . . . .'

'I know who your boy is, I know who your boy is. . . .'

Waiting by the garden gate,
Waiting by the garden gate . . .

'We'll never get to the Reservoir!'

'Whose idea was it?'

'I've strained my ankle!'

Someone began to cry. We stopped walking.

'I've strained my ankle!'

There was an argument.

'It's not strained, it's sprained.'

'strained.'

'sprained.'

'All right sprained then. I'll have to wear a bandage, I'll have to walk on crutches . . . .'

'I had crutches once. Look. I've got a scar where I fell off my stilts. It's a white scar, like a centipede. It's on my shins.'

'Shins! Isn't it a funny word? Shins. Have you ever been kicked in the shins?'

'shins, funnybone . . .'

'It's humerus . . .'

'knuckles . . .'

'a sprained ankle . . .'

'a strained ankle . . .'

'a whitlow, an ingrown toenail the roots of my hair warts spinal meningitis infantile paralysis . . .'

'Infantile paralysis, Infantile paralysis you have to be wheeled in a chair and wear irons on your legs and your knees knock together. . . .'

'Once you're in an iron lung you can't get out, they lock it, like a cage . . .'

'You go in the amberlance . . .'

'*ambulance . . .*'

'amberlance . . .'

'ambulance to the hostible . . .'

'the *hospital*, an *amberlance to the hospital* . . .'

'Infantile Paralysis . . .'

'Friar's Balsam! Friar's Balsam!'

'Baxter's Lung Preserver, Baxter's Lung Preserver!'

'Syrup of Figs, California Syrup of Figs!'

'The creek's going on high-flow!'

Yes, there were bubbles on the surface, and the water was turning muddy. Our doubts were dispelled. It was the same old creek, and there, suddenly, just ahead, was a plantation of pine trees, and already the sighing sound of it reached our ears and troubled us. We approached it, staying close to the banks of our newly claimed creek, until once again the creek deserted us, flowing its own private course where we could not follow, and we found ourselves among the pine trees, a narrow strip of them, and beyond lay a vast surface of sparkling water, dazzling our eyes, its centre chopped by tiny grey waves. Not a lake, nor a river, nor a sea.

'The Reservoir!'

The damp smell of the pine needles caught in our breath. There were no birds, only the constant sighing of the trees. We could see the water clearly now; it lay, except for the waves

beyond the shore, in an almost perfect calm which we knew to be deceptive – else why were people so afraid of the Reservoir? The fringe of young pines on the edge, like toy trees, subjected to the wind, sighed and told us their sad secrets. In the Reservoir there was an appearance of neatness which concealed a disarray too frightening to be acknowledged except, without any defence, in moments of deep sleep and dreaming. The little sparkling innocent waves shone now green, now grey, petticoats, lettuce leaves; the trees sighed, and told us to be quiet, hush-sh, as if something were sleeping and should not be disturbed – perhaps that was what the trees were always telling us, to hush-sh in case we disturbed something which must never ever be awakened?

What was it? Was it sleeping in the Reservoir? Was that why people were afraid of the Reservoir?

Well we were not afraid of it, oh no, it was only the Reservoir, it was nothing to be afraid of, it was just a flat Reservoir with a fence around it, and trees, and on the far side a little house (with wheels inside?) and nothing to be afraid of.

'The Reservoir, The Reservoir!' A noticeboard said DANGER, RESERVOIR.

Overcome with sudden glee we climbed through the fence and swung on the lower branches of the trees, shouting at intervals, gazing possessively and delightedly at the sheet of water with its wonderful calm and menace.

'The Reservoir! The Reservoir! The Reservoir!'

We quarrelled again about how to pronounce and spell the word. Then it seemed to be getting dark – or was it that the trees were stealing the sunlight and keeping it above their heads? One of us began to run. We all ran, suddenly, wildly, not caring about our strained or sprained ankles, through

the trees out into the sun where the creek, but it was our creek no longer, waited for us. We wished it were our creek, how we wished it were our creek! We had lost all account of time. Was it nearly night? Would darkness overtake us, would we have to sleep on the banks of the creek that did not belong to us any more, among the wild sweet peas and the tussocks and the dead sheep? And would the eels come up out of the creek, as people said they did, and on their travels through the paddocks would they change into people who would threaten us and bar our way, TRESPASSERS WILL BE PROSECUTED, standing arm in arm in their black glossy coats, swaying, their mouths open, ready to swallow us? Would they ever let us go home, past the orchards, along the gully? Perhaps they would give us Infantile Paralysis, perhaps we would never be able to walk home, and no one would know where we were, to bring us an iron lung with its own special key!

We arrived home, panting and scratched. How strange! The sun was still in the same place in the sky!

The question troubled us, 'Should we tell?'

The answer was decided for us. Our Mother greeted us as we went in the door with, 'You haven't been long away, kiddies. Where have you been? I hope you didn't go anywhere near the Reservoir.'

Our Father looked up from reading his newspapers.

'Don't let me catch you going near the Reservoir!'

We said nothing. How out-of-date they were! They were actually afraid!

The Bull Calf

'Why do I always have to milk the cows?' Olive said. 'Couldn't the others do it for a change?' But no, it is always me. Up early and over the hills to find Scrapers. At night home from school and over the hills again to find Scrapers, to bring her down across the creek (here it is difficult; I tie a rope over her horns and make my leap first; she follows, if she is willing) through the gate that hangs on one hinge, into the cow byre with its cracked concrete floor. Pinning her in the bail. Putting on the leg rope. Day after day rain shine or snow.

'I'm tired of milking the cows,' Olive said. 'Beauty, Pansy, and now Scrapers who is bony like bare rafters and scaffolding. One day I will refuse.'

Sometimes she did refuse, in the early morning with sleep gumming her eyes, her body sticky with night, her hair tangled.

'Milk your own cows!' she cried then, retreating to the bedroom and sitting obstinately on the bed, chanting rhymes and French verbs which her Mother could not understand because she had left school at sixteen to go to service. . . .

But the thought of Scrapers waiting haunted Olive, and soon she would get up from the bed, clatter to the scullery, bumping furniture on the way to show her resentment of everything in the world including corners and walls and doors, take the bucket with a swill of warm water in the bottom for washing the teats, and climb the hill in search of Scrapers who, if her bag was full, would be waiting mercifully not far away.

Olive went to High School. In the morning she worried about being late. And every morning when the teacher called suddenly, 'Form Twos, Form Twos,' Olive worried in case no one formed twos with her. Very often she found herself standing alone. Is it because I stink? she thought. Then she would press the back and front of her uniform, down below, to smooth away the bulge of the homemade sanitary towel, layers of torn sheet sewn together with the blood always leaking through. The other girls used bought towels which were safe and came in packs with tiny blue-edged notices inside the packet, WEAR BLUE LINE AWAY FROM THE BODY. The other girls did not seem to mind when in Drill, which was later called Physical Education to keep up with the times, the teacher would command sharply, 'Uniforms Off, Come on Everybody, Uniforms Off!' Why should they mind when they were using towels which did not show, or even the new type where the advertisement had a picture of a woman in a bathing suit, shouting with rapture from the edge of a high-diving board, 'No Belts, No Pins, No Pads!'

But on the days when Olive wore her homemade towel she would ask, blushing, 'Please can I keep my uniform on?'

'Oh,' Miss Copeland said. 'Yes.'

And Olive and one or two other girls with their uniforms on would huddle miserably on the end seat, by the bar stools, out of everybody's way.

Olive and her sisters had hickies on their chins and foreheads. The advertisements warned them never to wear 'off-the-face' hats. Whole pages of the newspapers were devoted to the picture-story of the disasters which befell Lorna, Mary or Marion who continued to wear off-the-face hats in spite of having hickies on their chins and foreheads. Lorna, Mary, Marion were lonely and unwanted until they

used Velona Ointment. Olive and her sisters used Velona Ointment. It had a smell like the oil of a motorcar engine and it came off in a sticky grass-green stain on the pillowcase.

But mostly Olive was tired. She stayed up late working on mathematical problems, writing French translations and essays, and in the morning she was up so early to go over the hill and find Scrapers. There were so many trees and hollows on the hill, and often it was in these hollows where the grass was juiciest, nourished by the pools of yesterday's rain or the secret underground streams, that Scrapers would be hiding. Sometimes Olive had to walk to the last Reserve before she found Scrapers. Then there was the problem of tying the rope across her horns and leading her home.

Sometimes Scrapers refused to cooperate. Olive would find her dancing up and down, tossing her horns and bellowing. 'Scrapers, Scrapers, come on, be a good cow!'

Still Scrapers refused, Olive could not understand why. I'll be late for school, she thought, after struggling with and trying to chase the entranced cow. But it was no use. Olive would hurry down the hill, across the creek, through the broken-hinged gate and up the path to the house where the family, waiting for breakfast, would ask, 'Where's the milk?' while Olive in turn confronted them with her question, 'What's the matter with Scrapers? She's dancing and tossing her horns and refusing to be milked.'

Her Mother received the news calmly. 'Leave the cow. She'll be all right in a few days.'

Nobody explained. Olive could not understand. She would pour stale milk on her Weet-Bix, finish her breakfast, brush the mud from her shoes, persuade the pleats into her uniform, and hurry away to school.

It was always the same. She stood alone in Assembly,

concealing herself behind the girl in front who was taller, Captain of the 'A' Basketball Team, Holder of a Drill Shield. Olive did not want the teachers on the platform to see her standing alone, hiding behind the girl in front of her.

Peace perfect peace in this dark world of sin
the cross of Jesus whispers Peace within

she sang, sensing the mysery. Her heart felt heavy and lonely.

When she climbed the hill in search of the cow she always stopped in the paddock next door to pat the neighbour's bull calf which was growing plumper and stronger every day. Everyone knew what happened to bull calves. They were taken to the slaughterhouse while they were still young, or they became steers journeying from saleyard to saleyard until they grew old and tough and despised, without the pride and ferocity of bulls and the gentleness and patience of cows. If you were caught in a paddock with them and they attacked you it was in bursts of irritation which left them standing as if bewildered, half-afraid at their own daring. They did not seem able to decide; they panicked readily; they had no home, they were forever lost in strange surroundings, closed in by new fences and gates with unfamiliar smells, trees, earth; with dogs snapping at their heels, herding them this way and that, in and out, up and down. . . .

Olive knew that one day Ormandy's bull calf would be a steer. 'Calfie, calfie,' she would whisper, putting her flattened palm inside the calf's mouth and letting it suck.

Night came. The spotted grey cockabullies in the creek wriggled under the stones to sleep, and soon the birds were hushed in the willow trees and the hedge and the sighing

pines. This evening Olive was late in fetching Scrapers. She was late and tired. Her best black stockings, cobbled at the back of the leg, were splashed with mud, there were no clean ones for tomorrow; her stockings never lasted, all the other girls bought their stockings at Morton's, and theirs were cashmere, with a purple rim around the top, a sign of quality, while Olive's were made of coarse rayon. She was ashamed of them, she was ashamed of everything and everyone. She kicked her shoes against a clump of grass. Toe and heel plates! Why must she always have toe and heel plates on her shoes? Why must they always be lace-ups? She yawned. Her skin felt itchy. The pressure of her tight uniform upon her breasts was uncomfortable. Why hadn't Auntie Polly realised, and made the seams deeper, to be let out when necessary? Olive's sisters wore uniforms made by real dressmakers. Her sisters were lucky. How they teased her, pointing to the pictures of the *True Confession* magazines, digging their elbows slyly at each other and murmuring, 'Marilyn's breasts were heavy and pendulous.'

'That means you,' they said to Olive. 'You'll be like Mum with two full moons bobbing up and down, moons and balloons and motor tyres.'

Yes, her sisters were lucky.

'Why don't they help with the cow?' Olive asked. 'Why don't they milk the cow for a change?'

She walked slowly up the hill, keeping to the path worn by herself and Scrapers; it was rucked with dry, muddy hoofprints and followed along the edge of the pine plantation. When she reached the top of the hill and there was still no sign of Scrapers she went to the fence bordering the native plant reserve and looked out over the town and the sea and the spilled dregs of light draining beyond the

horizon. The silver-bellied sea turned and heaved in the slowly brightening moon-track, and the red and green roofs of the town were brushed with rising mist and moon. She identified objects and places: the Town Clock; the main street; the houseboat down at the wharf; the High School, and just behind the trees at the corner, next to the bicycle sheds, the little shop that sold hot mince pies and fish and chips at lunchtime. Then she gazed once more at the sea, waiting for the Sea-Foam-Youth-Grown-Old to appear. It was her secret dream. She knew he would never reach her. She knew that his bright glistening body became old, shrivelled, yellow, as soon as he touched the sand; it was the penalty. She sighed. The grieving hush-hush of the trees disturbed her. Their heads were bowed, banded with night. The wind moved among them, sighing, only increasing their sorrow. It came to her, too, with its moaning that she could not understand; it filled the world with its loneliness and darkness.

Olive sighed again. What was the use of waiting for the Sea-Foam-Youth-Grown-Old? What was the use of anything? Would the trees never stop saying Why, Why?

She was Olive Blakely going to milk Scrapers. She was Olive Blakely standing on the hill alone at night. The cutty grass and the tinkertailor were brushing against her black stockings; there was bird dirt on the fence post; the barbed wire had snapped and sagged.

That evening she milked Scrapers on the hill. What a miracle! The cow stood motionless for her and did not give those sudden sly kicks which she practised from time to time. Scrapers was an expert at putting her foot in the bucket.

Olive patted the velvety flank. Scrapers was standing so calmly. Why was she so calm when a few days ago she

had danced, tossed, bellowed, jumping fences and running with her tail high in the air? Now she stood peacefully chewing, seeming to count the chews before each swallow, introducing a slight syncopation before returning the cud to her mouth which she opened slowly once or twice in a lazy yawn releasing her warm grassy-smelling breath on the cool air. Her teeth were stained and green, her eyes swam and glistened like goldfish. She let down her milk without protest.

Leaning to one side to balance the full bucket with its froth of creamy milk, Olive walked carefully down the hill. Damn, she thought. I will have to iron my uniform tonight, and sponge it to remove the grass stains. And damn again, I have trodden in cow muck. Cow muck, pancakes, cowpad . . .

She mused on the words. The Welsh children up the road said *cowpad.* They were a compact, aloof, mysterious family with the two girls going to High School. They had a cousin called Myfanwy. Olive wished that she were called Myfanwy. Or Eitne. Or anything except plain pickled Olive.

She crossed the creek. The milk slopped against her legs, dampening her stockings and staining the hem of her uniform.

'Damn again,' she said. She would have to look in Pear's *Dictionary*, 'Household Hints,' to find how to remove milk stains; she never remembered.

Then just as she was approaching the gate she noticed two men leaning over the bull calf in the corner of the paddock, near the hedge. 'Mr Ormandy, Mr Lewis,' Olive said to herself. 'Old Ormandy.'

He had been named *Old Ormandy* when he stopped people from picking his plums but there was no law against picking them, was there, when the tree hung over the fence

into the road, inviting anyone to take the dusty plums split and dark blue with pearls of jelly on their stalks and a bitter, blighted taste at the centre, near the stone.

Old Ormandy. The girl Ormandy picked her nose and ate it. Their uncle had been in court for sly-grogging.

Olive watched the two men. What were they doing to the bull calf? It was so dark. What were they doing in the dark? She waited until they had left the bull calf before she went over to say good night to it.

'Calfie, calfie,' she whispered. It was lying outstretched. She bent over it, seeking to pat its face and neck. Its nose felt hot and dry, its eyes were bright, and between its back legs there was blood, and a patch of blood on the grass. The calf had been hurt. Old Ormandy and Lewis were responsible. Whey hadn't they noticed the calf was ill? Or perhaps they had deliberately been cruel to it?

'I wouldn't put it past them,' Olive said aloud, feeling strangely satisfied that she was expressing her indignation in the very words her Father used when he became suspicious. 'I wouldn't put it past them.'

She trembled and patted the calf.

'Calfie, calfie,' she whispered again. 'Sook sook. Never mind, calfie, I'll get someone to help you.'

But her heart was thudding with apprehension. Supposing the calf were to die? She had seen many animals die. They were not pampered and flattered in death, like human beings; they became immediate encumbrances, threats to public health, with neighbours and councillors quarrelling over the tedious responsibility of their burial. Or were dead human beings – in secret of course – regarded in this way also, and was their funeral procession a concealment, with flowers, of feelings which the living were afraid to admit?

Olive's thoughts frightened her. She knew that all things dead were in the way; you tripped over them, they did not move, they were obstacles, they were no use, even if they were people they were no use, they did not complain or cry out, like sisters, if you pinched them or thumped them on the back, they were simply no use at all.

She did not want the bull calf to die. She could see its eyes glistening, pleading for help. She picked up the milk bucket and hurried through the gate to the house and even before she reached the garden tap (she had to be careful here for the tap leaked, the earth was bogged with moss and onion flower) she heard her Father's loud voice talking.

His friends, the Chinese people, had come to visit him, and he was telling the old old story. His operation. He had been ill with appendicitis and while he was in hospital he had made friends with the Chinese family who came often now to visit him, filling the house with unfamiliar voices and excitements, creating an atmosphere that inspired him to add new dimensions of peril to his details of the operation.

'Going gangrene . . . they wheeled me in . . .'

Almost running up to the house, fearing for the life of the bull calf, Olive had time only to hear her Father's loud voice talking to the visitors before she opened the kitchen door. She was almost crying now. She was ashamed of her tears in front of the visitors. She tried to calm herself. Everyone looked up, startled.

'It's calfie, Ormandy's bull calf, it's been hurt, there's all blood between its legs and its nose is hot!'

Olive's Mother glanced without speaking to her Father who returned the glance, with a slight smile at the corner of his mouth. The Chinese visitors stared. One of them, a young man, was holding a bowl with a flower growing

in it, a most beautiful water narcissus whose frail white transparent petals made everything else in the room – the cumbersome furniture, the heavy-browed bookcase, the chocolate-coloured panelled ceiling, the solid black-leaded stove – seem like unnecessary ballast stored beyond, and at the same time within, people to prevent their lives from springing up joyfully, like the narcissus growing out of water into the clear sky.

'The bull calf, what will we do about it?' Olive urged, breaking the silence, and staring at the flower because she could not take her eyes from its loveliness and frailty.

Her Mother spoke. 'It's all right,' she said. 'There's nothing the matter with the calf.'

Olive stopped looking at the flower. She turned to her Mother. She felt betrayed. Her Mother, who took inside the little frozen birds to try to warm them back to life, who mended the rabbit's leg when it was caught in the trap, who fed warm bran to the sick horse that was lying on its side, stretched out!

'But it's bleeding! The calf might die! I saw Mr Ormandy with it, Old Ormandy and another man!'

She knew the man had been Mr Lewis, yet she said 'another man' because it seemed to convey the terrible anonymity which had suddenly spread over every person and every deed. Nobody was responsible; nobody would own up; nobody would even *say.*

'The bull calf's all right, I tell you,' her Father said, impatient to return to his story of the operation. 'Forget it. Go and do your homework.'

Olive sensed embarrassment. They seemed ashamed of her. They were ashamed of something. Why didn't they tell her? She wished she had not mentioned the bull calf.

'But I saw it with my own eyes,' she insisted, in final proof that the calf was hurt and needed help.

Again everybody was silent. She could not understand. Why were they so secretive? What was the mystery?

Then her Father swiftly changed the subject.

'Yes, they wheeled me in . . . going gangrene . . . I said to Lottie, I said, on the night . . .'

Olive was about to go from the room when the young man in the corner beckoned to her. He smiled. He seemed to understand. He held out the bowl with the narcissus in it, and said, 'You have it. It is for you.'

Gratefully she took the bowl, and making no further mention of the sick calf she went to her bedroom. She put the narcissus on her dressing table. She touched the petals gently, stroking them, marvelling again at the transparency of the whole flower and the clear water where every fibre of the bulb seemed visible and in motion as if brushed by secret currents and tides. She leaned suddenly and put her cheek against the flower.

Then she lay down on her bed and with her face pressed to the pillow, she began to cry.

You Are Now Entering the Human Heart

I looked at the notice. I wondered if I had time before my train left Philadelphia for Baltimore in one hour. The heart, ceiling-high, occupied one corner of the large exhibition hall, and from wherever you stood in the hall you could hear its beating, *thum-thump-thum-thump.* It was a popular exhibit, and sometimes, when there were too many children about, the entrance had to be roped off, as the children loved to race up and down the blood vessels and match their cries to the heart's beating. I could see that the heart had already been punished for the day – the floor of the blood vessel was worn and dusty, the chamber walls were covered with marks, and the notice 'You Are Now Taking the Path of a Blood Cell Through the Human Heart', hung askew. I wanted to see more of the Franklin Institute and the Natural Science Museum across the street, but a journey through the human heart would be fascinating. Did I have time?

Later. First, I would go across the street to the Hall of North America, among the bear and the bison, and catch up on American flora and fauna.

I made my way to the Hall. More children, sitting in rows on canvas chairs. An elementary class from a city school, under the control of an elderly teacher. A museum attendant holding a basket, and all eyes gazing at the basket.

'Oh,' I said. 'Is this a private lesson? Is it all right for me to be here?'

The attendant was brisk. 'Surely. We're having a lesson in snake-handling,' he said. 'It's something new. Get the children young and teach them that every snake they meet is not to be killed. People seem to think that every snake has to be knocked on the head. So we're getting them young and teaching them.'

'May I watch?' I said.

'Surely. This is a common grass snake. No harm, no harm at all. Teach the children to learn the feel of them, to lose their fear.'

He turned to the teacher. 'Now, Miss – Mrs –' he said.

'Miss Aitcheson.'

He lowered his voice. 'The best way to get through to the children is to start with teacher,' he said to Miss Aitcheson. 'If they see you're not afraid, then they won't be.'

She must be near retiring age, I thought. A city woman. Never handled a snake in her life. Her face was pale. She just managed to drag the fear from her eyes to some place in their depths, where it lurked like a dark stain. Surely the attendant and the children noticed?

'It's harmless,' the attendant said. He'd been working with snakes for years.

Miss Aitcheson, I thought again. A city woman born and bred. All snakes were creatures to kill, to be protected from, alike the rattler, the copperhead, king snake, grass snake – venom and victims. Were there not places in the South where you couldn't go into the streets for fear of the rattlesnakes?

Her eyes faced the lighted exit. I saw her fear. The exit light blinked, hooded. The children, none of whom had ever touched a live snake, were sitting hushed, waiting for the drama to begin; one or two looked afraid as the attendant withdrew a green snake about three feet long from the basket and with

a swift movement, before the teacher could protest, draped it around her neck and stepped back, admiring and satisfied.

'There,' he said to the class. 'Your teacher has a snake around her neck and she's not afraid.'

Miss Aitcheson stood rigid; she seemed to be holding her breath.

'Teacher's not afraid, are you?' the attendant persisted. He leaned forward, pronouncing judgement on her, while she suddenly jerked her head and lifted her hands in panic to get rid of the snake. Then, seeing the children watching her, she whispered, 'No, I'm not afraid. Of course not.' She looked around her.

'Of course not,' she repeated sharply.

I could see her defeat and helplessness. The attendant seemed unaware, as if his perception had grown a reptilian covering. What did she care for the campaign for the preservation and welfare of copperheads and rattlers and common grass snakes? What did she care about someday walking through the woods or the desert and deciding between killing a snake and setting it free, as if there would be time to decide, when her journey to and from school in downtown Philadelphia held enough danger to occupy her? In two years or so, she'd retire and be in that apartment by herself and no doorman, and everyone knew what happened then, and how she'd be afraid to answer the door and to walk after dark and carry her pocketbook in the street. There was enough to think about without learning to handle and love the snakes, harmless and otherwise, by having them draped around her neck for everyone, including the children – most of all the children – to witness the outbreak of her fear.

'See, Miss Aitcheson's touching the snake. She's not afraid of it at all.'

As everyone watched, she touched the snake. Her fingers recoiled. She touched it again.

'See, she's not afraid. Miss Aitcheson can stand there with a beautiful snake around her neck and touch it and stroke it and not be afraid.'

The faces of the childern were full of admiration for the teacher's bravery, and yet there was a cruelly persistent tension; they were waiting, waiting.

'We have to learn to love snakes,' the attendant said. 'Would someone like to come out and stroke teacher's snake?'

Silence.

One shamefaced boy came forward. He stood petrified in front of the teacher.

'Touch it,' the attendant urged. 'It's a friendly snake. Teacher's wearing it around her neck and she's not afraid.'

The boy darted his hand forward, rested it lightly on the snake, and immediately withdrew his hand. Then he ran back to his seat. The children shrieked with glee.

'He's afraid,' someone said. 'He's afraid of the snake.'

The attendant soothed. 'We have to get used to them, you know. Grownups are not afraid of them, but we can understand that when you're small you might be afraid, and that's why we want you to learn to love them. Isn't that right, Miss Aitcheson? Isn't that right? Now who else is going to be brave enough to touch teacher's snake?'

Two girls came out. They stood hand in hand side by side and stared at the snake and then at Miss Aitcheson.

I wondered when the torture would end. The two little girls did not touch the snake, but they smiled at it and spoke to it and Miss Aitcheson smiled at them and whispered how brave they were.

'Just a minute,' the attendant said. 'There's really no need to be brave. It's not a question of bravery. The snake is *harmless*, absolutely *harmless*. Where's the bravery when the snake is harmless?'

Suddenly the snake moved around to face Miss Aitcheson and thrust its flat head toward her cheek. She gave a scream, flung up her hands, and tore the snake from her throat and threw it on the floor, and, rushing across the room, she collapsed into a small canvas chair beside the Bear Cabinet and started to cry.

I didn't feel I should watch any longer. Some of the children began to laugh, some to cry. The attendant picked up the snake and nursed it. Miss Aitcheson, recovering, sat helplessly exposed by the small piece of useless torture. It was not her fault she was city-bred, her eyes tried to tell us. She looked at the children, trying in some way to force their admiration and respect; they were shut against her. She was evicted from them and from herself and even from her own fear-infested tomorrow, because she could not promise to love and preserve what she feared. She had nowhere, at that moment, but the small canvas chair by the Bear Cabinet of the Natural Science Museum.

I looked at my watch. If I hurried, I would catch the train from Thirtieth Street. There would be no time to make the journey through the human heart. I hurried out of the museum. It was freezing cold. The icebreakers would be at work on the Delaware and the Susquehanna; the mist would have risen by the time I arrived home. Yes, I would just catch the train from Thirtieth Street. The journey through the human heart would have to wait until some other time.

Insulation

In the summer days when the lizards come out and the old ewes, a rare generation, a gift of the sun, gloat at us from the television screen, and the country, skull in hand, recites To kill or not to kill, and tomatoes and grapes ripen in places unused to such lingering light and warmth, then the people of Stratford, unlike the 'too happy happy tree' of the poem, do remember the 'drear-nighted' winter. They order coal and firewood, they mend leaks in the spouting and roof, they plant winter savoys, swedes, a last row of parsnips.

The country is not as rich as it used to be. The furniture in the furniture store spills out on the footpath and stays unsold. The seven varieties of curtain rail with their seven matching fittings stay on display, useless extras in the new education of discernment and necessity. The dazzling bathroom ware, the chrome and fur and imitation marble are no longer coveted and bought. For some, though, the time is not just a denial of gluttony, of the filling of that worthy space in the heart and the imagination with assorted satisfied cravings. Some have lost their jobs, their life-work, a process described by one factory-manager as 'shedding'.

'Yes, we have been shedding some of our workers.'

'Too happy happy tree?'

The leaves fall as if from other places, only they fall here. They are brittle in the sun. Shedding, severing, pruning. God's country, the garden of Eden and the conscientious gardeners.

Some find work again. Some who have never had work advertise in the local newspaper. There was that advertisement

which appeared every day for two weeks, full of the hope of youth, sweet and sad with unreal assumptions about the world.

'Sixteen year old girl with one thousand hours training at hairdressing College seeks work.' The *one thousand hours* was in big dark print. It made the reader gasp as if with a sudden visitation of years so numerous they could scarcely be imagined, as if the young girl had undergone, like an operation, a temporal insertion which made her in some way older and more experienced than anyone else. And there was the air of pride with which she flaunted her thousand hours. She was pleading, using her richness of time as her bargain. In another age she might have recorded such time in her Book of Hours.

And then there was the boy, just left school. 'Boy, sixteen, would like to join pop group as vocalist fulltime' – the guileless advertisement of a dream. Did anyone answer either advertisment? Sometimes I imagine they did (I too have unreal assumptions about the world), that the young girl has found a place in the local Salon Paris, next to the Manhattan Takeaway, where she is looked at with admiration and awe (one thousand hours!) and I think that somewhere, maybe, say, in Hamilton (which is to other cities what round numbers are to numbers burdened by decimal points), there's a pop group with a new young vocalist fulltime, appearing, perhaps, on *Opportunity Knocks*, the group playing their instruments, the young man running up and down the stairs, being sexy with his microphone and singing in the agony style.

But my real story is just an incident, a passing glance at insulation and one of those who were pruned, shed, severed, and in the curious mixture of political metaphor, irrationally

rationalised, with a sinking lid fitted over his sinking heart. I don't know his name. I only know he lost his job and he couldn't get other work and he was a man used to working with never a thought of finding himself jobless. Like the others he had ambled among the seven varieties of curtain rail and matching fittings, and the fancy suites with showwood arms and turned legs, and the second circular saw. He was into wrought iron, too, and there was a wishing well in his garden and his wife had leaflets about a swimming-pool. And somewhere, at the back of his mind, he had an internal stairway to the basement rumpus. Then one day, suddenly, although there had been rumours, he was pruned from the dollar-flowering tree.

He tried to get other work but there was nothing. Then he thought of spending his remaining money on a franchise to sell insulation. It was a promising district with the winters wet and cold and frosty. The price of electricity had gone up, the government was giving interest-free loans – why, everyone would be insulating. At first, having had a number of leaflets printed, he was content to distribute them in letter boxes, his two school-age children helping. His friends were sympathetic and optimistic. They too said, Everyone will be wanting insulation. And after this drought you can bet on a cold winter. Another thing, there was snow on Egmont at Christmas, and that's a sign.

He sat at home waiting for the orders to come in. None came. He tried random telephoning, still with no success. Finally, he decided to sell from door to door.

'I'm going from door to door,' he told his wife.

She was young and able. She had lost her job at the local clothing factory, and was thinking of buying a knitting-machine and taking orders. On TV when they demonstrated

knitting-machines the knitter (it was always a she, with the he demonstrating) simply moved her hands to and fro as if casting a magic spell and the machine did the rest. To and fro, to and fro, a fair-isle sweater knitted in five hours, and fair-isle was coming back, people said. Many of her friends had knitting-machines, in the front room, near the window, to catch the light, where, in her mother's day, the piano always stood, and when she walked by her friends' houses she could see them sitting in the light moving their hands magically to and fro, making fair-isle and bulky knit, intently reading the pattern.

'Yes, door to door.'

The words horrified her. Not in her family, surely! Not door to door. Her father, a builder, had once said that if a man had to go door to door to advertise his work there was something wrong with it.

'If you're reputable,' he said, 'you don't advertise. People just come to you through word of mouth, through your own work standing up to the test.' Well, it wasn't like that now, she knew. Even Smart and Rogers had a full-page advertisement in the latest edition of the local paper. All the same, door to door!

'Oh, no,' she said plaintively.

'It can't be helped. I have to look for custom.'

He put on his work clothes, a red checkered shirt, jeans, and he carried a bundle of leaflets, and even before he had finished both sides of one street he was tired and he had begun to look worried and shabby.

This is how I perceived him when he came to my door. I saw a man in his thirties wearing a work-used shirt and jeans yet himself looking the picture of disuse, that is, severed,

shed, rationalised with a great lid sinking over his life, putting out the flame.

'I thought you might like to insulate your house,' he said, thrusting a leaflet into my hand.

I was angry. Interrupted in my work, brought to the door for nothing! Why, the electrician had said my house was well insulated with its double ceilings. Besides, I'd had experience of that stuff they blow into the ceiling and every time there's a wind it all comes out making snowfall in the garden, drifting over to the neighbours too.

'No, I'm not interested,' I said. 'I tried that loose-fill stuff once and it snowed everywhere, every time the wind blew.'

'There's a government loan, you know.'

'I'm not really interested,' I said.

'But it's new. New. Improved.'

'Can't afford it, anyway.'

'Read about it, then, and let me know.'

'Sorry,' I said.

My voice was brisk and dismissing. He looked as if he were about to plead with me, then he changed his mind. He pointed to the red print stamped on the leaflet. There was pride in his pointing, like that of the girl with the thousand hours.

'That's my name and phone number, if you change your mind.'

'Thank you, but I don't think I will.'

He walked away and I shut the door quickly. Insulation, I said to myself with no special meaning or tone. How lovely the summer is, how cosy this house is. The people here before me had carpets that will last for ever, the ceiling is double, there are no cracks in the corners, that is, unless the place decides to shift again on its shaky foundations. How

well insulated I am! How solid the resistance of this house against the searching penetrating winds of Stratford. The hunted safe from the hunter, the fleeing from the pursuer, the harmed from the harmer.

'How well insulated I am!'

That night I had a curious ridiculous dream. I dreamed of a land like a vast forest 'in green felicity' where the leaves had started to fall, not by nature, for the forest was evergreen, but under the influence of a season that came to the land from within it and had scarcely been recognised, and certainly not ruled against. Now how could that have been? At first I thought I was trapped in a legend of far away and long ago, for the characters of long ago were there. I could see a beggar walking among the fallen leaves. He was the beggar of other times and other countries, and yet he was not, he was new, and he was ashamed. I saw a cottage in the forest and a young woman at the window combing her hair and – a young man with a – lute? No, a guitar – surely that was the prince? – and with the guitar plugged in to nowhere he began to play and sing and as he sang he sparkled – why, it was Doug Dazzle – and he was singing,

One thousand hours of cut and set
my showwood arms will hold you yet
baby baby insulate
apprentice and certificate,
God of nations at thy feet
in our bonus bonds we meet
lest we forget lest we forget
one thousand hours of cut and set. . . .

The girl at the window listened and smiled and then she turned to the knitting-machine by the window and began to play it as if from a 90 per cent worsted, 10 per cent acrylic score. I could see the light falling on her hands as they moved to and fro, to and fro in a leisurely saraband of fair-isle. Then the beggar appeared. He was carrying a sack that had torn and was leaking insulation, faster and faster, until it became a blizzard, vermiculite falling like snow, endlessly, burying everything, the trees and their shed leaves, the cottage, the beggar, the prince, and the princess of the thousand hours.

The next morning I found the leaflet and telephoned the number on it.

'I'd like to be insulated,' I said.

The man was clearly delighted.

'I'll come at once and measure.'

We both knew we were playing a game, he trying to sell what he didn't possess, and I imagining I could ever install it, to deaden the world. All the same, he measured the house and he put in the loose-fill insulation, and following the Stratford custom, although it was summer, I ordered my firewood against that other 'drear-nighted' winter.

PATRICIA GRACE

A Way of Talking

Rose came back yesterday; we went down to the bus to meet her. She's just the same as ever, Rose. Talks all the time flat out and makes us laugh with her way of talking. On the way home we kept saying, 'E Rohe, you're just the same as ever.' It's good having my sister back and knowing she hasn't changed. Rose is the hard-case one in the family, the kamakama one, and the one with the brains.

Last night we stayed up talking till all hours, even Dad and Nanny who usually go to bed after tea. Rose made us laugh telling about the people she knows, and taking off professor this and professor that from varsity. Nanny, Mum and I had tears running down from laughing; e ta Rose, we laughed all night.

At last Nanny got out of her chair and said, 'Time for sleeping. The mouths steal the time of the eyes.' That's the lovely way she has of talking, Nanny, when she speaks in English. So we went to bed and Rose and I kept our mouths going for another hour or so before falling asleep.

This morning I said to Rose that we'd better go and get her measured for the dress up at Mrs Frazer's. Rose wanted to wait a day or two but I reminded her the wedding was only two weeks away and that Mrs Frazer had three frocks to finish.

'Who's Mrs Frazer anyway,' she asked. Then I remembered Rose hadn't met these neighbours though they'd been in the district a few years. Rose had been away at school.

'She's a dressmaker,' I looked for words. 'She's nice.'

'What sort of nice?' asked Rose.

'Rose, don't you say anything funny when we go up there,' I said. I know Rose, she's smart. 'Don't you get smart.' I'm older than Rose but she's the one that speaks out when something doesn't please her. Mum used to say, Rohe, you've got the brains but you look to your sister for the sense. I started to feel funny about taking Rose up to Jane Frazer's because Jane often says the wrong thing without knowing.

We got our work done, had a bath and changed, and when Dad came back from the shed we took the stationwagon to drive over to Jane's. Before we left we called out to Mum, 'Don't forget to make us a Māori bread for when we get back.'

'What's wrong your own hands,' Mum said, but she was only joking. Always when one of us comes home one of the first things she does is make a big Māori bread.

Rose made a good impression with her kamakama ways, and Jane's two nuisance kids took a liking to her straight away. They kept jumping up and down on the sofa to get Rose's attention and I kept thinking what a waste of a good sofa it was, what a waste of a good house for those two nuisance things. I hope when I have kids they won't be so hōhā.

I was pleased about Jane and Rose. Jane was asking Rose all sorts of questions about her life in Auckland. About varsity and did Rose join in the marches and demonstrations. Then they went on to talking about fashions and social life in the city, and Jane seemed deeply interested. Almost as though she was jealous of Rose and the way she lived, as though she felt Rose had something better than a lovely house and clothes and everything she needed to make life good for her. I was pleased to see that Jane liked my sister so much, and proud of my sister and her entertaining and friendly ways.

Jane made up a cup of coffee when she'd finished measuring Rose for the frock, then packed the two kids outside with a

piece of chocolate cake each. We were sitting having coffee when we heard a truck turn in at the bottom of Frazers' drive.

Jane said, 'That's Alan. He's been down the road getting the Maoris for scrub cutting.'

I felt my face get hot. I was angry. At the same time I was hoping Rose would let the remark pass. I tried hard to think of something to say to cover Jane's words though I'd hardly said a thing all morning. But my tongue seemed to thicken and all I could think of was, Rohe don't.

Rose was calm. Not all red and flustered like me. She took a big pull on the cigarette she had lit, squinted her eyes up and blew the smoke out gently. I knew something was coming.

'Don't they have names?'

'What. Who?' Jane was surprised and her face was getting pink.

'The people from down the road whom your husband is employing to cut scrub.' Rose the stink thing, she was talking all Pākehāfied.

'I don't know any of their names.'

I was glaring at Rose because I wanted her to stop but she was avoiding my looks and pretending to concentrate on her cigarette.

'Do they know yours?'

'Mine?'

'Your name.'

'Well . . . Yes.'

'Yet you have never bothered to find out their names or to wonder whether or not they have any.'

The silence seemed to hang around in my head for ages and ages. Then I think Jane muttered something about difficulty, but that touchy sister of mine stood up and said, 'Come on

Hera.' And I with my red face and shut mouth followed her out to the station wagon without a goodbye or anything.

I was so wild with Rose. I was wild. I was determined to blow her up about what she had done, I was determined. But now that we were alone together I couldn't think what to say. Instead I felt an awful big sulk coming on. It has always been my trouble, sulking. Whenever I don't feel sure about something I go into a big fat sulk. We had a teacher at school who used to say to some of us girls, 'Speak, don't sulk.' She'd say, 'You only sulk because you haven't learned how and when to say your minds.'

She was right that teacher, yet here I am a young woman about to be married and haven't learned yet how to get the words out. Dad used to say to me, 'Look out girlie, you'll stand on your lip.'

At last I said, 'Rose, you're a stink thing.' Tears were on the way. 'Gee Rohe, you made me embarrassed.' Then Rose said, 'Don't worry, Honey, she's got a thick hide.'

These words of Rose's took me by surprise and I realised something about Rose then. What she said made all my anger go away and I felt very sad because it's not our way of talking to each other. Usually we'd say, 'Never mind Sis,' if we wanted something to be forgotten. But when Rose said, 'Don't worry, Honey, she's got a thick hide,' it made her seem a lot older than me, and tougher, and as though she knew much more than me about the world. It made me realise too that underneath her jolly and forthright ways Rose is very hurt. I remembered back to when we were both little and Rose used to play up at school if she didn't like the teacher. She'd get smart and I used to be ashamed and tell Mum on her when we got home, because although she had the brains I was always the well-behaved one.

Rose was speaking to me in a new way now. It made me feel sorry for her and for myself. All my life I had been sitting back and letting her do the objecting. Not only me, but Mum and Dad and the rest of the family too. All of us too scared to make known when we had been hurt or slighted. And how can the likes of Jane know when we go round pretending all is well. How can Jane know us?

But then I tried to put another thought into words. I said to Rose, 'We do it too. We say, "the Pākehā doctor", or "the Pākehā at the post office", and sometimes we mean it in a bad way.'

'Except that we talk like this to each other only. It's not so much what is said, but when and where and in whose presence. Besides, you and I don't speak in this way now, not since we were little. It's the older ones: Mum, Dad, Nanny who have this habit.'

Then Rose said something else. 'Jane Frazer will still want to be your friend and mine in spite of my embarrassing her today; we're in the fashion.'

'What do you mean?'

'It's fashionable for a Pākehā to have a Māori for a friend.' Suddenly Rose grinned. Then I heard Jane's voice coming out of that Rohe's mouth and felt a grin of my own coming. 'I have friends who are Maoris. They're lovely people. The eldest girl was married recently and I did the frocks. The other girl is at varsity. They're all so *friendly* and so *natural* and their house is absolutely *spotless.*'

I stopped the wagon in the drive and when we'd got out Rose started strutting up the path. I saw Jane's way of walking and felt a giggle coming on. Rose walked up Mum's scrubbed steps, 'Absolutely spotless.' She left her shoes in the porch and bounced into the kitchen. 'What did I tell you?

Absolutely spotless. And a friendly natural woman taking new bread from the oven.'

Mum looked at Rose then at me. 'What have you two been up to? Rohe, I hope you behaved yourself at that Pākehā place?' But Rose was setting the table. At the sight of Mum's bread she'd forgotten all about Jane and the events of the morning.

When Dad, Heke, and Matiu came in for lunch, Rose, Mum, Nanny and I were already into the bread and the big bowl of hot corn.

'E ta,' Dad said. 'Let your hardworking father and your two hardworking brothers starve. Eat up.'

'The bread's terrible. You men better go down to the shop and get you a shop bread,' said Rose.

'Be the day,' said Heke.

'Come on my fat Rohe. Move over and make room for your Daddy. Come on my baby shift over.'

Dad squeezed himself round behind the table next to Rose. He picked up the bread Rose had buttered for herself and started eating. 'The bread's terrible all right,' he said. Then Mat and Heke started going on about how awful the corn was and who cooked it and who grew it, who watered it all summer and who pulled out the weeds.

So I joined in the carryings on and forgot about Rose and Jane for the meantime. But I'm not leaving it at that. I'll find some way of letting Rose know I understand and I know it will be difficult for me because I'm not clever the way she is. I can't say things the same and I've never learnt to stick up for myself.

But my sister won't have to be alone again. I'll let her know that.

Valley

Summer

The sun-filled sky wraps the morning in warmth. Already the asphalt has begun to shimmer with light and heat and the children are arriving.

They spill out of the first bus with sandwiches and cordial, in twos and threes, heads together, strangely quiet. Uncertain they stand with bare feet warming on asphalt, clutching belongings, wondering. They are wondering what I will be like.

It is half past eight. I am watching from my kitchen window and see them glance this way, wondering. In a minute or two I will be ready to go over for them to look at me, but now they are moving away slowly, slapping feet on the warmed playground.

They are wondering what he will be like too. He is in his classroom already, sorting out names, chalking up reminders, and cleaning dead starlings from the grate of the chipheater in the corner. They stand back from the glass doors and stare, and he comes out with the dead birds on a shovel and gives them to a big boy to take away and bury. They all stare, and the younger ones wonder if he killed the birds, but the older ones know that starlings get trapped in the chimneys every summer and have to be cleaned out always on the first day of school.

I pick up the baby and my bag and walk across. Their eyes are on me.

'Hullo,' I say but no one speaks, and they hurry away to the middle room which is Tahi's, because they know her. Some of them call her Mrs Kaa because they have been told to; others call her Auntie because she is their aunt; and others call her Hey Tahi because they are little and don't know so much.

At nine he rings the bell and makes a come here sign with his arm. They see, and know what he wants, and walk slowly to stand on the square of concrete by the staffroom steps. They stand close together, touching, and he tells them his name and mine. Then he reads their names from a list and Tahi tells each where to stand. Soon we have three groups: one for the little room which is mine, one for the middle room which is hers, and one for the big room which is his.

We find a place for the sandwiches and cordial and then they sit looking at me and not speaking, wondering what I am like.

I put the baby on a rug with his toys. I put my bag by the table, then write my name on the board to show them how it looks. And I read it for them so they will know its sound. I write baby's name as well and read it too, but they remain silent.

And when I say good morning they look at one another and at the floor, so I tell them what to say. But, although some open their mouths and show a certain willingness, no sound comes out. Some of them are new and haven't been to school before and all of them are shy.

The silence frightens me, beating strongly into the room like sun through glass.

But suddenly one of them speaks.

He jumps up and points excitedly. Necks swivel.

'Hey! You fullas' little brother, he done a mimi. Nā!'

And there is little Eru with a puddle at his feet. And there we are, they and I, with a sentence hanging in the sun-filled room waiting for another to dovetail its ending.

I thank him and ask his name but his mouth is shut again. The little girl in shirt and rompers says, 'He's Samuel.'

'Mop?' Samuel asks, and means shall I get the wet mop from the broom cupboard and clean up the puddle. Which is friendly of him.

'Yes, please,' I say, but again he stands confused.

Shirt and rompers shoves him towards the door. 'Go,' she says.

He mops up the water and washes the mop at the outside tap. Then he stands on the soggy mop-strings with his warmed feet, and the water squeezes out and runs in little rivers, then steams dry. Samuel wears large serge shorts belted with a man's necktie and there is one button on his shirt. His large dark eyes bulge from a wide flat face like two spuds. His head is fat too and his hair has been clipped round in a straight line above his ears. The hair that is left sticks straight up as though he is wearing a kina.

Shorts and rompers tells me all the names and I write them on the board. Her name is Margaret.

Samuel
Margaret
Kopu, Hiriwa
Cowboy
Lillian, Roimata
Glen
Wiki, Steven
Marama, Evelyn
Michael, Edie

Hippy
Stan.

We have made a poem. The last two are twins; I don't know how I'll ever tell them apart.

We find a place for everyone at the tables and a locker for each one's belongings, but although they talk in whispers and nudge one another they do not offer me any words. And when I speak to them they nod or shake their heads. Their eyes take the floor.

The play bell rings and I let them go. They eat briefly, swig at the cordial or go to the drinking taps. Then they pad across the hot asphalt to the big field where the grass is long and dry. Then they begin to run and shout through the long grass as though suddenly they have been given legs and arms, as though the voices have at that moment been put into them.

Ahead of them the grasshoppers flick up and out into the ever-heating day.

Hiriwa sits every morning at the clay table modelling clay. He is a small boy with a thin face and the fingers that press into the clay are long, and careful about what they do.

This morning he makes a cricket – female by the pointed egg-laying mechanism on its tail. He has managed the correct angles of the sets of legs, and shows the fine rasps on the hind set by lifting little specks of clay with his pencil. Soon he will tell me a story so I can write for him; then later he will show the children what he has made and read the story for them.

We collected the crickets yesterday because we are learning about insects and small animals in summer. The crickets are housed in a large jar containing damp earth and

stones and a wine biscuit. The book tells me that this is the way to keep crickets, and they seem content enough to live like this as they begin their ringing in the warmth of mid-morning.

Two weeks ago we walked down past the incinerator to where nasturtiums flood a hollow ground at the edge of bush, covering long grass and fern beginnings with round dollar leaves and orange and gold honey flowers blowing trumpets at the sky.

The first thing was to sit among the leaves and suck nectar from the flowers, which wasn't why we had come but had to be done first. And it gave us a poem for the poem book too. Roimata, who finds a secret language inside herself, gave us the poem:

> I squeeze the tail off the nasturtium flower
> And suck the honey,
> The honey runs all round inside me,
> Making me sweet
> Like sugar,
> Like treacle,
> And lollies,
> And chocolate fish,
> And all the children lick my skin
> And say, 'Sweet, sweet,
> Roimata is a sweet, sweet girl.'

The next thing was to turn each flat nasturtium leaf carefully and look on the soft green underside for the pin-prick sized butterfly eggs. We found them there, little ovals of yellow, like tiny turned-on light bulbs, and found the mint green caterpillars too, chewing holes in their umbrellas.

The next thing was to put down the leaves they had picked and to begin rolling down the bank in the long grass, laughing and shouting, which wasn't why we had come but had to be done as well:

I rolled busting down the bank
On cold seagrass,
And I thought I was a wave of the sea,
But I am only a skinny girl
With sticking out eyes,
And two pigtails
That my Nanny plaits every morning
With spider fingers.

Now all the eggs have hatched, and every afternoon they pick fresh leaves for the caterpillars. Every morning we find the leaves eaten to the stems, and the table and floor littered with black droppings like scattered crumbs of burnt toast.

The caterpillars are at several stages of growth. Some are little threads of green cotton, and difficult to see, camouflaged by the leaf and its markings. Others are half grown and working at the business of growing by eating steadily all day and night. The largest ones are becoming sluggish with growth, and have gone away from food and attached themselves to the back of the room to pupate:

The caterpillar,
Up on the classroom wall,
Spins a magic house around itself
To hide from all the boys and girls.

Then yesterday on coming in from lunch we found the

first of the butterflies, wing-beating the sun-filled room in convoy. We kept them for the afternoon, then let them out the window and watched them fly away:

> Butterfly out in the sun,
> Flying high by the roof,
> 'Look up there,' Kopu said.
> 'Butterfly. Nā.
> The best butterfly,
> I want to be a butterfly flying.'

I said that he would tell me a story to write about his cricket. And that later he would show the children what he had made and read the story for them. But I turned and saw his arm raised and his fist clenched. His thin arm, with the small fingers curled, like a daisy stem with its flower closed after sundown. The fist came down three times on the carefully modelled insect. Head, thorax, abdomen. He looked at what he'd done and walked away.

'Why?' I asked but he had no words for me.

'That's why, he don't like it,' Samuel told me.

'That's why, his cricket is too dumb,' Kopu said.

Those two have made a bird's nest out of clay and are filling it with little round eggs, heaping the eggs up as high as they will go.

'I made a nest.'

'I made some eggs.'

I made a cricket as best I could with my careful fingers. Then my flower hand thumped three times down on the cricket. Abdomen, thorax, head. And my cricket is nothing but clay.

Autumn

Autumn bends the lights of summer and spreads evening skies with reds and golds. These colours are taken up by falling leaves which jiggle at the fingertips of small-handed winds.

Trees give off crowds of starlings which shoot the valley with scarcely a wing beat, flocking together to replace warmth stolen by diminishing sun.

Feet that were soft and supple in the summer are hardening now and, although it is warm yet, cardigans and jerseys are turning up in the lost-property box. And John, our neighbour, looks into his vat one morning and sees a single sheet of milk lining the bottom. He puts his herd out and goes on holiday.

Each day we have been visiting the trees – the silver poplar, the liquid amber, and the plum, peach, and apple. And, on looking up through the branches, each day a greater patch of sky is visible. Yet, despite this preoccupation with leaves and colours and change, the greater part of what we see has not changed at all. The gum tree as ever leaves its shed bark, shed twigs, shed branches untidily on its floor, and the pōhutukawa remains dull and lifeless after its December spree and has nothing new for this season.

About us are the same green paddocks where cows undulate, rosetting the grass with soft pancake plops; and further on in the valley the variegated greens of the bush begin, then give way to the black-green of distant hills.

They have all gone home. I tidy my table, which is really a dumping ground for insects in matchboxes, leftover lunches and lost property. Then I go out to look for Eru. The boys are pushing him round in the wood cart and he is grinning at the sky with his four teeth, two top and two bottom, biting against each other in ecstacy.

Tahi is in the staffroom peeling an apple. She points the knife into the dimple of apple where the stem is and works the knife carefully in a circle. A thin wisp of skin curls out from the blade. She peels slowly round and down the apple, keeping the skin paper-thin so that there is neither a speck of skin on the apple nor a speck of apple flesh left on the skin. Nor is there a ridge or a bump on the fruit when she has finished peeling. A perfect apple. Skinless. As though it has grown that way on the tree.

Then she stands the apple on a plate and slashes it down the middle with a knife as though it is nothing special and gives me half.

'Gala Day in five days' time,' she says.

'Yes,' I say. 'They'll want to practise for the races.'

'We always have a three-legged and a sack.'

Then Ed comes in and picks up the phone.

'I've got to order a whole lot of stuff for the gala. Gala in five days' time.'

We wake this morning to the scented burning of mānuka and, looking out, see the bell-shaped figure of Turei Mathews outlined by the fire's light against the half-lit morning. He stands with his feet apart and his hands bunched on his spread waist, so that his elbows jut. With his small head and his short legs, he looks like a pear man in a fruit advertisement, except that he has a woman's sunhat pulled down over his ears.

Beside him Ron and Skippy Anderson are tossing branches into the flames and turning the burning sticks with shovels. We hear the snap, snap of burning tea tree and see the flames spread and diminish, spread, diminish – watch the ash-flakes spill upwards and outwards into lighting day.

Yesterday afternoon Turei, Ron, and Skippy brought the truckload of wood and the hāngī stones and collected the two wire baskets from the hall. They spat on their hands, took up the shovels, and dug the hole, then threw their tools on the back of the truck and went.

Yesterday Ed and the boys put up the tents, moved tables and chairs, and set up trestles. The girls tidied the grounds, covered tables with newspaper, and wrote numbers in books for raffles.

We were worried by clouds yesterday. But now on waking we watch the day lighting clear; we pack our cakes and pickles into a carton and are ready to leave.

By eight o'clock the cars and trucks are arriving and heaving out of their doors bags of corn, kūmara, potatoes, pumpkin, and hunks of meat. Women establish themselves under the gum tree with buckets of water, peelers, and vegetable knives. Turei and his helpers begin zipping their knives up and down steel in preparation for slicing into the pork. Tahi is organising the cakes and pickles and other goods for sale, Eru is riding in the wood cart, and Ed is giving out tins for raffle money. I take up my peeler and go towards the gum tree.

Roimata's grandmother is there.

'It's a good day,' she says.

'Yes,' I say. 'We are lucky.'

'I open these eyes this morning and I say to my mokopuna, "The day it is good." She flies all around tidying her room, making her bed, no trouble. Every smile she has is on her face. I look at her and I say, "We got the sun outside in the sky, and we got the sun inside dancing around." I try to do her hair for her. "Hurry, Nanny, hurry," she says. "Anyhow will do." "Anyhow? Anyhow?" I say. "Be patient, Roimata, or they all think it's Turei's dog coming to the gala."'

Opposite me Taupeke smokes a skinny fag, and every now and again takes time off from peeling for a session of coughing. Her face is as old as the hills, but her eyes are young and birdlike and watchful. Her coughing has all the sounds of a stone quarry in full swing, and almost sends her toppling from the smaller primer chair on which she sits.

'Too much this,' she explains to me, pointing to her tobacco tin. 'Too much cigarette, too much cough.'

And Connie next to her says, 'Yes, Auntie. You take off into space one of these days with your cough.'

She nods. 'Old Taupeke be a sputnik then. Never mind. I take my old tin with me. No trouble.'

Hiriwa's mother is there too. She is pale and serious-looking and very young. Every now and again Hiriwa comes and stands beside her and watches her working; his small hands rest lightly on her arm, his wrist bones protrude like two white marbles. I notice a white scar curving from her temple to her chin.

Tahi comes over and says, 'Right give us a spud,' then spreads her bulk on a primer chair and begins her reverent peeling. A tissue-thin paring spirals downward from her knife.

'How are you, Auntie? How are you, Connie? How are you, Rita? Gee Elsie, you want to put your peel in the hāngī and throw your kūmara away.'

'Never mind,' says Elsie. 'That's the quick way. Leave plenty on for the pigs.'

'Hullo Auntie, hello ladies. How are all these potato and kūmara getting on?' asks Turei. He takes off his sunhat and wipes the sweat from his neck and head.

'Never mind our potato and kūmara,' Tahi says. 'What about your stones? Have you cooks got the stones hot? We

don't want our pork jumping off our plates and taking off for the hills.'

'No trouble,' Turei says. 'The meal will be superb. Extra delicious.'

'Wī! Listen to him talk.'

'You got a mouthful there, Turei!'

'Plenty of kai in the head, that's why,' he says.

'And plenty in the puku too. Na. Plenty of hinu there Turei.'

'Ah well. I'm going. You women slinging off at my figure I better go.'

He puts his hat on and pats his paunch. 'Hurry up with those vegies. Not too much of the yakkety-yak.' He ambles away followed by a bunch of kids and a large scruffy dog.

The sacks are empty. We have peeled the kūmara and potatoes, stripped and washed the corn, and cut and skinned the pumpkin. The prepared vegetables are in buckets of water and we stand to go and wash our hands.

But suddenly we are showered with water. We are ankle deep in water and potatoes, kūmara, pumpkin, and corn. Connie, who hasn't yet stood, has a red bucket upside down on her lap and she is decorated with peelings. Turei's dog is running round and round and looks as though he has been caught in a storm.

'Turei, look what your mutt did,' Tahi yells, and Turei hurries over to look, while the rest of us stand speechless. Taupeke's cigarette is hanging down her chin like an anaemic worm.

'That mutt of mine, he can't wait for hāngī. He has to come and get it now. Hey you kids. Come and pick up all this. Come on you kids.'

*

The kids like Turei and they hang around. They enjoy watching him get the hāngī ready and listening to him talk.

'They're the best stones,' he tells them. 'These old ones that have been used before. From the river these stones.'

The boys take their shirts off because Turei wears only a singlet over his big drum chest.

'How's that, Turei?' they ask, showing off their arm muscles.

'What's that?' he says.

'What you think?'

'I seen pipis in the sand bigger than that.'

'You got too much muscles, Turei.'

'Show us, Turei.'

'Better not. Might be you'll get your eyes sore.'

'Go on,' they shout.

So he puts the shovel down, and they all watch the big fist shut and the thick forearm pull up while the great pumpkin swells and shivers at the top of his arm.

'Wī nā Turei! Some more, Turei.'

'You kids don't want any kai? You want full eyes and empty pukus?'

'Some more, Turei. Some more.'

But Turei is shovelling the white-hot stones into the hāngī hole. 'You kids better move. Might be I'll get you on the end of this shovel and stick you all in the hole.'

He makes towards them and they scatter.

The prepared food is covered with cloths and the baskets are lowered over the stones. Steam rises as the men turn on the hose. They begin shovelling earth on to the covered food.

'Ready by twelve,' one of them says.

'Better be sweet.'

'Superb. Extra delicious.'

'Nā. Listen to the cook talk.'

*

Over at the chopping arena the men finish setting up the blocks and get ready to stand to. The crowd moves there to watch as the names and handicaps are called. Hiriwa stands opposite his father's block watching.

Different, the father. Unsmiling. Heavy in build and mood. Blunt fingered hands gripping the slim handled axe.

Hiriwa watches for a while, then walks away.

The choppers stand to and the starter calls 'Go' and begins the count. The lowest handicapped hit into their blocks and as the count rises the other axemen join in. The morning is filled with sound as voices rise, as axes strike and wood splits. White chips fly.

By three o'clock the stalls have done their selling. The last bottle of drink has been sold, many of the smaller children are asleep in the cars and trucks, and the older ones have gone down to the big field to play. Some of the tents are down already and the remains of the hāngī have been cleared away. At the chopping arena the men are wrenching off the bottom halves of the blocks from the final chop and throwing split wood and chips on to the trucks.

Turei's dog is asleep under a tree. Finally the raffles are drawn.

Joe Blow wins a bag of kūmara which he gives to Ed. Ed wins a carton of cigarettes which he gives to Taupeke. And Tahi wins a live sheep, which she tries to put into the boot of her car but which finds its feet and runs out the gate and down the road, chased by all the kids and Turei's dog.

The kids come back and later the dog, but the sheep is never seen again.

I said to Nanny,
'Do my hair anyhow,
Anyhow,
Anyhow,
Today the gala is on.'
But she said, 'Be patient, Roimata,
They'll think it's Turei's dog.'

Winter

It rains.
The skies weep.
As do we.

Earth stands open to receive her and beside the opened earth we stand to give her our farewell.

'Our Auntie, she fell down.' They stood by the glass doors touching each other, eyes filling. Afraid.

'Our Auntie, she fell.'

And I went with them to the next room and found her lying on the floor, Ed bending over her, and the other children standing, frightened. Not knowing.

'Mrs Kaa, she has fallen on the floor.'

Rain.

It has rained for a fortnight, the water topped the river banks then flowed over. The flats are flooded. Water stirred itself into soil and formed a dark oozing mud causing bare feet to become chapped and sore and hard.

'Like sky people crying,
Because the sun is too lazy

And won't get up.
And won't shine,
He is too lazy,
I shout and shout,
"Get up, get up you lazy,
You make the sky people cry,"
But the sun is fast asleep.'

The trees we have visited daily are bare now, clawing grey fingered at cold winds. Birds have left the trees and gone elsewhere to find shelter, and the insects that in other seasons walk the trunks and branches and hurry about root formations, have tucked themselves into split bark and wood-holes to winter over.

Birds have come closer to the buildings, crowding under ledges and spoutings. We have erected a bird table and every morning put out crumbs of bread, wheat, bacon rind, honey, apple cores and lumps of fat. And every day the birds come in their winter feathers, pecking at crumbs, haggling over fruit, fat and honey. Moving from table to ground to rooftop, then back to table.

On John's paddock the pied stilts have arrived, also in search of food, Standing on frail red legs, their long thin beaks like straws, dipping into the swampy ground.

'Our Auntie she has fallen.'

I took them out on to the verandah where they stood back out of the rain, looking at the ground, not speaking. I went to the phone. Disbelief as I went to the phone.

An emptiness and an unbelieving.

Because they had all been singing an hour before, and she had been strumming the guitar. And now there was a half sentence printed on the board with a long chalk mark

trailing, and a smashed stick of chalk on the floor beside her.

Because at morning break she'd made the tea and he'd said, 'Where's the chocolate cake?' Joking.

'I'll run one up tonight,' she'd said. 'But you'll have to chase the hens around and get me a couple of eggs. My old chooks have gone off the lay.'

'Never mind the eggs,' he'd said. 'Substitute something, like water.'

'Water?' It had put a grin on her face.

'Water?' It had brought a laugh from deep inside her and soon she'd had the little room rocking with sound, which is a way of hers.

Or was. But she lay silent on the schoolroom floor and he came out and spoke to them.

'Mrs Kaa is very sick. Soon the bus will come to take you home. Don't be frightened.' And there was nothing else he could say.

'Our Auntie, she fell down.'

Standing by the glass doors, the pot bellied heater in the corner rumbling with burning pine and the room steaming. She had laughed about my washing too, that morning. My classroom with the naps strung across it steaming in the fire's heat.

'I'm coming in for a sauna this afternoon. And a feed. I'm coming in for a feed too.'

Each morning the children have been finding a feast in the split logs that the big boys bring in for the fire. Kopu and Samuel busy themselves with safety pins, digging into the holes in the wood and finding the dormant white larvae of the huhu beetle.

'Us, we like these.'

And they hook the fat concertina grubs out on the pins

and put them on the chip heater to cook.

Soon there is a bacon and roasted peanut smell in the room and the others leave what they are doing and go to look. And wait, hoping there will be enough to go round.

Like two figures in the mist they stood by the doors behind the veil of steam, rain beating behind them. Large drops hitting the asphalt, splintering and running together again.

Eyes filling.

'Mrs Kaa, she fell down.'

Gently they lower her into earth's darkness, into the deep earth. Into earth salved by the touch of sky, the benediction of tears. And sad the cries come from those dearest to her. Welling up, filling the void between earth and sky and filling the beings of those who watch and weep.

'Look what your mutt did, Turei.'

'We always have a three-legged and a sack.'

'Water?' the room rocking with sound, the bright apple skinless on a plate, smashed chalk beside her on the floor.

'A sauna and a feed.'

'Our Auntie.'

'Mrs Kaa . . .'

It is right that it should rain today, that earth and sky should meet and touch, mingle. That the soil pouring into the opened ground should be newly blessed by sky, and that our tears should mingle with those of sky and then with earth that receives her.

And it is right too that threading through our final song we should hear the sound of children's voices, laughter, a bright guitar strumming.

Spring

The children know about spring.

Grass grows.
Flowers come up.
Lambs drop out.
Cows have big bags swinging.
And fat tits.
And new calves.
Trees have blossoms.

And boy calves go away to the works on the trucks and get their heads chopped off.

The remainder of the pine has been taken back to the shed, and the chips and wood scraps and ash have been cleaned away from the corner. The big boys make bonfires by the incinerator, heaping on them the winter's debris. Old leaves and sticks and strips of bark from under the pōhutukawa and gum, dry brown heads of hydrangea, dead wood from plum, peach, and apple.

Pīpīwharauroa has arrived.

'Time for planting,' he calls from places high in the trees.

'Take up spade and hoe, turn the soil, it's planting time.'

So we all go out and plant a memorial garden. A garden that when it matures will be full of colour and fragrance.

Children spend many of their out-of-school hours training and tending pets which they will parade at the pet show on auction day. They rise early each morning to feed their lambs and calves, and after school brush the animals, walk them, and feed them again.

Hippy and Stan have adopted Michael, who hangs

between them like an odd-looking triplet. The twins have four large eyes the colour of coal, four sets of false eye lashes and no front teeth. They are a noisy pair. Both like to talk at once and shout at each other, neither likes to listen. They send their words at each other across the top of Michael's head and land punches on one another that way too.

Bang!

'Nā Hippy.'

Bang!

'Nā Stan.'

Bang!

'Serve yourself right Hippy.'

Bang!

'Serve yourself right Stan.'

Bang!

'Sweet ay?'

Bang!

'Sweet ay?'

Until they both cry.

Michael is the opposite in appearance, having two surprised blue eyes high on his face, and no room to put a pin head between one freckle and the next. His long skinny limbs are the colour of boiled snapper and his hair is bright pink. Without his shirt he looks as though the skin on his chest and the skin on his back is being kept apart by mini tent poles. His neck swings from side to side as Hippy punches Stan, and Stan punches Hippy. And Michael joins in the chorus. 'Nā Hippy! Sweet? Sweet Stan ay? Serve yourself right.' And when they both cry he joins in that as well.

New books have come, vivid with new ink and sweet with the smell of print and glue and stiff bright paper.

We find a table on which to display the books, and where

they can sit and turn the pages and read. Or where I can sit and read for them and talk about all the newly discovered ideas.

'Hundreds of cats, thousands of cats, millions and billions and trillions of cats.'

'Who goes trip trap, trip trap, trip trap over my bridge?'

'Our brother is lost and I am lost too.'

'Run, run, as fast as you can, you can't catch me I'm the gingerbread man?'

Hiriwa makes a gingerbread man with clay, and Kopu and Samuel make one too.

Out of the ovens jump the gingerbread men, outrunning the old woman, the old man, the cat, the bear. 'That's why, the gingerbread man is too fast.' Then is gone in three snaps of the fox's jaws. Snip, Snap, Snap. Which is sad they think.

'Wī, the fox.'

'Us, we don't like the fox.'

'That's why the fox is too tough.'

'Cunning that fox.'

Then again the closed hand comes down on clay. Snip. Snap. Snap.

He writes in his diary, 'The gingerbread man is lost and I am lost too.' One side of his face is heavy with bruising.

On the day of the pet show and auction his mother says to me, 'We are going away, Hiriwa and I. We need to go, there is nothing left for us to do. By tomorrow we will be gone.' I go into the classroom to get his things together.

The cars and trucks are here again. The children give the pets a drink of water and a last brush. Then they lead the animals in the ring for the judges to look over, discuss, award prizes to. Some of the pets are well behaved and some are not.

Patsy's calf has dug its toes in and refuses to budge, and Patsy looks as though she is almost ready to take Kopu's advice. Kopu is standing on the sideline yelling, 'Boot it in the puku Patsy. Boot it in the puku.' And when the judges tell him to go away he looks put out for a moment. But then he sees Samuel and they run off together, hanging on to each other's shirts calling, 'Boot it in the puku. Boot it in the puku,' until they see somebody's goat standing on the bonnet of a truck, and begin rescue operations.

Inside the building, women from WDFF are judging cakes and sweets and arrangements of flowers. I go and help Connie and the others prepare lunch.

'Pity we can't have another hāngī,' Connie says.

'Too bad, no kūmara and corn this time of the year,' Elsie says. 'After Christmas, no trouble.'

Joe Blow stands on a box with all the goods about him. He is a tall man with a broad face. He has a mouth like a letter box containing a few stained stumps of teeth which grow out of his gums at several angles. His large nose is round and pitted like a golf ball, and his little eyes are set deep under thick grey eyebrows which are knotted and tangled like escape-proof barbed wire. Above his eyebrows is a ribbon width of corrugated brow, and his hair sits close on top of his head like a small, tight-fitting, stocking stitch beanie. His ears are hand sized and bright red.

'What am I bid ladies, gentlemen, for this lovely chocolate cake? Who'll open the bidding?

Made it myself this morning, all the best ingredients.

What do I get, do I hear twenty-five?

Twenty I've got. Thirty I've got.

Forty cents.

Forty-five.

Forty-five. Forty-five. Gone at forty-five to my old pal Charlie, stingy bugger. You'll have to do better than that mates. Put your hands in your pockets now and what do I get for the coffee cake? Made it and iced it myself this morning. Walnuts on top. Thirty.

I have thirty. Thirty-five here.

Forty-five. Advance on forty-five come on all you cockies, take it home for afternoon tea.

Fifty I have, keep it up friends.

Fifty-five. Sixty, now you're talking.

Sixty-five, sixty-five, seventy.

Seventy again. Seventy for the third time. Sold at seventy and an extra bob for the walnuts, Skippy my boy.

Now this kit of potatoes. What am I bid?'

'Do we keep the kit?' someone calls.

'Did I hear fifty? Fifty? Fifty I've got. Any advance on fifty?'

'Do we keep the kit too?'

'Seventy-five I've got. Come on now grew them myself this morning. Make it a dollar. A dollar I've got.'

'What about the kit?'

'One dollar fifty I've got. One seventy-five. Make it two. Two we've got. Two once, two twice, two sold. Sorry about the kit darling we need it for the next lot.' He tips the potatoes into her lap and gives the kit to one of his helpers to refill.

'Two geranium plants for the garden. Two good plants. What do I get? Come on, Billy Boy, take them home for the wife. Make her sweet.'

'I already got something for that.'

'That's had it man, say it with flowers.'

'I got much better.'

'Skiting bugger, twenty-five I've got. Thirty I've got. Advance on thirty? Forty. Forty. Forty again. Forty, sold!'

'Now here's one especially for Turei. Filled sponge decorated with peaches and cream. Come on cook, I'll start you off at forty. Forty cents ladies, gents, and Charlie, from our friend Turei at the back. And forty-five at the front here, come on Turei. Sixty?

Sixty. And seventy up front.

Eighty. Ninety.

One dollar from the district's most outstanding hāngī maker and a dollar twenty from the opposition.

One dollar fifty. Two? Two up front. Two fifty from the back.

Two fifty, two fifty . . . Three.

Three we have, come on friend.

Three fifty. What do you say, Turei?

Five. Five from the back there.

Five once, five twice, five sold. One cream sponge to Turei the best cook in the district. Thank you boys.

Time's getting on, friends. What do you say to a leg a mutton, a bunch a silver beet, a jar a pickle, a bag a spuds, there's your dinner. A dollar? Two? Two ten, twenty, fifty, seventy. Two seventy, two seventy, two seventy, no mucking around, sold.

Another kit of potatoes. I'll take them myself for fifty. Will you let me take them home for fifty. Seventy. Seventy to you, eighty to me. Ninety to you, a dollar to me. Dollar twenty, OK, one fifty. Let me have them for one fifty? One fifty to me, ladies and gents and Charlie. One seventy-five? OK, one ninety. Two?

Two we have once, two we have twice, two for the third time, sold. All yours boy, I've got two acres of my own at home.

Here we are friends, another of these lovely homemade sponges. What do you say Turei . . . ?'

But Turei is away under the gum tree sharing his cake with a lot of children and his dog.

And back again to summer, with all the children talking about Christmas and holidays, their pockets bulging with ripe plums.

The branches of the pōhutukawa are flagged in brilliant red, and three pairs of tūī have arrived with their odd incongruous talking, 'See-saw, Crack, Burr, Ding. See-saw, See-saw, Ding.' By the time they have been there a week they are almost too heavy to fly, their wings beat desperately in flight in order to keep their heavy bodies airborne.

On the last day of school we wait under the pōhutukawa for the bus to arrive, and a light wind sends down a shower of nectar which dries on our arms and legs and faces in small white spots.

They scramble into the bus talking and pushing, licking their skins. They heave their belongings under the seats and turn to the windows to wave. Kopu and Samuel, who are last in line, stand on the bus step and turn.

'Goodbye,' Kopu says, and cracks Sam in the ribs with his elbow.

'Goodbye,' Samuel says and slams his hands down on top of his kina and blushes.

As the bus pulls away we hear singing. Waving hands protrude from the windows on either side. Hippy, Michael, and Stan have their heads together at the back window, and Roimata is there too, waving a pigtail –

'I am a tūī bird,

Up in the pōhutukawa tree,
And a teacher and some children came out
And stood under my tree,
And honey rained all over them,
But I am a tūī bird,
And when I fly
It sounds like ripping rags.’

Between Earth and Sky

I walked out of the house this morning and stretched my arms out wide. Look, I said to myself. Because I was alone except for you. I don't think you heard me.

Look at the sky, I said.

Look at the green earth.

How could it be that I felt so good? So free? So full of the sort of day it was? How?

And at that moment, when I stepped from my house, there was no sound. No sound at all. No bird call, or tractor grind. No fire crackle or twig snap. As though the moment had been held quiet, for me only, as I stepped out into the morning. Why the good feeling, with a lightness in me causing my arms to stretch out and out? How blue, how green, I said into the quiet of the moment. But why, with the sharp nick of bone deep in my back and the band of flesh tightening across my belly?

All alone. Julie and Tamati behind me in the house, asleep, and the others over at the swamp catching eels. Riki two paddocks away cutting up a tree he'd felled last autumn.

I started over the paddocks towards him then, slowly, on these heavy knotted legs. Hugely across the paddocks I went almost singing. Not singing because of needing every breath, but with the feeling of singing. Why, with the deep twist and pull far down in my back and cramping between the legs? Why the feeling of singing?

How strong and well he looked. How alive and strong, stooping over the trunk steadying the saw. I'd hated him for

days, and now suddenly I loved him again but didn't know why. The saw cracked through the tree setting little splinters of warm wood hopping. Balls of mauve smoke lifted into the air. When he looked up I put my hands to my back and saw him understand me over the skirl of the saw. He switched off, the sound fluttered away.

I'll get them, he said.

We could see them from here, leaning into the swamp, feeling for eel holes. Three long whistles and they looked up and started towards us, wondering why, walking reluctantly.

Mummy's going, he said.

We nearly got one, Turei said. Ay Jimmy, ay Patsy, ay Reuben?

Yes, they said.

Where? said Danny.

I began to tell him again, but he skipped away after the others. It was good to watch them running and shouting through the grass. Yesterday their activity and noise had angered me, but today I was happy to see them leaping and shouting through the long grass with the swamp mud drying and caking on their legs and arms.

Let Dad get it out, Reuben turned, was calling. He can get the lambs out. Bang! Ay Mum, ay?

Julie and Tamati had woken. They were coming to meet us, dragging a rug.

Not you again, they said taking my bag from his hand.

Not you two again, I said. Rawhiti and Jones.

Don't you have it at two o'clock.

We go off at two.

Your boyfriends can wait.

Our sleep can't.

I put my cheek to his and felt his arm about my shoulders.

Look after my wife, he was grinning at them.

Course, what else.

Go on. Get home and milk your cows, next time you see her she'll be in two pieces.

I kissed all the faces poking from the car windows then stood back on the step waving. Waving till they'd gone. Then turning felt the rush of water.

Quick, I said. The water.

Water my foot; that's piddle.

What you want to piddle in our neat corridor for? Sit down. Have a ride.

Helped into a wheelchair and away, careering over the brown lino.

Stop. I'll be good. Stop I'll tell Sister.

Sister's busy.

No wonder you two are getting smart. Stop. . . .

That's it missus, you'll be back in your bikini by summer. Dr McIndoe.

And we'll go water-skiing together. Me.

Right you are. Well, see you both in the morning.

The doors bump and swing.

Sister follows.

Finish off girls. Maitland'll be over soon.

All right, Sister.

Yes, Sister. Reverently.

The doors bump and swing.

You are at the end of the table, wet and grey. Blood stains your pulsing head. Your arms flail in these new dimensions and your mouth is a circle that opens and closes as you scream for air. All head and shoulders and wide mouth

screaming. They have clamped the few inches of cord which is all that is left of your old life now. They draw mucous and bathe your head.

Leave it alone and give it here, I say.

What for? Haven't you got enough kids already?

Course. Doesn't mean you can boss that one around.

We should let you clean your own kid up?

Think she'd be pleased after that neat ride we gave her. Look at the little hōhā. God he can scream.

They wrap you in linen and put you here with me.

Well anyway, here you are. He's all fixed, you're all done. We'll blow. And we'll get them to bring you a cuppa. Be good.

The doors swing open.

She's ready for a cuppa, Freeman.

The doors bump shut.

Now. You and I. I'll tell you. I went out this morning. Look, I said, but didn't know why. Why the good feeling. Why, with the nick and press of bone deep inside. But now I know. Now I'll tell you and I don't think you'll mind. It wasn't the thought of knowing you, and having you here close to me that gave me this glad feeling, that made me look upwards and all about as I stepped out this morning. The gladness was because at last I was to be free. Free from the great hump that was you, free from the aching limbs and swelling that was you. That was why this morning each stretching of flesh made me glad.

And freedom from the envy I'd felt, watching him these past days, stepping over the paddocks whole and strong. Unable to match his step. Envying his bright striding. But I could love him again this morning.

These were the reasons each gnarling of flesh made me glad as I came out into that cradled moment. Look at the sky, look at the earth, I said. See how blue, how green. But I gave no thought to you.

And now. You sleep. How quickly you have learned this quiet and rhythmic breathing. Soon they'll come and put a cup in my hand and take you away.

You sleep, and I too am tired, after our work. We worked hard you and I and now we'll sleep. Be close. We'll sleep a little while ay, you and I.

Waimarie

Waimarie called to Max to come and unplug the iron. She spoke in their own language.

And she told him to have a smoke now, where she could see him. 'Lucy's picking me up,' she said, 'and don't you smoke while I'm out, putting the place on fire. And don't cook. You come down the marae after and have a kai down there, you hear me . . . Get me up,' she said.

For a moment Max stood and looked at her. He had the cigarette out of the packet but he hadn't lit it.

'Get me up,' his sister said again.

So he moved to the settee where she was sitting and took her by the arm, pushing up under her elbow until she stood.

'My stick.'

He unhooked her stick from the back of the settee and put it in her hand.

'Now you do what I say,' she said, and pointed at the tea-towels and tablecloths. 'Put them in the drawer.'

Max put his cigarette down and went to do as she told him.

'And those in the cupboard.' She poked her stick at towels and pillowcases.

'Nothing else,' she said, when he had put the linen away. 'You have your smoke now before Lucy come.'

She picked up Keriata's and Ariana's jeans and T-shirts and took them to put in their drawer. She put her skirt away and hung Max's shirt on the end of his bed, moving slowly to and fro.

Then she changed into her black dress, and while she was waiting for Lucy she hooked long shark-tooth earrings onto her ears.

'Hot,' Lucy said, as she helped her aunt to stand. 'But could get cold.'

'My shawl, there on the settee,' said Waimarie. 'And my bag too. And, dear, I want my teeth, in the bathroom, in the glass.'

'You finish your smoke?' she asked Max. 'You put it out properly?'

He showed her the ashtray with the cigarette butt and the dead match in it.

'Empty that in the rubbish,' she said. 'Wash it, and don't turn on any stove or jug. Don't you smoke. Don't cook nothing. And you wait here. When those girls come back you tell them Nanny gone to the marae. Tell them come straight down. Now, what you going to say to Ariana and Keriata?'

'Nanny gone marae,' he said.

'What else?'

'You go down.'

'Straight down.'

'Straight down.'

'And you speak English, don't forget. Speak English or they won't know.'

On their way down the path Lucy said, 'Your garden's good, Aunt.'

So Waimarie stopped and pointed here and there.

'See all my portulaca, Harriet give me it from her old place but not the dark one, the dark one it's from my mate

down the road. She got a big one at the back of her place. The yellow one, it's from Robert's wife. And begonia? I get two when I'm in the hospital and when I come home I stick them in the ground and they grow no trouble. That one, that one, I get them from the gala for the school, and polyanthus from the school too – red, purple, pink. But over there it's all from the old place – kākā beak, gladdies, gerbera, hydrangea – it's my own mother's flowers from the old place.'

'Does Uncle Max help you?'

'Useless, he don't know a kōtimana from a flower. Nah, I just sit on my cushion and do what I want to do, then move along. Next day another part, or whatever I want. Well if there's digging Max can do it. He's not so old like me, only handicap, but still strong. My mother's forty-six when she have him and I'm twenty. Well it's me who bring him up all his life . . . Now dear get me a leaves from my little tree.'

Lucy picked the leaves and helped her aunt to the car. She opened the door and held the old lady as she eased her way on to the seat. She helped her get her legs in and put the shawl across her knees.

'Lovely car, dear,' Waimarie said. 'Warm, nice sheepskins.'

'Kids bought us the sheepskins not long after we got the car.'

'Who's home with you and Jimmy now?'

'Only Teina. Teina's the only one still home.'

After they'd been driving awhile, Lucy said, 'We've got room Aunt, if you want us to have the girls.'

'They won't come,' said Waimarie. 'Won't even go to their own mother. Too haurangi that one. That's why I take them off her in the first place. She give them flash names and that's all. She come here wanting them last Christmas –

now she sees them pretty and growing up – but they won't go. "We're stopping with Nanny," they tell her. Anyway all beer talk. She only ask for them when she's haurangi.'

'Yes, I suppose . . . Or Uncle Max. We could have him. Jimmy likes Uncle Max, those two get on like a house on fire.'

'Well it's me who bring him up all his life.'

Lucy pulled over and stopped the car.

'That's true . . . but, if ever you want . . .'

'What time they bringing Bill in?'

'Two. Leaving the undertakers at two, and should be here by ten past. Sit there I'll come round.'

Lucy helped the old lady out of the car and they moved towards the wharenui where others waited in the sun.

'I was here earlier, Aunt,' Lucy said. 'Everything's ready, house is ready. Hone, Mattie and Watson are doing the kai, and there'll be more helpers this afternoon and tonight.'

'Kei te pai,' the old woman said.

Then Waimarie stopped and said to Lucy, 'Later on dear, later on I want them to come to you, Ariana and Keriata.'

'Kei te pai, Aunt.'

'The house can be for Max, well it's me who bring him up all his life. And . . . someone can come there and live with him. Later on. Dear, I want the girls to come to you and Jimmy.'

'Kei te pai, Aunt, don't say anything more.'

Waimarie moved to greet the men at the front of the wharenui.

'You see him out,' she said to one of them.

'Tough breed,' the old man replied.

'Me too,' she said.

'The wicked stay healthy.'

Lucy assisted her up the two steps on to the verandah where those who were waiting stood to greet her.

'You're here,' someone said.

'With teeth.'

'We can get the show on the road then.'

'Where's Uncle Max?'

'Burning our house down might be.' She sat down to wait. 'You all got a warm, nice place here in the sun. Poor old Bill, ah well.'

She looked out over the marae to where the mats had been put down for the casket. The seating was ready for the family coming in and the grass had been cut and the edges trimmed. As she waited she twisted the trail of leaves into a band for her head.

When the group saw that the people were ready at the gate they helped Waimarie to her feet. Lucy put the shawl about her aunt's shoulders. The old lady moved forward to the top step and the group closed in behind her.

There was hot sun on her lifted face, sun which swathed light through her hair and sifted the circle of leaves into layers of green. And then she called their kinsman to his home, called him to the warmth, the protection of the place where he would be wept for.

The light showed the lines on her face to be deep and hard, and light spun off the gold clasps which clutched the ornaments at her ears. These ornaments hung quivering in the brightness, curving the way her jaw curved, light sculpting them against the contour of her jaw. She called the spirits of the many dead to gather along with the kinsman, so that the dead could all be wept for together.

Light mixed the muted colours of her shawl and glossed the dark clothing. And her voice lifted out, weaving amongst the sheddings of light, encompassing the kinsman and his family, bearing them forward.

The Wall

The old man was the only one who liked our wall, or the only one said. Our wall got in the papers.

We saw the woman there with her camera, and a guy was with her having a look, writing stuff on a pad. That's good, us and our wall's going in the paper.

The day the man and the woman came was packing-up day, clearing up our rubbish, loading the gear. Only four of us and Lindsay. The others were already gone off on a new job, footpaths down Tamihana Road somewhere. Footpaths are all right but walls are better. Well to me it's a good wall.

It took three months, and at first we didn't know what the hell. Just hacking away at the bank, mixing concrete, carting rocks. Then Lindsay got us going on it, how to put down a bit of the mix, lay one of the rocks, and keep on going like that. But not just any rock. You have to pick out a good one, the right one, the right size and a good shape to fit in with the one you just done.

We all scrapped over which rock. That one. Nah. Ha, ha, haw, haw, like that. Then try them out to see which one. A lot of times my rock was the good one, fitted in just right, ha ha ha, hee hee, get stuffed. Hee, hee, ha, ha. Haw, haw, haw. It was only easy after a while.

So our wall got started and it was pretty good, only easy, and every day there was this new bit of wall. Not just straight. Higher some places, lower some places, and got a bend in it where the road goes round.

Every morning we mucked around and had a look what

we done yesterday. My rock, ha, ha. Mine, haw, haw. Stink one, slack one, ha, ha, ha, then Lindsay yells out to get on with it.

Plenty of people went past, in cars, or walking, but they never said. Drive past, have a look, keep going. Walk past, have a look, keep walking. Sometimes the kids stand around on their way home from school and have a stare, have a talk. Where you get your stones? Off the truck. But where? Don't know.

But I like the old fella best. He's the only one liked our wall.

At half past three we sent Jerryboy to get us a paper, two papers, three papers, no four.

And there was a photo of our wall all right, with a write-up about this headmaster and these parents saying how the kids couldn't see cars and buses because of our wall. Our wall was too built out.

Well too bad, at least our wall was in the paper. And us. Not looking, just loading the leftover rocks. Jerryboy's back, my hand, Pete's shoulder, and Notpeter standing up on the truck. Haw, haw. Ha, ha. Sucker. Hee hee, haw, haw, haw. I took the paper home with me at knock-off. Showed it to one or two. They didn't say much.

Anyway, this old fella came walking down the road one day. Not our side, the other side. Our wall was only about halfway then. He stopped and had a good old jack at us working. After a while he came over. He wasn't that old, just a slow walker with his breaths making a noise. Not rich.

Well, he said, and his hands were clanking round in his pockets like he had keys and ten-cent pieces, and might be a few washers and nails. And he had a big smile like he really liked us and our wall. Black old teeth. Fat stomach. Well

good on you. Good on all of you and your wall. Hee, hee, hee, hee.

So Peter got up on the wall and bent his arms up and made his muscles big, pulled a strong face. Patsy swung his bum. Hee, hee, hee, squeal, squeal.

And then Notpeter, who was hosing off the footpath, stuck the hose between his legs and went yah ha, hosing all over the road. Well the old fella laughed and laughed, and squeaked and squealed with his noisy breaths. What a pisser, he shouted, hee, hee, hee. Hey, Pisser, hee, hee, hee, squeal, squeal, big funny mouth, black old teeth. Well good on all of you. Good one. Good wall. And then he went away, slow walking, big funny grin.

Well I watched out for the old fella after that, but he didn't come past again. Only cars, only kids, and people hurrying. Could be in the hospital. Could be dead. Anyway the wall's done now. Finished. We're back on footpaths again.

But if I saw the old fella, round town, down the pub, anywhere, I'd give him a yell. If he didn't remember, I'd tell him it was us made the wall. And he might say was you the pisser, and I'll say no, that's Notpeter. And he might say was you the strongman? No. The wrigglebum? No. So I might tell him I'm the one who finds the good stones, ha, ha, ha, the right rocks to fit in the right place. And he'll say good one, hee, hee, squeal squeal.

Then I might say come on how about it, I'll shout you one. And he might say good on you, what are we waiting for? Then we'll go.

Kahawai

All right then. One morning I got up late and hurried to the kitchen. He was up before me and would have the jug boiling, the pan plugged in, the bread popped down, I thought.

Instead he was in the front room looking out.

Because the gulls had gathered out at sea, under cloud, and were chasing, calling, falling to the water. Up, chase, drop. Screaming. There's fish, he said. It brought juices. Kahawai, beating green and silver through purple water, herding the herrings, which excited the gulls, which excited me . . .

Could we . . . ?

Be sick?

We could.

Have we got. . . ?

Bait?

We have.

Have we got two-stroke?

No.

Get breakfast, get changed, get two-stroke.

Have we got spinners?

No. Someone borrowed.

Don't need spinners. Can trawl the heads of soldiers.

Then the others came in.

Well . . . what? Have you got a holiday or something? Or what?

We're sick . . .

Of work.

And the fish are out there, nose to tail.

Yes, we heard.

The birds.

Saw splashes. But . . .

It's only us who don't go. Sometimes. Or don't get up. Right? Because of hangovers, or laziness, or going somewhere else. Or from not being back from somewhere. Only us have sickies. Right? But anyway . . . Good. Good on yous. Kahawai, yum. Make some bread too. Yahoo.

Lines, bait, knife, hooks, sinkers, jerseys, towel, apples, can of two-stroke, putt-putt motor, rowlocks, oars. Push the dinghy out and sidle out past the weed.

He winds the rope and pulls, tries again and then we're away putt-putting out over the navy blue, under cloud, stopping for a while to remove the sinkers from the lines and to bait the hooks with the heads of soldier fish.

Then away again to where the gulls swarm above the swarming kahawai that herd the swarming herrings. But he and I are not a swarm, we are only two of us. One fish each will do.

Then we are in the middle of it, the darting, leaping little fish crack open the dark water, leap and splash, the gull's eye singling out one, the eye of the kahawai on another. Gulls swooping, following, rising, diving, rising, swallowing, turning, following. And the kahawai zigging, zagging, leaping, shooting through the water, beating silver on the surface of it. Hundreds. But for us two will do.

We trawl our long lines with the putt-putt on slow, putt-putting through chaotic water under the screeching canopy.

Of birds. One of them is eyeing the bait, the head of the soldier, and is following. I stand spread-legged and wave

one arm. No. Go. Silly bird. It's dead meat, hooked. Krazy Karoro.

Krazy Kahawai too, for that matter. And Krazy Kātaha. K.K.K. And what about Krazy Kouple in a boat? K.K.K. and K.K. I wave. Shout. Go, Karoro, go. So Karoro drops back, but still follows, still wants.

And then, Got it, he says. So I stop waving, stop shouting, plonk myself down. He switches the motor off so that he can pull in . . . number one. Pulling . . .

What have we here?
One little kahawai, my teacher dear.
Kahawai, Kahawai, nicky nicky nacky noo,
That's what they taught me
When I went to . . .

Pulling . . . Pulling in over the side . . .

Flip flop she flied,
Flip flop she flied,
Flip flop she flied,
She went up to heaven and flip flop she flied
Flip flop she fliedy flied flied . . .

Krazy Kahawai flapping, slapping the tin boards of the boat, bouncing in the wet sack on the tin bottom of the boat. I pull in too so that my line won't tangle in the motor while we start up again.

Off. Putt-putting full out to catch up with Karoro again. They have moved further out now, dinning and diving. We trail the heads of soldiers, turning to run with the fish . . .

Kahawai, Kātaha, nicky nicky nacky noo,
That's what they taught me . . .
Hat on one side what have we here?
One little chin chopper, my teacher dear.
Chin chopper, snot catcher, eye basher, sweaty boxer, nicky nacky noo
That's what they taught me when . . .

Karoro. Again. Eyeing, swooping. I stand, wave, shout. Not for you. Shoo. Wave and shout. Go. Blow. Karoro backs off, then moves up again. I pick up an apple, throw it, and Karoro turns, circles, returns. Krazy Kamikaze Karoro. I pick up the towel, swing it, and Karoro, nervous, drops back, still wanting, still turning the eye.

But then, is beaten to the bait by Kahawai. Number two. Got it. He switches off and I sit down pulling in swiftly . . .

One little kahawai my teacher dear,
Kahawai, Kahawai, nicky nicky nacky noo,
That's what they taught me when . . .
Kahawai, Kahawai, nicky nicky nacky noo,
That's what they . . .
What have we here?
One great big kahawai my teacher dear,
Kahawai, Karoro, Kātaha, Krazy Kouple, nicky nacky nacky noo,
That's what they taught me . . .

Bring it in over the side, hand into the gills, push the hook. Look Karoro, hook, turn your eye. Not meant, not bent for a feathered throat. Open the bag and . . .

Flip flop she flied,
Flip flop she flied,
Flip flop she flied,
She went up to heaven and flip flop she flied
Flip flop she fliedy flied flied.

And now, the gulls, the fish have moved out again, too far for a tin boat and a putt-putt on a cold day. It's Kold, and two will do. One flick and we're moving again, turning, the Krazy Kouple. Kold. Heading home.

As we come to the weed in the shallow water we switch off, lifting the motor, and row in swiftly. Kold. We step out, ahh, into water, kold hands gripping the sides of the boat. Can we lift it? We can, rushing it up over the stones. Rest, then again. Again, blue knuckled. And lift. Can we? On to the trailer? We can.

Then back to the edge we go with the two fish, scraping fast, because it's kold. The scales leap. We slit the white bellies, pulling the insides out, flinging. Kum Karoro. They come, dance on the surface of the sea, snatch the innards and fly up gulping. We wash the fish and the water runs red-salt-blood. We hurry with the trailer, home, to be dry and warm.

When it is time I put bread in the oven. He cuts up fish, puts it in the big pot with a good fist of salt, watches so that it won't boil fast. We scrub and slice vegetables and put them on to cook.

Then the others come, lifting the lids of the pots. Did you? Yous did.

Opening the oven door.

Did yous? Yous did. Yum.

*

When it is time we lift the fish carefully into bowls and strain the water into a jug. We break up the bread on the board and heap the vegetables on to dishes.

Then we sit down to celebrate.

OWEN MARSHALL

The Master of Big Jingles

I know what it's called now, it's called fennel. Knowing the name doesn't make it what it was, however. I see it rarely now. It peers occasionally from the neglected and passing sections, like the face of a small man over the shoulders of others in a crowd. Its fronds are the pale green of hollow glass, and it has a look of pinched resignation, as if it can foresee the evolutionary course before it.

When Creamy Myers and I were young, it was in its prime. There were forests of it pressing in on the town, and it reared up confidently in waxy profusion. The rough strip below the bridge was its heartland, and there Creamy and I had our hut. We could reach it by tunnel tracks from the river bank, and the fence. We built it in the summer which ended our standard four year, and in the summer after that we renewed it in our friendship. The year we finished primary school we restored it again. We cut out the tunnel tracks as usual, so narrow that the top foliage showed no tell-tale gap, and even Rainbow Johnston wouldn't find them. We evicted the hedgehog and its loosely balled nest from the hut, and spread new sacks to mark our occupation. In a biscuit tin we kept the important things, wax-heads, shanghais, tobacco, fishing lines and the tin of cows' teat ointment I found on the bridge.

Fennel is the great home of snails: it is their paradise, nirvana and happy hunting ground. The matchless abundance of the snails was a fascination to us, and a symbol of the place itself. The snails were the scarabs of our

own hieroglyphic society, and the snail hunt was the most satisfying of our rituals. From the length, breadth and depth of the river terrace we took them. From time to time one of us would return, and lift his shirt from his trousers, to tumble the catch into the biscuit tin. When we had a massed heap of them, perhaps 150 or more, we would sit in the hut and anoint them. We used the cows' teat vaseline, rubbing it on the shells to darken the pattern and make them shine. We would lie the snails in handfuls amongst the fennel, just off the sacks, and in the penumbral green light. As we watched the snails would begin their ceremonial dispersal: large and small, sly and bold, all with the patterns of their shells waxed and gleaming. Scores of snails, each with its own set angle of direction. The gradual, myriad intersection of the planes of their escape through the fennel was like an abacus of three dimensions.

The friendship of Creamy and myself was the smallest and strongest of several circles. We often played with Arty and Lloyd, and there were other faces that we expected at other times. If we went swimming at the town baths for instance, we joined up with the Rosenberg twins. They didn't seem to do much else but swim. But sometimes when Creamy and I were sick of what the others were doing, or after school when we'd rather be alone, then we'd make our signal, just a movement of the head, that meant we'd meet later at the hut. The hut was something apart from the rest of the world. In its life were only Creamy and me. As long as we agreed, our word was law, and no conventions but our own were followed.

I remember just when Creamy told me about going to Technical. We'd had a snail hunt, and were sitting by the river to wash. Creamy had his shirt off, and the snail tracks

glistened on his chest. The linear droppings, inoffensively small, clung there too. 'Dad told me I'm not going to Boys' High after all,' he said. 'He's sending me to Tech.' Creamy's voice was doubtful, as if he wasn't sure if it marked an important decision or not.

'But I thought we were all going to High?'

Creamy leant into the shingle of the river. He supported himself on his arms, and lifted first one hand then the other to wash his chest. 'Dad said if I'm going into the garage with him, I need the Tech courses. He doesn't go much on languages and stuff.' Creamy had a broad, almost oriental face, and his upper lip was unusually full. It sat slightly over the bottom lip, and gave his face an expression of thoughtful drollery.

'I suppose after school we'll be able to do things together just the same. Maybe it's just like being in different classes at the same school.' I had a premonition though that Creamy's father had done something which would harm us.

'I did try to get Dad to change his mind,' said Creamy. He said it almost as if he wanted it recorded, lest some time in the future he might be blamed for not putting up more of a fight. Creamy flexed his arms, and recoiled with easy grace out of the water. He pulled the back of his trousers down, and showed the marks of a hiding. 'I did try,' said Creamy, and his upper lip quirked a little at the understatement.

'I don't see why it should make that much difference.' I could say that because it was weeks away in any case. When you are thirteen, nothing that is weeks away can be taken seriously. Creamy and I controlled time in those days. We could spin out one summer's day for an eternity of experience.

'Maybe I'll play against you in football,' said Creamy speculatively.

'I'll cut you down if you do.' We smiled, and Creamy skipped stones across the surface of the river with a flick of his wrist. The sun dried the water from us, and snapped the broom pods like an ambush on the other side of the river. Already I was surprised at my innocence in thinking that all my friends must go like myself to the High School.

Time made no headway against us that summer, not while we were together. But then my family went on holiday to the Queen Charlotte Sounds, and I returned to find the world moved on. The new term was before us, and Creamy was indeed going to the Tech, and I to the High.

I didn't see Creamy after school during the first week, and on Saturday when we went after lizards on the slopes behind the reservoir, we didn't wear uniform. But the next Tuesday we met at the hut, and the nature of our division was apparent. Although I should have expected it, Creamy's Tech uniform was a blow. His grey trousers to my navy blue; his banded socks and cap, distinct in a separate allegiance. Creamy was never deceived by outward appearance. A smile spread out under his full upper lip, and creased his tanned face. 'I see you've lost your knob, too,' he said, and lightly touched the top of his cap.

'The fourth formers tore them off. Initiation,' I said.

'Same with us.' It was typical of Creamy that he should notice first about our uniforms a subtlety we had in common, whereas I couldn't help seeing us from the outside. Even my friendship with Creamy hadn't given me a totally personal view. Creamy didn't mention the uniforms again. We left our caps with our shoes and socks in the hut, and waded in the river to catch crayfish. As long as we maintained the old life separate from the new, then both could exist. It was like those studies I did at High School, about the primitive

societies existing for hundreds of years, and then collapsing when the white man came. Creamy and I couldn't change much in the old way, because our ideas came from different sources that year. Sooner or later the white man would come; the white man comes one way or another to all the pagan societies of our youth.

I never sat down to think it out, but if I had, it must have seemed that as Creamy and I had held our friendship through the end of that summer, and the first term of our new schools, then there was no reason why we shouldn't go on. That wasn't the way of it, however. In the winter months I didn't see much of Creamy. The days were short, and the rugby practices we went to almost always came on different nights. I made new friends too, like big Mathew and Ken Marsden. When I was with Creamy, I sometimes found myself assuming that he knew all about High, and then halfway through some story I'd realise that it must have been meaningless to him. Creamy never showed any impatience. Creamy had a natural and attractive courtesy. He would sit there smiling, his expanding lip faintly frog-like, and say, 'He sounds a real hard case,' or, 'I wish I'd seen that.' Unless I asked him, he never said much about Tech. The odd thing perhaps about sport, or the time he saw Rainbow Johnston smash the windows in the gym. Rainbow was the baron of all our childhood fiefdoms. He had a job at the pie-cart in the evenings, and made more money by stealing milk coupons. Birds stopped singing when Rainbow came past. He knew how to twist an arm till the tears came, did Rainbow, and it was said he made little kids put their hands in his trousers.

In the third term, when it became summer again, we began going back to the river. Not just Creamy and me anymore though, for I'd grown accustomed to spending

my time with Mathew and Ken. The first time I took them to the hut, Arty was with us too. Arty knew Creamy from primary school, but Mathew and Ken didn't. I could see them measuring themselves against Creamy, as the afternoon went on. Creamy didn't seem to mind. Creamy liked a challenge in his own unassuming way. Creamy could stand measurement beside anyone I knew.

The mentality of youth is able to unhook its jaws like a snake, and swallow up whole antelopes of experience. Youth is a time for excess: for breaking through the ice to swim, for heaping up a mountain of anointed snails from the fennel, for sledging until your hands are bleeding from the ropes, and sunstroke smites you down. Youth is a time for crazes: hula-hoops and under-water goggles, bubble gum and three-D cardboard viewers.

But that year it was knuckle bones. The year when Creamy and my new High School friends met, it was knuckle bones. Knuckle bones had risen obscurely, like an Asian plague, and swept as an epidemic through our world – brief and spectacular. Creamy excelled at knuckle bones of course: Creamy was insolently good at knuckle bones. Like chickens about a hen, the knuckle bones grouped and disbanded, came and went around Creamy's hand. Creamy had begun with plastic knuckle bones. The softdrink colours of the pieces would rise and fall, collect and separate, at Creamy's behest. He won an aluminium set in the Bible class competition. The aluminium ones were heavier and didn't ricochet. Creamy was even better with the aluminium ones. Cutting cabbages, camels, swatting flies, clicks, little jingles, through the arch, goliath, horses in the stable; Creamy mastered them all.

Creamy's expression didn't change when Ken challenged him to knuckle bones. He seemed interested in my new

friends. His fair hair hung over his forehead, and his complex face was squinting in the sun. Ken was good at knuckle bones, as good as me, but he wouldn't beat Creamy I knew. Creamy was a golden boy, and it's useless to envy those the gods have blessed. Ken and he went right through knuckle bones twice without any faults. 'What do you think is the hardest of all?' said Creamy. Ken considered. He pushed the knuckle bones about the ground with his finger as he thought.

'I reckon big jingles,' he said.

'Ten big jingles on the go,' said Creamy. 'I challenge you to ten big jingles without a fault.'

'You go first then,' said Arty. 'You go first and if you make a mistake then Ken wins.'

'All right,' said Creamy. The injustice of it didn't seem to worry him. He started out as smoothly as ever, allowing no time for tension to gather. His rhythm didn't vary, and his broad face was relaxed.

'That's good going,' said Mathew when Creamy had finished, and Ken had failed to match him.

'They're small enough, these aluminium ones.' Arty seemed jealous of the praise. 'Smaller than real or plastic knuckle bones. It's a big advantage to have them smaller in big jingles.'

'Stiff,' said Creamy.

Later in the afternoon we found ourselves fooling about by the bridge. Along the underside of the bridge was a pipe which Creamy and I sometimes crossed to prove we could do it. 'Creamy and I often climb across that,' I told the others. They looked at it in silence.

'Shall we do it now,' said Mathew at last. He thought he was strong enough to try anything.

There's no dichotomy of body and spirit when you're young. Adults see the body as an enemy, or a vehicle to be apprehensively maintained. There's just you, when you're young; flesh and spirit are indivisible. For Creamy and I then, for all of us in youth, any failure in body was a failure of the spirit too. Creamy went first. As always when he was concentrating, his lunar upper lip seemed more obvious, the humorous expression of his face more pronounced, as though he were awaiting the punch line of some unfolding joke. He leant out, and took hold of the pipe. He moved his grip about, as a gymnast does to let his hands know the nature of the task, then he swung under the pipe, and began hand over hand to work his way to the central bridge support. He used his legs as a pendulum, so that the weight of his body was transferred easily from one hand to the other as he moved. When he reached the centre support, Creamy rested in the crook of its timbers, and looked down to the river. Then he carried on, hanging and swaying below the pipe, becoming smaller in silhouette against the far bank as he went.

'Seems easy enough,' said Arty.

'You go next then,' said Ken. Arty measured the drop between Creamy's swaying figure and the river beneath.

'I would,' he said. 'I would, but I've got this chest congestion. I see the doctor about it.'

'Sure.'

Mathew could only think about one thing at a time, and as he was busy watching Creamy he found himself next in line for the pipe. The rest of us by slight manoeuvrings had got behind him. 'It's me then,' said Mathew. He took a grip and his body flopped down beneath the pipe, and stopped with a jerk. His up-stretched arms were pulled well clear

of his jersey, and his hands were clamped on to the pipe. The crossing was an exercise in sheer strength for Mathew. He pulled himself along clumsily, and his legs hung down like fence posts below his thick body. I went next. I didn't want Arty in front of me in case he froze, and I couldn't get past. The few feet just before the central support were the worst, for if I looked down there I could see the concrete base of the timber supports on which I'd fall, instead of into the water. I used to count the number of swings I made just there; one, two, three four, until I was able to put my feet on the wooden supports. The second half wasn't so bad, because at the end if you were tired, you could drop off on to the grassy bank which rose up towards the underside of the bridge.

Arty and Ken didn't go over at all. Arty pretended he'd seen a big trout in the hole beneath the bridge, and he and Ken went down and poked under the bank with a stick. When we came back over the bridge, we couldn't see any big trout in the hole. 'Want to go over the pipe again?' said Creamy mildly.

'That's hard work, that.' Mathew was always honest.

'Good though,' said Creamy.

As we scuffed about in the shingle at the end of the bridge, a horse and rider came past. The horse paused, and with flaunting tail deposited vast rolls of waste. Mathew watched the horse with awe. 'I bet horses are the biggest shitters around,' he said.

'No, in proportion guinea pigs are far greater shitters,' said Creamy.

'Guinea pigs?'

'Yea, in proportion they are.'

'Rabbits are good shitters,' said Arty.

'I don't see how anything could beat horses and elephants,' said Ken. As an ally he weakened Mathew's argument. The rest of us recognised the subtlety of Creamy's reasoning.

'Guineas are by far the best shitters in proportion.' Creamy knew he was right. 'Imagine a guinea pig as big as a horse. Now there would be a shitter.'

'Yea,' said Mathew in wonder, and capitulation.

We had a swim, and threw fennel spears at each other during the rest of the afternoon. We forgot about the time, and Ken's sister came looking for him. She left her bike by the road, and came down to the fence, calling out for Ken. 'You've got to come home,' she said. Her breasts caused furrows across the material of her blouse.

'Have you been eating too much or something,' said Arty. We had a good laugh at that witticism. 'Turning into a moo-vie star,' continued Arty, pleased with his reception. He tucked his thumbs into his shirt, and paraded before her and us.

'Oh, get lost,' she said. She began to go back up the bank towards the road. 'You'd better come, Ken. You know what'll happen,' she said.

'Hubba hubba, ding ding, look at the tits on that thing,' we sang.

'Watch out for Rainbow Johnston,' I called out.

'Hey, Rainbow, here she is.'

'Quick, Rainbow.'

For the first time Ken's sister seemed flustered. She looked back along the river bank, and then hurried on to her bike. I don't know why I called out about Rainbow. Perhaps in looking at her smooth legs and breasts, I found some part of Rainbow in myself, some desire to reach out and pinch her, or twist her arm, or worse.

Ken stayed a little longer, trying to show he wasn't afraid of being late, but we soon all began straggling back down the road. Creamy and I walked the last part together. 'I'm looking forward to the full summer,' I said. Creamy agreed. He played with his knuckle bones, and whistled as he walked, his upper lip funnelling out and creating a very clear, penetrating whistle. His shoes, worn by water and grass during the afternoon, were almost white at the toes. Creamy stopped whistling, and asked me if Ken and Mathew were the two I liked best at High School. I told him I quite liked them.

'I'm getting sick of Arty,' said Creamy thoughtfully. 'You know that. I'm finding Arty pretty much of a pill.'

'So am I,' I said. Creamy tossed his aluminium knuckle bones up and down again in the palm of his head. We were nearly at the street where Creamy turned off. 'You didn't mind Ken and Mathew being there?' I asked him. Creamy didn't give any glib answer. He walked on for a while.

'I suppose it's selfish to just have one or two friends,' he said. 'I suppose as you get older, you meet more and more people and make friends with them. Only I don't seem to find as many as you. There's an awful lot like Arty.'

As Creamy went off home, I thought about that. For the first time I realised that, despite being good at everything, Creamy didn't have that many friends. Being good at everything was in itself a disadvantage even. That's what was the matter with Arty. He resented Creamy's ability. Somewhere, sometime, he'd like to see Creamy take a fall.

The next Saturday I went again. Ken couldn't come, but Mathew and Arty did. I hadn't seen Creamy, but I thought he'd be there. He had another Tech boy with him. None of us knew him. He had eyebrows that grew right across the

top of his nose. I'd never seen anyone with one long eyebrow like that before. His name was Warwick Masters. When he thought something was funny, he let his head fall forward, bouncing on his chest, and gave a snuffling laugh on the indrawn breath.

Creamy and I hadn't had any snail hunts that summer: No decision was made not to, we just didn't do it. As third formers we were growing out of snail hunts, and on to more fitting things like knuckle bones, and calling hubba hubba, ding ding, at Ken's sister. Yet the way Warwick treated the snails made me so angry, I could feel my throat becoming tight. 'Christ almighty,' said Warwick, 'look at these snails.' He reached into the fennel walls of the hut, and plucked out the snails. 'Just look at these snails will you.' He let his head bounce on his chest, and gave his idiotic, sucking laugh. He arranged a line of them by the wall, then smashed each one with his fist. The shells cracked like biscuits, and what was left of the snails seemed to swell up in visceral agony after Warwick's fist was lifted. Creamy made no attempt to stop him. He hardly seemed to notice what he was doing.

'Don't do that,' I said to Warwick.

'Bloody snails.'

'It only makes a mess in the hut.'

'Stiff,' said Warwick. 'That's really stiff.'

'Just leave them alone.'

'Yea.'

'Yea?'

'Yea.'

'Yea?' The verbal sparring quickened into a semblance of humour, and Warwick bounced his head and laughed.

'Anyway,' said Arty, 'I don't think you Tech guys should come to the hut.'

'It's always been my hut too,' said Creamy seriously. Three summers are an accepted eternity when one is young.

'It's got to be either Tech or High ground,' said Mathew. He liked things simple for his own peace of mind. 'All the places got to be either Tech or High.' Mathew's simplicity had found the truth. All the places that mattered in our town were either High or Tech ground. The territories were marked, and only the adults in their naivety were unaware. My father never understood why I wouldn't take the short cut through the timber yard on my way to school.

'This side of the bridge is ours,' said Arty.

'But it's closest to the Tech swimming hole.'

'Stiff.'

Warwick picked up some of the squashed snails and quickly wiped them down Arty's face, then crashed away through the fennel a few paces, and stood bouncing his head and snorting. Creamy's subtle and unique face creased with delight, but he made no movement. Arty flung the remaining mess of snails at him, and urged Mathew to grab him. 'Grab him, Mathew, grab him.' Creamy dodged Mathew's first clumsy attempt. He seemed as if he were about to say something, but Arty got in first. 'High on to Tech,' he shouted.

'Yea,' I heard myself say, but without reason. It seemed to come from a surface part of me, and not deeper where I thought things out. Creamy slipped from the hut, and stood with Warwick.

'For today you mean,' he said, smiling. Creamy loved a battle.

'For always,' said Arty. Arty was pleased that at last he had something over Creamy. Creamy was Tech, and the rest of us were High. Creamy was quicker, stronger, better at knuckle

bones and swinging under the bridge, a true friend, but he was Tech. Arty, like most weak people, enjoyed advantages he couldn't himself create. 'For always. No more Tech farts on the bank. Fight you for it.'

It was three on to two, but that didn't worry Creamy. He had a sense of occasion though, did Creamy. If it had to be Tech against High after all, then it should be done on a fitting scale. 'Thursday night then,' said Creamy. His full upper lip expanded as he thought about it, and his eyes took on the visionary look with which he regarded his schemes. A look that hinted at the appreciation of more colours than existed in the spectrums of the rest of us. 'On Thursday after school we'll have the full fight between Tech and High for the bank. You get all you can, and we'll meet you. All out war.'

'I don't know,' said Arty. 'Maybe we should set rules and numbers.' Arty's brief moment of initiative was over; Creamy had as always taken control.

'All out war,' he repeated, and Warwick's head bounced and his laugh sounded through the fennel.

'Is it really all out war?' I said. I could see Creamy's face not many paces away, but he didn't answer. 'All out?' I said. Creamy's face was relaxed and droll, so difficult to read.

'Full scale,' cried Warwick. 'Tech against High.' And still Creamy didn't answer.

'We'll win easily,' said Mathew. 'We can round up a dozen or more easily.'

'Look out for Rainbow Johnston, that's all,' called Warwick. He went off laughing, to follow Creamy, who had turned away and begun walking towards the fence below the bridge.

I watched Creamy climb up to the road with Warwick, and I knew it had happened. I knew that him going to Tech

and me going to High had ruined our friendship after all. I looked at Arty and Mathew standing by the hut, and I knew that neither of them was half the friend that Creamy had been. 'Do you think they'll really get Rainbow?' said Arty hollowly.

'I've heard things about Rainbow. I think we need plenty of guys.' Mathew's slow logic was depressing.

'Can we get enough though?' said Arty.

'Jesus, Arty,' I said, 'will you stop moaning.'

That week at school we started getting as many allies as we could. Arty wrote the names down at the back of his pad. He had two lists – one headed possibles and one headed probables, like trial teams. There were some names in the possibles that I hardly knew. Not even all the probables were at the gate after School on Thursday though. Arty himself didn't show up until we were just about to go. We told him he was trying to get out of it. 'No I'm not. I'm coming; of course I'm coming. I just had to put off other things, that's all. What do you think of this stick?' Arty had a short piece of sawn timber. He hit it against the five courts, and then tried not to show that he'd jarred his hand. 'I reckon I'm ready,' he said.

We began walking towards the river but a car drew up over the road, and the man driving it called out to Arty. It was Arty's father. Arty went over and talked with him, then came partly back. 'Wouldn't you know it,' he said. 'I've got to go up to the hospital for my tests. It has to be tonight.' With Arty's father watching from the car, it wasn't any use saying much. 'Maybe the Tech will be there again tomorrow night. I'll be right for tomorrow.'

'Sure,' said Ken. Arty walked over the road quickly. As he got into the car he let his stick slip onto the roadway.

'He rang his dad,' said Lloyd. 'That's what he did.' Arty couldn't meet our eyes as the car pulled away.

'What a dunney brush he turned out to be,' said Mathew, and we laughed. I was on the point of telling them what Creamy had said about Arty, Creamy had him picked all right, then I remembered that Creamy had become the enemy.

That left seven of us. Mathew, Ken, Lloyd, Buzz Swanson and the Rosenbergs. And me of course. As we got closer to the bridge I had a strange feeling that our group was becoming smaller, although the number remained the same. Ken was walking beside me, and I saw how frail he was. His legs were so thin they seemed swollen at the knees to accommodate the joints. He had little, white teeth that looked as if they were his first set. Even as Ken smiled at me, I thought to myself that he was going to be useless. I didn't want to be by Ken when we were fighting. I'd keep by Mathew. Mathew's dirty knees were comfortingly large, and he plodded on resolutely. 'Perhaps we should scout around first, and find out how many of them there are,' I said to Mathew.

'I've got to be home by half past five,' said Ken. I bet you do Ken, I bet you do, I thought. I resolved that not only would I stick with Mathew when it started, I'd make sure Ken wasn't protecting my back. I had some idea it was going to be like the musketeers of Dumas, us back to back against the odds of the Tech boys.

We stood on the raised road leading up to the bridge, and looked over the bank from the fence, across the frothing fennel to the grey-wacke shingle of the river bed, where the larger stones crouched like rabbits in the afternoon sun. Creamy stepped out from the cover of the willows two

hundred yards away. He raised one arm slowly, and lowered it again. It caught the significance of our presence, as a hawk becomes the sky. It had nothing to do with friendship or compromise: it was a sign of recognition. It was a sign of deeper cognisance too, in that we were there. Unlike Arty and the others on the list, we had come. So Creamy acknowledged our equality of hostility.

Life was drama when we were young. The power of it made Lloyd's voice shake when he reminded us to keep together as we broke our way through the fennel. Creamy watched us coming for a bit, then disappeared behind the willows. 'Where are they?' said Ken. They were below the hank, where the terrace met the river bed. As if to answer Ken's question, they began throwing stones which snicked through the fennel.

'Let's head for the willows,' I said. The Tech harried us as we went. I could hear Warwick's indrawn laugh, and I had a desultory stick fight with a boy who used to be in cubs with me. The Rosenberg twins were the best fighters on our side. They probably had the least notion as to why we were there in the first place, but they were the best fighters all right. They seemed to fight intuitively as one person; four arms and four feet. They rolled one Tech kid over the bank, and winded him on the shingle below. Mathew seemed unable to catch anyone to fight in this sort of guerrilla warfare. Nobody took him on, but he was too slow to take on anybody himself. He kept moving towards the willows, and we skirmished about him.

I think the whole thing might have petered out, if Rainbow hadn't come. Even in an all out fight there were rules: you knew that no one would deliberately poke anything in your eye, or hold your head under the water longer than you

could hold your breath. Rainbow was different. He liked to hurt people did Rainbow. He stepped up onto the bank by the willows, and halted our forward progress. He had a thick stick. 'So it's Tech against High,' said Rainbow. His features were gathered closely on his round head, like sprout marks on a coconut. He held the stick in front of Ken, and Ken stopped. The rest of us did nothing. We did nothing not just because Rainbow Johnston was a fifth former, but because he was Rainbow Johnston. And deep down we were glad he'd picked on Ken, and not on us.

'I'm pax,' said Ken. It was the best he could think of, and its incongruity set the Tech guys laughing.

'Pax?' said Rainbow bitterly. 'We don't have any pax between Tech and High.' He drew back his stick, and speared it out at Ken, catching him on the side of his chest. Ken fell on his back, and as his head hit the soft grass his hair flopped away from his face, making him seem even younger.

'Ah, Jesus,' said Ken, and he got up and felt his side where he'd been struck. He laughed shakily, and picked up his own stick in a show of defiance. Then he dropped his stick again, and began to cry. He slumped down on his knees and held his side. He arched his back and squeezed his eyes closed with the pain.

'We've won,' said Creamy, before anyone else could think of a reaction to what had happened. Rainbow motioned with his stick towards the rest of us. 'We've won,' repeated Creamy quietly. 'You can stay and play in the hut, Rainbow.' Creamy had found the right note as ever. With the fight declared over, Rainbow felt a bit ashamed to be with third formers. He vaulted over the sagging willow trunk onto the river bed, and slouched off upstream. 'See you, Rainbow,' said Creamy.

'Yea,' said Rainbow.

Ken was still crying. There was some blood showing through his shirt from the graze, and Mathew and I helped him up. We began to go back to the bridge through the fennel. 'They can't come here again, Creamy, can they?' called out Warwick. 'It's Tech now.'

'They can't come here again,' said Creamy. His face was the same: relaxed, and with the upper lip creating the impression of incipient humour. He didn't speak with any special triumph.

We broke down the fennel in our retreat, paying no attention to the tunnels Creamy and I had made. I was glad Tech had won. I joined in the talk about the injustice of Rainbow being there, but I was glad they'd won. It gave a more general explanation for the end of our friendship – Creamy's and mine. There couldn't be any personal betrayal when it was a matter of Tech and High, a commitment to a cause. Ken was still crying, but with greater artifice as his sense of heroism grew. He leant to one side, and he held his shirt out so it wouldn't stick to his graze. The fennel fronds were like miniature conifers, smaller and smaller, each in the join of the other as marsupial embryos in a pouch. The oddly coastal smell of the crushed fennel was all about us. 'I don't know that we lost, not really fair and square,' said Mathew. 'If Rainbow hadn't been there, I mean.' They could say what they liked, but for myself I knew I'd lost all right. And it was worse that as I climbed from the fennel, up onto the road, I could understand what it was I'd lost, and why.

Kenneth's Friend

At the north side, towards the point, the shore was rocky. When the tide was going out I liked to search the pools for butterfish and flat crabs like cardboard cut-outs, sea snails with plates instead of heads, and flowing anemone in pink and mauve. Once Kenneth let a rock fall on my hand there on purpose, after I told him I didn't want to spend the morning making papier-mâché figures. He said it was an accident of course, but I knew he meant it. The rock had a hundred edges of old accretions, and cut like glass. I sat and waited for the sun to stop the cuts bleeding. I thought about Kenneth and me, and how I came to be there at all.

I had good friends when I lived in Palmerston North, friends that experience had shown the value of, but when we shifted to Blenheim I didn't have time to make friends before the holidays. I liked Robby Macdonald best. He and I became close later, but Kenneth seemed to attach himself to me in those first weeks. Perhaps he felt it gave him at least a temporary distinction to be seen with the new boy. He came home with me often after school, and lent me *Crimson Comet* magazines. At Christmas time he invited me to go with his family to their holiday home in the Queen Charlotte Sounds. His father was a lawyer and mayor of the town. My mother was pleased I'd been invited, and for sixteen days too. She gave me a crash course on table manners and guest etiquette. I had a ten-shilling note in an envelope, so that I could buy something for Kenneth's parents before I left.

The house had a full verandah along the front, facing out towards the bay. We used to have meals there, and standing out like violin music from amongst the talk of the Kinlethlys and their guests, I could hear the native birds in the bush, and the waves on the beach. It was a millionaire's setting in any country but ours, though Mr Kinlethly was a lawyer and mayor of the town admittedly. Glow-worms too: there were glow-worms under the cool bank of the stream. At night I crept out to see them, hanging my head over the bank, and with my arms in the creek to hold me up. The earth in the bush was soft and fibrous: I could plunge my hands into it without stubbing the fingers. The sand of the small bay was cream where it was dry, and yellow closer to the water. There was no driftwood, but sometimes after rough weather there would be corpses of bull kelp covered with flies, and filigree patterns of more fragile seaweed pressed in the sand.

What Kenneth wanted, I found out, wasn't a friend, but someone to boss about. A sort of young brother, without the inconvenience of his sharing any parental affection. With no natural authority at school, Kenneth made the most of his position at the bay. Each night before we went to bed, Kenneth enjoyed the privilege of choosing his bunk and so underlined his superiority. He might bounce on the top bunk for a while, then say that he'd chosen the bottom one; he might wait until I'd put my pyjamas on one of them, then he'd toss my pyjamas off and say he'd decided to sleep there himself. He liked to play cards and Monopoly for hours on end, or work on his shell collection. Whenever we had a disagreement as to what we should do, Kenneth would say that I could go home if I didn't like it. I think in a way that's what Kenneth wanted – for me to say that I wanted to go home, that I couldn't stick it out. He didn't understand how

much the bay offered me, despite its ownership. Kenneth's parents didn't know we disliked each other. We carried on our unequal struggle within the framework of their expectations. We slept together, and set off in the mornings to play together. We didn't kick each other at the table or sulk to disclose our feud. His parents were always there however, as a final recourse: the reason I had to come to heel and follow him back to the house when he saw fit, or help him catalogue his shells in the evening instead of watching the glow-worms.

The Kinlethlys seemed to take their bay for granted, corrupted by the ease and completeness of their ownership. Mr Kinlethly was away more days than he was there, and at night he shared the family enthusiasm for cards. I never saw him walk into the bush, and he went fishing only once or twice as a sort of tokenism. There was no doubt he was pleased with the place, though. He liked visitors so that they could praise it, and I heard him telling Mrs Kinlethly that the property had appreciated seven hundred percent since he purchased it. Mrs Kinlethly had some reservations I think. She wouldn't allow any uncleaned fish near the house. She said the smell lingered. We would get them at the shore, washing the soft flaps of their bellies in the salt water, and tossing their entrails to the gulls. Mrs Kinlethly gave us what she called the filleting board, and we would scale and dismember the blue cod and tarakihi in the ocean they came from: the filleting board between Kenneth and me, our feet stretching into the ripples. Mrs Kinlethly seemed sensitive to the smell of fish. When the wind was strong from the sea, blowing directly up to the house, she said it smelled of fish. It didn't really. It carried the smell of kelp, sand-hoppers, mussels, jetty timber, island farms, distant horizons – and fish.

One wall of Kenneth's room was covered with the display case for his shells, and our bunks were on the opposite side. I thought the collection interesting at first: the variety of colours and shapes, the neatly typed documentation. Each entry seemed to have one sentence beginning 'This specimen . . .' Mr Kinlethly wrote them out, and Kenneth proudly typed them on the special stickers, which I got to lick. 'This specimen a particularly fine example from the northern coast of Sabah', 'This specimen a gift from Colonel L. S. Gilchrist following a visit to our bay' or 'This specimen one of the few examples with mantle intact'. The collection seemed to admirably satisfy the two Kinlethly requirements concerning possessions – display and investment.

My dislike of the shells began when I had sunstroke. Kenneth and I had been collecting limpets on the rocks, and I forgot to wear a hat. The sun on the back of my neck all morning was too much for me. I lay on the bottom bunk, and tried not to think of the bowl Mrs Kinlethly had placed on a towel by the bed. The family considered it rather inconsiderate of me to get sick. After all I was there to keep Kenneth amused, not to add to Mrs Kinlethly's workload. I lay there trying not to be a bother, and hearing Kenneth's laugh from the verandah. In the late afternoon Mr Kinlethly brought a guest back from Picton, and they came in to see the shells. 'A friend of Kenneth's,' said Mr Kinlethly as my introduction. I was bereft of any more individual name at the bay. It was always 'Kenneth's friend'. 'I think he's been off colour today,' said Mr Kinlethly. 'Now here's one in particular, the *Cypraea argus*.'

'Oh yes.'

'And *Oliva cryptospira*.'

'Strikingly formed, isn't it?'

'*Cassis cornuta.*'

I wanted to be sick. The nerves in my stomach trampolined, and saliva flooded my mouth. The mixing bowl on the towel seemed to blossom before me. Mr Kinlethly was in no hurry. 'Most in this other section were collected locally,' he said. 'Kenneth is a very assiduous collector, and also people around the Sounds have become aware of our interest. A surprising number of shells come as gifts.' Despite myself I looked over at the shells. Many of them seemed to have the sheen of new bone; like that revealed when you turn the flesh away from the shoulder or knuckle of a newly killed sheep. I had to discipline myself, so that I wasn't sick until Mr Kinlethly and his visitor had left the room. The shells were always different for me after that.

The Kinlethlys had a clinker-built dingy. It always had a little bilge water in it that smelled of scales and bait. They had their own boatshed for it even, just like a garage, with folding doors so that the dingy could be pulled in, and a handwinch at the back of the shed to do it with. The dingy was never put in the shed while I was there. Kenneth said they left it out all summer. We used to pull it up the sand a way, and then take out the anchor and push one of the flukes in the ground in case of a storm or freak tide. Using the dingy was probably the best thing of all. When we went fishing I could forget the boring times, like playing Monopoly, and helping Kenneth with his shells. I could look down the woven cord of the hand line, seeing how the refraction made it veer off into the green depths, and I could listen to the water slapping against the sides of the dingy. Closer to shore the sea was so clear that I could see orange starfish on the bottom, and the sculptured sand-dunes there, the sweeping outlines formed by the currents

and not the wind. Flounders hid there, so successfully that they didn't exist until they moved, and vanished again when they stopped at some magician's trick.

Wonderful things happened at the bay, even though I was only Kenneth's friend. Like the time we were out in the dingy and it began to rain. The water was calm, but the cloud pressed lower and lower, squeezing out what air remained between it and the sea, and then the rain began. I'd never been at sea in rain before. The cloud dipped down into the sea, and the water lay smooth and malleable beneath the impact of the drops. The surface dimpled in the rain, and the darkest and closest of the clouds towed shadows which undulated like stingrays across the swell. 'I never think of it raining on the sea,' I said to Kenneth. 'Imagine it raining on whole oceans, and there's no one there.'

'Bound to happen,' said Kenneth. He couldn't see why I was in no hurry to get back.

'I always think of it raining on trees, animals, the roofs of cars,' I said weakly. I couldn't share with Kenneth the wonder that I felt.

Kenneth had no respect for confidence. That evening at tea, when Mrs Kinlethly told the others how wet he and I had got in the dingy, Kenneth said that I'd wanted to stay out and see the rain. 'He didn't know that rain fell in the sea as well as on the land,' said Kenneth. That wasn't the whole truth of it, but it was no use saying anything. I just blushed, and Mrs Kinlethly laughed. Kenneth's father said, 'Sounds as if we have a real landlubber in our midst,' in a tone which implied he wasn't a landlubber. I learnt not to talk to Kenneth about anything that mattered.

On the Thursday of the second week there were dolphins again at the entrance of the bay. I admired dolphins more

than anything else. They seemed set on a wheel, the highest point of which just let them break the surface before curving down into the depths. I imagined they did a complete cartwheel down there in the green water, then came sliding up again, like a side-show. 'There's dolphins out at the point,' said Mr Kinlethly. Mr and Mrs Thomson and their two unmarried daughters were with us on Thursday.

'I've never seen dolphins,' said Mrs Thomson.

'Quite a school of them,' said Mr Kinlethly. He decided that his guests must make an expedition in the dingy to see the dolphins. Mrs Kinlethly wouldn't go, but the Thomsons settled the dingy well down in the water and there wasn't room for both Kenneth and me.

'There's not room for both the boys,' said Mrs Kinlethly. Kenneth didn't care about the dolphins, but he wasn't going to let me go. He called out that he wanted to go, and his father hauled him aboard.

'Kenneth's friend can come another time,' said Mrs Thomson vacuously, and the dingy pulled away clumsily. I waded out a bit, and kicked around in the water to show I didn't care, but I could see Kenneth with his head partly down watching me, waiting to catch my eye, and with the knowing little grin he had when he knew I was hurt. The dingy angled away towards deeper water, the bow sweeping this way then that, with the uneven rowing of Mr Kinlethly and Mr Thomson.

'Dolphins, here we come,' I heard Kenneth shouting in his high voice.

That finished it for me, not missing out on the dolphins, but Kenneth going merely because he knew I wanted to. I'd taken a good deal, because after all I was just a friend of Kenneth's invited for part of the holidays, but I was beginning

to think myself pretty spineless. I thought of my Palmerston friends, and the short work they'd have made of Kenneth. I left Mrs Kinlethly watching the dingy leave the shelter of the bay to reach the dolphins at the point. I went up to the house, across the wide, wooden verandah and into Kenneth's bedroom. From the bottom bunk I took a pillow case, and began to fill it with shells from Kenneth's collection. I tried to remember the ones he and his father liked best, the ones most often shown to visitors. *Pecten maximus*, *Bursa bubo*, and *Cassis cornuta*, the yellow helmet. The heavy specimens I threw into the bag, and heard them crunch into the shells already there. Once committed to it, the enormity of the crime gave it greater significance and release. Whatever outrage the Kinlethlys might feel, whatever recompense they might insist on, Kenneth would understand: he'd know why it was done, and what it represented in terms of him and me.

I took the shells up the track into the bush, and I sat above the glow-worm creek and threw the shells into the creek bed, and into the bush around it. Most disappeared without sound, swallowed up in the leaves and tobacco soil. The yellow helmet stuck in the cleft of a tree, and as I sat guiltily in the coolness, and heard the ocean in the bay, it didn't seem incongruous to me, that *Cassis cornuta* set like a jewel in the branches. The bush was a good imitation of an ocean floor, or so I could imagine it anyway.

A sense of drabness followed the excitement of rebellion. I came down to the house, and replaced the pillow case. Without a plan I began to return to the beach, scuffling the stones and listening to the sound of the sea. Mrs Kinlethly came up the path towards me. I thought she must have found out about the shells already, and her response was

more than anything I'd expected. She walked with her hands crossed on her chest, as if keeping something there from escaping, and her tongue hung half out of her mouth. It was an obscenity, worse than if she'd opened her dress as she came. I tried not to look at her face, and I felt the muscles of my arms and shoulders tighten, like at school just before I was strapped. Mrs Kinlethly passed so close to me that I heard the leather of her sandals squeaking, but she didn't stop or say anything. She went up the steps, and the house swallowed her up in complete silence. I couldn't work out what was happening. I sat down there by the path. I looked out towards the bay and the drifting gulls, letting the wind bring the associations of the sea up to me.

Mr Kinlethly came up next, without his trousers and with everything else wet. Instead of his hair being combed across his head as usual, it hung down one side like ice-plant, and the true extent of his baldness was revealed. 'The dingy went over. Kenneth's gone,' he shouted at me forcefully, and looked about for others to tell. He seemed amazed that there was just me by the path in the sun, and the birds calling in the bush behind the house. His eyes searched for the crowds that should have been there to receive such news. When I made no reply, he turned away despairingly. 'Kenneth's gone. I must get to the phone,' he shouted at the monkey-puzzle tree by the verandah, and he strode into the house. His coloured shirt stuck to his back, and on the ankle of one white leg were parallel cuts from the rocks.

The house filled rapidly after Mr Kinlethly made his phone calls, until there were enough people even for him: relatives from both sides of the family, friends, and folk from the next bay. Two policemen from Picton came, quiet men who kept out of the house, and began the search for Kenneth.

I rang my father when I could, and asked him to pick me up at the turn-off by four o'clock. My mother had made it very clear to me about thanking the Kinlethlys before I left, but the way it was I couldn't bring myself to say anything. I just packed my things, and walked up to the road to wait for my father. I was up there by mid-afternoon, and I climbed up the bank above the road and sat there waiting. I hadn't had anything to eat since breakfast. I could see right over the bay, and although the house was hidden by the foreshortened slope and the bush, I could see the boatshed like a garage at the edge of the sand. Where the dingy had capsized at the point, the chop was visible, occasional small, white crests in the wind.

The Seed Merchant

Father very worse, the telegram read. I had it folded in my pocket during the flight south. The wording itched in my mind, and the irritation diverted my worry. I imagined my mother being told that both very and much were an unnecessary expense, and agreeing without caring to cut one out. I was mowing the lawn when it came. I caught a flight so soon afterwards that in the hair of my wrist were fine pieces of cut grass, held out from the skin. At such times the senses are capable of meticulous observation. Birdy Watson was thirteen when he tried to climb the cenotaph, fell off and killed himself. As the taxi passed I saw far above the stone figures the ledge that Birdy reached, and the concrete steps below that broke him on his fall. Even his nickname had not saved him. The town had grown rapidly the driver told me, though it held no progeny of Birdy's or of mine.

My father had rallied by the time I reached him. You will recognise the terminology. He had rallied surprisingly well, the doctor said. So my father was able to return home and wait a little longer. He lay in his own bed, and as I talked first in the hall with my mother and sister, I could hear him clearing his throat as he waited to welcome me. A questing smile as he tried to see in my face a picture of himself before I could disguise it. He clasped my hand rather than shook it, and looked away, asked about Susan and the children as a defence against his own predicament. The rowan trees by the fence were in berry amidst the fingered leaves, and I could see the hardwood chopping block where roosters had

been sacrificed. All of us had lived together in the place, yet each had a separate experience of it: in the same way we share life, I suppose.

'Lately I've often thought of things to say to you,' my father said. 'No one argues about books any more. No one cares. It's all politics and entertainment now, you see.'

'Reading and writing are too slow for them,' I said.

My father nodded against the pillow. 'Even in sport,' he said. 'Even in sport all they're interested in is finishes, and the money.'

I sat in the cane chair by the window and talked with my father. I hadn't been there long before he mentioned Ivy. He asked if I remembered her, and said what a close friend of my mother's she'd been. He turned his head and looked at the window with flat eyes, the symptom of the inverted vision of memory. The skin lay loosely on the tendons of his neck, and stubble was salt and pepper beneath his jaw-line. After a time he said, 'You remember Ivy.' He took my silence as forgetfulness. 'You stayed with her at times as a boy. You mustn't forget Ivy. People used to take her and your mother as sisters. Did you know that?'

Ivy must have been thirty odd when I stayed with her. She laughed a lot. There was always reason for a laugh at things, even though she did have her mother to look after. The trams came right past their house. Over thirty years ago. The noise and smell of the trams on the street straight through to the square. Ivy and her mother made painted eggs of wood. Ivy was a nurse as well at a private hospital, but I remember them sitting with trays of eggs. The old woman sanded the eggs wet and dry. She had a slight moustache. Ivy painted them: several coats and then designs and varnish. Patterns like Fair Isle, or hooped colours, or little circles like the seeds

of silver birch. I don't know what they were for: darning, or paperweights, or to be valued for their own sake perhaps, on a mantelpiece in deep blue and gold.

'She came sometimes to stay with us. A great friend of your mother's.' And of my father. 'You remember staying there now?' he said. Yes, I remembered things that had a new interpretation with the years. Like the seed merchant. Some friend was with Ivy. They laughed in the bedroom as Ivy finished dressing to go out, and the trams rattled past to the square. I was to remain behind with the old lady, and fill the coal scuttle from time to time. Ivy called to me from her room. The two of them were laughing again. How they were laughing, and there was powder smudged on the dark polish of the duchess, and underclothes on the bed like the limp, pink petals of a rose. Ivy stopped me with her hand, and brushed the hair from my forehead.

'This is Frank's boy,' she said. Her friend started to laugh. 'Oh stop it,' said Ivy, laughing herself, and swaying back to ease the effort of the laughter. She brushed my hair again to show she wasn't meaning to laugh at me.

'How is your father: How is the seed merchant?' said Ivy's friend. Her top teeth were slightly buck, yet white and of a size.

'He's not a seed merchant,' I said. 'He works for the paper.'

'Oh, Ivy always told me he was,' she said.

'He proved to be, by God!' said Ivy.

I was disappointed not to be going with them into the city, for at night the noise and the lights of the tram blurred its outline, fusing the tram with the other colours and movement of the city night.

My father slept a good deal. I spent much of each day working in the section which had been neglected because

of his illness. I cleared and levelled several garden plots, and put them down in grass. I lacked the resignation of my mother and sister to sit and talk quietly in the living-room, with his medicines on a tray, while they waited for him to wake. Each task served to exorcise some small ghost of time past, trivial familiars that were in wait within the simplest things. My father's fishing rod above the garage door, and the breadboard shaped like a Pig.

Sport was my father's realm as a journalist. He was given his own column when I was in the fourth form, and stayed so long in the hotel that my brother and I divided his scallops between us, and enjoyed the celebration on his behalf. I read to him about sport, and wildlife which was his other interest. For years he said that he would write a book on the great man Anthony Wilding, but it was never done. 'Ivy married, you know,' he said. 'Went to live in Tasmania, but it didn't last.' We were quiet for a time. My father seemed to want me to remember Ivy, and I did, but not in his way. 'It didn't last,' my father said. 'She came to New Zealand again, but we never saw her.' Ivy took me to the pictures in the square at night. On the tram I stood by the driver and watched him use the solid metal levers in place of a steering wheel. The noise, and the lights of the square in the distance. Ivy bought chocolates loose in a bag, and she laughed with the manager, who looked at the front of her dress. She told me that she used to go to the pictures often with my mother when they were nurses together. I hadn't thought about Ivy for a long time before coming to see my father: the trams, the painted wooden eggs, the seed merchant. Sitting with my father I realised more clearly that my age had prevented me from knowing Ivy as she was to a man, though even then I was conscious I think of

warmth, fluidity of movement, and laughter both generous and knowing. 'They were fine lasses those two. Ivy and your mother. A lot of people thought they were sisters,' said my father. I had no clear recollection of my mother at Ivy's age. We make present appearance retrospective for those close to us. 'You were only a boy,' said my father, recalling not so much my age then, as his own. Frank the snappy dresser and journalist perhaps.

'Trams ran right past her gate,' I said. 'Right past and rattling on down into the square.'

'I know.'

'And Ivy's old mother who was always cold, always sitting over the fire or heater.'

'Of course. Old Mrs Ransumeen. But she was deaf you remember. Yes, that's right. Ivy's mother, Mrs Ransumeen. She didn't sleep well, but she was rather deaf.' My father laughed quietly. I couldn't remember the old lady being all that deaf. My father's laugh was even and subdued. It seemed the laugh of a younger man, just that once.

I asked my mother about Ivy one afternoon. My father had fallen asleep while I read aloud from his articles on Anthony Wilding. He started to weep in his sleep: the tears soaked into the white cotton pillow, yet he lay without sound or movement apart from his breathing. I hope never to see that again. I told my mother that he asked about Ivy quite often. She said he never mentioned Ivy to her. She'd known Ivy longer than the rest of us, but then perhaps a friend's view of Ivy was not what my father wanted.

The wind was strong outside. It set up a persistent and familiar whine around one of the protruding barge-boards. 'Could you cut back the twisted willow by the study again sometime,' my father said. 'The branches rub on the side of

the house in the wind, and the leaves block the guttering.'

'You cut it down years ago,' I told him. He was quiet for a time, smiling.

'What an old fool I've become,' he said. 'Jesus, just an old fool. Even my sense of taste is playing up. I get a sudden taste of onions or marmalade when I'm lying in bed. It makes me sick at times, the taste of things I haven't eaten, suddenly there in my throat.' Ivy's mother had kept clearing her throat all the time – arp, arp, arp. Indignities come with age it seems. She used to wet the eggs to give them a last buffing with a leather cloth. She always reminded us to check the coal bin before we left her alone in the winter. I don't think my brother ever went to stay with Ivy, it was always me.

Ivy took me to the knick-knack and souvenir shop by the river once. She had her eggs in a shoe box, each wrapped in tissue. She took some out to impress the shopkeeper, and spread them on the counter, and moved them with her fingers to show how even, bright and smooth they were. He touched each in turn after she had, his hands following hers. Ivy laughed, making the eggs brighter than ever on the counter, and her dress rustled on her stockings. I wonder if he knew better than I did what use they were, and I wonder why I never thought to ask her.

My father had become a noisy breather, not snoring, but the air forced in and out, whispering in his nose, resounding in his chest, so that the mechanism by which life is sustained was always emphasised. His thoughts turned back, and I couldn't follow him all the way. We started out as equals, with the same perspective in that at least we were adults, but as we went back my sight became that of a boy, while he remembered Ivy as a man. I don't know if my father realised that, or what he expected of me. Any interpretation

of what we knew as a child is dangerous. 'I took them both to the Industries Fair once,' he said. 'I was working for the old *Herald* and had complimentary tickets. There was a demonstration of working machinery from the woollen mills, and a glass blower who made goblets and ships as you watched. Your mother and Ivy wore dresses with puffed sleeves.' My father paused. 'The skin that girls had then,' he said. I had a vision of my father then as in his old photos, with a soft brim hat, and two-tone shoes. With a smooth, thin face, and one hand in his pocket.

These questions and offerings of Ivy occurred amongst many other things not relevant to them in my talks with my father, but the reiteration was not in my imagination I thought. I told my sister that in a way it embarrassed me, for I wasn't sure what was required. I was going to tell her of the seed merchant, but closed my mouth on it. She is a shrewd and handsome woman, my sister. About the age that Ivy had been, when I think of it. She said that he had a history with Ivy, odd expression, but that it was the time back he wanted, not just Ivy. She said the ache was for the time of it: Ivy and our mother like sisters, and he himself as he was. My sister may be right, and I too insensitive to understand. Perhaps my father did in fact see Ivy as the image of what they both were, my mother and her: even the image of what all three were then. He never knew Ivy old, never saw her since he knew her, and she had never seen him old.

My father would sweat a lot at times as he lay in bed. Not on his face, but at the base of his neck, the pit where neck met chest, and the sweat would glisten there with the movement of his chest and the forced breathing. When I went down to the living-room my mother would ask me if he was awake. Ivy's mother fell asleep in front of the fire in

the evenings. Ivy placed a patterned tea cosy on her head, and we laughed without noise or malice. 'We lost touch with her after her marriage broke up and she came back. Even that we heard about through someone else,' my father said. 'Like a sister to your mother, like a mother to you.'

'I remember her better when I stayed with her, than when she came to visit us.'

'It was different,' my father said.

My father asked me to clean out the desk in his study, and yes, I found one of Ivy's eggs lying with Forest and Bird annual reports, typewriter ribbons, dry fountain-pens, and pieces of kauri gum. The egg was royal blue, with gold and red rosettes. Still shiny, but old-fashioned in a way I couldn't pick. The decoration gave a false impression of jewelled solidity, for when I lifted up that Trojan egg it lay lightly in my hand, as if already hatched. I could see faint cracks in the paint, which compensated for the drying of the wood through many years. The tram-lines were shiny in the street outside Ivy's house, as if someone from the council polished the top surface. On a hot day the sun caught the lines for blocks ahead, and the trams shook and shimmered all the more in the currents of heat. Ivy used to push my hair off my forehead, and make a part using her own comb. I felt ashamed of the egg in a way. I put it in my pocket as I stood in the study, and my fingers caught on the edges of the telegram still there. Father very worse, it said, and it was true again.

A Day with Yesterman

Chatterton woke to the birds. The absence of pain may have been the reason. He moved his legs, sucked in his stomach, but nothing caught, just the squeak of the plastic sheet beneath the cotton one. Chatterton was accustomed to the need to occupy himself much of the night, to sidle and belay from ledge to ledge of darkness, but not all that often did he hear the birds begin. He marvelled at the intensity – a sweet hubbub as a base, and superimposed the longer, individual exclamations of thrush or blackbird. He had the pleasing thought that the birds gathered at his house to inaugurate a special day. Chatterton folded the sheet under his chin, so that the blanket no longer tickled, and he made himself a little wider and longer to pop a few joints and check that he was in good shape.

A mild suffusion of light from behind the curtains strengthened as Chatterton sang 'Danny Boy' and 'The White Cliffs of Dover'. He stopped with a feeling something of value was slipping away, and then it came to him, a recollection of the night's dream in which he had made love to an ample woman beneath an elm tree in Hagley Park. It was to some degree an explanation of his mood. Chatterton was sensible enough to enjoy authentic emotion however it reached the mind. Before the experience quite faded he closed his eyes to breathe again the fragrance of the elm and observe a wisp of auburn hair quiver with the pulse of her neck. He lay listening to his birds as morning came. How young at last I feel, he assured himself.

By the time Chatterton was in the kitchen, he could get by with natural light. He poached himself an egg without boiling off the white, and he watched his yellow feet like flounders on the floor. He would never recognise his feet in a crowd, for they were just any old, yellow feet. Truck rigs passed with a roar on the nearby motorway as they tried to get a clear start to the day. Chatterton rubbed his knee to loosen the joint. The skin seemed to have no attachment to the bones, and slid all ways. Only the young body savours its union.

As the birds wound down, Chatterton finished his third cup of tea, and went back to his bedroom to choose his clothes. 'I'll make a bargain with you.' He addressed a small, familiar god. 'Best clothes for best day.' The trousers were a quality check, but big at his waist and so the band tucked somewhat under his belt. A grey jacket, with a chrome zip, that his daughter had given him for Christmas. Tropic Sands aftershave, which the label exhorted Chatterton to splash on liberally, but which he did not. 'Chatterton,' said Chatterton to his own reflection, 'you are an old dog.' He looked at all the bottles on his drawers, and decided to take no medication at all. Before he left the house Chatterton buffed the toes of his shoes with the socks he was putting out to wash. He should have known better, for the bending sent him dizzy, and he over-balanced and fell onto the smooth lino by the bench. He had a laugh at himself, and felt the cool lino on his cheek as he lay and waited for his head to clear. In the corner was a false cut in the lino: Chatterton could remember clearly the wet day seventeen years before when he had laid the lino and made just that false cut. How difficult it is to fault life's continuity. The rain had caught the window at an angle, and drained like rubber tree striations across its surface.

As Chatterton walked to Associated Motors he calculated a route which would keep him on the sunny side of the streets, and he watched other people on their way to work, disappointed that he couldn't recognise them as friends. He nodded and smiled nevertheless.

Chatterton helped part-time with the accounts at Associated Motors. So very part-time over the last months that Susan was surprised to see him. 'And you're looking so smart today,' she said. Chatterton knew he was. He began to use the computer to calculate GST payments. Chatterton enjoyed the computer, and was impatient with people who claimed they couldn't adapt to them.

'Life is adaptation,' he said.

'Right, Mr Chatterton.'

'How I could run when I was young.'

'Could you?' said Susan.

'I was a small-town champion,' said Chatterton, 'and could have been a large-town one with training.' He was wistful rather than proud.

'I like netball,' said Susan.

'Ah, your knees are wonderfully smooth,' said Chatterton: his fingers nimble on the keys.

The Sales Manager broke up their flirtation. 'How are you feeling?' he asked.

'I am in complete remission today,' said Chatterton. 'I can sense my prime again. I'm growing young again very rapidly.' The Sales Manager laughed, for he thought Chatterton intended a joke.

'How about taking a Cressida down to Dunedin then for me. It's needed there today,' he asked Chatterton.

The mechanics watched in envy as Chatterton took a set of provisional plates and two of his own cassettes. They

hoped for such perks themselves. 'Hey, Chatters, you lucky old bastard,' and Chatterton winked and executed a no-fuss manoeuvre before them in the yard.

'I thought the old bastard was dying or something.'

'Dying to get away in that car, all right.'

In fifth gear the Cressida was only loping on the Canterbury Plains. Chatterton fed in his Delius cassette and the quiet interior was sprung with sound. Chatterton wondered why he dreamed so often in old age of hang-gliding. Something he'd never done, yet increasingly his night views were from above, the cold air whistling in a rigging he didn't understand. Progress was relentless, and from landscape and people half-recognised he was borne away. He supposed it might be a side effect of the medication. When he was younger he would have tackled hang-gliding. He had been an athlete, hadn't he, and a soldier?

At Karitane, Chatterton turned off to take the old road. He could avoid the increasing traffic. He liked that swamp flat: rushes, brown and yellow mosses, mallards, and pūkekos with their bookish, striding way. Later there was a stranded man – enquiring face and car bonnet raised. Chatterton stopped, and the man came with grateful haste to meet him. His name was Norman Caan. He began to thank Chatterton, who smiled, but was distracted by the peace as he stood there – the quiet road, the crimped blue light over the sea, the headland beyond with an apron of gorse on the steeper ground. The wind from the sea was wine, and it scented the beachside grass and bore spaciousness inland.

'I do appreciate you stopping. I've got something of a problem as you see, and I've a city appointment at one.' Caan was close to Chatterton, his voice a trifle plaintive. He put out his hand and Chatterton shook it.

'Sorry,' said Chatterton, 'but what a day it is. Isn't it? How things continue to fit newly together, year after year.'

'I suppose it is.' Caan looked at the sky, blown almost clear, and the hills and the inlet and the horizon seaward, as though he had just entered a large building and had its architecture commended to him. The coast curved, and a far cutting bore a drape of pink ice-plant, and the sun shone back from it as if from glass.

As they examined the engine of Caan's Volvo, Chatterton noticed a balding spot at Caan's crown, as if a tidy bird had been scratching a nest there. Chatterton passed a hand over his own stiff, grey hair. A dunny brush he'd heard it called. He had to admit Caan's clothes better than his own, however: an integration of style and texture which Chatterton could recognise, yet not explain.

'There's nothing we can do,' said Chatterton. 'Lock up and come with me. We can have someone out in no time.' But back at his own car, instead of getting inside, Chatterton was drawn to the bank again. 'Will you look at that though,' he said. 'No pain there at all. Will you look at the ripples on the bars as the tide comes in, and the bubbles over the crab holes in the mud.' The single cloud against powder blue made a cameo brooch of the sky; birch leaves tossed as a mane on the back of a macrocarpa hedge. 'You don't mind just for a moment?' asked Chatterton. 'It's just such a day.'

'No, no,' said Caan.

'It's just such a day,' said Chatterton. Caan had no option, but his face had initially a shrug of the shoulders expression as he watched Chatterton move to the edge of the bank above the coast. He was only a few feet above the sea, yet Chatterton sucked several breaths as a diver would on a high cliff. 'I shall become part of it. I see it all as if I'm twenty,' he said.

Despite concern for his situation, Caan was affected by Chatterton's wonder, and something more – something naive in his cheerful age and the trousers belted too large, and his hair bristling. 'It is rather splendid,' said Caan; diffident in praise of his own country.

'You know,' said Chatterton, 'today I keep thinking of when I was young.'

Somewhere between Lake Grasmere and Seddon the black AJS left the road at speed and took an angle into grass standing high as a field of wheat. There was no way of stopping quickly. The bike's metal scything through. He heard only one sound, that of the rushing grass, and he was aware in the clarity of fear how bright the sun shone on that roadside grass like wheat. Yet there was nothing hidden – no snare, no ditch – and fear gave place to exultation as the grass slowed him and he *knew* that nothing there had harm in it: an instant almost too brief to allow him the dangerous conviction that he couldn't die. The black, heavy AJS off the road, the hissing, even fluster of the wheat-grass in the vivid sun. All in a few seconds, he supposed. All happening in a few seconds and in heightened perception. And the bike had stopped and he found himself quite alone in that landscape, stalled high from the road with grass packed around him, the cicadas coming back to chorus, and the fine pollens settling on the black tank of the AJS.

'Like riding through a wheat field,' said Chatterton.

'Sorry?'

'I was thinking back,' said Chatterton. 'Other days.'

As they passed over the hills into the city, Chatterton and Caan, together completely by chance they would suppose, talked freely. Chatterton found it easier to be honest as he grew older, and the knowledge that relationships had no

necessary continuation ceased to disconcert him. Besides, Caan was prepared to listen as well as talk. Chatterton liked a positive listener: he could be one himself. They covered the decline of state medicine, the loss of flavour in Bluff oysters, the self-serving of the political powerful, and the suicide of Tony Hancock. There is a good deal of satisfaction to be had from free-ranging criticism. 'But then I'm a deal older than you,' said Chatterton.

'Not so much surely, I'm retired.'

'There are two possibilities as you get old,' said Chatterton. 'You become archaic, or you leave the world behind in your progress. Either way increasing isolation is the result.'

'Well, isolated numerically perhaps.'

'And in confidence. It's hard to be confident and old. The opposite of what most people expect I suppose.'

'But you are,' said Caan.

'An act of faith. Besides, superstition and disease have me now, so I indulge myself. There's days sometimes that favour you, you know.'

'Propitious,' said Caan.

'Pardon.'

'Propitious.'

'Yes,' said Chatterton. 'That's it.'

'Anyway today you're welcome to travel back with me, and have lunch with me too. I'm allowed a guest at the Rotary Lunch I'm addressing. I'll have my car delivered, and afterwards we'll pick up my sister who's coming back with me to recuperate for a while.' Caan was pleased to be able to establish the immediate future, and to provide for Chatterton's repayment within it.

The President of Rotary was a splendid host, just one size larger and more glossy than his fellows as befitted his

office. 'So much of what service groups do now is taken for granted,' he said. 'Assistance is an expectation now, almost a right.' Chatterton noticed the barman's black reefer jacket, and it produced before Chatterton his grandmother's sewing basket. The fine wicker-work and the embroidered top – black, black, with a country spire perpetually slate blue. The colours were ribbed, and the tranquillity of even execution rather than the subject had made an ache which allowed of no expression. So he had built childlike barricades of pins around the black field's spire in attempts at the protection which his memory was later able to assume.

'We get told who we should be supporting, and how much,' said the President. 'We get told we're not doing enough rather than thanked. Not coughing up sufficiently.' Chatterton enjoyed a free whisky, and watched the last members picking up their badges. The President led the way into the dining room, and they took their places before three slices of ham on each plate. Chatterton rather enjoyed the Rotarian mood: an aura of confidence and good intent that arises from reasonable success in the world and a wisely unexamined life. Chatterton looked with favour on his ham, and waited for the vegetables. Caan talked to the President.

'I ran my own business for twenty-seven years, then it grew too complex and I sold out. That's one of the things I want to mention in my address: the need to understand there's a point at which a business becomes too much for the managerial skills of its founder alone. A lot of concerns go wrong at that stage.'

Chatterton admired the Rotarians across from him, particularly an assured man in his thirties, eating carefully and smiling carefully as he listened to his neighbour. A man well carapaced in a three-piece suit, and trusting the ground

beneath his feet. Chatterton wondered if he himself at any age had looked that way; and knew the answer. The man had a sheen almost, the beauty of a live lobster, an exoskeleton creature, any vulnerability safe within. He was all jointed precision of appearance. Chatterton caught his eye.

'Good on you,' said Chatterton, and they lifted their forks in mutual salutation.

'Few businessmen can make the transition from personal to corporate management,' said Caan. 'And why should it be expected, or easy.' Caan stopped, and looked first at the President and then at Chatterton as if some explanation was expected from them. His face was pale, and he swallowed several times. 'I feel rotten,' he said. 'I think I might be sick.' His head gave a shiver, and he sighed as if lonely.

'Perhaps the cold meat,' said the President. Caan and he left the table and went through the conversations to find a place for Caan to lie down. Caan walked as if he were carrying a tray of marbles and the loss of any of them would be his death.

Chatterton was offered more vegetables, and accepted all but the peas. Sprouts he had, and potato balls and corn heaped like nuggets of gold. And no pain was swallowed with them, no pain whatsoever. The President returned alone. 'He's lying down,' he said. 'He says he feels a little better.' The President looked searchingly at Chatterton. Chatterton lacked an executive mien, and there was grey hair tufted in his ears. He alone in the dining room had a jacket with a zip. There was a sense of ease though, and goodwill and self-will. The President was not a fool. 'Caan suggested you might speak instead,' he said. Chatterton was happy to be of service. He liked to talk to people. And he had his best trousers on, even if they were gathered at

the waist somewhat. He had visions to draw upon, his life among them.

When the President's routine business was over and the Serjeant-at-Arms had imposed fines with sufficient humorous innuendo, Chatterton was introduced as a colleague of Norman Caan. As he waited to speak, as the polite applause eddied about the tables, Chatterton was reminded of his last Battalion reunion, and by another step of recollection Birdy Fowler, who died of heatstroke before they came out of the desert. Chatterton hadn't been invited to speak at the reunion, and he thought there was a need for Birdy's name to be heard again. So Chatterton began his talk with several of the stories Birdy used to tell when drinking: the Rotarians laughed at the ribaldry of natural man, and Chatterton laughed in tribute to a friend. Then Chatterton talked about his illness: the prostate and spleen which had been taken, the disaffection of other organs; about how to make it through the nights, the spiritual and practical ingenuities by which it's possible to inch closer to the day. About his wife who had been very beautiful when she was young and he was a coarse, stupid boy. About his dream of steam trains ascending steep tracks through the bush, so that the engine fumed and panted, the white steam like egret's feathers flared against the leaves, wild cattle crashed away, and deep, faded varnish of the inner woodwork still showed a living grain.

The green, sashed curtains quivered at the windows of the hotel. The long tables of Rotary luncheon had flower vases, and pollen beneath some of them was spread like pepper on the white cloth. A waitress with her hair up in gel was at the kitchen swing doors, ready to clear away. She picked her lip, and wondered if she would be through by four. We make the mistake of assuming that our present experience is

the world's. The tussock would be blowing on all the crests of Dansey's Pass, glue sniffers sitting with statues of the city fathers, a fine rain flaking on to the pungas of the Ureweras, a sheer excalibur of sunlight from the high window of a panel shop in Papanui transfixing young Marty working there.

The Rotarians were normally uncomfortable with personal revelations, which could easily obscure sound business practices, but as Chatterton was unknown to them they felt none of the embarrassment that acquaintanceship would have brought. They were quite struck by his eccentricity, his passion, and the evident movement of the bones in his thin cheeks as he talked. Chatterton had an innocent pride as he left with the President to find Caan. He was resting on an alcove chair in the foyer. His coat and tie were off, and his head relaxed backwards. 'I think I'm all right now,' he said.

'Well, Mr Chatterton was a considerable success,' said the President.

'That's the second time he's saved the day,' said Caan.

'I just sang for my supper,' said Chatterton. The President's laugh was high-pitched, almost a giggle, and odd from such an imposing man.

Caan's car was delivered as he and Chatterton sat peacefully in the foyer. Caan washed his face with cold water, and then decided that he was recovered. 'You'll understand that Joan's had a hard time of it,' he said when he returned. 'She left her husband to make a midlife career for herself in physiotherapy and then found she had cancer. The treatment's knocked her pretty badly.' Chatterton knew the treatment, but he didn't think about it as they drove to the nursing home. Instead he enjoyed the dappled shadows on the road through the green belt, the shimmer caused by the breeze on the tops of the trees, and imagined himself

joining in with the afternoon joggers – putting his weight well forward on the slope and judging a pace to keep both legs and lungs comfortable. The bellows of the chest in full use, cooling tree air on the damp singlet, hair heavy with sweat patting on the back of his head as he ran.

On the front lawn of the nursing home a badminton court had been marked out. Young people played vigorously there, their bare feet silent on the grass, their voices loud and sudden. Joan was waiting in the lounge with her two cases beside her. 'She'll need a good deal of rest of course, but we're all optimistic,' Caan said as he and Chatterton walked past the lawn. Chatterton watched a brown girl leap forever so that her arms and breast were outlined against the sea. He wondered why God still chose to punish old men. As Caan came closer to the lounge he smiled and raised his hand, but his sister was behind the glass, and nothing could be said. She wore a light dress of floral pattern that would be considered cheerful perhaps – when purchased for someone else. She wore lipstick but her eyebrows were very pale, and to hide her baldness she was topped with a tam-o-shanter, green and red. She had the eyes of the travellers of illness.

'I'm sorry we're a bit late,' said Caan. 'It's been an odd sort of day.' As he told her of it, and Chatterton's part as an explanation for his presence, Joan and Chatterton regarded one another. When Caan finished, Chatterton touched the woollen cap in a friendly way.

'I had a hat, but not as colourful as yours,' he said. He took one of her cases, Caan the other, and they waited at the door while Joan farewelled a nurse. 'Chemotherapy as well as the ray can be pretty much a sapping combination,' said Chatterton when she was back. 'Is your hair all out?'

'All out,' she said.

'So was mine,' said Chatterton, 'but it grows in again. Mine grew back very wiry.'

'Very wiry,' said Joan. Well, frankness could work both ways.

'And you get a good deal of strength back.' To demonstrate, Chatterton stopped by the car and threw the case up, and caught it again in both arms. 'See,' he said eagerly.

'You get used to him,' said Caan.

'Are you so very different?' she asked Chatterton.

'I'm in search of natural man now,' he said.

'Too late, too old,' she said, but Chatterton threw up the case again and capered with it. The badminton players cheered; a nurse stood watching from the office and telling others over her shoulder what was happening.

Caan asked Chatterton to drive. After his illness at lunch Caan wanted a restful trip. Chatterton was obliging once more. As he drove he calculated aloud the unexpected profit he was making on the day – the price of the bus fare to Christchurch, and of a midday meal. Enough for a week's groceries, or for semi-gloss to paint his small porch. 'Do you enjoy painting?' he asked Joan. The triviality of it stimulated Joan; she was tired of weighing up life and death. She began to talk of the renovations she had done years before on her house at Port Chalmers. Although her voice was well back in her throat, and somewhat husky, it increased in tempo and her tam-o-shanter nodded green and red. 'Oh, no, no,' interrupted Chatterton decidedly. 'You should always strip back before repapering for a first rate job.'

'It's not always needed.'

'Shoddy, shoddy,' cried Chatterton.

'What would a man know about making a home,' said Joan. 'What does a man remember.'

Chatterton was in the presence of things which gave an answer. The water in the pink heart of flax, and a monkey puzzle tree to hold up the sky. Sheep coughing out the night, and in a winter drizzle the horses smoking in the dray. His mother standing at the laundry, pushing back her hair with her wrist, smiling at him, and the smell of hot woollens and yellow soap again. Old coats without shoulders on nails there like dried fish, and gulls following his father's plough.

At Tīmaru they had cream freezes, and turned off from the main road at the Showground Hill to rest and eat. Chatterton leant his arms on the top wire of the fence, and watched the downs and the mountains beyond. He led a game to distinguish as many shades of green as possible. 'Nine different colours. To stand and see nine different colours of green,' said Joan. 'All growing from the same soil; all compatible and with the promise of some use or crop.'

When he looked south, Chatterton sensed a change in the weather, and he told the others to expect a southerly. A fisherman gets to read the elements of his locality. Chatterton encouraged Joan to talk as they went on north. He refused to be deferential just because of her trial. 'You have to be careful illness doesn't make you selfish, you know,' he said. 'And you could do a lot more with your appearance – a young woman like you.' He could say such things because of his own illness, his lack of malice, but mostly because of a special innocence which arises from experience and is the mark of rare and successful old age.

'I was never at all religious before,' said Joan. 'Now I'm an atheist by faith rather than logic. And I've got tired of most of my friends: they almost bored me to death when they came. What you expect rarely happens. You, Norman, you're one of the worst.'

'But I'm a brother. All brothers are boring. They lack sufficient biological variation to be otherwise.'

Eventually release was almost overpowering for Joan. 'It's stuffy,' she said. 'I feel dizzy.'

'It's the closeness before the change,' said Caan, 'and you're not used to travelling yet.' Joan took off her woollen hat, and leant back on the seat. Her naked, bird's head had a little downy hair, and the skull plates joined in apparently clumsy workmanship.

'The treatment can have a long term effect on your food preferences,' said Chatterton. 'Peas and beans for instance. I can't eat them at all now; the smell disgusts me, while fruit is a positive craving. Nectarines and satsumas: ah, there now.'

The southerly came through late in the afternoon, catching them before Ashburton. The churned cloud, wind that flogged the trees and bore a scattered rain too pressed to set in. The temperature dropped as if a door had been opened. 'Oh, that's much better,' said Joan.

'Let's sing "Danny Boy". You know "Danny Boy"?' said Chatterton.

'Oh Danny Boy, the pipes . . .' Three of them together. Chatterton likes to sing, although he has a poor voice. He watched the broad, shingle river bed, the islands of gorse and lupin in the scattered rain. He thought of his nineteen-pound salmon near the mouth of the Waitaki; the gravel unsure beneath his waders as he turned, and the cry going up from his fellow fishermen as they gave way for him. The salmon don't feed: they strike in anger or homecoming exultation perhaps. The river aids its fish against the line, and swans form a necklace above the struggle as they pass to Lake Wainoni.

'We're all a bit high,' said Joan. 'I like the song, but we've all light voices and we need someone deeper. A bass

baritone, say.' The southerly was blowing itself out, but the coolness remained. Near Dunsandel they saw a hitchhiker with a giant pack and the legs to make light of it. Chatterton pulled up ahead of him.

'Can you sing "Danny Boy"?' he asked. The hitchhiker was willing, although for a time he was embarrassed by Joan's head.

'Where do you come from?' she said.

'Dubbo, Australia.'

'We've all of us got problems,' said Caan.

There were enough voices for a barbershop quartet. 'Oh Danny Boy, the pipes . . .' The Australian sang well. He was out of the weather and travelling in the right direction. Over the sinews of his brown arms were raised a few graceful arteries, and the whites of his eyes glinted in a tanned face. 'The green, green grass of home . . .' they sang as Caan conducted. Joan and the hitchhiker, who couldn't remember each other's names and would never meet again, combined their voices, and smiled at each other because of Chatterton's caterwauling.

They dropped the Australian baritone at the city overbridge. Chatterton took his pack from the boot, and Joan gave him a bag of seedless grapes she had from the nursing home. 'Goodbye Danny Boy,' she said. What could he make of them: what could they make of themselves. A hitchhiker's experience is only life accelerated. 'Oh my God,' said Joan as they went on. 'I've had my hat off all that time. What a sight.' She laughed at her own humiliation, and wiped her eyes. She put the tam-o-shanter on once more, for the formality of parting with Chatterton.

The wooden house was like the others that surrounded it; insufficiently individual, it seemed, to be his. Chatterton

stood in the drive as Caan came round to take the driver's seat. The evening was calm, but the evidence of the southerly was there. Leaves stripped by the wind and gathered on the concrete in the lee of the house. Leaves of peach and maple. Leaves of birch with aphids still clustered on the underside. The wind's violence had in its eddy a delicacy of graduated winnowing, and the litter diminished to a whip tail of fragments which included two ladybirds, a length of tooth floss, tuft of cat fur, and ended in a line of most fragile, perfect dust.

'But we'll keep in touch,' Caan was saying. 'You cheer Joan up because you know what she's been through, and she won't have many people to visit her while she's here.'

'If you can be bothered some time,' said Joan. The sheen of her hospital skin wrinkled in a grin.

'You know, right from the very start I had a feeling this was going to be a good day,' said Chatterton. 'It's a sort of Indian summer perhaps.'

'Life is sad though, isn't it?' said Joan. She looked up at him with a terrible openness.

'Oh yes, sad, but not dreary, not lacking purpose. But sad sure enough,' said Chatterton firmly. He went to the protected corner of his small garden and came back with a red rose for Joan, an old English rose, dark and red. 'Old style roses have the true scent,' he said. 'Aren't I right.' She had it to her face. 'Eh?' he said.

'Yes.'

Two white butterflies tumbled in the air above the letter box, and Chatterton smiled, not withdrawing his attention from the car as Caan backed out. 'He's a hard case that one,' said Caan. 'He gave a speech off the cuff at the Rotary meeting you know. Hardly a moment for thought.'

'He's certainly got no singing voice, but he sees through things all right.'

Chatterton waited to see them drive away, not the last minute shamefaced turning of some people's farewells, as if they feared what might be being said of them. Only his trousers suggested age, crimped at his slender waist and bagging somewhat at the seat the way trousers of old men do. When they were gone Chatterton arched back cautiously, and pressed with the flat of his hand on his stomach. He decided to stay in his garden while he felt so well. Did he tell them he was an athlete once, he wondered. Unthinkingly he kept his arched stance as he tried to remember. All the things he could do then, all the things he could feel. Chatterton could see his dark roses on the fence, and the two ladybirds upside down and closer in the whip tail dust upon the concrete.

The scent of the rose seemed to linger, maybe only in his heart, for he was no longer sure of such distinctions. What would he think of next, he wondered. He would fetch a beer and have it in his garden, because of the extra money and the friends he had made that day. As he turned to go, he had in recollection the sight of the Marlborough hills, and a hawk the colour of a moth against the sea of the sky.

A Poet's Dream of Amazons

My friend Esler is sick again. His mother rang, and implored me to hurry to the bed-side. She spoke in a whisper, not in deference to the sinking Esler, but from fear that her husband might overhear. Mr Esler hates me.

'He says he mightn't see the night out,' said Mrs Esler. 'He's had a dream again about a Big Woman, and she turned out to be a preammunition of death.' Mrs Esler is loyal in her way, but for a mother of that son her vocabulary is less than impressive. 'The doctor's been twice already,' she whispered. I suppose that a really Big Woman, and irrational as women often are in dreams, could quite well be a sinister omen.

I put down my work at once. I knew it was no joke if Esler said he was dying: well rather I knew that he might laugh about it, but die all the same. Esler fights a persistent and terrible battle against the world, but it is a losing battle.

My moped was in the shed, but before opening the door to it, I rattled the neighbours' fence to start their dog barking. A melancholy and majestic sound that dog made: deep bells in the cold air. Why should anyone sleep if Esler was dying? I interspersed the hound's barks with appeals to Odin, the god of my ancestors. I didn't want Esler to die, for he is one who speaks my language in this town.

On my moped I set a course from the forlorn suburb in which I lived, to the forlorn suburb in which Esler lived. Mrs Esler was watching for me: she was at the door when I approached, hoping that she would be able to smuggle me through to the laundry without a confrontation with her

husband. I saw half of him in the doorway of the living room; one arm, one side, one leg, one eye looking down the passage to the front door, and half a sneer to have seen a grown man arrive on a 50cc step-thru. 'It's only you,' said Mrs Esler. She pulled a face. 'The doctor's been twice. Oh, it's bad, it's bad.' She made another sudden face. Pulling faces is the qualifier Mrs Elser uses when her husband is at hand. They are the briefest flashes across her long face; semaphore by tic which hint at the hospitality, gratitude and compassion she can't speak of. They are spasms of emotional intent, and probably quite unconscious. 'You can't stay long,' she said, as we went up the passage, and then a fleeting contortion to nullify her tone. 'Mr Esler and I don't want you coming around really,' she said, and touched my arm. I turned at the laundry door, and went back, and put my head into the living room. I could see the back of Mr Esler's head as he watched sport on the television. There was a worn patch at the crown, as if he had a habit of twisting his head into the pillows at night.

'Mr Esler.'

'Uh,' said Mr Esler.

'I'm going through to see Branwell.' I said it loudly so that it would carry to Esler in his bed.

'Oh, it's you,' said Mr Esler. He didn't turn towards me.

Esler had his blue tartan dressing gown on in bed. He looked bad enough to be dying, but he was trying to laugh. He flipped his hands on the covers, and further down I could see his feet jerk. 'Branwell. Branwell,' he wheezed. 'I love it.' As well as liquid at the corners of his eyes, there was white gathered there, like a little toothpaste. On his cheeks were patterns from the creases in the pillow. Esler is balder than his father, but in a different way; going back a long way at the temples, and the hair between quite downy. 'Branwell's

good,' he said, 'and look!' He put his hand under the pillow and produced a flat bottle of brandy. 'You see before you indeed, the Earl of Northangerland.'

Esler's voice was squeezed out, as if someone was sitting on his chest. The Big Woman perhaps. His wrist buckled with the effort of getting the brandy bottle back under his pillow. I'd thought up the mention of Branwell as I went over; something to give Esler a lift. He becomes depressed without literary allusions from time to time. He began to tell me about his fantasy of the Big Woman. 'As did the Pharaoh I have a dream,' said Esler. 'Each night this vast and determined woman comes to wrestle with me.'

'All I get are nightmares of rooms without doors, and sinking ground beneath my feet.'

'Night after night,' said Esler, 'she seeks me out, and we must love and fight.'

Esler's room had been the laundry, but his mother now has an automatic washing machine in the old pantry, alongside the deep-freeze. The laundry tubs have been taken out, and Esler's bed moved in, and a small table by the window. Esler's boyhood room has become a guest room, which means it's never used. His father refuses to let Esler keep it because he is thirty-six years old, a poet, and still at home. Living in the laundry is one of those strange and bitter compromises that families have, and which remain incomprehensible to outsiders.

Mrs Esler came and interrupted her son just when he was describing to me the body lock that the naked Big Woman put on him in their struggle. All poets have a tendency to pornography. 'Mr Esler says you've started him coughing again. He won't have it.' Her lengthening face, pulled inexorably towards the grave, convulsed to disavow the

message she delivered. When she left, Esler continued to tell me of his Big Woman: a giant poster nemesis of sex. It was typical of Esler that even those things threatening his very life, could only appear ludicrous.

His room retains a faint smell of soap and washed woollens. A fine mould like candle smoke covers the underside of the window sill, residue from a more tropical climate.

'Is he still there?' shouted Mr Esler. He must have been taking advantage of an injury stoppage on the television.

'Night after night she comes, this immense woman,' wheezed Esler. 'Hair like a waterfall, navel a labyrinth, thighs like a wild mare.' Esler's warm breath had scents of meatloaf, medication and mortality. His gums had shrunk from the palings of his teeth.

Esler's clothes are on plastic hangers on nails along the laundry wall opposite his bed, and his books are heaped beneath on shelves made from bricks and planks. What can I tell you of my friend which won't make you feel contempt or pity. What can I tell you of this man who is better than us, whose interests and principles have made him in a modern world a mockery, whose skills are as little considered as those of a thatcher or a messiah.

'Waikato have scored again,' shouted Mr Esler, and Mrs Esler made an odd sound of wifely concurrence, like the instinctive response of a duck to another's call.

Esler and I have been friends since we ganged up at eleven to beat the second largest boy in the class: a prematurely hairy slob who used to hold us under water during swimming periods. We became one of those braces so common amongst boys – Brunner and Esler. We heard our names coupled more at school than we heard them separately. I can imagine the staffroom association.

'Caned Brunner today.'

'Who?'

'Brunner. Fair haired kid, hangs about with Esler. Caned him too.'

Or perhaps, 'That's Esler isn't it, smashing those milk bottles?'

'No, that's Brunner.'

'Both look the same to me, little buggers. Call him over.'

We fought together, smoked together, marvelled at the sky and stars together, took out the O'Reilly girls together. I have a scar on the underside of my left arm because Esler accidentally shot me with a home-made spear gun. We both saw Bushy Marsden collapse and die in the gym. We began the dangerous experiment of taking words seriously, and so resisting the process of attrition by which life betrays us.

'The Big Woman has a scent of almonds and macrocarpa,' said Esler in wonder and dread. His tartan wool dressing gown is also his lucky writing jacket, ever since he had it on when he wrote his Van Gogh sequence. Constant use without washing, a little lost food and the oils of feverish sweat from his asthma bouts, have taken the nap from it, have buffed it until it shines like silk, and the original tartan pattern is almost lost. 'Read me something to take my mind off breathing,' said Esler. He had a hundred poets to choose from, and I read Seamus Heaney to him. He nodded his downy head and squeaked 'Yes, yes,' at the touches which moved him. The liquid and the white gathered at the extremes of his eyes, spread a little to the corner skin.

'Will you stop that never ending jawing in there,' shouted Mr Esler to me.

'Exactly,' Mrs Esler said. I could almost hear the snap as her face, just for a moment, was contrite, bewildered.

'Read on,' said Esler.

The laundry never seems a bedroom no matter how long Esler is in it, or how many clothes or books he lines the wall with. Images of soap flakes linger in the air as a false Christmas, and one corner of the lino always seems to be damp. There is more utilitarian aura than even poetry can dispel. 'That's so,' said Esler as I read. In a paper packet on the second plank are one hundred and seventy three green copies of Esler's poems printed by the Whip-poor-will Co-operative Press. I have the dedication by heart: *These poems are for Bruce Brunner and Frank Heselstreet, fellow poets and friends who share my belief that emotion is like ours a round world, and as far enough east becomes west, so is laughter to tears and genius to insanity.*

I have eighteen copies in the top of my wardrobe. Frank and I buy one from the bookstore when we can afford to, and have our reward later when Esler tells us of another green pamphlet sold. Frank says we might end up with the whole edition of Esler's poems: a private joke, but what are friends for. Esler has always been absurd, but it is only one trait of character, as is deceit or shrewdness, composure or ambition. Just one aspect of my friend, but it makes it difficult to decide if he is dying or not. In a way I understand the Grim Reaper concluding that it is below his dignity to come for Esler, and sending a very Big Woman instead, who can laugh in her killing work and not be out of character.

Mr Esler appeared at the laundry door. His face was like that of a rock groper: reactionary and full of low cunning. 'You're doing him no good at all. Leave him alone can't you. I blame you for a lot of it,' he said. I never resent Mr Esler's antagonism. I see it rather as one of the few remaining signs of concern for his son – this determination to blame me.

'I know you do,' I said.

'How many did Waikato win by?' said Esler in his squeezed voice. His father knew that Esler didn't care, but couldn't deny himself the satisfaction of saying the score out loud.

'Thirty-two, ten,' he said. 'Thirty-two bloody ten.'

'That means a season's tally so far of one hundred and forty-two for, and fifty-three against,' said Esler. 'How many did Mattingly score?'

'Fifteen.'

'That makes him the highest scoring fullback in Waikato provincial rugby apart from Rawiri,' said Esler.

'You don't care. You don't care!' shouted his father.

'It's so though,' said Esler. He didn't care, but it was so though. He spent fifteen or twenty minutes each day on rugby statistics so that he could know more than his father and still disregard the game.

Mr Esler knew better than to dispute Esler's facts; instead he looked around the laundry as a rock groper does another's cave. 'This place stinks of idleness,' he said.

'Mattingly has twenty-four points to go before he reaches Rawiri's record, and he's already played three more first class games,' said Esler. His voice became treble with an effort at volume as his father left.

'Shut up,' cried Mr Esler from the passage.

'Each night now she comes, my Amazon,' said Esler. 'Beautiful, but so huge. Dear God. I try to oppose her with intellect and poetry when lust has failed. It's no use. She's killing me, the Big Woman, ending me with breasts and kisses.' Esler cleaned his lips by rubbing them with his fingers, and concentrated on breathing well for a time.

'I've never been afraid of women, or been against women, have I,' he said.

'I know.'

'The power, the weight, yet the subtleness of her. I can't stand it.'

'Take a sleeping pill or something,' I said.

'I can't. Not with my regular medication.'

Esler is loyal and honest, totally without envy or malice in his friendship, perhaps because the only basis he knows for friendship now is poetry. I have watched his other means of communication atrophy. Elser can discuss anthropomorphic imagery with wit and eloquence for hours, but when the grocer questions him of necessities, Esler grips the counter, is helpless before yet another stranger, stumbles to tell of sliced bread or free flow green beans. People exchange glances and knowing smiles at this evidence of the dangers inherent in any serious scrutiny of the mind. Esler tries to give Frank and me money from his savings account which has less than three figures: he writes to the *Listener* to point out that regional poets Brunner and Heselstreet have not received sufficient recognition. He is ugly, incongruous, annoying, ludicrous, and a true friend.

Esler asked me to bring a packet from the laundry table. 'It's my new poems to *go* to Australia,' he said. 'I want you to post it for me: you're luckier than me. Bless it before you put it in the box.' He made no mention of the postage charge: such things are incidental when you are dying. 'Send it airmail, and don't let them use any stamps with heads on. They're unlucky for manuscripts, I always feel.' All the seams in the brown paper were traced with sellotape, and the parcel was quartered in string woven of green and red strands. I bet Esler had said a prayer or a curse over his parcel, and sprinkled on some of the lucky dust that he'd collected from beneath Honey McIlwraith's bed. Esler is that sort of

intellectual and innocent. He really believes that there could be someone out there interested in poetry, willing to publish or pay for it, someone who will untie Esler's two-tone string, unpick his sellotape – and cry genius.

'If the Big Woman comes again tonight,' said Esler, then trailed off and began wheezing. It became worse until he was flapping his shoulders, and his veins began to swell.

'Puffer, puffer,' called his mother as she ran in. Her face twitched to one side then the other, as if offering her endless Christian cheeks to be slapped. She meant the asthma gadget with the diaphragm, and she and I tugged Esler to a sitting position, and she did his throat thoroughly, as if to ensure it would remain free of greenfly.

When he felt easier, Esler lay back again. 'Okay, Mum, okay,' he said. 'I'm fine now.' He turned away from us until he could regain the personal distance he required after the ignominy of his attack, his weakness, his mother with the puffer. Mrs Esler touched his downy head once, but he turned more resolutely, and she went out: first her dull curls and then the rest of her face, feature by feature, as a freight train curves from view. Esler rested: his skin gleamed with the sweat of illness and puffer liquid. I watched the soap flakes, and the light of the moon through the window without any curtain.

'Where's Frank?' said Esler finally.

'In Wellington at the technicians' course,' I said.

'They'll destroy him in the end, those computers,' he said. 'He left me the last poem in his Scheherazade series. So detached, so nimble. It makes me doubt my own progress. But those computers are the danger for poor Frank.' He picked up his puffer, held it to his mouth, but forgot to use it. Instead he said, 'I wish I could have a civilised life.' Beneath the bottom plank of his bookcase, close to the bricks, are Esler's two pairs

of shoes. Brown shoes with roughly sewn seams, and each left heel worn to a slant, and the inside liners curling up. Where the outlets for the tubs had pierced the wall, Esler has fitted wooden plugs covered with muslin to improve the seal.

'Pass the ball, pass it!' cried his father from the living room.

'France,' said Esler, looking at his poets gathered on the planks. 'France has always seemed to me a place where people have a civilised life.'

'A cultivated people. A people who accept without reserve the necessity of art,' I said. I had almost starved to death on my one sojourn there. Having been nowhere, Esler still believed that life can be essentially different in other parts of the world.

He began on the Big Woman again. He was amused by his own recollections of the dreams. It was a tribute to his creative impulse that even the thing he thought was killing him was transmuted into an entertainment for us both. He had his brandy bottle in one hand, his puffer in the other, and he was trying not to laugh. 'You know,' he said, 'the odd thing is that I do feel that I might be dying this time after all. It's more than asthma the doctor said, but he doesn't know about the Big Woman, of course.'

Later he started tossing about. I put his brandy away and called his mother. She began to fuss over him, but he became worse. Mrs Esler called to her husband that he'd have to ring the doctor about Esler needing to go into hospital, and Mr Esler came and stood by the bed. He has a face not wildly dissimilar to our own: eyes facing forward, a two-entry nose, mouth, and teeth still nominally intact. Yet what a gulf of species is there. He might as well have been a rock groper or a pear tree standing in the laundry.

'Thirty-six years old, writing bloody poetry, still has

asthma, and now dirty dreams,' he said. 'Jesus.' The sound of the puffer was loud. 'I blame you,' he said to me.

'So do I,' said Mrs Esler, her face hidden.

'Heckel and bloody jeckel. It was a sorry thing when you two and that Frank Heselstreet met up,' said Mr Esler. He went out to phone the doctor.

I decided to go the back way. Mrs Esler came out with me. At the other end of the hall I could see Mr Esler with the telephone cord drawn tight. That way he could stand at the living room door and watch the television as he waited to get through to the doctor.

'This asthma can't be all that serious, can it?' I asked Mrs Esler. 'I mean he's had bouts before and come through. There's nothing else is there?' Mrs Esler held her nose to stop herself from crying, and I didn't say any more. She gave a final, ambiguous face, and then turned her interminable chin away. Mr Esler talked at the other end of the passage on his extended line, as Mrs Esler went back into the laundry.

For a time I waited in the moonlight of winter outside the Eslers' back door. What it came down to I suppose, was that I thought my friend Esler couldn't die because nothing was ready, and because it wasn't just. There was still too much that was ludicrous, and too much confusion. But you and I and Esler can't always rely on an appropriate setting for our deaths. Esler might have to go in a laundry bed, with soap flakes in the air, brandy under the pillow, a puffer in his mouth, and a Big Woman squeezing him in his dreams, with mould like candle smoke beneath the window sill, with one green vanity collection of his poems from the Whip-poor-will Press, with a polished blue, tartan dressing gown, and no reason for it to be happening at all. And just a friend or two, who can do nothing but remember better times.

As I walked the path at the side of the house, Mr Esler leant excessively from his window to bring his harsh whisper closer to me. 'Murderer,' he hissed. 'Don't come back. Leave him alone. You bloody writers have done for him.' The moon struck down, and held the Eslers' garden in a frost of light. I didn't take the accusation too much to heart. I knew Mr Esler becomes desperate late at night when all the sports programmes end, when he finds himself with hours ahead and no team left to join, and none to hate, just his wife's Greek faces and his son in the laundry with the ailments of asthma and poetry.

'Murderer,' I heard Mr Esler hissing. There were guilty ones of course: Pound and Olson, Eliot and Larkin, Yeats and Frost, Stevens and Neruda, Lowell and Williams, Turner and Sewell, had all made their attacks on Esler. And Dylan Thomas. Now there's a murderer if ever I read one.

At the end of Te Tarehi Drive, and turning into Powys Street, which lay stark in the moonlight, I couldn't help laughing at the dying Esler. Laughter can be a guise of love: laughter can be helplessness expressed. Perhaps Esler is simply dying of his poets' amazement at the world in which he finds himself.

I let the moped engine run on in the shed for a few minutes, so that the battery would charge up a bit after the light had been on. I shook the neighbours' fence to rouse Cerberus again, and savoured the echoing sound. A deep barking dog suits a full moon. Esler had been dying before, and got over it. We all have to get over a little dying of ourselves in life. Is he dying of the asthma and the other things his mother wouldn't say, or is the Big Woman, that preammunition of death, suffocating him in his dreams with excess of loving?

Off by Heart

Trevor McDermott I've known, and Willy Seymour, Rachel Pesetsky, Mary-Lou Sutton, Peter Tamihana, Esplin Dee, Nathan Ives and Susan tits McMurken, Albert Dwyer, Zim Soloman, Dipper McGee, Helen Scarlett, Genevieve Prattley and Simon Prattley of a different family altogether. Cuddy Moone I remember, and Alan Donahue, Lloyd Olorenshaw, Natalie Johnstone, Liz van de Linden, Hek Francis, Selwyn Downey, William W. Williams, Cruise Enari and Arron Meek.

Picked one? Ah yes, Cuddy Moone. All right. Cuddy nearly blinded me when we were 13. I walked to Cuddy's one Sunday afternoon because he promised me that his twin sister would take off her bra. It wasn't the magnificence of that revelation, or the prurience of my interest, which threatened my eyesight. The sister wasn't even there. The family, except for Cuddy, had gone to watch a dying relative, and Cuddy knew that I was sour at his failure to demonstrate a hypnotic power over his sister.

To make up for it Cuddy built this volcano of dirt among the pumpkin leaves, and filled it with salt, matchheads, lighter fluid and so on. He lit it when I was bending over the top. He was vindictive was Cuddy. My eyebrows vanished, my face was pocked with burns and I had the taste of sulphur for days.

Cuddy Moone must have said something to his sister as well, for later in the term she slapped my face for nothing while the class was practising 'Good King Wenceslas' in the music room.

Hamish Gascoigne, Simone Field, Bridget McMaster, Snoz White, Hughie Gladman, Fitz Esler, Steven Aubert, Robby Dunn, Philippa Niall, Nancy Thomas, Richard III. I can't give any other name for him. I only met him once: we sat together on the railcar between Christchurch and Timaru. He had such bad teeth that he laughed only when he forgot himself, and then stifled that laughter with a hand over his mouth. He talked with fervour about adobe: how he intended to set up his own business once he had the expertise concerning the type of architecture and building techniques. He'd seen it used in America and the Mediterranean, he said. By the time we had passed Ashburton he had invited me to come in as partner, but I begged off. He might be an adobe millionaire by now, though I haven't read of it. Only when he left the railcar did I realise that he was a hump-back, and as he passed quickly along the single platform he didn't see my wave as almost partner from the window, but kept his suppressed smile over his bad teeth, and focused on the spaces between people with the introspective glare of a visionary.

Others are John McLeod, Coddy Youdale, Jane Caird, K. C. Venning and Ivan Platt. Sam Kīngi, Eileen O'Loughlan, Irina Mintossian, Val Elsen, Kate Fairbrothers and Zipper Farrington. And Zipper had a younger brother who went to California on a sports scholarship.

That's a good choice: I like to remember Irina Mintossian. She was the office manager at Esterhaub, Hayhoe and Grant, where I worked for three years. I had hoped that I would be offered a partnership, but I never was. Instead of a reputation for steadfast loyalty or undeniable flair, Irina said that the partners considered me a self-opinionated fart. She passed the information on to me with such friendly glee that it set us both laughing.

Of the titular partners only Grant was alive: a mediocrity who wore coloured bow ties and spent his time on boards or committees. Irina and one of the junior partners called Dudley Watson were the brains of the firm. Dudley drank coffee liqueur between appointments, persisted in heterosexuality despite himself, and had wonderfully successful ideas. Irina Mintossian matched everything up: product to presentation, clients tó staff, fees to scale, letters to addresses, documents to files, secretaries to typing, moods to days, attitudes to lives. She was the office hub, and the faster everything turned, the more blurred the extremities, the clearer Irina at the centre.

Her mother had Alzheimer's disease, and Irina would recount the incidents of that tragic comedy until our sides ached with laughing and our hearts for other reasons. And she would stand at the end wiping her lined cheeks with a man's handkerchief, and say ah dear, ah dear, the things that happen, you know. So much humour and so much efficiency was a rare combination, I have since realised. Her mother once got lost at the harbour, and wandered into one of the woolstores. She was there two days with only Parmesan cheese from her bag to eat, and wasn't found until a forklift driver heard from among the high bales her imitation of a morepork.

Tricia Wallace, Elinor Brown, Warwick O'Nian, Norman Preddie, Cecil Doak, Wendy de Wet. Sandra Dennis, poor soul, Alice Reddaway, Richard and Mandy Tomkinson, somebody Addis, Paul Hamilton, Gene Alpers and Tub Mann. A concept of Christian duty was the reason Tub Mann took Life Boys: the same reason prompted his dislike of me, I suspect. No matter what I was thinking or said, people assumed my intention was ridicule. Tub said I had a cheeky face. As captain of the Life Boys, Tub Mann refused

to award me the yellow cloth badge for Bible Knowledge, yet I was always top. In my time in Life Boys I won every Bible quiz except the one after the saveloy-eating contest. Do you know that the third river to come from Eden was Hiddekel, or that Daniel was called Belteshazzar? No, you don't. Years later, when I studied corruption within the early Vatican, I understood it so much better because of my experience of religious hypocrisy under Tub Mann.

Emma Turnbull, Dr Aldridge, Graeme Earl, Belinda Dix and the Scammel twins. Margritte Leaper, Adrian Pyne, RSM Glassey, Jane Racinski, Peter Peterson, Peter Beloff, Peppy Jewell, Suzanne Alperonne, Nick Smythe, the youngest and runt of the seven Wilberforce boys, Vincent Messenger, S. D. Ogden and Patsy Bentley, Cilla Hill, Alain Grocott, Susan in the lounge bar of the King Dick. Denis Gadd, Podge Furnnell, Lawrence Trevor, wonderful Billy Hawken, Evan Ransumeen, Malcolm Crowhurst and Virginia no longer.

Someone organised a reunion of our masters class, and it took the form of a twilight cruise on Lyttelton Harbour. It was embarrassing at first because we remembered so little of one another after 20 years: perhaps we had never known much. The feeling wore off during the trip, not because we recalled much more, or even learnt much more, about our fellows, but rather that we drank enough to be reconciled by familiarity to the faces around.

I was in a dull group at the stern around the wine casks – neat and high spirits were further forward, it seemed. We were denouncing politicians, I think. 'I'm Suzanne Alperonne,' said the quiet woman next to me.

'This is Suzanne Alperonne,' I said to my wife. Two things I could remember about Suzanne – she was a better scholar

at the end than I was, and once the professor apologised to her for his comments on feminism. My wife seemed to know more people on board than I did. She and Suzanne began talking to others about saving whales, while I watched at a distance a good-looking bald-headed man give a speech. Perhaps he was the organiser, and I never thanked him.

At dusk as we returned from the cruise the tug hesitated out from the wharf to allow access for another ship, and a group disenchanted with the whales and the politicians dared each other to dive in and swim ashore. Silly, competitive male banter it was, stilled finally by Suzanne Alperonne, who said she'd do it for $100 and would anyone else match her? I almost spoke, I swear, but was shy of my soft, middle-aged stomach, and my short, blue socks if I swam without my trousers. The water too: heavy, and with a greasy sheen in the fading light. 'No takers?' she said quietly, and dived in as we cheered in our defeat. The tug seemed to keep pace merely by its movement in the swell, then she receded, her arms turning as if on the face of a corrected clock.

Someone must have had the idea of the reunion, and found us all out, and organised the tug and casks of wine. I can't remember who, and never gave the thanks that were due. Suzanne Alperonne, though, swimming in the darkening harbour, was a lesson to me in courage and reticence.

Bob Isherwood, Neddy Dawson, Prue Whitby-Orme, Kevin Attwell, Carla de Joux and Fiona Ballance. Then there was old man Towler and Arch Hollis. Arch is my father's cousin. His farm in the Wairau Valley seemed baronial to me – a town boy. Baronial not in terms of evident money, or antique furniture, or tours abroad, but in the vast scale of ownership and decision: tractors, trucks, sheds, haybarns, married-couple cottage, sets of yards, silos, flocks, fields of

crops, beehives, creeks, whole lines of windbreak trees and fences, gates, the very sky over it all. How magnificent a wardrobe of possession it seemed to me. I understood why Arch left his fief only when forced to by the need to placate his wife, or deal cautiously with the professions of the town. He ruled in muted, muscular grandeur; ploughing and fencing, dipping and harrowing, shearing, sowing, harvesting, building and breaking down. He dispensed justice and decided life and death on his land. He culled and mated with care and no vindictiveness.

From that place I would return home dissatisfied with our urban section, an area which Arch might use for piling stones, or setting a few hives on. My father's resources were all within his head, and difficult for a boy to appreciate. Arch is still gradually wearing into his context, still there and becoming more and more a part of what he both rules and serves until, when he stands still, he is quite indistinguishable from the texture, strong grain and natural contours of the land itself. I doubt if they will ever find a body to take away.

Will Ng, Richard Jones, Pinhead Guy, Catherine Dickison, Ace Gallagher, Joanne Ryder, Pearl Edgecombe, Gaston Labermoute and Maurice Hume. Such a compact figure, Pearl Edgecombe, the flesh smooth and dense like silver, and if she had been dropped into the sea she would have sunk instantly without flutter or bobbing. Her appearance mirrored her imperturbable nature. As an historian she was contemptuous of the present, for its transience and unsettled way prevented valid judgements being made.

In a morning of blossom and warm stone at the old campus she talked of Cannae in passing. Not many had bothered to come, but she saw that as no reason for relaxing her scholarship. Her view was as ever orderly, exact, just

what was required, yet so removed from the physical event. I had a sense of dynamic awe that the hopes and blood, the tumultuous horror and unbearable pain, the loss, the waste, and pageantry to follow, had dwindled through 2000 years to five minutes in that quiet room with flowers and old stone.

Have I said Tony Calder? He stole a girlfriend I never had. She was an AFS from Wolf Point, Montana, with a pony tail and a languid voice. I told my friends I planned to ring her at her host family's place and make a date, but in the days I was using to perfect my telephone technique, Tony Calder rang and invited her to go water-skiing. After that, every time they were together, someone would remind me of my boast.

I never said anything to Tony, but years later when a different Calder applied for a job with my firm I turned him down, and had the illogical satisfaction of writing Dear Mr Calder I regret to inform you etc. We must assuage our grievances as best we can, after all. I had for a long time a vision of Wolf Point, Montana – blue sage hills, cattle yards, Chevrolet pick-ups, and lost blond girls with bobby socks and pony tails. He cost me, did Tony Calder.

Russell Priest, Noleen Suter, E. P. E. Tattersall, Raf Maslen, Iggy Rousse, Tracey Bates and Lily Gustafasson. Ah, yes, Awol Grisson, Naomi Allport, Sutz McCallum, Ivan Linkall and the big girl who played the part of the beadle in the Dickens play. I was in National Service with Awol Grisson: months at Waiouru, which is a sort of Gulag Archipelago the fortunate New Zealander never experiences. We 20-year-olds were divided into a majority who could get by, even adapt and find friends and humour, and a minority who could not stand it.

Awol couldn't stand it. He'd come from a close provincial family of religious fundamentalists and suddenly he was on the parade ground and unable to remember whether he should turn left or right about; unable to recall the sequence of assembly for the Bren gun, unable to fold an immaculate bed-roll, unable to answer to his Christian name because it was never used. He was burnt with a thunderflash during exercises, and put on charge for losing a bayonet during bivouac training. Each day his large face was a map of uncomprehending misery, and each night his sobbing punctuated our plaintive dreams. He tried to escape, but was always brought back.

Awol was convinced he had passed into the shadow of death, and his anguish finally expressed itself in fits. He had one while we were lining up at the mess hall on a wet evening, and as he twitched the rain matted his hair, and fine gravel stuck to the side of his face. Like a stricken cat he drew his lips back to show his teeth, and we knelt awkwardly to put coats on him until the medics came So the army set him free at last, and the rest of us voiced contempt for his weakness, and felt envy for his deliverance.

I haven't been called upon to defend my country. I have forgotten my camouflage technique and ambush drills by whistle; the octopus of battalion signals has sunk to a mystery once more But I see Awol Grisson spasm-bent in the rain outside D block, and his teeth bared to all the world.

Aubrey Gilden, Con Dawson, Judy Posswillow. Did I say Judy Posswillow? Well I didn't mean to, you see. I must withdraw my pledge to have no secrets. I couldn't bear it. Some shafts must be left buried in the heart, for if drawn the very blood will follow to the death. And she was beautiful and wilful, Judy Posswillow. How beautiful she was.

Debbie Faas, Dutch Bleeker, Alun Heuw, Frank Lox, Donald Rangi and April Burton. Winn Mannering, Jocelyn Hills. Kate Lim, Catherine Smythe, Nolan Wright, Al Bruce, Essie Bray, Alice Lenns, Toad Hall. Essie Bray, you say. Essie was my landlady in my second year. I've forgotten the medieval history and Georgian poets, but the taste of the beetroot sandwiches Essie sometimes made for tea is fresh in my mouth. The blood comes through the bread if you don't eat them right away. Yet Essie lent me her bike with a chain-guard and basket, which I used in the twilight sometimes, clanking along back streets to the bar, or parties. She went through my room most days and read the letters in my drawer, I could tell. Several times she left a clothes-peg with red wool wound on it under my pillow: I never could work out why. Essie Bray will be dead now, and later so will I. I've done nothing in the meantime to make me feel superior, and I'll say this for Essie, when I had beetroot so did she. Betwixt landlady and lodger was no distinction. How truly she mourned when Kennedy was assassinated: utter and inconsolable bereavement, as if she had lost a lover.

Nigel Uftern, May Brookes, Father Wilton, Buddy Garter, B. B. Gandy, Lester Hefferman, Winston Eddy, Karl St John Darling, Barbara Troon, Dork Cowan and Janet Mathews, who died in Ethiopia. Pop Casey and Stan Livesey, Banzai Frew, fat Gwillam, Wesley Collet, Amanda Hawkey, and Geoff Hyde, who was the best wing the school ever produced, many said.

We were all failures, Gwillam, Ian and myself. So we kept a fine old humour together at our wretched work, and never wished to see each other outside those hours. Gwillam was a boozer, and on his bad days Ian and I would hide him on sacks behind the pallets, where he could sleep. And we

would do his share because if he was fired we might have someone in his place without a sense of humour or failure. Gwillam would sleep on the sacks with his fat cheeks and lips sagging like a baby's.

The two essential qualities of friendship are to make allowances and to respect privacy. In return Gwillam told endless stories from his own Arabian Nights of sexual conquests. Almost certainly Gwillam had an ordinary experience, a baby face advances one only so far in a woman's affections, but as a voluptuary he would not allow fact to deny him pleasure. Over our breaks during three days he recounted the saga of the Mint Princess, a rabbiter's wife he claimed to have loved in Culverden. Ian and I laughed and listened to pass the time, breathed in the ash of the ground grain, watched the glimmer through the trailing webs of the skylights. They had a rendezvous in the creekbed, Gwillam said, in the old channel lined with upright mint, and in the still evening, he said, with the bronze north Canterbury hills too far to pry, he would roll the mint with her, releasing essences to blink a slanted sun. Her white hips above him, heavily pale, turned like the pharaoh's alabaster bowl, Gwillam said, sheened white with joy, he said, and Ian and I would turn our smiles to the corner of the warehouse, but listen all the same. We were all failures, Gwillam, Ian and myself.

Yes, you're right about Reg Osborne being a mutual friend. Strangely enough I had a dream about him not long ago. I dreamt that I was farewelling some friend at the wharf: the crowd immense, everything bedecked with tickertape, hooters and flowers in the television way. So great was the crush that I was being pushed over the side, between the heavy timbers of the wharf and the massive, breathing side of the ship, and I called in fear, reached to hold the man next

to me. He turned sufficiently for me to see his face, and it was Reg Osborne. But he pretended I wasn't there. He drew his arms away and I wasn't able to grip the smooth back and shoulder of his coat. I fell, conscious of great horror and pity for myself.

Reg was a friend, and I'd not thought about him for years, yet how clearly I saw his expression, and how true to him it seemed that instant as he turned away. He wanted me to fall. He must have hated me for something. A dream means nothing, perhaps, yet if I ever meet Reg again I won't feel the same towards him. His expression so authentic, looking away, pretending he couldn't see my need, yet with malice apparent even in the determined face of that pretence. Just a dream, of course, you may say. All the same; all the same.

Lauris James, of course, Raymond Sadler, Gillian Burridge, Marya Robeliski, Peewee Riddle, Peter Guile, Archdeacon Langley, Margaret Reesman, Nonce Falconer, Pauline Stowell and Desmond Mulcahy. P. G. Fisst and Barry Beardsley. Akker Lisdeen, Prof. Webbernath, Mo Thyne, Esplin Dee, no, I said him. Yvonne Shelley, though, Alistair Smith and Gussie Hambinder. Each of them has a life.

Yvonne Shelley was the undertaker's daughter and let me take her home after the carnival on New Year's Eve. She took off her shoes and walked the final blocks in her stockings on the warm concrete. I had the feeling that she did it because of some film, or some book she'd read. She swung her shoes by their straps, and laughed when cars came by. Even in the seclusion by her house I sensed that she was using me as a stock on which to base a more intriguing partner, but I didn't care. I would have answered to any name, bayed at the moon on cue, to be as I was hard against her in the hedge: feel her

hip on mine, smell the warm, night leaves we oppressed, hear the rustle of her dress upon her thigh and the sound of my own snagged breath. I wasn't too proud. How rare the times when we truly envy no one; when there is nothing in this world's variety that we would swap for the present held.

'How you do go on,' said Yvonne Shelley. Her head tilted back into the hedge in submission to my kisses, yet her smiles in the dark were languorous as if for an audience. Shelley's Funeral Parlour, the sign said in unlit lettering, but it was life I served that night not death. With an elbow awkwardly lifted to allow me to feel her breast from the top of her dress, I heard the lowing of harbour boats, though the New Year was long in. 'Don't squeeze,' she said. The hedge was well forced back. A pearl band of sky lay in the east beyond her father's kindly business. Her breath fluttered on my neck, and a hedgehog turned mystified away. 'Do you love me,' Yvonne Shelley said.

Hey nonny, names are the proof, we say, of anything having happened at all. Gunter Berge, Murray Young and Simon Hillier I remember now: Lennie Haseltine and Marianne Ranunski, cousin Violet and that Winston Talbot. All have a response in the roll-call which substantiates the trivial course of a private life. My name on the margin of theirs too, perhaps.

For names, the word, reversed can fertilise the combs of memory, and our lives are like expanding universes in miniature – the parts receding from the centre with a hapless, silent speed.

Notes on the Authors

KATHERINE MANSFIELD, New Zealand's most celebrated writer, was born in Wellington in 1888, and died in 1923 at Fontainebleau of tuberculosis. She published several collections of stories in her lifetime; other work was published after her death. The texts for the stories in *Six by Six* are from *The Stories of Katherine Mansfield*, edited by Antony Alpers (Oxford, 1988). Mansfield's letters were published in five volumes for Oxford University Press by Margaret Scott and Vincent O'Sullivan between 1987 and 2008.

FRANK SARGESON (1903–82) lived and worked as a writer in Takapuna for most of his life. His first book, *Conversation with My Uncle and Other Sketches*, appeared in 1936, and he published several other volumes of short stories. The third edition of his collected stories, *Frank Sargeson's Stories* (2010), includes thirteen previously uncollected pieces. As well as stories, Sargeson published a number of novels (including *Memoirs of a Peon* and *Joy of the Worm*) and three volumes of autobiography. A collection of his critical writings, *Conversation in a Train*, edited by Kevin Cunningham, was issued by Auckland University Press in 1981.

MAURICE DUGGAN was born in Auckland in 1922; he died in 1974. During his life he published a tale for children, *Falter Tom and the Water Boy*, and three collections of stories: *Immanuel's Land* (1956), *Summer in the Gravel Pit* (1965) and *O'Leary's Orchard* (1970). Stories from these volumes,

along with early uncollected work and the posthumously published 'The Magsman Miscellany', were brought together in a *Collected Stories*, edited and introduced by C. K. Stead (Auckland University Press, 1981).

JANET FRAME (1924–04) was the internationally renowned author of thirteen novels, four story collections, two books of poetry and a three-volume autobiography – *To the Is-land*, *An Angel at My Table* and *The Envoy from Mirror City*. She had a number of works published posthumously, including *The Goose Bath*, which won the Montana Book Award for Poetry in 2007. Frame was awarded the C.B.E. in 1983 and received two honorary doctorates. She was appointed to the New Zealand Order of Merit in 1990, and in 2003 became one of the first recipients of the Arts Foundation of New Zealand Icon Award.

PATRICIA GRACE was born in Wellington in 1937; she is of Ngāti Raukawa, Ngāti Toa and Te Āti Awa descent, and is affiliated to Ngāti Porou by marriage. She is the author of eight novels, a number of children's books, and seven short story collections, the first of which was *Waiariki* (1975). Her memoir, *From the Centre: A Writer's Life*, was published in 2021. She has been awarded the New Zealand Book Award for Fiction (*Potiki*, 1987) and in 2001 was longlisted for the Man Booker Prize with *Dogside Story*, which went on to win the 2001 Kiriyama Pacific Rim Fiction Prize. In 2008 Grace became the twentieth laureate of the Neustadt International Prize for Literature. She has received two honorary doctorates and a Distinguished Companion of the New Zealand Order of Merit for her services to literature.

OWEN MARSHALL was born in Te Kūiti in 1941. His first publication, *Supper Waltz Wilson*, was issued in 1979 and was the first of eleven short-story collections, with additional selected volumes published in 1997 and 2008. As well as four books of poetry, Marshall has published seven novels, the most recent of which is Ockham-shortlisted *Pearly Gates* (2019). He won the Deutz Medal for Fiction at the Montana New Zealand Book Awards in 2000 for his novel *Harlequin Rex*, and that same year was awarded the ONZM for Services to Literature. Marshall was the recipient of the CNZM in 2012 and the Prime Minister's Award for Fiction in 2013.